A MARKED MAN

STELLA CAMERON

A MARKED MAN

MIRA®

MIRA

ISBN-13: 978-0-7783-2358-7
ISBN-10: 0-7783-2358-7

A MARKED MAN

www.MIRABooks.com

Printed in U.S.A.

First Printing: November 2006
10 9 8 7 6 5 4 3 2 1

In loving memory of a faithful friend, Spike.
1990–2006

CHAPTER 1

The moon was a thin white wafer with a big bite missing.

Walking silent streets at night—alone—could be a bad idea. Staying in bed, half awake, half asleep, sweat stinging your eyes, sticking hair to your face, while the monster panic ate you up could be a whole lot worse idea. Nothing bad ever happened around here anyway.

Annie Duhon moved quietly through the town square in Toussaint, Louisiana. That violated moon, coy behind riffles of soft gray cloud, pointed a pale finger at the wide road lined with sycamores, stroked a shine on the windows of businesses and homes on either side.

A warm breeze felt friendly. Yesterday there had been a sidewalk sale and food fair. Holiday lights strung between trees on a triangle of grass in the center of the street were turned on at dusk; they were still on and bobbled, out of place for the time of year, but festive and comforting…briefly.

She ought to know better than be lulled by a few strands of quivering colored lights. She ought to turn back and lock herself inside her apartment over Hungry Eyes, the book shop and café run by the Gables, Toussaint's only lawyer and his wife. They lived next door and she had an open invitation, almost an order to go to them at any time if she needed help.

Help, I had another bad dream. They've been happening for more than a couple of weeks and they get worse all the time. Someone dies but I don't know who. It's a woman. Could be me.

Sure she would tell them that, and what could they do about it?

A battered pickup clanked by and made a left turn at the next corner. When Annie reached the spot and looked for the vehicle, she saw it pull into the forecourt of Murphy's Bar where a neon sign blinked on and off behind a grimy window. The small hours of the morning and some folks were still looking for company.

Annie kept walking. She had been here for seven months and felt happier than she had in years, until the nights came when she could not shut out terrible visions of death.

Ten minutes got her to St. Cécil's church, glowing white in the darkness, Bayou Teche a faintly polished presence behind the church and the rectory on the other side of Bonanza Alley.

The bayou drew her, always had. She slipped past the church, reached the towpath and stood awhile, her thin cotton skirt caught to her thighs by warm currents of air.

A slap and suck sound, subtle, inexorable, reminded her how the bayou water kissed its banks on a night like this. Something swam, plopped, beat up a spray. A bass, maybe, or an alligator, or even a big rat. Rats reminded Annie of things she wanted to forget. She walked a few more steps and stopped. Noises swelled, pushed at her. Frogs grumbling, little critters skittering through the underbrush, a buzz in her ears, growing louder.

Annie turned around abruptly and retraced her steps. The breeze became a sudden wind, whipping leaves against her bare legs. A bird cried and she jumped, walked faster.

On Bonanza Alley again, she looked at the rectory. A subdued light shone in the big kitchen at the back but she knew Father Cyrus Payne always kept a light on in case a stranger happened by and needed a little welcome. That good man would be sleeping now.

There were not many good men like him.

Heat rose in her face and her cheeks throbbed. Speeding her pace only made the noises around her head louder. Low lights gleamed steadily behind the stained glass windows of the church. Annie stood still again and willed her heart to be quiet.

Slowly, she pushed open a gate in the white fence surrounding the churchyard. She stepped inside and walked along a path between tombs to a side door into St Cécil's. Annie wasn't a churchgoer, hadn't been since she was a teenager. She gritted her teeth, climbed the steps into a small vestibule and turned the door handle, never expecting it to open. It did and she went inside. Church used to be real important to her, until she offended and the holy congregation suggested she shouldn't be there.

Her mama had suffered even more than she had over that.

A wrought iron gate closed off a side chapel. Annie threaded her fingers through the scrollwork and peered into the candlelit cell beyond. Those candle flames glittered on gold thread in an embroidered hanging behind the little altar. She smelled incense, and old roses, their bruised heads hanging from frail, bent necks around the rim of a glass vase.

The roses reminded her of funeral flowers kept too long because when they were thrown out, the loss would feel more final. Death was final but while the tributes remained, before the false cheer of a life's "celebration" died away and the sympathizers stopped coming around anymore, well then, the grieving ones could try to keep truth at bay.

Nights when she gave up on sleep brought images so clear they seemed real. She didn't want them, or the thoughts that came with them.

Inside the chapel with the gates closed behind her, Annie sat on the cushioned seat of a bench, its high back carved into a frieze of wild animals and birds. She put her head in her hands. What would she do, what could she do? Push on, exhausted by frequent nights filled with ghastly images followed by occasional recurring flashes of the same sick dramas when she was awake? Yes, she guessed that was what she would do, and she would pray for the burden to be taken away.

She did not want to go home until morning. St. Cécil's felt safer. Evil knew better than to enter God's house.

Minutes passed and her head felt heavy. If she went to the rectory, Father Cyrus would take her in, she knew he would. He'd make her stay and want to listen to what troubled her.

Talking about her imagination wasn't worth taking sleep from a busy man at this hour. And talking about the reality that haunted her from other times and places was out of the question—with Father Cyrus or anyone else.

Annie had come to Toussaint to take over a new position as general manager at Pappy's Dance Hall and Eats just north of town. Since she'd first visited the place while she was back in school and planning a fresh direction for her life, Annie dreamed of owning something like Pappy's one day. She'd never expected the dream to come true and working there felt unreal and wonderful.

Another unexpected surprise had been meeting Dr. Max Savage and falling into an unlikely friendship with him. He often stopped by Pappy's after the lunch rush. Sitting with him while he ate had become a habit. His idea, not hers, but she probably looked forward to seeing him more than she ought to.

Max and his brothers, Roche and Kelly, planned to open a clinic in the area. Roche was also a doctor, and Kelly took care of business matters. There would be more doctors on the staff by the time they opened. Max persuaded her to go out a couple of times and said he wanted her to consider him a friend. She wanted to, but the last time she accepted an offer like his...well, the outcome hadn't been good. She surely didn't want Max to find out about either her past or her present troubles.

She and Max couldn't be more different, he a highly regarded facial reconstructive plastic surgeon while Annie came from poor beginnings and had clawed for each handhold on the way to a modest, mostly trade education. Not that she wasn't proud of what she had accomplished.

Truth was, she intended to remain in Toussaint and make already successful Pappy's into a destination people came from all over to visit. She would get accustomed to being alone and whatever happened, she wouldn't be falling back on her family in Pointe Judah, not so far from Toussaint. She loved them but didn't need them, or anyone, to survive anymore.

She yawned and before her staring eyes, the candle flames blurred. Still watching the light, Annie lay on her side on top of the cushioned seat and pulled up her legs. There was no reason not to stay, just until it started to get light.

He trained the flashlight ahead and she couldn't see his face behind the yellow-white beam. The beam bounced and jerked. She heard the sound of something dragging over leaves and sticks, rocks and sharp, scaly pinecones. Another noise, a clank-clank *of metal on the stones was there just as it had been each time the man had come.*

She heard him breathing, short, harsh breaths. But she also heard the sounds she made herself, a high little wheeze because she was so scared, her throat wouldn't work properly.

What if he heard her?

She knew what he dragged behind him.

Her eyes burned. They burned every time. Too many times.

He dropped his burden and walked forward, his flashlight trained on a thick carpet of leaves.

Rain began to fall. It splattered the leaves on the ground, turned them shiny so she saw them clearly, distinct one from another.

Overhead, branches rattled together and wind whined.

If he looked up he'd see her. She was right there.

A scent swept at her nostrils. Coppery, like blood. And burned hair: there was no mistaking that, not when you'd smelled it so close before.

The man said, "Here we go," as if he was with his children and he'd just found the ice-cream shop they'd all been looking for. More clattering and he poked through the leaves and mulch with the shining point of a brand-new shovel.

A woman's body lay on the ground beside him, her eyelids burned off, and empty dark holes where her eyes had been. Her hair, nothing but a thin matted spongelike layer, shed filaments in the wind.

"Here we go," the man said again. He didn't start digging a hole but cleared debris from an area no more than two feet across. Poking and scraping quickly brought his satisfied sigh and he lifted the woman as if she weighed nothing. Rags of blackened clothing stuck to her rigid body.

"There we go," the man said and dropped the corpse, headfirst into a hole that swallowed her.

Annie, her hands outstretched before her, ran at the man. "Bring her back. Give her back," she cried. But when she reached for him he turned into fire, and she cried out in pain.

Her forehead struck the side of the altar. She fell to her knees, her arms upraised, and felt her left hand scorch. At the same moment she heard the sound of flame shooting along filaments.

She opened heavy eyes and saw a movement. On the far aisle of the church, she thought. A hooded figure. "No," she murmured. There was no one there.

Then she was wide-awake, pulling herself to her feet, righting the candle she'd knocked over and using one end of a linen runner with silk fringes to beat sizzling threads cold. Immediately she ran to the sacristy and poured water over her hands and into the sink there. She held them under the cold water and realized she had been lucky to sustain little injury. No one need find out what had happened.

The pain ebbed. She found a first-aid kit and wound a bandage around her left hand to keep the air from hurting the wound. Returning to the chapel, she took the runner from the top of the altar and used it to clean black residue from the marble.

She would pay for another runner to be made.

"Don't jump," a man said behind her.

Annie screamed. She screamed and shook her head, and staggered backward against him. Sweat stuck her clothes to her body. That woman she had seen in the nightmares was her, Annie. Premonitions, not nightmares. They were coming true. The gagging sounds she heard were her own.

"Annie, it's me, Father Cyrus. People are lookin' for you."

CHAPTER 2

Hi, Max,

It's been a long time. Forgive me for not writing sooner.

Have you picked your next victim yet?

How was London? Clever of you to go there. Far enough away for you to get lost in another closed-ranks medical fraternity, but not so far you couldn't keep an eye on things here. I expect you were surprised how quickly the media in the States forgot about you and your nasty little habit. I wasn't surprised.

The media is fickle, with short attention spans, but that means they're always on the hunt for the next story, or the next installment of an old, sick story like yours.

Did you lose a close friend in London? You know the kind of friend I mean. A woman. If you did, you hid the evidence well. We didn't hear a thing about it.

There are a few questions I want you to think about and maybe you'll tell me the answers one day. Do you disfigure them so badly because you enjoy knowing that you are one of the few who could put some of their bones and flesh back together again, if you wanted to? Does the thought turn you on?

Do you tell them what they'll look like afterwards and remind them that you know how to mend wounds like that—then laugh when you say you don't heal dead women?

You're back. That's too bad, but we'll make the best of it. You've chosen a quaint place to hide—conveniently out of touch, too, but that doesn't mean a few words here and there won't have the whole town watching you. If you stray, even sleepy Toussaint will notice the attention you get.

Be very, very careful who you associate with, Doctor. Stay away from whores. You know how quickly your history can jump into the public eye from every media outlet across the country—the way it did before. They loved crucifying you then and they'll love it even more the next time—if there is a next time. But that's up to you. Try to control yourself, and keep your nose clean.

Remember how charges in the first death, poor Isabel's, were dismissed for lack of evidence? And the second one went the same way? Carol was so sexy.

How did you wait all those years before you killed the second time? Or did you wait? Did other women die in between without any connection being made to you?

The third time (that they find out about) won't be a charm for you.

I don't know why I waste my time trying to help you. Once a killer, always a killer. You'll do it again and probably soon—unless I find a way to stop you.

Why not show my letter to someone who can help you? Not your brother, Roche. It might seem convenient to use a shrink in the family but he would only say whatever you wanted to hear. Kelly would *worry about himself first, then panic. He would sacrifice you to save his own skin. Best keep this away from him, too.*

Go to the law. Tell the truth and show them this. Say it's a letter from the best friend you ever had, the only honest friend you ever had, and ask them to lock you away before you do something unspeakable again.

God help you, and them.

I don't sign my letters to him. Why should I? He'd know I was only trying to be clever.

By now he'll feel safe, as if he's finally outrun me and his past, but he never will.

CHAPTER 3

"The reconstruction should have been finished months ago," Kelly Savage said. "Before we had to worry about the weather." He gestured to the restaurant windows with his sandwich.

A gray-green sky rested on treetops outside Pappy's Dance Hall and Eats where Kelly had insisted he and his brothers meet for lunch. Max had known better than to raise curiosity by suggesting they go somewhere else, even if he did have good reasons to keep the place to himself.

Max saw his twin, Roche, skirting a giant, blue-varnished alligator inside the front doors and raised a hand. A jukebox interested Roche more than his brothers did. He leaned on the neon-flashing machine and fished in his pocket for coins.

Kelly craned around to see and shook his head. "I don't know where that boy came from but it surely wasn't the same set of eggs as you and me."

"Speak for yourself," Max said and laughed. Kelly was their half brother, their father's son by a short first marriage, but most of the time they all forgot that.

Max had called ahead to warn Annie Duhon he'd be arriving with an entourage—they had both decided they wanted to keep their friendship fairly private, at least for now—but Annie hadn't been in when he'd called and she still hadn't shown up. He wished he had the right to find out why because during the past seven months he had never visited Pappy's without finding Annie there.

He knew why he preferred not to advertise their connection. What was her reason? She'd never said, but neither had he.

Kelly clapped his hands over his ears and he was not the only one who did. "Jailhouse Rock," as only Elvis could sing it, blared through the speakers from the jukebox, cutting off Jellyroll Morton on the sound system.

Max smiled at his diminishing pile of softshell crabs. Folks called Roche "oblivious" and Max guessed they were right, but he liked him the way he was.

"Dammit, he can make me mad," Kelly said. "Listen to that racket. Who's the Elvis look-alike over there?" He shifted to see better. "Black wig and a white suit. And damn me if he isn't wearing blue suede shoes. This place got stuck in a decade I don't remember. Kitschy doesn't come close."

"Loosen up," Max said, losing patience. "I was told about him. Name's Carmen. Apparently he's worked here for years and he's part of the atmosphere, I guess. He's around in case someone forgets their manners. When Roche gets over here we'll listen to whatever's on your mind and get out. We could have talked at the clinic anyway." He glanced toward Annie's office again. The door was still closed. She loved this place and treated it with the kind of care she'd use if it belonged to her. He had seen her yesterday. If she intended to be out today she would have said so.

"The clinic ought to be finished," Kelly said. "Aren't you worried about your arteries with all the fried food?" He eyed Max's crabs and took another bite out of his own toasted cheese sandwich. His basic tastes in food hadn't progressed much since grade school.

"Sure I'm worried. Don't you think that lump of yellow goop you're eating could be a problem, too?"

Max was used to watching his own double walk around. Finally heading in their direction, Roche loped, tall, loose-limbed and relaxed, his short black hair mussed. Crossing the dance floor in the middle of the low-lying building, he returned nods from folks he knew only by sight. He rarely smiled because it slipped his memory, but people felt drawn to him anyway.

He sat beside Kelly, opposite Max. "Did you take a look at that jukebox. Wurlitzer '1015.' How do they keep the thing running?"

"Probably a new knockoff," Kelly said.

Roche swivelled and hooked a thumb in the direction of the machine. "Uh-uh. Take a closer look. They first made those in the forties. There's nothing new in this place. Anyway, sorry I'm late," he finished absently.

"You were late before you got here," Kelly said in a monotone. Max didn't like the way Kelly looked. It wasn't like him to be pale under his tan or to have dark marks under his usually clear, hazel eyes.

"I stopped in at Rosebank for the mail," Roche said. "Nothing but bills."

All three of them had small apartments at Rosebank, a resort that belonged to Spike Devol, the local sheriff, his wife Vivian and her mother, Charlotte. Green Veil, an antebellum house next door to the resort was the site of the new clinic. Already converted into a plastic surgery clinic a few years earlier, Max had decided that, with work, the place was exactly what he wanted. The work had turned out to be a lot more extensive than he had figured, but despite Kelly's panicking, Max expected the place to open within months. It had to. Already there were doctors with different plastic specialties from Max's who had committed to coming on board at Green Veil.

Roche looked around for a waitress. "I ran into Father Cyrus at Rosebank. He and Vivian closeted themselves away and didn't look so happy."

"Wonder what that was about?" Kelly said. "Those two don't go in for closed-door meetings, do they?"

Roche shrugged and asked a waitress in squeaky-bottomed shoes for the same thing Max had ordered. "This is a great place," he said, hanging his head back to look at a thick layer of mostly yellowing business cards tacked to the ceiling. "It's got character, atmosphere. I'd like to come when the band plays. Did you see the size of the gator out front? Blue." The restaurant surrounded a dance hall and the section where the Savages sat was built off one side of the building.

"Blue what?" Kelly said, after considering. "The shoes? Yeah, fucking idiot Elvis impersonator. Jeez."

"He was talking about the alligator," Max said. "It's called Blue. I told you that when we got here."

"Yeah," Roche said to Kelly, his tone light and even. "And I'm humoring you, friend. Otherwise I'd tell you to go to hell and take your third-degree with you."

Time to change the subject. "Wasn't it great to see Michele Riley yesterday? I knew she'd come for an interview just to be polite, but I wasn't sure she'd accept the job."

Roche said, "I was," and looked too pleased.

"Because she can't resist your charms?" Max asked. "I don't think you had much to do with it. She likes the idea of having her own physical therapy department even if it will be small. And she's damned good, so all the luck is on our side. I'm relieved she wants to come here—there's nothing much she doesn't know about me."

"Oh, yeah?" Roche crossed his arms.

"You know what I mean."

Roche looked into the distance. "It's a good sign she's so positive. She'll bring others with her—including the fiancé she ought to dump in favor of me. She seems to really like it here." He and Max had known Michele professionally. At their invitation she had come to Toussaint the day before, expressed delight over the clinic and agreed to coordinate the physical therapy department. Her fiancé was a nurse.

"Just remember Michele's taken," Max said to Roche and smiled. "It's beginning to feel as if we should have done something like this a long time ago," he observed. "This will be a good place for patients to recuperate."

"Fucking weather," Kelly muttered as if he hadn't heard a word either Roche or Max said. He gulped beer from a sweating glass. "You know you can't hide forever, don't you, Max."

"If I didn't, I do now," Max said. "Where did that come from?" He could always rely on their older brother to state the obvious.

"Someone has to remind you what we're facing. You get off in your own world and forget—"

"Keep it down," Roche said through his teeth. "We've been here a long time now without any problems."

"You and Roche have been here a fair amount of time," Kelly said. "Making sure you two can do what you want to do keeps me pretty busy elsewhere."

"Can it," Max said. "You don't have to spend so much time in New York and you wouldn't if you didn't like it there. We all like it there, remember? It's home, or it was. You're in a rotten mood and it isn't helping a thing. So we're gonna get more rain, big deal, it rains plenty here and work doesn't stop."

"Delays cost us," Kelly said. He finished the sandwich rapidly and wiped his mouth on a paper napkin. "You know how hard it is to keep a work crew focused. If the weather gets bad they find inside jobs, and they come back when they damn well please."

"*Dammit,*" Max said. He noticed that noise had dwindled at nearby tables and saw patrons lose interest in their own conversations while they listened to the brothers argue. He dropped his voice. "What's up with you, Kelly? You get jumpier by the day. If you want out of this project, say so. I never imagined we'd have to resort to hiding away to do our work but it's the best we've got—or I've got. You two don't have to be here."

Roche rolled his eyes and kept quiet.

"You can be an ungrateful son of a bitch," Kelly said.

"So you say. You push me too far. We're finally within shouting distance of opening the clinic's doors and you're looking for more problems."

Roche half turned away and pulled an ankle onto the opposite knee. Roche the quiet peacemaker with a steely will said less than he thought, much less. Max was the one man who read his twin regardless of the man's enigmatic demeanor. Neither of them went in for idle talk.

"Well, hell, it is starting to rain," Kelly said, looking up at the first big drops on a skylight. He dropped his voice. "I get edgy is all. You're right, I look for problems. I'll try to knock it off."

"Forget it," Max said. "We're going to be looking over our shoulders for a bit. We'll learn to forget about it in time." He did not say they'd be looking for unnatural deaths that might be blamed on Max the way two others, fifteen years apart, the second one three years ago, initially had been. He also didn't mention that he hesitated to give the impression that he cared about any woman in more than an offhand way because knowing him well might be dangerous to a lady's health. Kelly and Roche thought Annie Duhon was just a nodding acquaintance.

"Okay," Roche said, easing a baseball cap out of his back pocket and tossing it on the table. "Is that it, Kelly? You're edgy and you wanted us all here so you could talk about it."

"For a shrink, you have a lousy bedside manner," Kelly said, jutting his square jaw. "I already said I was uptight, but that isn't why we're here. I wanted to go somewhere we could talk without being overheard by the Devols, or those sorry-ass construction workers."

"Really?" Roche looked at the nearest table where four men instantly got real interested in their food. "So talk. Quietly. And the contractors are doing a great job. Looks like they'll finish almost on time and that doesn't happen so often."

Kelly put his elbows on the table and rested his face in his hands. "I'm not sure about this place anymore, that's all."

Roche and Max looked at one another quickly, and Roche shook his head slightly.

Sure, Max thought, as usual they were supposed to consider Kelly's unpredictable moods and give him space. "What d'you mean?" he asked, unable to resist. "If you're saying we're making a mistake opening Green Veil, I wish you'd said something a year or more ago."

"You were so set on it," Kelly said, his face still in his hands. "Your buddy, Reb Girard, told you this was a good place to get lost and you believed her. I don't know what I think about it now."

"I still believe her," Max said, getting heated.

Roche's crabs arrived, sizzling on the plate. He thanked the waitress who gazed into his very blue eyes for a bit too long, then glanced at Kelly before she scuttled away.

"Reb's dad was the town doc around here and she's the second generation taking care of the folks. She ought to know if it's a backwater. Half her bills, or more, get paid in chickens and eggs—a ham if she's lucky."

"My heart bleeds for Dr. Reb Girard," Kelly said, running his fingers lower on his face until his eyes appeared. "She and that architect husband of hers are rolling in it. He owns most of the town."

"So what?" When Kelly went into one of these phases they never got anywhere. "I've got to go."

"Wait," Kelly said, slapping the table. "I'm telling you I think we should consider selling and getting out while we still can. Someone's going to figure out who you are. I feel it coming. That cousin of your friend, Reb, is always looking for dirt to put in that miserable little newspaper of hers. I'd say you'd give her enough to last a long time."

The cousin was Lee O'Brien and she lived out at Cloud's End, the Girard estate, while she ran the *Toussaint Trumpet,* the town's one paper.

"You don't know half of what's gone on in this *quiet backwater,* do you?" Kelly said.

Max figured he knew about everything that was worth knowing, and some of it he didn't like, but that didn't change Toussaint into a metropolis. "They've had their share of bad luck—of the criminal kind—but it's over now. Finally. Sooner or later my history will come out. I'm betting everything on having some champions who will speak up, and on winning over the folks who live here. So far, I'm doing okay."

"Yes," Roche said. "I think you really like it here, and I sure do. What have you got against the place, Kelly?"

That bought him an unblinking stare. "I *love* it. Especially when I feel like seeing a first-run play."

Max laughed. "If you knew how you sound, you'd change the subject. You can get to a play anytime you want to, or whatever—or whomever—you have an itch to see in a hurry. You don't have to be here at all if you don't want to be."

"So you don't want to reconsider?" Kelly asked.

"No."

"Neither do I," Roche said.

A smile, all unaffected charm and guaranteed to disarm, transformed Kelly. He laughed and flipped back overlong, dishwater blond hair. "Just checking."

Roche was first out of his seat and shaking Kelly by the shoulder. "Rat. You don't change. Outside. I want to beat the crap out of you."

Reason stopped Max just in time and he sank back into his seat, but he chuckled watching the other two wrapped in a mockferocious embrace. "Nice language from the gentleman shrink," he said. "You've been listening to our clown act here for too long. That wasn't funny, Kelly, but you always did have a cruel sense of humor."

"Just wanted to get us together for once," Kelly said, punching Roche good-naturedly. "I'm relieved to hear you say you're not wearing rose glasses, though, Max. Hell, I worry about you and so does Roche, you know that. You got a rotten deal and we don't want to see it happen again just when you think you're safe."

Max's stomach revolved but he kept the corners of his mouth turned up. "My eyes are open," he said. He never intended to share some of the thoughts that went through his mind. Green Veil would work. He and Roche made a great team and together with a handpicked staff they were going back to what they loved. Kelly's financial skills made everything easier and maybe it was a good idea to have him keeping everyone's feet on the ground.

Pappy's was busier than usual today, not that it was ever too quiet. Every few moments the front door opened to admit more customers. Then it opened and Annie came in. Carmen went to her at once and they shared a few words before she went directly into her office and shut the door.

Max tensed. She hadn't looked to see if he was there, but she probably assumed he'd be gone by now. He would hang around until his brothers drove away, then come back and talk to her. The tension in his shoulders relaxed. There was nothing to worry about.

Not far from where Max sat, someone watched his reaction to Annie Duhon. Pleasure, the watcher thought, the good doctor felt real good at the sight of her. He wanted her—it showed in his face. How convenient.

CHAPTER 4

Gator Hibbs and his wife, Doll, proprietors of Toussaint's one hotel, the Majestic, arrived at the table. He shifted his round body uncertainly and took off a battered, sweat-stained Achafalaya Gold Casino baseball cap, revealing his sweating bald head. Doll stood behind him as if she were shy, which was anything but the truth from Max's dealings with her. Nondescript, with fine brown hair held by a rubber band at the back of her head, Doll's eyes were her one notable feature. They were incongruous. Light gray and wide, as if in perpetual surprise, they didn't reflect a thing about Doll's acerbic personality.

"Hi, Gator, Doll," Max said.

"Nice day," Gator said, fastening his attention on the rain-splattered windows. "I like this kinda day." He winced and jerked—and Max figured Doll had elbowed her husband.

"Y'didn't have to do that," Gator said, turning his back on Max. "What d'you do that for? Pokin' me in the kidney like that. Me, I already got water troubles—you heard Dr. Reb—"

"We come to talk to Dr. Savage," Doll said, her eyes still wide open and blank. "He's not interested in your waterworks, Gator. I hear tell he does the faces and stuff."

Max raised his eyebrows at Kelly and Roche and stood up. He tapped Gator's shoulder. "Let's find somewhere quieter."

"We can say what we got to say here," Doll said. "Ain't nuthin' private."

"The hell it ain't," Gator said, and turned red. "Thanks, Doc. Appreciate your understandin'."

They moved outside under the covered entry. Gator shoved his hands in the pockets of his washed-out overalls and spread his feet to brace his weight. Doll stared at him.

"Relax," Max said. "Just tell me what's on your mind."

"We're real fair folks," Gator said after a pause. "Give anybody anythin', we would. Ain't that right, Doll?"

"Right."

"You can ask anyone in this town and they'll tell you how the Hibbses is generous."

Max smiled. He felt sorry for the man. "You're uncomfortable with whatever you need to tell me. You can't say anything I haven't heard before, so why not get it over with?"

Gator took a deep breath and gave a bronchitic cough. "It's the damp," he said, indicating the rain beating into a layer of fog resembling ice vapor. "You did say your Miz Riley was only stayin' one night?"

"Yes."

"And she was goin' to pay when she left this mornin'?"

"She didn't pay," Doll said rapidly. "And extra days is extra pay. She's takin' up a room even if she ain't sleepin' in it."

These two didn't amuse Max anymore. "When I made the booking, I told you to send the bill to me."

"You said it would be one night but check-out's at eleven. We're owed for two nights now—as long as she's gone by tomorrow mornin'."

His throat tightened. "Miss Riley is still here?"

Doll actually smirked. "Why don't you tell us? What you do in private is your business, except if you try using us as a cover. Don't make no difference to us if she's stayin' with you, now. But it makes more sense for her to get the rest of her things, don't it?"

Max couldn't draw a full breath. "I drove her back to the hotel last night." He didn't want to think what he was thinking. "I saw her go inside. Perhaps she just forgot one of her bags. I'll arrange to get it sent on." He retrieved his wallet from a back pocket and pulled out some bills.

Doll looked uncertain. "She didn't clear any of her stuff out of the bathroom. And her rental car's still parked out back of the hotel."

CHAPTER 5

Annie would know those shoulders and that back anywhere. Looking at Max Savage from any direction was more than a pleasure, except when she didn't want to talk to anyone, even him.

The doors to Pappy's swung shut behind her. Annie hovered, the hood of her jacket pulled well down against the rain, and considered backtracking. She still had a chance to get inside without being seen.

With a cell phone clamped to his ear, Max turned and saw her. He must see her. That or he was looking right through her with an expression on his face that turned him into a stranger. Intense agitation—and anger—distorted his features. Annie breathed great gulps of air through her mouth. She half raised her hand to wave, but let it fall again. The intense, blue-eyed man who caught the attention of many women and left them trying to decide if they had seen him on the cover of *GQ*, had stepped out in a frightening disguise today. With a vague smile about her lips, Annie walked on and made to pass him.

Fortunately, since he was on the phone she didn't need to speak. And she wasn't sure she could.

Before she managed to escape toward the parking lot, Max caught her by the arm and smiled, with his mouth, not with his eyes. Some emotion made his eyes darker. He averted the phone mouthpiece and said, "Please give me a moment, Annie." The downpour had turned the shoulders of his denim jacket dark. Rain plastered his black hair to his head and ran down his face.

She nodded, but would rather leave without the inevitable questions about why she looked exhausted. When Father Cyrus drove her home early that morning, Joe and Ellie Gable had greeted her, Ellie with Annie's cat, Irene, clutched in her arms. Irene was queen in Annie's flat and never stepped outside. But the Gables had been awakened by the cat yowling at their back door.

With an easy excuse that Irene must have slipped, unseen, out of the building when she left, Annie had lied to her friends. But no matter what else was on her mind, she never neglected Irene who had been asleep on the tumbled bed when Annie left.

Someone had got in and let her cat out.

No, this time she had been so agitated that she left a door ajar somewhere. That's probably what happened.

Twice since the episode at St. Cécil's she had dozed, only to be jolted by visions from the nightmare. Cyrus had spent a long time with her that morning and inevitably, spurred on by the trust he fostered just by being himself, she had told him what was happening to her.

Cyrus, who had probably never turned anyone away, promised her he would be there for her and that they'd get together again to see how she was doing.

For the first time, the scenes had continued for seconds when she was completely awake. She turned her head from Max and closed her eyes. What did it mean? What was happening to her?

Max's grip tightened on her arm. "Spike, I don't think anything has happened to her," he said into his phone. "Yes, of course it's possible. Sorry. Michele drove into Toussaint yesterday morning. She rented a car at the airport. I drove her back to the Majestic last night—after dinner—but according to Gator and Doll, she didn't sleep there. Her things are still in the room and the rental car's parked in the hotel lot."

The conversation was not her business but she heard every word loud and clear. Michele would be Michele Riley, the woman Max had mentioned hoping to hire for the new clinic.

"Of course I'm worried," Max said. "Look, I'm gonna have to come in and have a chat, but not today."

While he listened to Spike his color deepened. "Kelly's the detail man," he said. "He dealt with the employment information we need to have on file for her. He knows what's happened. I'll have him call you…okay? We'll get back to you."

Slowly, Annie turned her eyes toward Max. While he listened to Sheriff Spike Devol, a pale line formed around his mouth. When he spoke again, even his voice sounded different, with no trace of the warmth she expected.

He shoved the phone onto his belt. "I want to get away from here, now. Annie, I could use your company. Or can't you do that?"

She paused. A quick explanation that she had to get back to work would set her free. Only she would rather be with him. "I can take a little while." She wouldn't pry. If he wanted her to know about his problems, he would let her know.

Max moved quickly, his strides long enough to press Annie into a trot. He aimed his key, and the lights on his gray Boxster blinked. He didn't slow down until he took a moment to see her inside the car and close the door. Within seconds he got behind the wheel, and sat swiping water from his face. He turned on the engine and drove from the lot, too fast for the slick conditions.

Without looking at her, or saying a word, he grabbed his phone again and pressed a button. "Come on, come on. Kelly? Yeah, hi, it's Max. Just got off the phone with Spike... No, dammit, I told him what I found out from the Hibbses, nothing else. Get Michele's information. Home address, contract, whatever you've got. Take it to Spike at his office." He stopped talking and his attention seemed to wander. "Spike can find out if she was on her plane back to New York today. I forgot to ask if he'd already done that."

He looked at her. She got another mouth-only smile and pushed a fist into her stomach. This was panicking her and she'd already been through enough in the past twenty-four hours.

"Did you sleep last night?" he asked, pressing the mouthpiece against his shoulder. He figured he already knew the answer. Annie looked sick. She blinked rapidly as if her eyes stung.

"Of course I slept," she said, sounding defensive and not like the Annie he was trying to know.

"Is that why your eyes look like black holes and you're so stressed you'd probably break if someone touched you. What did you do to yourself?" He had noticed before, but never mentioned several small, silvered areas on both sides of her hands. Old, insignificant burn scars. Severe burns, taking away the disfigurement they caused, were part of his life, but Annie's weren't even near his league. However, today she did have a new gauze dressing on the left side.

"I'm fine," she protested. "Never been better. Mornings aren't my favorites, that's all." She didn't explain the bandage.

Max didn't believe her. Absently, he heard Kelly's muffled, angry voice.

Annie didn't intend to talk about what had happened at the church. She returned Max's blue stare. "Do you think I'm lyin'?"

The road curved but he took the bends with absent ease.

Annie felt every turn of the wheel, the frequent corrections the car made, and looked doggedly at her lap.

"Have you finished?" Max said into the phone, repeatedly glancing back at Annie. "Oh, yes you have. No, I'm not telling you the details—let Spike tell you. I can't face it. Not yet. Hell, I don't know but it's all too familiar. I'm going for a drive... Because I need to."

He turned off the phone—all the way off—and headed north. Annie wanted to know where they were going but didn't ask.

Yellow and brown leaves fell from deciduous trees. Some caught in the windshield wipers and slapped back and forth. The rising fog layer steamed as if the rain falling from misty skies were boiling. Billowing vapor rolled from the road and coiled away between trees on either side. Patchy visibility cleared for brief moments before disappearing into ghostly clouds that took the car in a suffocating embrace.

If she asked him to slow down, or even to wait for the conditions to improve, would he turn his strange hostile voice on her, and allow his face to look as it had outside Pappy's?

Max leaned forward slightly. His damp knuckles were white, the tendons on the backs of his hands and wrists, distended.

"I'm sorry," he said suddenly and glanced at her. He heard himself swallow. "Really sorry, Annie. I don't know what got into me, bringing you with me like this. I'm not good company." This was probably the only appealing woman he had known who didn't feel her own power over a man. Reticence hovered behind her eyes. Yet she was lovely, her shoulder-length hair smooth and fair, her eyes remarkable for their catlike, almost amber color and her mouth soft, full and inviting. And Annie was slim with gentle curves and long legs.

But Annie Duhon, a thoughtful, gentle woman, had a tough side. She ran Pappy's with an ease he admired and he had witnessed how she used humor to cut through difficult encounters. Max didn't think he would enjoy being on the wrong end of Annie's displeasure. He smiled slightly at the thought.

"Me, I kind of like wild days like this," Annie said, feeling silly but desperate to break the tension. Each time he glanced at her she felt as if he touched her. Her breathing grew shallower, her lungs tight.

"I can tell I'm upsetting you," he said. "I'll go back."

"Don't," she said. "You said you needed my company. I'm here for you. If you want to talk, I'm ready to listen." She had never been able to walk away from someone in need. Sometimes that had been a mistake but it couldn't be with Max…could it?

"Thanks," he said and drove on more slowly.

He thumped the steering wheel and Annie jumped. Her hands trembled and she wound them tightly together. If things did get sticky, she would find a way to bail out. She'd learned the hard way about not allowing a man to trap her where she could be overpowered.

Max wasn't the type to overpower anyone.

She touched his arm. "It's none of my business, but you're worried. Is somethin' wrong with the person you interviewed yesterday? Michele?"

"I don't know." He didn't, and he didn't want to talk about it—or think about it, for God's sake.

"Okay." She wished she hadn't asked.

"You're shaking," he said. "I've scared you. Dammit! This isn't like me. Those bastards are getting what they want, they're turning me into a madman."

"Who?" she said automatically.

"Let it go."

If it might not turn out to be a really bad idea, she would tell him what she thought about being a captive audience for someone in a foul temper.

"Bail," she said, not meaning to speak aloud. She cleared her throat.

A strong hand settled over both of hers. "There's no reason for me to bail. I'm going through a rough patch is all. And I'm getting ahead of myself. Do you like bagels?" He continued to hold her hands. "Remember a little restaurant in St. Martinville called Char's Bagels?"

"No." She looked around. *St. Martinville?* The weather, the fog, had disoriented her, if it hadn't, she'd have asked him to go somewhere other than St. Martinville—anywhere but there. The town where she'd grown up wasn't so far from Toussaint but she'd left a long time ago and never returned since.

"You'll love it. Every kind of bagel and every flavor whipped cream cheese you can think of. Smoked salmon. Capers. Paper-thin onions. Great coffee."

"New York food," she said faintly.

"People eat bagels all over," Max said. "Could you go to Char's with me and eat something now?"

Her life in the town was over. The people she'd known were dead or gone—most of them. Those who remained would never recognize her after so long. Almost everything about her had changed.

She definitely wanted out of this car. "Didn't you get lunch at Pappy's?" What did it matter? Once she was out of the car she could take charge of herself. "Well, I'll come. Why not. I always like pickin' up fresh ideas." If she made a big deal out of driving somewhere else, Max could get suspicious.

"I had a good lunch." He couldn't read her mood. "But I can't remember what it was, so I'll take more time with the bagels."

This man was in control, always. He had never blabbered about inconsequential things—like bagels. "Lead me to Char's," she said.

When he glanced at her again, his eyes were narrowed and she felt him assessing her, her reactions. He suspected she was humoring him. She stared back into his eyes and felt drawn to him, even as she couldn't put fear completely aside.

In St. Martinville, folks had said she was a bad seed, that she went after the kind of excitement that could ruin her. She had heard whisperings: "Disgustin'" "Stay away from her and make sure your George does. She's ruined more than one decent man." They had no proof because there was none, but they linked her to men she'd never met and she had no defense because she had made two mistakes that turned out badly enough to trash her reputation.

Max drove into St. Martinville. The rain had cleared the streets of people on foot.

"You know your way around this town," she said and her voice felt unused. Annie kept her face straight ahead and wished she could put her hood up again and hide inside.

"Blink and you'd miss the place," Max said. "What's to know? It's a pretty town, friendly."

She shrugged. The fog over the road had dissipated as soon as they entered the town, but the rain beat down here just as heavily as it had in Toussaint.

That's where she should be, in Toussaint, at Pappy's doing her job. This was out of character for her and it mustn't happen again. "Where is this Char's?" She didn't recall the place.

"Close to St. Martin de Tours Church. And there's the church now."

The white, single-story church boasted a bell tower over the front door. A few people formed a line out front to file up steps and into the building. Visitors liked to tour the building, and a wet day was a good time to be inside. When she'd been a little girl, Annie used to creep into the Perpetual Adoration Garden. She liked to sit and stare at the statue of Evangeline, the Acadian heroine. Peace waited there, and although Annie had never told anyone, she had secretly thought Evangeline watched over children—and fairies. She bit her lip. She had been certain fairies flitted about among the flowers because she'd seen them, and since she would never share that secret, no one would argue the point.

A right turn on Hamilton and they traveled a couple of blocks. Annie's stomach hit her diaphragm. Not much had really changed and she didn't want to be there. Abruptly, Max turned in at a narrow alley she didn't recall and made a quick right into a fore-court large enough for half a dozen cars. One open space remained and the Boxster slid in tidily.

A single window on the left side of a boxy little building gave a clouded impression of rapidly moving figures inside. The door, with an oval of glass at its center, stood to the right. Whoever painted "Char's Bagels" over the window wouldn't be making a living in signs. Each turquoise letter was of a different size from its partners. And the closer the offender got to the end of the two words, the smaller his or her efforts became. Apparently he had eventually noticed his mistakes and attempted to fill up ragged spaces with yellow-brown pocked circles with holes in the middle. Those would be bagels, Annie decided.

Max switched off his engine but didn't attempt to get out of the car. He turned her heart, and caused an ache in some places she shouldn't allow to react at all. An incredibly good-looking man with a square jaw, a dip in the center of his chin and a wide, firm mouth that turned up at the corners, he was tall, with a muscular body—and if he knew how much time she spent fantasizing about him, he would probably laugh, or pity her.

He got out but she couldn't make herself move. Max opened her door and offered her his hand.

Reluctantly, she joined him. He looked steadily down at her, his black brows drawn together. "What's wrong? There is something, isn't there."

One of the blushes that cursed her life blossomed on Annie's face. "Nothin' wrong."

He eased her away from the door and shut it. Once again they were pounded with rain and he swiped a hand across spiky eyelashes. "Yes, there is. What happened this morning? Why weren't you at Pappy's? You don't miss work." He'd done everything wrong with her so far today. The clock needed to be turned back. No hope there.

"Whoa, boy," she said. "I don't have to explain my actions to you." Adrenaline started to rush and gave her some strength, together with a whole heap of nervous jumpiness.

Someone needed to get them out of this tight corner and it should be him. "You're right. This is my fault. I got a bad shock this morning and when I saw you, it was like reaching someone sensible and sane who made me feel…calmer, I guess. I wanted to stay close to you."

"I guess we both had rotten mornings." Yet again, she said something she should have kept to herself. "Happens that way sometimes. Irene got out and had to be chased down." She hated lying and lies were coming too easily lately.

"Your cat? You found it?"

"Her, yes," she said and looked around the area. She had been down here at some time but the bagel shop had to be relatively new. Petals from magnolia blooms rolled over the forecourt. She could smell their sweet, musky scent.

Two laughing women spilled from a beauty shop on the corner and Annie spun away in case they looked in her direction. She put a hand to her throat and tapped the toes of her damp pumps. If they did see her, they'd only get a view of her back and never guess who she was, not that she recognized them.

If he had made her this edgy, Max thought, then he hated himself. "Come on. We'll get some hot coffee and warm up a bit. Then I'll drop you at your place so you can change. I'll hang and get you back to work."

He realized she was looking at something behind him and it didn't make her happy. He resisted the urge to find out what had caught her attention. Annie didn't seem to want to be here. And he didn't want to be in Toussaint now, but he had no right to pull her into his problems.

He put a hand on her shoulder and found it rigid. "You coming?"

Her lips parted and her eyes filled with tears. *Tears?* Hell, what had he done to her? When he looked over his shoulder he saw nothing but a man leaving the shop with a bulging white paper bag.

"Annie?"

If she could close her eyes and be miles away, she would. "No! No, I can't stay today. You go on in. I know how to get back to Pappy's on my own." As soon as she got away from this parking lot she'd call Carmen to come and get her. He didn't ask questions and he didn't discuss people's business.

Max didn't move.

"Really," she told him. "I'll see you back there—maybe tomorrow if you're in."

He reached for her right hand, turned it palm up, dropped his car keys there and folded her fingers over them. "Take my car. I've got a few things I should do while I'm here. Roche will be along and I'll go back with him. Just leave the car at Pappy's." Meanwhile he'd get his act together and make sure he never made another stupid slip like this one. But then he intended to find out why Annie was nervous in this town. More than nervous, just about paralyzed. "Off you go."

"No. That's not necessary," Annie said. She tried to push the keys at him but he stepped away. He blinked and worked his jaw, said, "Just take the car. I've got to go now." He walked from the lot and turned toward Bayou Teche.

Confused, her skin damp and clammy, Annie watched him move rapidly out of sight. She looked at the keys, then at the Boxster. Of course she couldn't take his car and leave him here. But the man with the white bag had stopped outside the bagel shop door and she felt him staring at her.

Max wouldn't have gone so far. She'd go after him now and give back the keys.

Only her feet wouldn't move. She pulled up her hood and bowed her head, moved close to the car.

It was Bobby Colbert who stood, looking directly at her.

How old was he now? A couple of years older than her, thirty-one maybe? *Move. Get out of here.*

Annie pivoted from the vehicle. No one would think anything of someone who took off running in this kind of weather.

"Annie? Is that you?"

She froze. He might as well have taken her by the throat and squeezed. Annie didn't react.

The sound of his footsteps, coming in her direction, horrified her. *He's not bad. He was just a boy back then. We were both kids. And the last time I met him he was trying to help me—he did help me. I would probably have died if he hadn't showed up. But he saw what that crazy man did to me. Bobby knows all about what I have to hide . . . No one else could know. She couldn't bear it if . . . If Max found out, she would leave Toussaint rather than put up with either his revulsion, or his pity.*

"Annie, it's me, Bobby. I didn't know you were back."

She raised her face as he reached her. Not a boy anymore. Slim as he had been, but with the mature development of the man he had become. Sandy hair, curly and well cut. Earnest brown eyes. Even, white teeth. The all-American kid had grown up and his open face only intensified her shock and fear at seeing him.

"I'm not back," she said and shuddered at the thin, wobbly sound of her voice.

Bobby smiled. "I think about you a lot, cher. How you doin'? How did it all…?" He glanced downward over her body.

Annie unlocked the Boxster, dropped inside and locked the door. Not until she saw him jump away did she register that when she shot backward, she almost hit Bobby Colbert.

He could destroy everything she had worked for.

CHAPTER 6

Max's shoes slipped on wet leaves and mud.

Sounds traveled from the bayou but there were no visuals of the water. He heard voices calling out there, from one boat to another. They headed for a dock and shouted back and forth to avoid a collision. Even the fog had a presence, as if it repeatedly whispered for the world to "shush."

He knew exactly where he was and kept moving quickly, corrected once for almost losing his balance and hurried on. A large piece of land lay ahead about a mile, and back through pretty dense trees. He had wanted to build the clinic there but the others preferred to work on an existing building. Today, he was convinced he should have insisted on that piece of land over Green Veil. A simplistic reaction and the result of pressure, but so what? If he could, he would change everything he had done since arriving in the area. Everything except meeting Annie and he'd managed to scare her away, too.

Under the leaves lay a concrete track, pitted, cracked and long past needing repair. If he had bought and built there, a good road would have been put through. He had thought about gardens and terraces where patients could wander and sit outside while they re-cuperated.

At a spot where he knew he could get through the trees easily, he climbed up a shallow bank from the track, stepped over a sagging wire fence and slapped a jungle of vines and bushes away as he passed.

He knew the sound of his own engine when he heard it. Annie had followed him. It was no good, he had to stay away from her until he found out if the unthinkable had happened, if Michele had been hurt, or... Max couldn't bring himself to form the other word.

Ducking under a low branch, he pressed on and hoped Annie hadn't seen where he went.

The noise of the car got closer.

A clearing opened in front of him and he stepped onto uneven ground where shadow from the surrounding trees had killed any grass and left moss and hardy weeds in its place.

The car passed. Max sighed. His gut told him the next news of Michele might not be what he wanted to hear. And a blow like that was what it took to knock sense back into him? Annie was off-limits; off-limits because he wanted her too much and the wrong people could find out how he felt.

Being important to Max Savage increased a woman's chances of premature death.

If Max wanted her company, he would not have taken off the way he had.

Annie braked gently and looked in her rearview mirror. He had left the road about a mile back.

She chewed a fingernail and immediately jerked it away from her mouth, muttering at herself.

Slowly, she eased the car into reverse, took her foot partway off the brake and coasted backward, stopping before she reached the exact place where she thought Max had gone.

Without giving herself time to back out, she left the car and went up the bank. He had stepped easily over the fence; the operation took her longer because she had to use a foot to draw the loose top wire to the ground so that she could move on.

Trees closed around her—old timber, a mixture of conifers and heavy deciduous trees—their branches seeming to push at one another for more space.

Debris crackled under her feet and she made no attempt to be quiet. She didn't want to surprise Max.

Annie leaned a hand against the furrowed bark of a dripping live oak. She had nothing to offer Max but friendship. By now he had to want more than that—and a few memorable kisses quickly cooled by Annie. The scent of rotting leaves rose around her, tannic and disturbing. In dreamy moments alone, she visualized, even felt, unbearably good sex with Max. She wanted to share his bed, to tear away her hang-ups and give herself to him—and take him in return. Annie's skin heated yet she shivered. The chance was too great that real intimacy with him would be a disaster.

But she couldn't leave him here. More quickly than she expected, spaces between the trees grew lighter. She saw Max move in a clearing, but hung back.

Standing close to a tree, she watched him. He trailed one end of a long stick along the ground, stopping from time to time to make marks before carrying on with one line after another. And at intervals he glanced up as if taking measure of the area and his chart, or whatever he was making.

Darkness fell rapidly. It wasn't time. Annie gasped, or rather opened her mouth and heard a gasp. She did not feel the muggy air enter her mouth. "Max," she called.

He didn't hear her.

Light went out completely, scarred by an immediate flash of flame. It crackled, and hissed, and went away, but not before she felt its heat.

She knew what was happening. Once again the nightmare closed in on her while she was awake. Only she wouldn't let it.

A rushing cloud of leaves billowed past her, grazed her hair and neck. Annie batted at her head, shook her hair. A sound squeezed from her throat, a sob.

Dragging.

From nearby she heard something being dragged, and the brittle sound of a hard object hitting rocks as it bounced along.

She closed her eyes but saw clearly just the same. A man dragged a woman's stiff body into the clearing and dropped it. He took up a shovel and cleared away leaves at least a foot deep that hadn't been there before. He poked at the leaves, making a hole through them to dig beneath.

Annie dropped to her knees and huddled against the tree. Her tan linen skirt soaked up water. She screamed, but the man took no notice.

The darkness faded, gradually thinned, and she couldn't see the man with the shovel, or the broken figure on the ground. Like stage lights, a glow rose slowly until she saw Max again. He was farther away, still scraping his stick on the ground.

She called his name again, "Max!" But he didn't as much as look up. Annie wanted to go to him but her limbs wouldn't move. Pain pounded in her head and she grew hotter. Was she there at all? If she was, why didn't he hear her?

Why didn't anyone know she was there?

A step, at last she took one step, her leg heavy, her foot scuffing over the ground. And another step. And another. Huge, ponderous steps but each one covered perhaps an inch. She wobbled and spread her arms to balance.

"Max!"

He turned his back on her and began to stride, only for him each stride became a bound, as if he were a spacewalker, and his figure grew smaller.

As Max grew smaller the light failed, just as fast as before. Annie squeezed her eyelids together. She shook her head and heavy, damp hair slashed from side to side across her face.

There was no sound, no dragging, no cracking of metal on stone.

Holding her breath, she slitted her eyes to look ahead. Nothing, only darkness, hot, wet darkness. Somewhere behind her lay the road and the car. She knew with shocking clarity that everything hung on her retracing her steps and getting away. And never coming back. She should never have come back to St. Martinville, never.

A lone horn wailed a single, endless note. Deep and mournful.

Annie marshaled her spirit and looked over her shoulder. The man approached from behind. This time he shouldered the shovel and carried a woman under the other arm. She kicked, flailed, but silver tape wrapped around her head sealed her cries away.

Annie opened her mouth to scream. The man passed only yards from her, his face averted. She had to stop him from killing the woman.

He dropped the woman on the leaves and set to work, raking together a pile of sticks and leaves. He brought logs and tree limbs and tossed them on the heap. The pieces of wood arced in slow motion and settled softly.

He stepped away, lit a crude torch that shot forth flames, and buried the pointed end in the ground. Then he picked up the woman and threw her in the same slow arc as the bits of wood. She spun in the air, illuminated by the torch, her arms and legs flopping and twisting with each turn.

Annie shoved her hands out and screamed. She moved forward, faster this time, she thought. Sparks reached her, pricked her face and legs like white-hot needles.

"Don't kill her," she cried. "Don't burn her."

* * *

Max dropped the stick and spun toward the garbled voice he heard.

"Hey, hey," he called, running toward Annie. She stumbled, knees sagging, arms outstretched.

He covered the space between them in seconds. Her eyes were unfocused, her face white, her hair hanging in sodden clumps. "Annie," he cried, reaching to grab her.

Her awful cry ripped through him. She screamed and screamed, and flung her arms back and forth as if in some imaginary fight.

"Annie!" He caught and shook her. "Take a breath. A deep breath, now."

A growling noise came from her throat. She appeared to look at him, but he could tell that her eyes were only turned in his direction. He doubted if she saw anything.

At first he'd thought she must have epilepsy, but this was no seizure.

Bending his knees, dropping his weight, he rose under her arms and caught her around the waist.

Her right forearm connected with his ear and the power of the blow astounded him. She struggled with enormous purpose, as if fighting for her life. Max steeled himself to stop her from hurting herself—or him.

Slamming her against him, he trapped one of her arms with his body and slid his left hand around her back to grasp the other arm. He lifted her and rolled her toward him until her face pressed into his chest.

He began to walk toward the trees.

"N-no-o!" She made room to free her mouth and yelled. "Stop it. Don't hurt her anymore."

Max tried to shut out the words. They had no meaning—or did they?

Carrying Annie was easy; she didn't weigh much.

"It's okay," he said, gently but loud enough for her to hear. "I'm going to help you. This will all be over soon."

"No, no, no."

Her bucking jarred him.

"No, don't burn me." She went limp, her eyes dulled. "I don't want to die like that."

At the car, Max set Annie inside. She seemed docile now, limp.

His cell rang and he answered. "Who is this?"

"Did you get my letter yet?" The voice on the phone sounded like a speaking harmonica.

CHAPTER 7

Sheriff Spike Devol lived with his family at Rosebank Resort, where Max and his brothers had apartments. Spike had assumed part ownership of the resort when he'd married Vivian Patin. Charlotte, Vivian's mother, remained a partner and also lived on the premises, as did Wendy, Spike's daughter by his first marriage.

Drinking coffee at a window table in Hungry Eyes, a combination café and bookshop, Max kept an eye on the sheriff's cruiser parked at the curb.

Spike was coming to meet him.

The suggestion that they have a chat in the café had been Spike's, but the location also helped solve one of Max's problems. He had to see Annie and he intended to hang around until he managed just that.

Annie drove an elderly red Volvo sedan. No sign of it yet. Max knew Annie usually entered the building through the shop if it was open, and used a door at the back of the café. Steps from a vestibule led up to her flat.

At Pappy's, a night manager took over from Annie most evenings and Max counted on her coming home by six. Once she was upstairs he'd feel better. At least he'd know where to find her.

Engrossed, Spike talked on his radio while staring into the glow of a computer screen. He made Max nervous. When he issued the "invitation" to Hungry Eyes he had avoided saying what exactly was on his mind. Max volunteered to meet the sheriff at his office but Spike kept deliberately cheerful and said there was "No need for formality—yet." The "yet" didn't sound so friendly to Max who knew the topic would be Michele Riley.

What if there weren't any leads?

Spike wasn't coming here for nothing.

When he was alone again, Max intended to go outside to the street and take a right between Joe and Ellie Gable's house and Joe's law offices, into an alley leading to back entrances into the buildings. The back door to Hungry Eyes was also Annie's front door. She could have gotten past without him seeing her.

She could well refuse to talk to him and shut him out. He drew his lips back from his teeth. Chatter at several other tables helped him feel anonymous. Max didn't want to attract any attention.

He had already made up his mind not to be put off. Whatever it took, he would get to Annie. After her meltdown earlier in the day she had refused to be examined by a doctor, even after he'd set out for Reb Girard's office. Annie would not discuss what had occurred, and something had definitely happened. All she had agreed to was going back to Pappy's where she'd insisted she was fine. *"I haven't really eaten today,"* she'd said. *"I think my blood sugar gets low. A little shakiness, that's all it was."*

Sure, and a little shakiness made a woman say bizarre things, stagger about with unfocused eyes, then collapse. He had never believed in such things before but he was almost convinced she had seen some sort of vision in that clearing.

"*Did you get my letter yet?*" Max couldn't keep that Darth Vader voice out of his head for long. He'd heard it before, several times. The one call he'd tried to get traced had come from a phone box and the trail was an immediate dead end.

The rain had stopped and with the early evening came a lemon sun dressed in puffs of navy blue. Why wasn't Annie here yet?

"She be here soon, cher."

A soft female voice startled Max and he looked up at Wazoo (L'Oisseau de Nuit to strangers), whom Annie had told him ran the shop during recently extended hours.

Wazoo also lived at Rosebank where she ran housekeeping and obviously had a special place in Vivian and Charlotte's hearts.

Calling Wazoo eccentric would be redundant. She was also a beautiful woman with olive coloring and an extraordinary face. And she was small, very feminine and the unofficial property of an NOPD homicide detective, Nat Archer. Or maybe that was the other way around. Wazoo wouldn't take kindly to being called any man's property.

"What did you say?" Max asked.

The woman didn't meet his eyes and refilled his coffee as if she'd never spoken. But she had, and she must mean Annie. Wazoo didn't know he and Annie were friends. Even if she did, how would she figure out he was thinking about her, waiting for her?

Wazoo balanced the curve of her carafe on the edge of the table. Slowly, she raised her face and her blank expression confused him. Then light sharpened in her eyes as she looked intently at Max. He saw her shudder.

"You like somethin' else?" she asked, her voice flat.

He shook his head, no. "You said—"

"Nothin'," she interrupted him. "I didn't say nothin', me."

Max drummed his fingernails on his cup. He raised one eyebrow in question.

"I got to get back to work," she said, frowning deeply, still staring at him. "Take care of what you love." A wide smile transformed her. "Wazoo's gettin' tired. Enjoy the coffee."

When she turned away her dress swished. As she returned to the counter, she stopped to fill cups for other customers.

Laughter came from deep in the shop, on the book side. Max couldn't see anyone between the stacks.

A man sitting alone rustled his paper loudly and felt around for part of a sandwich on his plate. He carried the food behind the paper.

What had Wazoo meant, dammit? What did she know?

He glanced toward Spike's cruiser again. How much should he volunteer to the sheriff? Nothing? Everything? Mentioning the call would be pointless. Once his history spread through Toussaint, he would be second-guessing every look that came his way. And if Michele didn't show up fast, he'd become the prime suspect in her disappearance.

Spike got out of his car and Max studied the man: A tall, muscular guy, good-looking with blond hair and a Stetson tipped forward over his eyes. His khaki uniform fit him well. He flashed a smile at a woman leaving the shop and carried on to the door.

This day continued to stink. More clouds piled over what was left of the sun and daylight faded fast. Max's pulse beat off the seconds, double time, while he waited. He expected bad news to keep on coming.

The shop bell rang and Spike stepped inside.

Max turned to greet the man but Wazoo cried, "Be still, my heart. Here come that sexy lawman. You come on in, Spike, I been needin' a gorgeous man to play with my mind. What you want? I got gumbo—best around. And...no, no, de gumbo best. I give you a bowl a gumbo."

Spike swept off his hat to reveal hair that stuck up in front, and bright blue eyes. His easy grin sent Wazoo twirling, her long black curls flying and the purple lace dress swirling about her feet. She held her hands over her heart and went into a mock swoon.

Several customers laughed and so did Spike. "Guess I'll be havin' the gumbo, Wazoo. I'll be with Max over there—" he nodded in Max's direction "—and I'll take black coffee with that."

The woman was odd, Max thought. She said whatever came into her head and everyone around knew she did. No one took her seriously and neither should he.

Spike took the chair opposite Max and they shook hands over the blue-and-white check tablecloth. "You know Wazoo?" Spike asked.

"I live at Rosebank, remember?" Max said. "So does she. I don't think she'd allow me to ignore her."

"True."

"She seems to have a lot of jobs." Max glanced back to the road. "I only found out about this one a few nights ago."

"Wazoo works for Jilly Gautreaux over at All Tarted Up, too. She helps with the early bakin'. Then she's back at Rosebank makin' sure the rooms are made up the way she likes 'em. And here in the late afternoon." Spike leaned closer. "Don't say anythin', but I think Ellie Gable came up with this evenin' openin' thing 'cause Wazoo needs more money."

"Sounds like something Ellie would do," Max said and almost followed up by saying he should be able to find something for Wazoo at the clinic. There were only so many hours in the woman's day and she'd probably be a disaster around patients.

Max hadn't known about Wazoo's job in the kitchens at the

pastry shop where just about everyone in town passed through between early morning and midafternoon. He didn't add to Spike that he'd been told Wazoo was an animal therapist—therapy for emotionally disturbed critters—and that she also dealt in a little hoodoo and gave foreboding predictions. And sang at funerals.

Wazoo moved around rapidly behind the café counter, pausing frequently to snap her fingers in time to a country beat coming from an old radio. A glass jar filled with saltwater taffy kept the radio safely wedged on a small shelf. At a signal Max couldn't hear, she opened the door to the back vestibule and stared down. A moment later she draped a tiny, mostly white cat around her neck. The animal stretched her small body to an impossible length and looked as if her dark markings were Egyptian, including the kohl-like lines around her eyes.

No doubt the health department would have something to say about a cat in a café, but several of the patrons crooned, "Irene, baby, Irene, cher," so he guessed the cat was a fixture.

Irene baby curled her lip at every would-be friend, and she wasn't smiling.

"You called," Spike said.

Max looked at him quickly. "I called you back."

Spike gave a slow smile and nodded. "Is that the way it went? Why don't you tell me what's on your mind, then I'll tell you what's on mine."

Playing it cute wouldn't earn him any points with the sheriff, Max decided. "Michele Riley is on my mind. I'm hoping you invited me here because there's good news."

Wazoo brought Spike's coffee, glanced from one man to the other and slipped away quickly, but not before the cat gave Max a narrow-eyed stare. "This isn't what I wanted to tell you," Spike said. "We don't have any leads, Max. All we have is what you told us. She had dinner with you and your brothers and afterward you drove her back to the Majestic. You saw her inside. And she disappeared."

"We both know that didn't happen," Max said. He stared outside again. He hadn't driven away from the hotel until the lights went off in the hall. What the hell could have happened to Michele? "She went into the hotel. If there was—I don't know, an attack—why didn't Gator and Doll and their boy hear? Why isn't there evidence of a struggle?"

"You tell me."

Max's skin tightened. "Come again?"

"I said, you tell me why there's no evidence and no one heard anything. I'm fresh out of ideas and, unlike you, I never saw the woman at all."

Max frowned. He caught Wazoo's eye and pointed to his cup, more because he needed whatever thinking time he could buy than because he wanted more coffee.

Wazoo came with Spike's bowl of gumbo in one hand and a carafe in the other. She set down the bowl and filled both coffee cups. "Be right back," she said, her eyes making a swift study of their faces. "You got trouble," she said, her voice little more than a whisper. "Big trouble. I keep smelling somethin' real bad." She sniffed the air and returned to the counter.

Max didn't meet Spike's eyes. First Annie passed out in front of him and came around begging not to be burned, then Wazoo talked about smelling something bad—like burning, maybe? If he was the type to run, he'd already be on his way, but running wouldn't stop the madness.

Carrying corn bread and a dish of honey butter, Wazoo returned and this time she slid into a seat at the table.

"You're deserting your post," Spike said.

She snorted. "No such thing, lawman. I'm right here and I got real good eyes."

"I think I see someone back in the books waving for you."

Wazoo gave Max a pitying look. "They know where to find me, not that I'm any book expert. The reading group's at the back— they answer anyone's questions—makes 'em feel important and suits me. This Michele, they sayin' she come lookin' for a job at Green Veil. That place used to be called Serenity House, y'know." She disentangled the cat and sat it on her lap where it rested its nose on the table and switched its green-gold gaze between the men.

"We know what the house was called," Spike said. "But thanks for the reminder."

"She's dead, that one. I know what I see."

"Who's dead?" Max shot back at her. "What do you see?" If she said something about fire, he might lose it.

"It isn't that easy," Wazoo said. "I can't turn it on like a picture show. Gotta wait for stuff to come clear, but that Michele ain't with us here no more."

"You shouldn't play around with things as important as this," Max said. He prickled all over.

Spike spooned up gumbo, chewed vegetables and managed to appear almost disinterested.

"Vivian," Wazoo said abruptly, pointing a long forefinger with a red-painted nail. "How is she? This baby is blessed, I feel it." She closed her eyes, raised her chin and breathed hard through her mouth. "The last little one couldn't stay, had other places to go. This one has things to do right where he is."

The expressions that flitted over Spike's face intrigued Max. The even-tempered, almost flip facade was gone, replaced by a sharper and definitely worried frown. "We don't know if we're having a boy or a girl," he said. "Thanks for the kind words, though. Only a few weeks to go now."

"Now you listen to me," Wazoo said, settling a hand on top of one of his. "There's nothin' to be afraid of this time around. That little one is takin' all the energy it needs from Vivian. It's wearin' her out but like you say, it'll soon be over. She's worried now because of losing the last baby, but she doesn't need to give it a thought."

Max had seen that Vivian was very pregnant but knew nothing of her history. He would try to find an opportunity to reassure her. He and Spike needed to get rid of Wazoo. With one forefinger, he attempted to rub between the cat's ears. That got him a view of a mouthful of tiny pointed teeth together with a hiss too big for the cat. He drew his hand back.

"Don't you take Irene's hiss serious," Wazoo said. "I gotta talk Annie into some therapy for this one. She's sufferin'. She tol' me she thinks she gonna be pushed out of her mama's lap—and bed—by some man."

There were moments when cool disinterest was the best reaction.

Max hooked an elbow over the back of his chair and raised his jaw. He looked detached, he was sure he did.

"Wazoo," Spike said after a slightly lengthy pause. "Thanks for the good words. Forgive us but this is a business meeting for Max and me."

Smiling, she popped up. "You know where to find me."

"You know Annie Duhon?" Spike asked when he and Max were alone, drumming his fingertips on the table. "Yeah, you do."

Shit. "I know who she is," Max said. "She runs Pappy's."

"Sure she does. How come you look so guilty?"

"You're off base," Max told him evenly. Lying didn't amuse him but he didn't want Annie's name linked to his.

"If you say so," Spike said quietly. "I wish we knew where to find Michele Riley. I'd settle for any clue, any idea. So far we've got a search for a missing person, and I kept it in this jurisdiction, used my people. But I can't cover for this any longer."

Max looked at him sharply. "I didn't ask you to cover for anything."

"No, you didn't. By tomorrow we'll be knee-deep in folks asking questions. Is there anythin' you'd like to share with me? Any incidents from the past?"

The man only asked the question to be polite. Max could tell he'd done some homework. It wasn't so hard to get at the record of Max Savage's career with the law. And innocent verdicts bore less weight if the same types of crimes followed you around.

"Have you searched the Majestic for leads?"

Spike took several spoonfuls of his gumbo before he responded. "There are prints on her own possessions—all the same. So what? They're probably hers. She couldn't use 'em without touching 'em. We didn't find any sign of a struggle or that her things had been messed with." He played with his coffee spoon, tapped it against his mug. "Same prints were on the front door and the handle. Both areas had been cleaned."

"When?" Max asked, shifting forward on his chair. "When did they clean the door?"

"Last night. Doll said she likes to brighten up the entrance and the reception area right before she goes to bed, just in case there's a real late arrival. The Hibbses turn in around eleven."

"Before I dropped Michele off," Max said, almost under his breath. "So if someone who didn't normally go there had got in that way before eleven and waited for her, those prints would be gone." A defeated feeling came and went, almost quickly enough. He had felt a setup closing in on him, but he couldn't allow himself to go there, not unless he eventually had to.

"You've got that right. Gator's were on the inside from openin' up this mornin'. That's all. He propped the door open."

A car approached, passed the triangular section of grass, trees and grimy plastic holiday statues in the center of broad Main Street. The car, a red Volvo, swung to a stop behind Spike's cruiser. Max deliberately turned his face from the window.

"Max?" Spike raised his eyebrows and pushed his fingers through his hair. "Want to share anythin'?"

"Why didn't we do this at the department?"

"I told you, informal appeals to me, particularly when I have pretty much nothing to go on. I thought we'd be more relaxed here."

Max didn't feel relaxed. Anything he said had a chance of being overheard. "You've been checking me out, haven't you?" He heard a car door slam. Annie, her hands crammed with bag handles, came toward Hungry Eyes.

"Yes." Spike's blue eyes stared steadily into Max's. "You understand why I'm real worried here? Either you're a serial killer, or you've made a serial killer real mad."

He wasn't being funny.

Max had never felt more serious.

"We have to find Michele," he said, the start of panic curling in his belly. He looked directly into Spike's eyes. "This hell has been going on since I was in college. I don't want the folks around here to find out about the accusations that were made against me. One of the reasons I decided to stay here was because after months, no one had ever mentioned my history. And they would have if they'd known about it. Michele comes first, of course, but I have to stick here, Spike. If I run again, I'm... Hell, I'm scared sick someone else will die. I'm scared Michele's already dead."

"Uh-huh," Spike said. "Can't blame you for that."

"You think the same thing, don't you?" Max said.

Spike pursed his mouth a moment then said, "I'm not into guessing. Until we've got a body, dead or alive, I won't be givin' a definite opinion. The longer the woman's missing, the worse our chances of finding her get."

Suddenly he was convinced of what he must do about Annie. He had to see her and make sure she was okay, then he would find a way to tell her both how he felt about her, and why he couldn't do a damn thing about it.

"Michele wasn't on her plane today—not that I thought she would be," Spike said.

"Damn. I didn't expect her to be either, but I hoped." He felt as if he'd been kicked, again.

"She had a purse with her when you picked her up?" Spike asked.

Max pinched the bridge of his nose. "She must have. She did. Kelly and Roche were there. They'll back me up." He thought about the four of them sitting around a table in the glass-walled restaurant at Rosebank. Michele laughed a lot and looked pretty when she did.

He didn't see Annie come into the shop, but he knew she had.

"You picked her up, spent the afternoon with her and your brothers and took her to dinner, where?"

Max wanted to turn and look at Annie. He listened for her voice and heard her respond to Wazoo's enthusiastic greeting. She sounded cheerful, too cheerful.

"We had dinner in the restaurant at Rosebank," Max told Spike. "They do a great job there."

Spike was too focused to acknowledge the weak joke. "When did you first know Michele was missing?"

"At Pappy's, yesterday lunchtime. Gator and Doll Hibbs came by and told me."

Spike stared at him for a long time. "From what was said by the people in New York, they knew she was coming here. I've waited as long as I can to call them and confirm she's missing."

Max buried his face in his hands. "When you do, it'll be all over," he said. The people Michele knew, knew Max, had known him a long time. They were only human and they were bound to get scared for Michele.

"I kinda thought you'd say that," Spike said. He extended a hand, palm up. "My time has run out. Can you give me anythin', Max? Anythin' at all? My gut tells me an intelligent guy like you isn't goin' to risk everythin' by… I don't think you're a killer but I don't have a whole lot of choice but to proceed as if you might be."

"And do what?" Max pushed aside his coffee. "Arrest me?"

"Keep it down," Spike said. "I'm not goin' to arrest you. I can't. You're an innocent man, remember. I can't hold past criminal investigations against you. But give me a way to tie you to foul play here and you're in the slammer."

Max felt sweat along his hairline. "What are you trying to get out of me? I didn't do anything to Michele. And I want her found, dammit. D'you understand me?"

"You're not in a position to play it heavy with me," Spike said.

"Why not?" Max curled his lip in a sneer. "I'm an innocent man, remember."

"I came here for one reason," Spike said, any trace of humor long gone. "You're the only suspect I've got. Thought I ought to tell you that."

Max swallowed and it hurt. "You haven't started to look."

"Sure, I have. And those telephone numbers are bein' followed up on right now. Why don't you cut the crap and save us both a lot of time. Where is she?"

A steady drumming pain set up in Max's temples. The horror had started all over again. "I don't know. She's a friend of mine and I like her. I wouldn't do anything to hurt her. I want to help with the search. My brothers have already asked why we haven't been called out."

"I don't think it would be a good idea, that's why. You wouldn't be the first murderer to help look for the victim. You think we're hicks here, don't you? That's why you never thought I'd get around to looking at you."

Max rubbed his palms together. "I've got enemies, I tell you. Enemies who want to ruin me. And they don't care what they do to people along the way."

"So you say," Spike said. "We're takin' the area apart. And we expect to find a *dead* body."

CHAPTER 8

Spike stood up and threw down some bills. He nodded at Max, stepped away from the table and stopped. "Hey, Homer," he said, but he frowned at his father. "Didn't see you come in. What's up?"

The drone of his heart and the pulse in his ears flattened sounds and movement around Max. He glanced up at Homer Devol and was grateful the older man didn't look in his direction.

Rolling the brim of his straw Stetson in gnarled hands, Homer stared at his son. "We gotta talk," he said. "No use puttin' it off any longer."

Max had learned the hard way that people didn't seem to bother much about privacy around here. Homer looked about ready to spill his guts and whatever he had to say might not be pleasant.

The tables had cleared out, all but for the man on his own sitting near the counter. He continued to read his newspaper.

"You gotta be wonderin'," Homer said to Spike.

"I am now. Let's go outside."

"Here's good enough. I want what I'm going to say to get around this town fast. I'm sick of havin' folks snicker about me behind my back."

Max could see Spike in Homer. Also tall but thinner and sinuous, his face seamed with deep lines, Homer would be counted as a nice-looking man who obviously hadn't led a soft life. Crew-cut gray hair stood up thick and helped make Homer seem more vigorous than he should.

At the counter, Annie held the cat. The animal closed her eyes tightly, suggesting she was in bliss. There was a rigid set to Annie's back. Max figured she could hear the Devol men argue and wasn't sure what to do next.

"Homer, please—"

"Stand there and take what I've got to say like a man," Homer snapped back at Spike. "Ain't you noticed nuthin' lately?"

Spike caught Max's eye and reddened. "No, I can't say as I have," he said. "I'll be out to the store to see you later on."

The store was the convenience store and gas station Homer ran on the outskirts of Toussaint. On a deep lot that reached Bayou Teche, the business also made good money renting out boats and selling bait.

"I don't plan on being there later," Homer said. "I don't know where I'll be later. Are you tellin' me you ain't noticed I've been scarce around Rosebank lately?"

Color rose higher in Spike's face. "No, I haven't noticed that. Why would you be staying away?"

"On account of my skin ain't as thick as yours."

Max didn't like seeing Spike's embarrassment.

"I'm not standin' by while folks say I'm a kept man," Homer continued. "You're fine with it. Maybe you don't care, or maybe you don't hear, but that's what some say about you, too. You're a man who lives on his wife's money. And Charlotte's her mother so if you can't see where I'm comin' from, work it out." Homer and Charlotte were engaged. Even Max knew the story about the two being soul mates.

"Think what you're saying," Spike said. "I didn't marry Vivian on account of her havin' a hotel, or comin' into a lot of money. When we met she was strugglin'. We're together because we love each other. Now leave it."

"I gotta speak my mind. It's time you had your eyes opened."

"Homer—"

Homer cut Spike off. "Let me have my say. I do fine for myself. I don't need no woman's money and if that means I gotta stay away from Charlotte Patin if I want to feel like a man, then I'll stay away. For her sake as well as mine."

At the counter, Annie rested her elbows and put her face in her hands. Irene inched around until she made a striped fur collar for her boss's white blouse. Wazoo stared hard at Homer.

Escape was on Max's mind, but he'd stay put until Annie went upstairs. He wanted to make some calls of his own to some of the people who were being contacted by the sheriff's department. They didn't have his number, not that he thought too many of them would try to make contact. They would be too frightened for Michele. And there were bound to be those who wondered if Max Savage was a killer who duped them into believing in him.

Spike and Homer stood silent, inches apart, looking hard at each other. "You finished?" Spike said finally. "I say you are anyway. And you're full of bull. Vivian and I don't need your interference, especially not now. Not ever. Do you remember Wendy? She's the granddaughter you supposedly love and she's happier than she's ever been. Don't mess with that. And if you do something stupid about Charlotte, you'll answer to me. Now I'm out of here."

The son strode outside, throwing the door open as he went and letting it slam shut.

The father stared after Spike for a moment, chomping down on a wad of gum with his back teeth. He took off, repeating the door-slamming performance, and Max avoided turning to see the men through the window.

Within seconds, several women—evidently the book group—filed quietly from between the stacks and left in a shuffling bunch. Once the door closed again Max heard them burst into conversation. Homer would get his wish. His argument with Spike would be all over town by morning.

Wazoo leaned toward Annie and spoke quietly to her. Annie nodded, then she stooped to gather the canvas bags she'd set at her feet and moved in the direction of the door at the back of the café.

"Annie Duhon," the man on his own said, folding his newspaper. "Didn't take me so long to find you this time. You've got to stop running away from me."

She stopped, just stopped. She didn't even start to turn toward him.

"You afraid of me, Annie? You afraid of a good old friend? Or are you too important to talk to me anymore?"

Max noted how she straightened her back—or stiffened it. The bags must be heavy, they dragged on her arms. "Hi, Bobby," she said, and looked at him.

She is afraid of him. Well, damn, Max didn't know a whole lot about Annie before she settled in Toussaint but she had seemed open, if quiet, and sure of herself—until today. From what he could see, *Bobby* didn't seem fearsome at all. Clean-cut with short sandy curls, the man's dark brown eyes smiled at Annie, did more than smile, they invited. A fit guy with a good body.

The emotion Max felt wasn't so familiar but he recognized a flash of possessiveness.

"Nice cat," the stranger said. "I'm gonna have another cup of coffee. How 'bout you join me? We got a lot of catching up to do."

Annie swivelled to see the whole café—and Max. Her mouth tightened when their eyes met. She looked from Bobby—whoever he might be—to Max and what he saw was a woman who felt trapped.

Max grinned and got a slight smile in return.

"Maybe this isn't a good time," Bobby said. "I can come back."

"Leave me a number," Annie said. "I'll give you a call sometime."

"Annie, I wouldn't do a thing to interfere with your new life. I want to talk about old times, is all. Reminisce. We had good times together." A lopsided smile was a combination of boyish charm and hinted-at intimacy that didn't make Max feel any better.

"We were kids," Annie said. Bobby's familiarity speeded up her pulse. "And I haven't avoided you. Our paths haven't crossed and there was no reason to think about you."

"You know how to make a man feel small," Bobby said.

"You're responsible for your own feelings," Annie told him. "I'm not into hanging out in the past. I've got things to do. A lot of paperwork." She lifted her heavy bags a fraction.

"Not good enough," Bobby said, and Annie glanced nervously at Max. Why did this have to happen in front of him? Bobby continued, "The last time I saw you, before this mornin', we weren't kids anymore. I'll never be able to explain how I felt that night. I—"

"Thanks for being there when I needed you," Annie said, praying she never had to see him again. Why had he decided to follow her around after so many years? She set the bags down, unwound Irene from her neck and handed the cat to Wazoo. "I almost forgot somethin'. Be back in half an hour or so." Max, sitting there listening to Bobby say things that could only raise curiosity, destroyed any shred of peace she had managed to restore while she was at work that afternoon.

"How was your day—the rest of your day?" Max asked.

This impossible encounter was a nightmare. No…she would not even think about nightmares. It was up to her to change what was happening.

"Annie?" Max said. His smile did not disguise tension. He'd not only heard every word Bobby said, he must have drawn conclusions she couldn't bear to think about.

She breathed in through her nose and concentrated. "Hi, Max." If she was lucky, she sounded more cheerful than she felt. "This afternoon was great, thanks. Business is steady and that always makes me happy. Kelly came in. He knows how to make a person feel good."

"I'm glad to hear it," Max said but nothing about him relaxed.

He was worried about Bobby, she could feel it.

"I came here to meet with Spike. There's still no news on Michele Riley."

Of course, Michele. His concern for her made him anxious and that's what she was picking up on. "I'm so sorry," Annie said, constantly aware of Bobby listening. "Kelly talked about it, too. All of you have to be upset."

Max's dark, dark eyes flickered away for a moment. "We are," he said.

Annie looked at his mouth. The corners turned up even when he was troubled. "What are they doing to find her?" she said.

"Searching," he said. "And checking with friends. The usual procedure, I guess."

"How about that coffee?" Bobby said with a forced laugh. "Guess you aren't in so much of a hurry to leave after all."

She continued to look at Max and said, "Bobby's right. I'd better get on. 'Bye."

Max turned his head to see where Annie went. She got into the Volvo and drove out of sight, but didn't appear to head back down

Main Street. Out of sight from the shop windows, one small street cut to and from the square. Annie might have taken that but she could just as well have used the alley that led to parking places behind this building. He wanted Annie to have gone home rather than set off to drive aimlessly.

He didn't want to look at Bobby and even more, he didn't want to talk to him. The sensation that he'd like to slam him against a wall and demand to know why he was bothering Annie unsettled him. Max got up and went to the counter. Wazoo stood opposite him at once and kept her voice way down. "There's really big trouble," she said. "That Annie, she is in danger."

"What kind of danger?" Max leaned to bring their heads closer.

"I get these notions. Folks laugh at me, but they not thinkin'. Too many times I see things that's goin' to happen. Sorta see 'em."

Max waited for her to continue.

Wazoo took her time before she said, "It's just I see somethin' happenin', or feel things. My mama was the same. And her mama. This time it's worse—stronger. Makin' me weary tryin' to sort it all out. I don't know what's goin' on, or what's goin' to happen, but it's somethin' terrible. And your Annie's in the middle of it." She paused and moved far enough back to see his face. "You, too, maybe. But what I'm pickin' up is comin' from her."

He was a surgeon, a scientist, and he didn't buy into this drivel. "Thanks," he said and smiled at Wazoo. *Your Annie,* that's what she had said. She had no reason to link them as a couple unless Annie had said something to her, and Annie seemed as eager as he was to keep their association quiet.

"You and Annie got something going?" Bobby said.

Max looked at the other man who stared right back. "What?" Max said. "No, you don't have to say any more. I don't know who you are and I don't want to know." The guy was looking for trouble.

"Of course you don't. You're afraid I'm competition and I reckon you're right."

The tingle down Max's spine was a natural reaction to confronting a clearly unhinged man. He composed himself. "Good night to you," he said.

"I plan for it to be a great night." The innocent look slipped into a leer.

Max glanced at Wazoo, and thought of Annie. She might or might not be alone upstairs but he wasn't comfortable leaving while this guy was here. "It's later than I thought," he said, checking his watch. "Are you about to close up?"

"In another hour," Wazoo said.

He looked down into the bakery case and pretended to be deep in thought. "Guess I should eat something before I go. I may not get time later. I'll have a piece of spinach pie."

"That pie is collard greens with onions, red beans and boudin sausage."

Max didn't like the sound of it, but he didn't care that much, either. "Fine," he said. "And I'll have some iced tea, if you've got it. Does everything feel kind of still to you?"

"Uh-huh," Wazoo said. "Me, I won't be shocked if there's another storm."

"I hope you're wrong," Max said and returned to his table.

Wazoo came to clean away the dirty dishes. This time she didn't have anything to say.

He sensed the man, Bobby, staring at him and looked back. He hadn't expected to see a smile, but the guy smiled broadly at him.

Max nodded, but wished Roche was with him. His psychiatrist brother's reaction to this man might be interesting.

"Annie doesn't talk much about herself these days, I reckon," Bobby said. "That doesn't surprise me, no sir. When a body's tryin' to get lost it doesn't make a whole lot of sense to talk about the past. What d'you say to that? Had she told you much about where she came from and what she did?"

"Why are you pushing this?" Max said. "Annie doesn't owe me any explanations about her life before I met her."

"I bet you've fucked her. She fucks most men she meets."

Max shot out of his seat and made it to Bobby in a couple of steps. "A man, a *man* that is, doesn't talk about a woman that way. He doesn't use language like that in public places when there's a lady present, either."

"Lady?" Bobby's expression turned blank.

"What's the matter with you?" Max said. "Did Annie turn you down and you can't get over it?" He stared down at him and breathed hard.

Bobby laughed. "I don't guess so, buddy. Oh, no. That girl was all fire between my legs, but you'd know about that."

"Why are you saying this?"

"I'm lookin' out for you, is all. Wouldn't want a fine man suckered in by real used merchandise."

Max grabbed Bobby by the shoulders and tipped him until the front legs of his chair left the floor. Bobby flung out his arms and tried to grapple himself up again. Max let the chair dip lower and the man flailed.

"Damn you," he yelled. "You back off or I'll call your sheriff friend."

"Okay by me," Max said, jiggling the chair while Bobby made a grab at his shirt and got off a weak blow to the belly. "Do that again and you'll be there a long time. What's on your mind about Annie? Spit it out and let's get it over with." Suddenly, with a force that stole his breath, he wanted to rattle the creep's teeth. "She doesn't say anything negative about anyone, so what's your problem?"

"Whooee! That pretty girl got to you. She's the first woman I loved, the only one, that's my problem. Now she's behaving like she can't even see me. That's also my problem."

"Then get lost. She's not interested in you."

"I'll get out when I'm ready. Annie Duhon owes me and she knows it. There's things you can't set right, but you can try."

Max began to haul the man and his chair upright.

"You should have made it with her when she was sixteen," Bobby jabbered and grinned. "Man, she was something else."

Max let the chair sag again. "That was what? Thirteen years ago? You'd better get a life and move on."

"I gotta life and I like where I am. All I want is a little respect. I suffered. And I helped her out big-time, too. But seeing her around here lookin' like butter wouldn't melt in her mouth is something I can't take. My folks never forgave me for bein' with her. She's dirty, that one. Soiled."

He would drop the man on the floor and beat the crap out of him. Max felt it coming.

"She's soiled," Bobby yelped. "But I'm still gonna take her back. I'll forgive her because she was young and adults interfered. I was an adult, too, but they didn't let that count."

"Are you telling me you were over eighteen and having sex with a minor?"

"Drop the fancy talk," Bobby all but screamed at him. "I know why she's afraid to let on she still loves me. I'm not talkin' about that. But I am counseling you to find fresh meat."

"I think I'm going to kill you," Max said, deadly quiet.

Max let go of Bobby's shoulders and he crashed to the floor, the back of the chair splintering around him. As he fell, his head slammed into the counter.

"Tell Ellie I'll be by to settle up on this chair," Max said to Wazoo, stepping over Bobby who scrambled to extricate himself and rubbed his head at the same time. "And you didn't hear a word he said here. Got that?"

"You can bet your pride and joy I do," she replied. She set a small pistol on the counter and crossed her arms.

CHAPTER 9

Rather than turn right as soon as he was outside Hungry Eyes and appear to follow Annie, Max went to the left. He walked briskly, not so much as glancing at his car when he passed. Bobby wasn't sitting near the windows and there was a good chance he had no idea the Boxster belonged to Max. The car was better where it was while he circled out of the square. He went around the block to look for a rear access to the dead-end alley beside Joe Gable's law offices.

He wasn't about to accept an obscene attack on Annie. He didn't believe Bobby, but he did think the man should be watched. Maybe what had been said would come up when Max reached Annie—if he did. Maybe it wouldn't. Her safety was his main concern, that and getting an explanation for what really happened on that piece of land in St. Martinville.

When he felt it was safe, he called Spike and asked him to have an officer check on Wazoo at Hungry Eyes. He kept the explanation short, but did mention Wazoo's pistol.

He could leave the square without being seen from the café. That was the easy part. Finding and entering the alley from the blind side wasn't so easy. When he did reach a spot where he could see the backs of Hungry Eyes, the Gables' house and Joe's offices on the other side of the alley, a tall brick wall confronted him and he figured out that it enclosed a stonemasons' yard between him and the back entrance he needed to reach.

At least there shouldn't be anyone on the masons' premises. He hoped.

After backing off to get a run at the wall, Max sprinted and leaped to grip the coping on top. He thought he might fall back but his sneakers found purchase on the bricks and he crawled up until he could sit on the wall. In the murky area on the other side, he made out close-packed stacks of stone slabs.

He couldn't get it out of his head that Bobby might decide to go after Annie.

Peering into the darkness, Max let himself down on the other side of the wall and found his way across the crowded lot to another wall on the other side.

Once again he squared off, jumped and hunkered down on top. *Bingo.* Hungry Eyes stood to his left with the section that contained two apartments on the upper floor, one Annie's, the other empty, stretching back at a right-angle.

A small guesthouse, tucked into the corner of the rambling garden, looked empty and the Gables' house was also in darkness.

He heard a door fly open behind him. Over his shoulder, at one end of the workshop, he saw a rectangle of light at the end of the masons' building with the dark shadow of someone standing there, peering around the stonemasons' yard. He should have considered the possibility of a guard in the building.

Max slowly flattened his body on the wall.

His heart thundered.

He didn't need to be apprehended while climbing into Annie's backyard at night.

"There ain't no way out," a gruff voice called and the man in the doorway stepped into the yard. "Put your hands up and walk into the light." The figure raised a weapon and Max rolled his eyes. Obviously the man had heard movement outside but he hadn't seen Max, or anyone else. If an intruder were armed and desperate he would have a clear shot at the guard.

Slithering as quietly as he could, Max dropped onto soft earth on the other side of the wall and ran swiftly, hunched over, beside a wooden fence that closed the garden off from the alley. He didn't have to go farther than the gate for the information he needed. Through a gap in the slats he could see a dull shine on the hood of Annie's Volvo.

Before he could change his mind, Max went to the door below a single illuminated window in the upstairs apartments and knocked lightly. She'd never hear that. He rang the bell and winced at its grating buzz.

This time he waited, staring at his feet, one hand braced against the door. He strained for any sound from inside but there was nothing—until a cat meowed. Max smiled to himself. Even if Annie wouldn't come down for him, she still might feel she wanted to get the cat.

Don't say good night, Irene. Don't you run up those stairs.

If Annie did come for the cat, surely she wouldn't ignore Max at the door. He had to be clearly visible through amber glass panes in the top half.

Ten minutes later he gave up on Irene saving him and rang the bell once more. He'd allowed for all of this and sworn he wouldn't leave until he saw Annie. He pressed his right forefinger into the bell and leaned on it, continued leaning on it. Please don't let Wazoo hear him and come out of the shop.

Max raised his chin, and saw the distorted silhouette of someone coming down the stairs. Very, very slowly down. The identity was obvious.

Annie came to stand on the other side of the door.

Ringing or knocking again would send her back upstairs and he'd never get in. Quietly, he waited.

At last she moved, took off the deadbolt, unlocked the door and opened it a few inches. The chain was still on and she peered out at him through a narrow space.

"Did Wazoo tell you to come around here?" she said.

"No."

"No," Annie repeated. "I didn't think so, but if she had it would only be because she was tryin' to help me."

"She's a nice woman. Funny sometimes."

"Having premonitions doesn't make you funny," Annie said. She scooped up the cat and it flopped over her shoulder with its back legs hanging straight down.

"I didn't say—"

"Yes, you did."

He hadn't noticed a tendency for her to jump to conclusions before this. When someone insisted they were right, about something pretty stupid, and they wouldn't listen to reason, Max got overheated. "She's *funny*," he repeated. "People laugh at some of what she says and does. I think she likes it." And he was the one overreacting.

"She's a natural comedian," Annie said, "but she does like it when she makes people laugh."

Max didn't want to invite himself in.

"You've had a rotten day," he said. "Too much has happened to be good for you."

"I don't think having a friend go missin' can be easy to cope with, either," she said. Annie raised her head. "Today's been bad for both of us. Would you like to come in for a bit?"

"Yes," he said. "I was hoping you'd ask."

Why had the man in the café tried to smear her reputation? Why had he turned up after so long?

Someone needed to find out what was eating him, and shut him up—permanently.

Annie closed the door and took off the chain, then let him in. "I have tea and coffee. And I've got some bottles of good wine if that's what you'd like. Take your pick."

Making faces at her bad-tempered cat, he walked upstairs behind her and she showed him into an L-shaped living room overlooking the square. "This is really nice," he said. The cat peered around to get another look at him. Her green-gold eyes crossed and she showed all of her teeth in a silent hiss.

Max wriggled his nose and looked around. The place looked new, as in brand-new.

"Ellie and Joe renovated the whole upstairs. They had what was the kitchen turned into a dining room. The kitchen—" she pointed right "—is where the master bedroom used to be, and they pushed through to the second apartment to make a really big bedroom, a second bedroom and a little office."

"So they got rid of the second apartment completely? You've probably got the biggest digs in town." However, all that stood in the living room was a white couch that looked untouched, and a red lacquer chest placed in front as a coffee table. A white carpet showed shoe impressions from the front door to the kitchen and bedrooms. They bypassed the rest of the living room, and the empty dining room.

"Are you looking for a bathroom?" Annie said.

Way to go, Savage, gape around her home like you're taking inventory. "No, thanks. You've got wonderful spaces to…"

"Work with?" she said, filling in the words he'd managed not to say. Her smile would turn on lights—and other things. He ought to know. "I haven't gotten around to furnishing the place. After all, I've only been here seven months. Gimme time."

He nodded, returning her smile. "Take all the time you want. These things can't be rushed." These polite conversations made him nervous because they meant the people involved were avoiding what they really wanted to say.

Annie crossed her arms. Except for her breasts, she was fairly small but he liked what folded arms did for them. And he liked the way her white blouse fitted without a wrinkle, and her jeans didn't have to cover many straight lines.

Annie didn't move a muscle. This wasn't the first time a man had sized her up, but it was the first time Annie had been as aware of each spot where his attention landed.

Max didn't behave like this. Or he hadn't before. Annie was used to his intense eyes and quiet way of considering what he wanted to say—and his open smile. They had kissed and hugged on parting, nothing more. They had never shared a sexually loaded moment like this and he had never tried for more intimacy.

He was too sensitive to push for sex when he had to suspect she was upset.

But it was on his mind. She could feel that, *see* that.

Rather than the heat Annie expected, she turned cold, so cold she couldn't feel her fingers, and the prickling that flooded into sensitive places was almost a wash of delicate pain.

Almost a climax. Standing there, watching him watching her, Annie's legs ached. The cold, dumbfounding stimulation pulsed and she longed to kneel. She wanted to tear off her clothes and pose before him until he dragged her down to him, stripping as he did so.

"You work too hard." His voice caught and he cleared his throat. When he looked at her face, his eyes were shadowy yet vulnerable. Guilty?

Annie drew in a great breath, the one she'd forgotten to take, and Max's gaze moved rapidly downward—and back. She saw him swallow hard.

"I've never had my own place before," said Annie. "In Pointe Judah I lived with my cousin, Eileen, and her son."

"But you lived in St. Martinville before that?"

She struggled to calm down. If she opened a window there would be more air in the room, and she'd break this invisible field they had formed between them. Max wouldn't be feeling what she did, Annie reminded herself. Or would he? Something was making his body react.

"I didn't tell you I lived there, did I?" she said.

"Maybe you did." He narrowed his eyes. "But it could be I got the impression you had when we were there today. When we drove in. It doesn't matter."

But it did matter. "I grew up in St. Martinville."

"You don't like it now?"

"You're only guessin'." She had to avoid talking about details from the past. "You're right though, I hate it now." Not a word would she say about Bobby Colbert. She shuddered just thinking his name.

"Are you okay?" Max asked.

Annie nodded. Opening the window would be impossible. She couldn't make her legs move, didn't want to. And she didn't want the desire that made her breasts heavy, her erogenous places ache, to slip away.

Another shudder, this one convulsive, embarrassed her. She closed her eyes and imagined his light touch passing over her skin, and slipping inside her where he flitted over raw nerves. Again, a climax came so close that she put a hand over her mouth to stifle a moan and hardly dared to look at him again. He was involved with his own thoughts.

Max ran the fingers of his right hand through his black hair and it sprang up in spikes. "If I have wine, will you join me?"

That was the moment when the reluctant heat broke free and rushed to her face. She touched her cheeks and laughed. "Cold, white wine?" she said.

"I'll get it," he told her and went into the kitchen. White maple, black granite and stainless steel confronted him. It seemed almost as unused as the living room.

Steadying himself with one hand on the refrigerator door and the other on a counter nearby, he stiffened that elbow and stole a moment to recover. The animal every man hid, some larger, more dangerous animals than others, had just put in a real inconvenient appearance. He opened the refrigerator and stared inside. Max had confronted his animal on numerous previous occasions but during the sexual hiatus while he worked to make a new life, the beast had apparently been on steroids.

He found a good bottle of Pinot Grigio, took it out and tried to decide where he'd be if he were a corkscrew.

Max shook his head.

"The bottle opener's in this drawer," Annie said, coming up behind him and reaching around to display a drawer where the only utensil was the corkscrew. She opened a cupboard empty but for a few glasses, some of them wine. Max took out two and uncorked the wine. He poured a little, stuck his nose in the glass and grinned. "Smooth, opinionated—brash even. A hint of white baking chocolate and squash casserole. Memorable."

Her giggle and the poke in the ribs she gave him didn't cool the tension any more than his silly assessment of the wine had. "Here you go." The first glass he poured he gave to Annie, then he took his own.

She walked out of the kitchen. "I'll show you the rest of the place, if you like. But maybe we should drink some of this first."

Following her, Max paused to look toward the square. "Are they going to have the holiday lights on for the rest of the year now?" he said.

"I don't know. This is my first year here." She came to his side. "It's silly, but I love those lights. They've just forgotten to reset the timer after the fair, or whatever it was."

"I've always enjoyed lights, the more the better," Max said. "Every Christmas my parents' home looks like Aladdin's cave. I always look forward to seeing it. Roche likes all the glitter, too, but Kelly's the tasteful one. He'd bring in a designer if Mom would put up with it."

They were making conversation again. Tipping up his glass, Max took a long, cold swallow of wine. Could be that alcohol was a bad idea while he wasn't exactly in control of all systems.

Annie took hold of his forearm and turned him toward her. "You're a lot taller than me."

"I do like my women to be observant." *She isn't my woman. Dumb remark.*

"Be nice. And kneel down. You should be able to rest your arms on the windowsill and have a place for your glass, too."

"Why would I do that?"

"Because I'm going to and I'm inviting you to join me—because you like holiday bling."

Barefoot and fleet, she went around the room switching off lights. With the last one, she paused. "You aren't afraid of the dark?"

Not until now. "I can handle it."

She plunged the room into darkness and returned to him. In the glow from outside, her blouse turned brilliant, translucent white. When she knelt beside him only her face and neck cleared the sill.

Silent, they stared into the skeins of tiny colored lights swaying and bobbing in the trees. Annie sighed and he glanced at her. "Makes me nostalgic," she said. "Not that we ever did much decorating, but I think I'm nostalgic for the feelings I got in the holidays. All we need now is snow."

He laughed. "Dream on. But I know what you mean about nostalgia."

She didn't reply, but she took several sips of wine.

"Are you all right like that?" he asked. "Or is your back killing you?"

"I'm okay."

Cautiously, he put an arm around her waist. "I'll hold you up," he said. "And don't argue."

Had anyone ever held her that way? With a warm, strong arm that made her feel...different?

For a long time they didn't speak. A wind picked up and the lights danced. And she was dancing, Annie thought—with danger. Bobby's angry face kept shoving itself into her mind. They'd met once since she left St. Martinville and that had been earlier today. Now he'd decided he was driven to force a new friendship. Funny to think about now, but they had been close friends once.

Max's fingers spread at her waist and she almost arched her back.

"I came for one reason," he said. "But I think I should tell you something else first in case you'd rather not be around me when I'm finished."

"You couldn't say anythin' that would affect me like that." But she was foolish to pursue what was happening between them. It couldn't come to anything.

Max didn't expect her to remain so understanding. "I've been involved in some nasty stuff, Annie. Believe me, this is going to be hard for you to take. It wasn't my fault, but you only have my word for it. I should have told you about this weeks ago when it first looked like we enjoyed each other's company."

"Don't tell me anything that will make you unhappy." She stared at the black sky.

"It may make us both unhappy but I've got to take that chance. I've had two brushes with the law." Max pressed his lips together and collected himself to go on. "The first time, my college girlfriend was murdered and I was accused, then cleared."

He caught the glitter in her eyes when she turned to stare at him. "How awful. Who killed her?"

"They never found out." What felt like a brick in his throat made it tough to swallow.

"I'm so sorry." She rubbed his shoulder and rested her cheek there. "I wish I'd been around to support you."

His eyes stung and he blinked. "Thank you." Her breast was full and firm against his side. Staying focused mattered now, really mattered.

"I could have told them you would never do something like that," she said.

A bitter taste entered his mouth. "Thank you." He closed his eyes and pinched the bridge of his nose. "Three years ago it happened again. My girlfriend was…someone killed her."

CHAPTER 10

Her absolute stillness should be what he expected, but it turned his stomach and started a gut-twisting burn of anger at the same time.

Settle down. You don't get to live a charmed life.

And he didn't want to answer the questions Annie was bound to ask.

"I'd better leave," he said.

"No." Annie rubbed her fingertips over his back. "I know you and I trust you. You wouldn't hurt anyone. Everythin' that really matters to you is about helping folks."

She wasn't afraid of him. He'd told her the worst but she remained by his side. With her he could have a chance at happiness, at closing the door on the horrific times. But if they spent too much time together, Annie might get hurt.

"I wish everyone felt the way you do. Not that I blame people for being suspicious. If something happens once but it can't be proved, sure you ought to get the benefit of the doubt. But the second time, even though you're found innocent… Well, my faith would waver, too." He held her tighter and she didn't resist. If he wanted to tell her how she soothed his soul, he wouldn't know how. Instead he nuzzled the side of her neck.

"Until Michele is found, you're going to think it's starting all over," Annie said, and she sounded breathless.

She voiced his fears aloud and he only felt more desperate.

Max started to get up but Annie reacted without thinking. She slid her right hand around his neck and reached up to kiss his cheek. "Promise me we're going to keep on bein' friends." His breath crossed her cheek and ear and she could still feel his mouth on her neck.

Turning away from the window, he pulled her against him, knee-to-knee, and held her.

Max's body felt hard and he held her in a viselike grip, but a tremor rippled beneath his skin. Telling her about himself had cost him too much. He'd expected her to recoil from him and now that she hadn't, he must be trying to convince himself she actually believed in him.

"You *are* my friend, aren't you, Max?"

"You'll never know how much I want to be," he said. "I can't do a thing to hurry it all up. The truth is, you shouldn't trust a man you don't really know—especially if you find out he's been accused of killing two women."

He was right, of course, but she was sure of how she felt about him, she'd seen him with his brothers and knew what they planned to do at Green Veil. Men like Max didn't commit vicious crimes.

"Whatever you need, I'm here for you." Annie meant every word. If she could, she would help him.

"Even if they find Michele dead?"

Annie's heart tightened. She took his face in her hands and looked into his eyes. Even in the shadows, she saw his pain, and his determination. He had come here because he wanted to see her, and to tell her the truth about himself. The only reason he'd do that was because her opinion of him mattered. She touched his brow with her lips and stopped breathing.

Max cared about her. Why else would he tell her things any man would rather hide if he could? "I intend to keep on praying Michele will show up," she said. "And I'll never change my mind about you."

"Something could change it," he said. "You know it could. I... No, Annie, this isn't fair."

He kissed her cheek lightly, then the side of her neck, not so lightly—and for a long time. With his hands on her shoulders, he pulled away.

"Bad luck is no stranger to me," she told him. "Sometimes I've thought it was the only kind of luck I'd ever get. But I got the job I'd always dreamed of at Pappy's, and then I met you. I did think we were miles apart because you're from a different world to mine— and you probably are. You're really special."

"So are you." He shook her gently. "Don't ever put yourself down to me. Annie, I should get back to Rosebank."

"I don't want you to." She didn't think before she told him. "I don't have anywhere else to go, or anyone I want to be with—apart from you."

He was quiet awhile but released her and stretched out on his back on the carpet. "I want to stay," he said, one forearm over his eyes. "Don't you think I like being here with you? Talking by holiday lights?" He laughed softly.

"Then stay and talk. You haven't even finished your wine."

"It isn't wine I want."

Annie sat beside him. She thought she knew exactly what he meant, exactly what he wanted. Slowly, she put a hand on his flat belly. His muscles contracted. She had her own secrets and the thought of revealing them to Max paralyzed her. How could she go where they were headed? She didn't even know for sure how she would behave if he moved to make love to her. Collapse, turn wild and attack? There were reasons why she mustn't take the risk. What she feared the most was repulsing him.

"I'll be lonely if you go." She believed it but she didn't have to say it aloud.

Max covered her hand on his belly. "Women who've got close to me have ended up dead," he said.

"I'll get me a great big gun," she said and gave a strained laugh. "An AK somethin'. Just you see, I won't get messed with while I'm carrying one of those on my shoulder."

He took her hand to his mouth and pressed his lips into her palm. "How come no man has snapped you up before now? You're wonderful. Crazy, wonderful."

The reason she was still alone and might remain that way was a subject she had sealed away long ago. But now she wanted, maybe needed to be with this man. She just didn't know how to go about it without causing one of them grief.

Max drew her first finger into his mouth and pulled it slowly free.

She bent over him, kissed him, all but fell on him when he held the back of her head, ran his fingers through her hair. The languor was gone. His tongue and lips turned hard. The side to side movement of his face, the way he reached deep into her mouth while he turned her face to meet his demands, telegraphed his urgency and changed Annie. Sex didn't have to bind two people together, but it had to leave a mark behind.

He cupped a breast, unsteadily passed his thumb back and forth beneath her nipple.

Mark me. He wasn't a child and neither was she. A man wasn't completed by petting in the dark. And Annie would be unfinished until she found out what it was like to have Max Savage inside her.

All the reasons to stop, now, coiled in her mind, swelled, warned her like a siren that what happened next could put her back where she'd once been; on the bottom. She stuffed down the fear and pressed her breast against his hand. Air hissed through her teeth. She wanted his skin on hers—all over.

"Annie," Max said. "We shouldn't make this harder than it's going to be anyway. But I need your help."

"To do what?" Other women kissed men—because they wanted to.

"Back away from each other." His words were strained. "Tell me to get out. Please."

"If you wanted to, you would."

"I don't." He turned his face away and took his hand from her. And he sat up, scrubbing at his face, raking his hair back. "I sound like a fool," he muttered.

Pulling in little gasps through her parted lips, Annie tugged her blouse free of her jeans. She fumbled the buttons, undoing them as if learning the task for the first time. Urgency drove her, and so did the rhythmic smarting she felt inside.

Max looked at her, watched her fingers part the blouse. He could tell she was frightened but forcing herself to do this. He hated to see her suffer, but he couldn't make himself intervene.

If things were different, this would be fantastic, a dream come true, and he would be the one pushing for more. Annie wasn't pushing. She hungered for intimacy but he wasn't sure why. He wasn't sure if it mattered. But what he felt had just one description: Lust. Lust wrapped up in fear for Annie—and for himself.

"Help me," Annie said. "Stop analyzing what's happening, or might happen. Give in." Her voice grew high and desperate.

"Damn." He didn't have what it took to refuse her. "You are sexy."
She shed her blouse.

He couldn't take his eyes off her.

Annie moved fast. She sat astride his hips, settled herself on top of his throbbing penis. And he sat there, supporting himself on locked arms.

"My turn," she said. "You tell me to leave you alone."

Sure. "That isn't going to happen." She started unbuttoning his shirt. "Annie!"

"Annie!" she mimicked. "So push me away, or I'll keep right on going."

This was unbelievable. Where had this new wild woman come from?

"I get the message," Annie said. He wondered if she knew her voice wobbled. She carried on until his shirt hung loose. "Now take it off."

"You get one last chance to nix this," he said. "When we come together, it shouldn't be while—"

Her next kiss cut him off. She pushed his shoulders and he let her land him on his back again, their mouths still together. Annie sucked in his bottom lip, nibbled, let it go so she could explore the inside of his mouth again.

Then she pulled her lips from his and sat up on him once more, with the same result as before, the hardest working part of his anatomy hurt like hell and he loved it.

She unhooked her white bra and took it off. A sound came from her throat, like a click. Her full pale breasts took his mind apart. Annie pinched his nipples, tweaked them rapidly and while Max shuddered and responded, he looked at her breasts. They belonged against his hair-rough chest—pulling cries from her—and in his mouth where he would make her scream out her pleasure.

When she lowered herself over him, pressed against him, any light he'd thought shone on them, went out.

"Please don't...don't turn into something I dreamed up, and disappear," he told her. "I've done that plenty of times before."

"About me?"

He smiled. "Yes, about you." His belly felt like fire. "In my mind I've made love to you in every way I could come up with. And I got one thing right—you want sex as much as I do. We're not playing around here anymore." With his hands around her waist, he lifted her, pulled her higher until her breasts hovered inches from his face. They swayed and he fought for some restraint.

He was losing the battle faster with every second.

Annie pushed her hands beneath his head and brought his mouth to a breast. He opened wide and sucked, used his tongue to flick her nipple until she writhed.

She collapsed on him and he shrugged his shoulders from the shirt. Annie pushed up and reached behind her. She lifted his penis, squeezed it again and again. He unzipped her jeans and pushed a hand inside.

Annie would make sure they remembered this night. But it had to be on her own terms. She pulled his hand out of her pants and shifted until she knelt over his thighs. He was so hard that unzipping his pants took determination.

Each time he tried to intervene, she slapped his hands away and worked his pants down. Not looking at him was impossible. He made a formidable bulge inside white undershorts. Annie rested her cheek there and her heart pounded, at the feel of him, and at the way he was helpless to stop the pulsing against her face.

Tentative at first, she settled a hand on one muscular thigh and inched her fingers inside a leg of the shorts until she met hair, and taut flesh. Holding him in her hand came naturally, even if she'd never done it before, never taken any initiative with a man.

She laughed, then kissed him through the shorts, made the fabric wet—with a lot of help from Max. Between her own legs, she was slick and hot. Annie wanted him to touch her there, but she was afraid to give him control.

He twisted beneath her and his much stronger hands took hold of hers and pulled them away.

Annie sprang to her feet. She backed slowly from him.

"Come here," he said, getting to his haunches. His voice wasn't uncertain anymore, and it wasn't gentle.

Annie rushed into the dining room and faced his direction again. In here the drapes were closed and almost no hint of jolly lights punctured the darkness.

Max remained where he was, but only for moments, then he was on his feet and closing on her. The white shorts were gone.

She shivered, but her face pulsed with heat. *I'm mad.* Being mad was exactly what she wanted. Mad in his company.

He reached her and she flattened herself to the wall, spread her arms wide as if she could force herself through. "I'm going to make love to you," he said. "Any objections?" He sounded strange. Whatever she said he intended to follow through.

With his legs braced apart, he anchored her hips, covered her. He tweaked at her and nipped. Her mouth, her earlobes, her shoulders. The sucking bites he landed on her shoulders would leave bruises.

Behind Annie's eyelids she saw black, then blinding red. Sweat sprang out on her skin. Nothing was clear, or quiet. Singing, whining sounds invaded her brain.

All over her body, nerves quivered. She beat at Max, screamed at him but couldn't hear her own words.

His mouth stole hers, worked hers until she forced her face aside. With one foot on the wall, she shoved at him and he moved off a few inches.

"Now it's what I want," Annie yelled. "Do what I want."

Sinking her nails into his side, she swung around until his was the back that faced the wall. And she shoved him until he threw his arms wide as she had.

"Annie," he said. "Do your thing. You're angry and I don't blame you. Beat it out on me."

"Shut *up,*" she cried. "You don't know anything."

With the living room window at a distance, and behind her, he wouldn't be able to see her as anything but light and shadow. Quickly, she pushed her jeans and panties down together and stepped out of them.

Her eyes flashed. Repeatedly, she tossed her hair back and he saw a sheen on her shoulders, the tops of her breasts. Annie sweated. He had sensed the instant when she passed over the edge of reason and went willingly to a place the timid avoided. She was intoxicated by the moment, by being with him, naked and longing for possession.

"Let me hold you," he said. Even while he wanted to throw her down and sink himself inside her, the warning came that they were beyond any caution. He didn't want to make her loathe him but if he couldn't slow this down, that's what could happen.

"Fuck me," she whispered, her voice hoarse. "Fuck me, you fool. I don't want to be held." Her laughter shook and he thought she was crying. She had shocked him into silence.

He didn't see her raised hand. Annie slapped his face hard. "Come on, hate me. I'm hateful. Repulsive. You don't want me, so hurt me." She slapped him again, and caught the corner of his eye. "Knock me down and leave me."

Everything she did and said excited him. And it set off warnings. If this was a sexy game, he wanted to play. If someone had wounded her enough to destroy her confidence, he *had* to know that.

"Max!"

What he did was catch her wrist and hold it while he grabbed for the other. She eluded him each time and landed closed-knuckled punches wherever she found a part of him. After driving a fist into his diaphragm, she reached between his legs again, took hold of his shaft and pumped. She strained downward until he was afraid he'd dislocate the arm he held, and let go. On her knees, Annie drew him into her mouth, reached around to pinch his buttocks and almost released him from her lips before she drove along him again, her mouth hot and wet.

If he wanted to stop her, he could, in a moment.

No way would he do that.

Annie sprang to her feet again. What she felt now approached nothing she had experienced before. The few times she'd been with a man, her role had been that of the victim, debased, hurt—once almost killed. But she had never guessed at her own hunger for sex.

She shivered. Painted only by a faint glow, the strong lines of his face became terrifying. His features were twisted and he had tensed. He waited as if ready to attack her. Annie heard small sobs from her own throat and started to scuff away from him.

"Oh, no you don't," Max said. "You want it. You asked for it and you're going to get it because you made sure I don't have a choice anymore."

He squeezed her waist, pushed a thigh between hers and ground into the flesh that already wept for release.

She lifted her arms as if in surrender.

"What's the matter with you?" he said. "How can you be two women in one?" Holding her breasts, he used the tips of his thumbs to draw circles around her nipples, coming closer and closer but never quite touching them.

"Please." Annie bucked toward him. "Do it." And she meant

she wanted him to play with her nipples, to ignite the white hot prickling.

With no warning, he dipped, caught her behind her knees and landed her on the carpet.

Horror engulfed her. "Max—"

His mouth cut off whatever she might have said, and he kissed her repeatedly, and while he did, he positioned himself and thrust inside. She felt his body give a great shudder and opened her mouth to scream, but his bellow drowned her out.

Once, twice, three times he battered into her, testing her, finding his rhythm, and with each thrust, Annie bit down on her bottom lip to stop him from hearing her moan.

She let her hands flop above her head. Tears streamed. He fell to pumping steadily, groaning, but with satisfaction, with pleasure.

On and on he went until a sensation both unbearable and thrilling, speared her and shot exquisite burning into her labia and down her legs. A heavy pulsing began, just as Max shouted her name, gave a last upward lunge and slumped with his body half on and half off hers. He slid off her but kept her in his arms.

"Annie, Annie," he muttered, as if slipping into sleep. "Whatever it takes, you're going to be mine now."

For moments she lay still. The pain had ebbed but she still hurt. And she had to get away. At first she thought she would slide free without him noticing, but he reached for her face. "Rest," he said.

Within moments, his arms relaxed. Annie rolled away, grabbed her clothes and made a dash for her bedroom. She passed straight through to the bathroom and locked herself inside. The fan hummed to life, then the shower water beat down. A woman could take a shower when she felt like one, couldn't she? It didn't have to mean anything. And while she was under the water, she wouldn't hear Max if he came after her.

***

He turned on his back and put an arm under his head. He couldn't take in what had just happened, or how. The Annie he knew wasn't the Annie who had goaded him, tried to subjugate him. He smiled at the thought. She didn't seem to realize that she only did what he allowed her to do. Every move, every unbelievable word, inflamed him beyond reason. He breathed slowly in through his nose. What he'd said to her, he meant. Now they'd been together, like wild things, he wouldn't rest until he had her again and again. He smiled faintly. Or she had him.

Why she'd rushed away, he didn't know unless she'd managed to shock herself. He didn't believe he'd just seen Annie as she'd ever been before. And now she hid to pull herself together.

The shower water was loud even from here. Max retrieved his jeans and walked into the kitchen. He turned on a light and found a glass for water. His dry mouth needed immediate attention.

He raised the full glass and drank it empty.

Tossing his jeans on the counter, he started putting on his shorts.

"For... Dammit all!" A small streak of blood smeared his penis and spotted the waistband of his shorts where it touched his groin.

CHAPTER 11

"I see you sneaking around out there, Madge Pollard," Father Cyrus Payne said.

The door to his office was partly open and he saw his assistant moving about in the hall.

"Just takin' Millie out," Madge responded. "Won't be a moment."

"Wait, I'm comin'." Cyrus moved rapidly from behind his desk and opened his door all the way. "I told you this isn't the time to be alone out there." He avoided looking at Madge's black and white puppy. "A woman's missing in this town. Give me that hound. I'll take her out."

"She's not a hound," Madge said and eased the front door open. Attached to a very long lead, the dog took off around the corner and Madge followed. "Have you finished your homily?" Her voice floated back.

Cyrus wandered after her. Her legs flashed pale beneath the swishing hem of a dark blue dress. "You don't get enough fresh air," he said.

"What?" The dog had wiggled under an azalea and Madge assumed a relaxed, waiting attitude. "Fresh air?"

"You're pale. I know I don't always take as much notice as I should but you're looking pasty. Get out in the sun—with a hat on—for an hour a day. You need the vitamins."

Madge didn't say a word but he could feel her big, dark eyes on him and if he looked closer, she'd be grinning. "Someone has to look out for you," he said. "You surely don't take care of yourself. Ask anyone and they'll tell you the same, and say you don't get enough sleep because you work such long hours, too. You forget you have to add on the time it takes you to get back home to Rosebank in the evenin'. What's that hound doin'?"

"Millie's a papillon—butterfly dog to you—and a member of the spaniel family. I've told you the same thing several times. Why don't you like her?"

He did, but he wasn't planning to tell Madge. "If she was a real dog, I might like her. Under five pounds of nothing doesn't count. Next time you take a good look at her, see if I'm not right. Maybe when she grows to full size she won't look like a long-haired mouse. What *is* she doin'?"

"Pooping." Madge emphasized both syllables.

"Under one of my azaleas?"

"A girl's gotta do what a girl's gotta do. This is her favorite spot because she can really get into it without some nosey poke watchin'." She giggled.

"Nothin' that small could take that long over—what she's doing," Cyrus said, getting close to laughter himself. He crouched on the gravel path beside the bed of azaleas and shifted branches until he could locate Millie. "She's not poopin'. She's sitting under there congratulating herself for getting you out of the rectory."

"She's an ounce or two away from full-grown," Madge said. "She'll soon be a year old. And I'm shocked at you for encouragin' folks to gossip about me. I like my work. And I like being here. Rosebank is just where I sleep."

Cyrus couldn't think of a thing to say. He liked her here, too. All he needed to feel at peace was to know that while he went about parish business, Madge was nearby. And he wasn't fair to her. Long periods passed when he could put aside the notion that he was probably standing in the way of her marrying and having a family, but it always came back. They were locked together by friendship...and love. The love wasn't mentioned but they understood that it must stay in their hearts and be expressed only through kindness.

He clapped his hands at the little dog. "Come on out, you. Come on, come to me." Flattened on her stomach, the dog wiggled, commando-style, about an inch closer to him. Her white teeth showed in what he would swear was a grin. She loved to play—not that he was interested in playing with dogs. "Look at that. She's disobeyin' me," he said.

"You're frightening her," Madge said. "She's hidin'."

Cyrus bounced to his feet. "I don't frighten anybody. I reckon that's the problem, I don't get respect because you all think I'm a pushover. It's time to change that." He liked being trusted. Sure, he allowed himself to be used, but it was his choice.

"Go back inside," Madge said. "You've been busy in there. Don't let me interrupt."

He looked around. The night had a way of growing soft fingers and a whispery voice when trouble came around, and trouble had really slipped into town today. First he'd found Annie Duhon in the church, looking wild and fighting him like she thought he wanted to hurt her. Afterward she wouldn't say much, although she'd promised to come back and talk to him. Then came the news of a stranger gone missing from the Majestic. Spike had said he'd call when Cyrus was needed for a search party. No call had come yet.

"Cyrus?" Madge said softly. "You've got a lot on your mind. Time to get it on paper."

"No big ideas in my head. I was just fiddlin' in the office. Is she ready to go in yet?"

"Writing a homily doesn't count as fiddlin', Father. I just bet you were prayin' for a diversion so you could get away from it."

He smiled a little. "No such thing." He longed to put off writing the weekend homily. Dark as it was out here, a walk would be preferable—with Madge and the mutt as long as they didn't make any noise. He needed to think, and hope he got some inspiration—pray he got some inspiration, that was. This was the first weekend of the annual pledge drive. *God, send me a new way to beg—please.*

Millie emerged from her bower, her ridiculously small body whipping from side to side, her long-haired curly pig tail swishing over her back. Cyrus looked down into a pair of shiny black eyes. Why the creature thought she loved him, he had no idea, but despite the way she sometimes pretended otherwise, he believed she did.

An engine ground unevenly in their direction.

"Someone's coming," Cyrus said. Headlights appeared and the beams swung down Bonanza Alley.

"Are you sure?" Madge said.

What could a man do when his assistant had been with him so long she'd taken control? He smiled but didn't respond.

Rattles and bangs joined the rough engine noise and Wazoo's van crunched onto the gravel parking lot above the rectory.

"Hoo mama," Madge said, sounding delighted. "This is something. Now why would Wazoo be comin' here at this time of night? She can't stand you."

"No such thing. Wazoo has a grudgin' admiration for me. It comes out sounding rude, nothing more."

Madge cackled, there was no other description that would fit the sound she made. She cleared her throat and said, "Sorry. That wasn't nice."

"You down there, God man?" Wazoo yelled, standing beside the open driver's door of her liberally decorated van. Planets, zodiac signs, snakes, gators, an ad for her "critter therapy" and another letting the world know, "There's no sadder singing than Wailing Wazoo. Your burial is my burial. Let me sing them into heaven— or wherever they going—for you."

"Hey, Wazoo," Madge called. "We're down by the azaleas."

Wazoo, who let it be known that she was available to offer helpful spells—conjures, as she called them—and that those in need of a little voodoo were always welcome, treated Cyrus with suspicion. She preferred to keep distance between them. Occasionally she ruined what Cyrus had decided was an act by turning to him for help. Or she ruined the act by going over the top into comedy.

"Does she do her own paintin' on that sorry vehicle?" he asked Madge, keeping his voice down.

"Surely does. On the other side she advertises vehicle logos. Air brushing. Wazoo doesn't believe in newfangled computer generated efforts, or wraps."

"No I do not," Wazoo said, although she shouldn't be able to hear them yet. "Inspiration, intuition and raw talent, that's what it takes to turn a vehicle into a rolling endorsement."

"Evenin', Wazoo," Cyrus said. "Nice to see you here after so long."

"It's not nice to be here, but thanks. Me, I get the creeps when I get close to—" she nodded toward the church. "I put myself at your mercy. Protect me, Father. Don't let the good fairies get me."

"Fairies?" Cyrus shook his head. "Are you coming in?"

"Oh, no," Wazoo said. "Me, I only drove here to frighten myself out of my red silk drawers."

Madge coughed and made a great deal of gathering up Millie, Millie who licked her boss's face then leaped out of her arms before Madge could stop her. Millie landed against Cyrus with the innocent confidence of one who has never been dropped.

"Will you look at that?" Wazoo said. "You better sign that dog up with me. And fast. She ain't got no taste when it comes to people. Not good, Madge."

Keeping a straight face, Cyrus turned toward the rectory. "I've got a new wine I'd like you to try," he told his visitor.

"You ain't used it for one of them hootin' and hollerin's you hold over there, have you?" Again Wazoo indicated St. Cécil's.

"The bottle hasn't been opened," Cyrus told her.

"That's good then. Stop right where you are, God man."

Cyrus, with Millie on his shoulder, licking his ear with great concentration, did as he was told. "Yes, Wazoo? What now?"

"You still drivin' that disgustin' old Impala, right?"

"Right."

"Self-respectin' folks don't drive ancient red Impala station wagons with bent frames."

He had long ago decided, perhaps because he was getting ornery, that he would drive his reviled vehicle until it shuddered and fell apart while he was in it.

"I've got the perfect solution," Wazoo said. "You was admirin' my van. And if I do say so—which I should—that's one fine logo job I done there. I'm gonna do the Impala. I'm gonna put frames on the sides, the kind posters slide into, so we can change out the message from time to time. I could put the times of those hootin' and—"

"Hollerings," Madge finished for her.

"See if I don't have folks pourin' in on a Sunday mornin'. And money's gonna pour right in with 'em. You'll wonder why you didn't do it before. There'll be a permanent shout line that runs all the way around. At the top. Right under the roof. 'Best donuts and coffee in town. Come gossip along with us. BINGO every night! BIG prizes.'" Wazoo drew up her shoulders. "I'm tellin' you we gotta do it."

He had asked for guidance in the begging department but this wasn't what he'd had in mind.

Praying quietly, Cyrus went into the rectory and walked along a passage to the kitchen. In daylight, the big window gave a wide view of Bayou Teche and the rectory's big back lawn, dominated by a two-dimensional bronze statue of five figures, some with flat braids flying, all capering. A gift from a previous housekeeper, the piece had a history and no one had the heart to take it away. At the moment, Ozaire Dupre, who worked part-time as a caretaker at the church, and part-time for Homer Devol, had attached goggle-eye glasses, with shocking blue eyeballs on springs, to each figure. This wasn't because he was either a humorist or a practical joker, but because his prime entertainment came from infuriating his wife, Lil, Cyrus's housekeeper.

With Millie perched at the back of his neck, her winglike ears trailing long black fur, Cyrus was forced to lean forward to balance her while he found a bottle of Merlot and carefully removed the cork. "Glasses?" he said, angling his face toward Madge. "Don't think I can manage them."

Madge took glasses to the big oak table by the window and the three of them sat down. Cyrus poured generous measures of wine and Wazoo made humming noises. They drank and she said, "To the missing," before taking another big swallow.

For the sake of his own skin, Cyrus carefully disengaged Millie's claws from beneath his collar. He put her on his lap and she curled up at once. This could get sticky if Madge started to question her dog's loyalty.

"Confused," Wazoo muttered, pointing a long forefinger at Millie.

"Why did you pray for the missing?" Cyrus asked.

"I didn't. I toasted them. I don't want to be here but I've got responsibilities to people I like. And I trust you." She dropped her voice to an annoyed whisper on the last sentence. Shaking back her long, curling black hair, she frowned at Cyrus who thought what a lovely woman she was, despite all the affectation and attempts to shock.

Madge got up and set her glass aside. "I've got a few things to finish before I go home to Rosebank."

"No you don't," Wazoo said. "This is your home. Rosebank is where you sleep and keep your clothes. A sad thing for a beautiful woman like you. Pining away for something that can't be. Or it could be if *someone* sexy enough to melt fillings right out of you teeth would give in and do the things he wants to do."

Cyrus put his elbows on the table and swirled the wine in his glass. If Madge weren't here, he could warn Wazoo that she had stepped way over the line, but Madge was right behind him and he would not upset her more than she already would be.

"Would you mind stayin', Madge?" Wazoo said in her sweetest tones. "I've got so much on my mind I can use all the help I can get, and I do appreciate another woman's point of view. Cher, let's face it, I need an interpreter here."

Madge returned to the table and slid into a chair. She kept her eyes down and her cheeks were pink. Wazoo wasn't wrong when she said Madge was beautiful to look at. What the woman didn't know was how special his best friend was on the inside.

And this was a place he couldn't afford to go.

"I am scared to my bones," Wazoo said. She peered around the old-fashioned kitchen. "Lil isn't here, is she?" she said as if expecting Lil Dupre to emerge from one of the white-painted cupboards that reached from floor to ceiling.

"No," Cyrus said. "Lil is never here in the evenin'."

"Whew." Wazoo swept the back of a hand over her brow. "Now you know how I detest gossip."

He and Madge said, "Mmm," in unison.

Wazoo made circles on the table with the base of her glass. She drank slowly and licked her lips. "There's something bad goin' on in this town. More than one bad thing. Could be more than two."

Cyrus sat back in his chair and pushed his hands into his pockets. "If you think there's something I can do to help, you know I will." Millie didn't move.

"It wasn't easy to come to you," Wazoo said. "If I wasn't worried sick about those Devol men I wouldn't be here. Except I should see what we can do about Annie. Now there's a woman who could turn into a tragedy if we don't get lucky."

"Wazoo—"

"It's all wound in with those Savage brothers. Max, anyway. I tell you, them who's supposed to keep us all safe ain't doin' much of a job 'cause they're all fouled up with they own problems. That is, some got problems, some only think they got problems. Hoo-ya-ya." She wound her head slowly from side to side. "Question is, who's at the top of the list? Who's most likely to get ruined first? I'll tell you—this is one heavy burden."

Madge had turned her face to the black window and stared at nothing. If he dared, Cyrus would take hold of her hand. They lived so close to, but so distant from each other. For too long he had begged her to make a life with someone who could be what she wanted a man to be for her, but she insisted she had chosen to be as near to him as he would allow. Madge wanted what little they could have together and refused to consider changing courses.

And Cyrus went to battle daily, wedded to his vocation, loving Madge in a celibate relationship that tore him apart.

"You were praying for someone who's missing," Madge said. "I could tell."

Wazoo slanted a glance at her. "And you could be right. But I'll get to that. I don't like to make any trouble but it would be good if someone who spends time here didn't repeat things they overhear."

Cyrus lifted Millie and gave her to Madge. "If you don't have something definite to say, don't say anything." He didn't need more of Wazoo's nonsense tonight.

"That's all I'm sayin' about it, me. Except you could make a big mistake if you look for this one in the most obvious place. If it's mentioned again, it won't be by me, no sir. The Devol men are makin' fools of themselves over somethin' I can't repeat, but they're makin' themselves miserable. They're gonna make all kinda people miserable before long."

"You can't say what the problem is, but you want me to do something about it?" Cyrus could feel Madge's awkwardness and he was tempted to tell Wazoo that office hours were over.

"All you gotta do is tell Homer and Spike—not together though—tell them that you know a person told Homer a lie about him and Spike and they should forget it. Me, I don't want Vivian upset when she's this far gone with the baby, and she could be. She's doin' well, except in her mind sometimes. If you set it all straight, they'll listen." Wazoo crossed her arms tightly. "They won't believe me, that's what I'm sayin'."

The phone rang and Madge got up to answer. "Rectory," she said. Then, "I'll tell him you need him in the mornin'. Night, Spike."

Wazoo's lips parted. She stared at Madge, clearly waiting for her to say why Spike wanted Cyrus in the morning.

"Thanks, Madge," he said quickly. "I'll be there." He didn't even ask the time Spike wanted to see him. He and Madge shared an understanding glance.

"I don't think I can talk to Homer and Spike," Cyrus said. "Even if I knew what you were talking about, I wouldn't interfere."

"You'll have to in time. Longer you wait, worse it'll get. Was Spike calling because that woman's gone missing? The nurse or whatever she was? They gettin' up a bigger search party?"

This wasn't the first time Wazoo had shown uncanny insight into something she shouldn't know about. "If that's true," Cyrus said "who told you?"

"You gonna have to work it out." Wazoo drained her glass and got up. "Me, I made the big mistake comin' here. That Max Savage could be a real good man, but how can I be sure? He's gettin' tight with Annie."

"You're not making much sense," Cyrus told her.

Wazoo clicked her fingers. "Concentrate. That dead woman came to see Max. Now she's gone."

"Please don't say she's dead." Hugging the dog close, Madge looked horrified. "We haven't heard that and you don't know it. She could have decided to run away. That happens all the time."

"She didn't run away. I know what I saw. There was… There was pain and terror, and he didn't care."

"That's it." With his skin getting tighter by the moment, Cyrus pushed to his feet. "Are you sayin' you saw Michele Riley murdered? And you saw who killed her? You should be talking to Spike, not me."

"I'm askin' you to believe I saw somethin' awful. Someone else saw it, too, but it's not my place to tell that story. And when I say I saw, I don't mean I was standin' there watchin'. No, sir, it come to me real quiet—until the screams started. I didn't see faces, but I knew who she was. I'm still workin' on the other one and often as not I don't get what I ask for specific."

Pacing, struggling to decide if he should brush this off as another Wazoo flight of fancy, or encourage her to keep confiding in him, Cyrus looked at her each time he turned.

"You a good man," she said, real low. "I'm askin' for too much. You can't make a leap into my world, any more than Madge can."

"We can't be sure some people don't have special gifts," Madge said, not so much as glancing at Cyrus. "You've known things other people didn't before. Not that I'm saying I can accept that completely, but I'll always listen to you."

He went back to the table and braced his weight on locked arms, looked down at Wazoo. He couldn't form an opinion as quickly as Madge had. "Why are you worried about Annie spending time with Max?" At least he could deal with something straightforward.

"I said I might be," Wazoo said, but she looked concerned. "He's a surgeon and he's opening that clinic people will come to from all over. Should be above question. Me, I question. Spike met Max at Hungry Eyes and I could tell they didn't have no pleasant chat. Then, when everyone else had cleared out but Max Savage and that Bobby, Max got real mad at the other one for what he said about Annie. But I can't repeat what he said."

Cyrus pushed his hands into his hair. "Bobby? Who is Bobby? Gimme some clear hints about what's going on here. You're scared out of your mind."

"Wazoo ain't never scared. I'm worried, is all." She plucked at a violet ribbon threaded through the lace bodice of her dress. "I thought Max was goin' to hit that Bobby. I don't know who he is except he said he'd known Annie for a long time, and he said a lot of other stuff. Max walked out and I know he didn't take his car. I reckon he walked around the back of the square and found a way in to visit Annie."

"What's Annie's phone number?" Cyrus asked. He stood straight again.

"Don't bother with that," Wazoo said and passed him a crumpled piece of paper with a number on it. She smiled with one side of her mouth. "I brought it in case we needed it."

"What am I supposed to say?" Looking at the phone keypad, Cyrus searched for an excuse. "Got it," he said and punched in the number.

After five rings Annie answered, "Hi."

"Father Cyrus," he said. "This mornin' we said we'd get together for a chat but we didn't set a day and time."

Annie thanked him and said she'd call him in a day or two.

"You're sure you're doing okay, then?" he asked, not feeling so happy at showing off his ability to fabricate, even if it was for a good cause and not entirely untrue.

"I'm just fine," Annie said. "Thank you."

When he hung up Wazoo spread her arms wide and laughed loudly.

"What?" he said. He looked to Madge who suddenly remembered her wine.

"You told a fib," Wazoo said. "The two of you didn't really agree you was gettin' together." She wiggled a forefinger at him.

He grinned. "Not exactly, but close."

"Now," Wazoo said, "about Homer and Spike…"

"Okay, okay." Cyrus said. "I'm going to talk with Spike. But I don't know if I'll say anything personal. You agree with me that he's got a steady head and nobody wants to solve this disappearance more than he does?"

"I guess. Unless it's her boyfriend. I heard tell he's gettin' here in the mornin'."

"Who told you that?"

"I can't say."

"What can you say?" Cyrus asked.

Millie had slid from Madge's lap and now she squealed pitifully beside Wazoo until she got swept up.

Wazoo breathed in deep and long. "The only thing I can tell you is I'm not the only one who saw a woman buried headfirst in the ground. And I saw fire, just like someone else did. The other person's suffered a long time because evil was done to her. Now it's bein' relived and I'm pickin' up on that. I'm not sayin' I like it but I don't have no choice.

"I don't know who did that to Michele Riley, but if we can't find out, Annie could end up burned and buried somewhere. Don't even ask why I think that."

A few miles away a man heaped charred remnants of logs and brush together and pushed them into bags. He checked around, studied the way the trees grew around the area. The crowns of live oaks, lush with Spanish moss, bunched heavy and black against a metallic sky. No breezes eased the sultry pressure that mixed with sweat to drip from his skin.

This was a good place, really good. Exactly what he needed was here in abundance.

He smelled phlox, faintly because the scent of burning still hung around. He had seen the purple blossoms on a previous visit. In the trees, berries grew all over tangled vines. Vines were something he had to watch for.

The bags were full and he hauled them to a spot where he made a pile. He made his way out to the road, to his car, and exchanged the shovel for a rake, then sprang back the way he'd come. He used the rake to scatter any minute remnants of singed material.

It was done. Again. He returned to the car, opened the driver's door and sat sideways on the seat. Surgical gloves had purposes some would never think of. He snapped off the pair he wore—and bent to pull off blue shoe-covers. Time to get rid of the last pieces of evidence.

CHAPTER | 2

The doorbell rang.

Oh, no, Annie thought, she wasn't going down there. The clock showed a few minutes before five in the morning. She didn't need a talented imagination to visualize Max waiting outside in the darkness.

If she couldn't forget last night, and pick up where she'd been before meeting Max, she couldn't stay in Toussaint. She didn't intend to leave, so... There would be no more days when she kept him company while he ate lunch—not that Max was likely to want her to. He wasn't likely to go near Pappy's.

That was it. Annie pulled the sheet over her head. She would never forget him, probably not for a single day, but she would cope and move on.

She had a dream, a goal, and cracking up over an infatuation could only get in the way.

This is more than infatuation.

The doorbell rang, a little longer this time.

Had to be Max.

Throwing herself on her face, she folded the pillow over her ears. They'd had sex, strange but powerful sex, and she had leaped away from him the instant it was over. Penetration had hurt at first, but not for long enough to make her want to stop. For at least an hour afterward she had stayed in the bathroom—what a surprise to discover he'd left when she finally came out!

He wouldn't come back. Not after the way she'd treated him. But someone was trying to get to her.

If it was important, she had a phone—and maybe she should use it to call 911.

Annie would not go downstairs.

The bell rang in repeated short bursts. Determined knocking on the door followed.

Her phone did ring. She sat up and looked at it, then snatched it up. "Yes?"

"I'm a tired man," Max said. "Can I come up? You don't have to talk to me, just let me use your spare bedroom."

"Did you lose your keys to Rosebank?" She sounded mean. She felt mean, and sad, and confused.

"I can't show up there, now."

"Where have you been?"

"Just driving around."

Annie wasn't soft, but she couldn't ignore him. "Okay." Hanging up, she swung her feet from the bed and grabbed her white silk robe. She pulled it on and tied the belt tightly while she went down the stairs. At the bottom she saw a familiar, tall shadow through the glass.

Annie opened the door.

Wearing dark beard stubble and with his curly hair on end, Max stood with his arms hanging at his sides, feet braced apart and an inscrutable expression on his face.

She stood aside and he came in. He followed her upstairs and she said, "You know where the other bedrooms are. Take your pick and make yourself at home, please." Her eyes stung and her skin smarted—and unless she sucked in her bottom lip, it trembled.

Max couldn't even figure out why she'd let him in at all—unless she wasn't ready to chuck him. He could hope. "Are you okay?" he asked, looking at her slim figure from the back. She looked nice in white silk.

"Fine. You?"

"The same," he said.

Sure, he needed a bed but he needed some answers from Annie first. After everything seemed so amazingly good between them, something had gone horribly wrong and he intended to make sure he hadn't caused her real damage. He thought he already knew how pummeled her emotions were likely to be.

He didn't think it was all his fault, but he'd played his part. Max almost laughed at that. Once inside the apartment, he closed the door. "How come Irene's not on guard duty?" The lighter he could keep things, the better.

"She's in bed, like most sensible creatures."

"Annie," he said. "Can we talk?"

"No. If you hear me in the mornin', wait till I'm gone before you come out."

With her arms crossed, she stood close to the wall and looked at her bare feet, as if waiting for him to choose one of the spare bedrooms.

"What happened to us?" he said.

She didn't answer.

"Why did you bleed?"

He heard her suck in a breath. Her eyes looked into his, but briefly, just long enough for him to see shock.

Damn, they had bad timing. "Okay, I'm sorry I was blunt." He crossed pristine carpet to sit at one end of the couch. "I had to make sure I hadn't hurt you badly."

"No," she said, too quietly. "I didn't know anythin' had happened at all."

Max looked at her over his shoulder. "Were you a virgin?" His pulse thudded.

Annie put her face in her hands and slid down the wall until she sat on the carpet, her head on her knees.

Shit. He scrambled across the room and sat on the floor beside her. He rubbed her back and at least she didn't try to stop him.

He massaged the tight muscles in her neck. "I'm a liar, Annie. I don't just want a place to sleep. I came because I had to see you. You couldn't have thought I'd ignore what happened."

So still, so quiet. Sitting like this, not having any idea what she was thinking, tore him up.

"Annie," he said quietly. "The way we made love was something new to me. You were incredible."

"I don't believe you," she said. "But thanks for the compliment, I think."

He put his mouth close to her ear. "I'm not making anything up. Take it or leave it. But I want more of whatever that was."

She gave him a tight little smile.

Her back heaved but she turned silent again. Might as well lay it all out. "Then there's the visit to St. Martinville. After you found me, you flipped. I need to know why and on this one I'm not giving you any breaks. This is about your health. When we get through talking—then it'll be time for sleep."

Annie tried to go limp. At most other times, his fingers on the back of her neck would have relaxed her—not this time. "You'll have to let me have more space, at least for now. Be patient, please."

He didn't look happy. When she caught his eye he raised one brow. She didn't get a response to her request.

"I'm sorry I…Max, I don't know why I ran off to the bathroom last night. It's been… This is so awful." She made herself meet his eyes which did nothing to calm her down. "It was like—I said things I've never said. I wanted to shock you and give myself some courage. Afterwards, I got more confused. Forgive me for bein' difficult."

"*Difficult?* You think that's what I thought about you?"

"I should have stayed and explained what was wrong."

"We're both here now. If you want to tell me, I want to listen."

The complete truth was out of the question. At least now. But she could fill him in without going into all the details. He looked so tired. Annie rested a hand on the side of his face. "You've got enough to deal with."

"I do. So please help me to stop worrying about you."

Lifting her head, she scooted closer until their hips touched, and she curled against his chest. "It was a big deal at the time, but I got lucky. I was attacked. Before the man could finish what he started, my mother came home and he stopped." Revisiting that night brought back the horror she had faced. But she was right, she'd been lucky. "He didn't rape me."

Max put his arms around her and hugged. "How long ago was this?"

"About ten years."

"And each time you have sex now you fall apart?"

She pulled away from him. "You didn't need to say that. I got frightened, is all. You sound like you're takin' a patient history."

Max laughed. "I guess I do. Come back here." She let him hold her again. "I'm a clinician, too. I do take histories. I slipped into a habit."

"I wasn't a virgin," she muttered. "But I haven't had sex since before it happened."

"Sweetheart, sweetheart," he said and turned her face up to his. Softly, he kissed her. "Now I get it. Jeez, if I'd known I'd—"

"You wouldn't have made love to me," she said flatly.

"Don't put words in my mouth. If I'd known, and I'd been sure you wanted it, I'd have made sure we took things slowly."

Annie pinched her lips together before she said, "I wanted it just the way it was."

He laughed again. "You're a wild thing." Tired or not, his body reacted to being close to her, and talking about sex together. "Annie, can I ask you one more thing about this?"

"Ask. I may not answer."

And he had thought she was too subservient when he met her! "Bobby. I don't know his other name." He gave her time to reply. She didn't. "Was it Bobby who attacked you?"

"No...no."

"You don't sound sure. Tell me the truth."

"I have."

Max tamped down a flare of anger. "If it was him, I want to know."

"It wasn't him, I tell you."

"He ran off at the mouth about you. After you left the café."

Her heart felt as if it dropped—hard. "Try not to think about that," she said. "I hardly recognize him as the high schooler I first knew. He's turned mean. He seemed fixated on me at one time, but he hasn't tried to get in touch with me for all these years."

Max timed his next question as carefully as he could. "How did he know where to find you?"

"He was the guy who came out of the bagel shop in St. Martinville while we were standin' there, talking. Who knows what caught his attention like that. Could be he got mad because I didn't immediately melt all over him. But why would I? Sure he helped me out once, but it's bizarre for him to get possessive now."

"That doesn't explain how he found you here in Toussaint."

"Unless he knows someone I know." She shuddered. "He wants somethin' from me—has to—but I don't know what it is."

And Max couldn't take a risk that the man was dangerous, even if he saw no connections to his own problems.

"He did something to help you once?" Max said.

"Yes. He and my mother stopped that man from finishing his attack on me."

"Why were you attacked?"

No, no, no, she couldn't go back there, not now and maybe never. "The man was mentally ill. He'd done bad things to other women."

Max's penetrating stare disturbed her even more. "I know you don't want to talk about it, but I think you'd help me if you could," he said. "What kind of bad things?"

She heard her throat make a sound when she swallowed. "Forcin' himself on them. Tyin' them down." And that was all he would get.

"Annie." Max stood and pulled her up by both hands. He kissed her knuckles and watched her reaction. "I don't want to let you go."

"I'm hopin' we'll get a chance to find out if...I feel silly sayin' this, but I'd like to know if we could really have somethin' together." And she did feel silly. What made her think a man like him wanted more than a warm bed and a warm woman?

He pulled her far away from the windows where the curtains were still open. "I've told you the truth about what's happened to me," he said. "Today I expect all hell to break loose over Michele. I'm praying for her to show up. Or call and say she had a wild need to run off to Vegas or something. She wouldn't be the first."

"Is she the kind of woman who might do that."

"No." He slipped an arm around her waist and rested his chin on top of her head. "Michele is responsible. She's the sort of woman who does exactly what she says she'll do and she said she accepted the job at Green Veil. She was going home to deal with handing in her notice and making the move. She's also engaged and planning a wedding. Her fiancé's a nurse and we really expect him to come to Green Veil. Michele intimated he would. They like the idea of a quieter lifestyle."

"Did Spike say if they'd found any evidence yet? Fingerprints they could use, clothing left somewhere…blood?" She coughed. "I thought about simple things, like the front door at the Majestic. She had to touch that to go in."

"So far, nothing they can use. They're searching, but I can't be with them."

"Why?" Of course she knew why.

"I'm the number one suspect," Max said. "I doubt they'd think my heart was in it. Today, I expect to spend time with Spike and probably a whole bunch of people who've jumped into the case by now." He raised his face to the ceiling. "Michele told me not to go into the hotel with her but I should have insisted."

"But you saw her inside?" Annie said.

"Of course. She walked straight in and turned toward the stairs. Why didn't I stay a bit longer—just to be sure?"

"It's not your fault at all," Annie told him. "Would it help if you and I were open about our friendship instead of tryin' to hide it? The authorities would see there's nothin' to suspect you of. That you're not a man women have to be afraid of."

His shirt was free of his pants and he shoved his hands underneath to put his thumbs in the waist of his pants. The shirt wasn't buttoned to the bottom and his flat, muscular belly made it hard for Annie to look away.

"I want to accept your offer. I want us to be together whenever we aren't working. I would love to ask you to build toward a future with me but I can't. I told you, two women I got close to, died."

"That was a long time ago."

"Three years isn't so long and plenty of people haven't forgotten. They haven't found anyone to pin those deaths on."

"I'm sure they're workin' on it," Annie said. She felt a growing desperation. "If you give up hope, you might as well be guilty."

He raised his chin and looked down at her. "I think you care."

She felt her own blush. "I do."

Max confronted what he had to say. He couldn't do any sugar-coating at all—not if he gave a damn about Annie. "Listen. I told you what's happened to me and how I've had to run and look for a safe place twice already. Now I might have to move on again—not without fighting to stay—but if it gets impossible to carry on in the area. Someone hates me enough to want to ruin my life. And they don't care if other people die to make sure it happens."

She moved in close and slid her fingers beneath his shirt, ran her hands around his waist. He jumped and shook his head. "You know how to get a man's attention." The white silk she wore clung to her breasts and the tips poked at the sleek fabric, showing she was reacting to touching him. "How did you manage to keep that to yourself for ten years?"

"I didn't meet anyone I wanted to be close to." She averted her eyes.

He inclined his head and ducked to settle his lips on hers. He kept it light but she was sexy as hell, warm, with a clean, faintly rose scent he'd like to settle down with beneath her sheets. And this wasn't what he'd come here for. Having sex with her again would blessedly numb his brain, but it wouldn't take reality away. Anyway, she needed a little time to heal.

Annie rubbed his bare back. She leaned her hips into his and then her breasts. He felt every millimeter of her skin where it met his.

"I'm afraid to love you," he said.

She stood still. "What did you say?"

"You heard me."

"Don't say things you don't mean."

"I wouldn't do that," he said. "I've admitted how people have died for being my friends. That means I'm trapped. If I do what I want and keep on getting closer to you, I could be...you could become a target. Annie, whoever hates me might decide to kill you. I'd do my best to keep you safe, but I can't take that kind of chance."

The blood drained from her face. "So you want us to say goodbye? Forget it." Not so long ago she'd been promising herself she'd stay away from Max, now she knew she couldn't.

"Do what I tell you to do," Max said. "For your own sake."

"Do what you tell me? I don't think so. I've faced danger before and I'm still here."

"I'll do what you said before," Max said. "I'll wait till you've left for work in the morning before I leave the building myself. Afterward, please let me make any moves. I'll figure out something. Don't come to me in public, Annie."

"Are you sure people haven't figured out we're close already?"

"I'm not sure," he said. "I know some suspect. Wazoo knows."

"Wazoo has gifts most people laugh at. She just knew I cared about you. I didn't tell her."

"Would she keep quiet if you asked her?"

"I'll ask anyway. You'd be surprised, she's pretty careful who she trusts. She can say too much, but she's not the kind to tell all kinds of people about a thing like that."

"I've got to go back where you don't want me to go." He didn't like what he'd decided he had to do. "You passed out in St. Martinville. I want to know what was happening to you. Did you see something that frightened you?" He remembered something. "Were you upset by Bobby? Was that what set you off?"

"No...I don't know. It was nothing. I hadn't—"

"Don't try blaming what happened on lack of food again. I'm not buying it. You need a thorough examination, a full workup, and I'm asking you to get it done."

She looked at him directly and sighed. "I don't want to, but I'll do it. I'll make an appointment and talk to Reb."

"And have her take a look at you to make sure there's nothing to worry about with the bleeding."

"I can't do that."

He raised his eyebrows at her.

"Okay, I'll do it." The man was a surgeon, why wouldn't he be matter-of-fact. Annie felt sick with embarrassment.

"You couldn't surprise Reb if you tried. She's been both the only doctor in town and the medical examiner for years. Roche knew her before I did and he says she's one of the best doctors he's ever met."

Annie nodded. "I really like her. I like her cousin, Lee, too."

"I don't know her," Max said. "Runs the newspaper, right?"

"Uh-huh. She's got a business partner but he isn't here much. I think everyone in town is afraid they'll see their name in the *Trumpet*. She has a gossip column and makes folks mad. She doesn't name names, but you know who she's writing about." She grinned. "Roche likes her, too. Maybe he's mentioned that."

Max gave a wide smile. "Oh, no. My dear twin likes to keep his women to himself. And he's a ladies' man—in his own quiet way."

"He's good-lookin'," Annie said, hiding a smile. She didn't need to remind him that he and Roche were hard to tell apart. "I don't blame Lee for being interested. She's pretty cute, too."

Seeing her relax lightened the black weight he felt most of the time.

"You're very tired," he said. "Me, too. I can't say goodbye to you, but we are going to have to do things at my say-so. Let me make the decisions. If we have to meet in the night, or way out of town, we'll do it. But if we have to wait until the heat's off in town, that's what we'll do."

He read her expression. She wanted to argue with him so badly. "Get some sleep," she said. "You don't have long before you'll have to get up for work." Annie went into her bedroom.

He hesitated a moment then knocked on the door. "Can I come in?"

A great deal of rustling came from inside the room. "Okay."

Max went in to find her kneeling on the floor beside an open bottom dresser drawer. The contents overflowed onto the floor. A jumble of delicate underwear spread in a semicircle around the chest. Bras, panties, one or two filmy negligees and tangled hosiery. Little packets of powder had been punctured and Max smelled a sweet scent like lily of the valley.

"Did someone get in here?" he said, kneeling to help her pick up.

"Oh, they did indeed and they are on my bed."

He turned and saw her cat, eyes crossed, curled into a tight, spiky ball in the sheets. The cat looked at Max and showed a lot of pointy teeth.

"That cat did this?"

"That cat," Annie said, "does things like this when she is *really* mad. Maybe even pissed. She's ruined all my sachets and put snags in just about everything. You don't need to help, Max."

"Have you told her off?"

"I'll do that," Annie said. "Irene, you are a naughty cat. How dare you empty my drawer and throw my stuff around. Never do that again." Her mouth twitched.

"So the cat is boss. I've got it." He got up, pulled Annie with him and plunked her on the side of the bed. "What upset you in St. Martinville—when you came to find me. Were you seeing something I couldn't see? You seemed like your mind had moved away."

Annie braced herself for his disbelief. "I have nightmares—and visions. After I was attacked, I had them a lot. They're back but they're different now."

"What happens in these visions?" Goose bumps shot out on Max's skin.

"I feel as if I'm inside someone who's losing consciousness. A man makes her...I don't know, but she can't move. He drags her along the ground and leans over her. Or me." She looked at him, her eyes too wide open. "I don't know if it's me but I think it could be."

"Lie down," he told her. He lifted the sheets and tucked her legs inside. Then he sat on the edge of the bed and leaned over her. "What else? Is there anything else?"

"No." Pictures burst into her mind, and a distant voice. She didn't recall knowing about them before, but they were clear now. The voice whispered and there was a face. "The vision gets smaller and smaller until I only see a circle with someone's face in it. *It's here now.*"

"Do you know the face?"

"No, but he looks... Oh, Max, he looks like a surgeon. In the blue helmet thing on his head and a mask and he's comin' closer and closer to me." She slipped lower in the bed. "I'm awake, aren't I?"

Max's stomach clenched. "Is it me?"

"No. I don't know. He said a name, not mine. He's saying...Isabel. And, Carol." Max faded. Annie saw the mask, and the eyes, but they fuzzed together. She tried to speak but her voice wouldn't work.

"You're making it up!"

The image stopped, dissolved, and Annie saw Max again.

He had stood up and stepped away from the bed. "Why?" he said. "Who put you up to this?"

Annie rose to her elbows. "What's the matter? You asked me what happened and I've told you. I haven't told anyone else."

"Who told you those names? Who did they say they were?" He took her by the shoulders. "Answer me."

"No one told me. I heard them just now. I'm scared. Let me go, you're hurtin' me." The fury in his eyes alarmed her. "Let me go, Max."

Carefully, he put her down against her pillows but didn't release her shoulders.

"I'm sorry," Annie said. "Max, when I see the bodies, they're burned, set fire to, then buried. I think they're dead first but I'm not sure."

The sound he made wasn't human.

"Max!"

"Isabel was my high-school girlfriend, the one who died. Carol was the nurse who was murdered while we were dating. Both of their bodies were burned."

Spinning away, hitting walls as he went, Max all but ran from the apartment.

His footsteps thundered on the stairs.

For seconds Annie couldn't move, then she threw off the sheets and rushed to her small office. The window overlooked the garden.

The gate to the alley stood open. A low, gray car shot under a light mounted on the alley wall and roared away.

The names, the impression of a man in surgical scrubs were new. Annie pressed her temples. Max being a surgeon must have influenced what she saw. He couldn't be blamed for questioning her behavior.

Shadows shifted outside. A tall figure stepped from the garden into a wedge of pale light at the gate. Annie got a single, brief profile of the man before he disappeared. A hood covered his head.

CHAPTER | 3

All Tarted Up belonged to Jilly Gautreaux, Guy Gautreaux's wife and Joe Gable's sister. Jilly and Joe used to own the café and bakery together until Joe's law practice got too busy.

Guy's office was in the upstairs apartment Jilly had vacated when she first moved into the house they now shared. The shingle for his private investigation service hung to the right of the shop where an open door invited clients to come inside.

By midmorning, All Tarted Up usually quieted down before the lunch rush. Not this morning. On a humid day, with rain-washed red honeysuckle blossoms shouting among clump bamboo in planters outside the shop, Father Cyrus paused on the hot sidewalk and peered through steamed up windows into the crowded interior.

There were some empty chairs. He entered the bright pink door, walking sideways to avoid a queue that divided the shop into two sections all the way to the counter. An assortment of familiar faces, and strangers, left with bags and boxes of pastries, and Jilly's big cardboard party containers of iced tea and coffee. He figured this crush of customers might be something to do with the searches going on for Michele Riley.

"Hey, Cyrus." Joe Gable stood up at a table against the wall and waved Cyrus over.

"Thanks," he mouthed, threading his way back and sitting down. He gave the girl who poured him coffee a grateful smile. "Marzipan tarts?" he asked without much hope that they wouldn't be sold out by now.

The girl, a nice kid called Sidney who lived in a trailer park south of town, gave Cyrus what resembled a quick curtsey and said softly, "Miz Jilly, she always has us keep some back in case you come in, Father." She smiled and her soft dark eyes lit up. "Mr. Gable, more coffee?"

"You bet." Joe slid his mug close and waited while it was filled. "Here we go again, huh?" he said when the girl had left. The noise in the place made quiet conversation safe. "For a little town, we do attract the screwballs. What are you thinking so far—about this missin' woman? They haven't found anything on her yet and they've been searchin' around the clock for three days."

"Marc Girard and I went out yesterday. There were fifty of us and we hit every inch along the Teche for miles. Didn't find anythin' but what you'd expect." Toussaint had seen more than its share of serious trouble but Cyrus always felt there was a whole lot more good than bad in the bayou town. "Michele Riley wouldn't be the first person who decided to drop out and start over somewhere else. Could be somethin' to do with her upcomin' marriage. Folks can get scared of commitment."

"You think Spike believes somethin' like that?" Joe asked.

"Spike's playin' it close to the vest. He's involvin' the police and if she doesn't show up by the end of the day, we'll be seein' the FBI.

Spike hates that but he doesn't mess around—even if there are one or two who think the FBI should have been in on day one. Spike leans on Guy when he needs to. He respects his opinion."

Pushing a spoon back and forth on the tabletop Joe said, "Spike's no fool. He's got access to some real useful talent there so he uses it. Ellie told me NOPD still calls and says Guy's got an open invitation to go back."

Cyrus cleared his throat. "I heard Spike's deputized him."

Joe glanced at his sister behind the counter, laughing at her customers, loving the business. "Jilly won't think much of that," he said. "If she could get her husband to take down his P.I. shingle, she would. She keeps talkin' about him doin' somethin' with white-collar crime."

Cyrus chuckled. "Madge said Jilly told her about that. I guess it didn't last long after he said he'd look into the FBI. He's doin' a service with the job he's made for himself here. He's a deterrent to a certain kind of people, and a help to others."

"You put that up right now," Jilly said loudly, grinning and tapping the back of a customer's hand. The man gave a theatrical howl and didn't relinquish his beignet, despite the powdered sugar that puffed onto his overall bib. "What d'you think you're doin', Zeb? Eatin' the merchandise before you get it paid for? Sheesh, no manners."

Zeb Delacour ran the big ice plant just out of town and he blushed easily.

"I'm only joshin' you," Jilly said. "Finish that and have another one. You work hard."

"Isn't she somethin'?" Joe said.

"Sure is. Temper like a mother gator on eggs, but the best heart in the world. It's nice to see a brother and sister as close as you two are. How's Ellie? We don't see that wife of yours often enough."

"She's great," Joe said, and closed his mouth. He touched Cyrus's arm and looked toward the door.

"You want me to turn around and stare at somethin'?" Cyrus said. "Not cool, as my young friend Wally would say." Wally was Gator and Doll Hibbs's only chick and Cyrus's shadow when the boy could get away. Cyrus had mentored Wally since he was a skinny kid and they remained friends now that Wally had become a gangly teenager.

"Yeah," Joe said. "Turn the back of your chair to the wall. You'll look real *cool*. And these three won't notice you anyway. Hoo-mama, those Savage brothers got plenty on their minds and it's makin' 'em unfit for public appearances."

Cyrus whipped his chair around, back to the wall, crossed one leg over the other and laced his fingers over his middle. "Cool enough?" he said, *sotto voce*.

He and Joe fell silent, watching Kelly, Max and Roche Savage stand inside the door and look around for an empty table. Max resembled an unexploded bomb and Kelly looked at him as if he were ready to light the fuse.

"I don't think I could tell Roche and Max apart," Joe said, stirring his coffee. "Except for their personalities. Roche seems so even-tempered."

"I pick him out because his hair's curlier and he's got a white scar through his right eyebrow. You can hardly see it," Cyrus said. "He's lookin' a little irritable right now. And you know what they say— watch out for the quiet ones."

Kelly came in their direction. He passed without any sign of recognition, and stood, apparently waiting for the folks at the last table between Joe and Cyrus and the kitchens to leave. His brothers hung back.

Cyrus felt badly for the party Kelly was encouraging to get lost, but interfering wouldn't be a good idea.

"Wow," Joe said. "You'd think this was the only eatery in town."

From his vantage point Cyrus saw his housekeeper, Lil, bustle into the shop with Doll Hibbs behind her.

"And here comes Lee O'Brien. I just bet you her recorder is runnin'. And she wouldn't be here if she didn't think she was goin' to pick up somethin' good—or juicy, I should say." Cyrus frowned. "You know what I mean. It can't be easy to fill a paper in a little town like Toussaint."

Lee, her blond hair pulled back into a ponytail, went straight to Roche and threaded both of her arms around one of his. "Mornin'," she said, and from the way she gazed up into his face, Cyrus could tell they weren't meeting for the first time. "I'm lookin' forward to dinner. Don't you be late now." Lee tipped her chin up so far her ponytail hung straight down.

Roche smiled at her and gave her ponytail a tug.

"Well, well," Joe said quietly. "They sure are broadcastin' the news right here."

Chairs scraped and customers vacated the table Kelly had decided was his. He sat down before the last patron left her chair and Sidney ran out to gather up dirty dishes.

Max left his twin's side to join Kelly and did manage a nod when he saw Joe and Cyrus. Cyrus liked Max.

"We should probably go," Cyrus said. He didn't relish the impossible task of trying not to listen to the Savage brothers.

"Before you get your marzipan tarts?" Joe said. "You'd break Jilly's heart. Sidney's, too. And I'm workin' my way toward some hush puppies."

"It's too early for hush puppies."

"I'm an adventurous eater," Joe said. He smiled with one side of his mouth. "It's hot in here."

"Why do I get the feelin' it could get hotter?"

Joe made to turn the back of his chair to the wall but Cyrus shot out a hand and gripped his wrist. "Too obvious," he said, and switched back to facing Joe.

The three brothers got seated. Cyrus glanced over his shoulder to see Lee join Lil and Doll. "Is it just me or are you gettin' any vibes that this town is all riled up?"

"Trouble in the makin'," Joe said. "I don't like it."

Cyrus had never liked the combination of Lil and Doll. He liked it less with the addition of Lee O'Brien. Lil and Doll had that pinched-and-looking-for-trouble air.

"It's none of your damn business," Max Savage said. He dropped his voice and although Cyrus could hear the rumble of his low register, he couldn't make out any words.

Just as well.

"I'm glad we both came in," Joe said. "I'm going to take it as an omen. Ellie and I have been tryin' to decide if we should mention anythin' to you—because we value your advice—or just keep quiet."

Cyrus smiled at Sidney who put his tarts on the table. He immediately chose one and took a bite that left only half of the pastry behind. If Joe and Ellie had to make up their minds whether or not to confide in him, Cyrus would rather not know.

"We're concerned about Annie Duhon." Joe leaned way over the table. "When you brought her back the other night—or mornin'— she obviously felt safe with you and I heard you remind her to come back and talk to you. Did she do that?"

"I wouldn't tell you if she had. As you well know."

Joe gritted his teeth. "I'm stupid. I didn't even think about that. Okay, Ellie and I really like her. I did some legal work for a friend of hers once. Someone who lived in Pointe Judah. Annie used to live there. That's how I met Annie and I feel responsible for keepin' a watch out for her because I helped her get the job at Pappy's."

"They tell me she's really good at it," Cyrus remarked.

"So I understand. But she's on her own here and I don't believe she's happy. Cyrus, she was smilin' all the time when she first came and for some time afterward, but now she's tense. We can feel it. And I'll tell you somethin'. You know how she said she thought Irene must have sneaked out of the door behind her that night?" Joe didn't wait for a response. "It never happened that way because that animal won't go outside. Ask Wazoo. She'll tell you."

"You're tryin' to make me see somethin', but I'm not gettin' it."

"We think someone deliberately put Irene outside to make a point."

Cyrus finished the tart and wiped his mouth on a napkin. "I'm not followin' you. What point?"

"That they'd been inside Annie's place while she was out."

"Was she robbed?"

"If she was, she hasn't mentioned it. Now that wouldn't make a bit of sense, would it?"

Kelly Savage's voice rose just enough for Cyrus to hear him say, "Devol didn't have the right to say that. He didn't have the right to dig around, either. It's a missing person case is all. There's no reason to treat you like a criminal and keep you at that damn station most of a day."

"Keep it down," Roche said. "He had to go back last night, too. I think Spike's got him guilty and convicted. And you went again this morning early, didn't you, Max?"

"Since you already know everything," Max said, "why should I repeat what you've said."

"I think it's time we talked to Dad," Kelly said.

"Why?" Roche turned in his seat to look at Kelly. "Why do you always want to run to Dad?"

"Why shouldn't I?" Kelly said. "I respect his opinion and he is my father as well as yours."

Joe met Cyrus's eyes.

"Did Max or I ever suggest he wasn't?" Roche said.

"Stop it, you two," Max said.

"Dad won't appreciate getting all this dropped on him with no warning," Kelly said.

Max glanced around and jutted his jaw. "I don't run to my father with problems."

Kelly swore.

"Calm down," Roche said. "I agree with Kelly. I'll talk to Mom and Dad. Kelly, you should let your mother know so she isn't shocked if the press comes calling."

"Do what you like," Max said but didn't sound happy.

"The search is on here—big-time," Roche said. "We all know what's going to happen eventually."

Max started to get up. "It doesn't have to," he snapped. He actually looked Cyrus in the face.

"Sit down," Kelly said. "You don't get to have your own way all the time. You may be a great surgeon but that won't cut any ice here."

"It's a mistake to get involved with the locals," Kelly continued and Cyrus smiled into his coffee at the man's oblivious behavior. He had to know he could be overheard at least by anyone close enough who wanted to make an effort to listen. "Stay away from her, Max. We don't need the complication."

"How do you know anything about it?" Max said.

"Shit!" Kelly thumped the table. "Do you think we don't know you've been having lunch with her for weeks? Nothing gets by the watchers around here. And while we're on the subject—" He turned his attention to Roche. "—fucking the newspaper the whole town reads isn't such a good idea, either."

"That's enough," Roche said and Cyrus heard how difficult it was for him to hold his temper. "Lee's a nice woman. Fun. Bright. I enjoy her company. You don't know what our relationship is. And you don't insult her. Got that?"

Kelly muttered something.

"The next negative thing you say about Annie will cost you," Max said in a grating tone. "What is it with you? Fallen out with the latest... Forget it."

Kelly let it go. "I'll be the one to contact Dad. He relies on me to keep a level head—and to keep him informed."

Cyrus was grateful that although the crowd had thinned considerably, there was still a lot of noise in the place. So Wazoo hadn't been pulling information from the air when she talked about Annie being involved with Max Savage. She was probably right about most things she'd suggested.

He wondered why the Savages sounded angry rather than upset over the recent disappearance.

"Some people go missin' and never show up again," Joe said, as if tuning into Cyrus's thoughts. "No body, no case—unless some really convincin' forensics come into play."

"I know," Cyrus said. "It happens too often. Means someone gets away with murder."

"That, it does." Joe flinched and set his teeth together. The shop door had opened hard enough to swing back and rattle its glass.

Things quieted down immediately.

Cyrus swivelled to see the door. A craggy-faced man built like a short wrestler walked in. He wore a black polo shirt with short sleeves that showed off massive arms, and his thighs strained at the seams of his jeans.

The door started to swing shut but he gave it another punch with a fist as big as a ham, reproducing the nerve-severing noise he'd managed the first time.

"Good God," Roche Savage said. "What's *Tom Walen* doing here?"

"If you can't figure that out, I can't help you," Max responded. "I'm the one he's looking for. I'll get him outside."

"You won't get him anywhere he doesn't want to go," Kelly said.

The man stared around but Cyrus got the impression that anger was knocking everything out of focus for him.

"Good mornin'," Jilly said.

Joe tensed, obviously ready to defend his sister.

"I want Savage," the man said. "Max Savage. I just got into town. The guy at the hotel said I might find him here."

"He was right," Max said, raising an arm. "Over here, Tom."

Blood flooded the newcomer's shiny face. "I'm not here for a tea party, Savage. I shouldn't have let her come but she wouldn't change her mind. She never had a bad thought about anyone. I'll kill you for this."

Several small shrieks sounded before utter silence fell once more.

"Outside," Max said, edging behind Roche's chair. "No point in upsetting everyone."

"Sit down!" Kelly yelled at his brother. "I'm calling the cops."

"That's appropriate," the man, Tom, said. "We're gonna need 'em. Why aren't you in custody, Max? You got away with two murders, but you won't get away with a third."

"Let's talk about this outside," Max said, shrugging off Roche's restraining hand and heading toward the newcomer. "Come on, Tom. We need to help each other out in this, not argue."

"My fiancée came to this town to see you and she's disappeared and you were the last one to see her alive," Tom said. "Why would I want to talk to you anyway?"

"I didn't ask you here," Max said. "You came looking for me. You've changed your mind about wanting to see me, fine. Goodbye. Michele will be back and when she is I hope you'll still work for us at Green Veil. We're counting on you."

Without warning, Tom landed a punch on Max's jaw and knocked him off balance. "Counting on us? You freak. I tried to stop Michele from coming here, but she's so trusting. She always wants to believe people are good. She's bought all the crap about you being framed before."

Max had caught himself against a pillar. "You don't have to tell me the obvious," he said. "Why do you think we want her with us here? She's the best. And we don't only want you because you're a couple." His jaw stung but he wouldn't let himself touch it.

Tom Walen raised his arm to strike again but Max was quicker. He blocked the other man's wrist and pushed him off. Walen didn't even stumble.

"Back off," Max heard Kelly say. "Max, get away from him. Watch your hands."

For God's sake, his reputation and his life from here out were on the line and Kelly fussed about scraped knuckles.

Tom lowered his head and charged Max.

"Time to call Spike," Joe muttered. "If we all get into it we'll wreck the joint and hurt people."

Just as Tom would have head-butted Max in the sternum, Max stepped neatly aside, took Tom's neck in an armlock and swung him around. Chaos followed. Tom's feet slid out from beneath him and he fell, spinning as he went and cutting a path through the few gawking customers remaining at the counter.

Joe Gable stood up, phone in hand, but slowly put it on the table. Max followed the direction of the other man's gaze and found him looking at his sister, Jilly, who shook her head vehemently. The lady didn't want the law to descend with sirens blaring.

Tom, halfway to his feet, looked up at Max.

"Stop *now,*" he told the man. "Outside."

Blood drizzled from Tom's nose but the heat remained in his eyes.

Hunched, he spread his arms, fingers cupped but open, and lined up on Max again.

"Leave it." Roche shot from the table and tried to muscle past Max. The two scuffled for a second or two before Roche threw himself around his brother and launched himself at Tom.

"Shit, stay out of it," Max said through his teeth when Tom body-slammed Roche on the hard floor. Max pulled him aside and kept on moving, shoulders curled, legs braced, and dropped below Tom's center of balance. Hauling the man off his feet and carrying him, fireman's lift style, he staggered toward the front of the shop. Zeb Delacour hopped to the rescue, opened the door and stood out of the way to allow the two men to explode onto the sidewalk.

"Lookit, will ya?" a man yelled. "Neat as you please. I don't want that Max Savage rearranging my nose, no, sir."

A few muffled giggles ensued.

Max landed on the sidewalk on top of Tom Walen and made sure he kept the squirming, heaving man where he was.

Vaguely, Max saw men's legs gather around him. His brothers and one or two others. At the same moment, a cruiser screeched to a tire-scraping halt at the curb and Spike called out, "Don't move. Keep your hands where I can see 'em and stay where you are."

"As if we didn't have enough trouble," Kelly said.

"The guy attacked Max," Roche said. "He came piling into the shop looking for a fight and making accusations."

"We'll take it from here," Spike said.

Max said, "Can I get up, please?"

"No," Spike told him. "We'll sort you out, then you can get up. And then the pair of you can come to the station for a chat. Another chat."

A deputy joined Spike and they both knelt over Max and Tom.

"Jeez," Joe said. "Are you arresting these men?"

"I should think so." Doll Hibbs interrupted. "Me, if I had a say, I'd put 'em in a cell and beat the truth out of them. That one—" she pointed to Tom "—said things about the doctor. You better find out about all that."

"Back inside, please, Mrs. Hibbs." Guy Gautreaux arrived, skidding from the entrance to his office. He met Max's eyes and gave a slight shake of the head. "Go now, Doll."

"We're not deaf, y'know," Doll hollered. "That poor man's engaged to that poor murdered woman. And he thinks *Dr.* Savage had something to do with it. And so do I."

CHAPTER | 4

Cyrus remained in his chair toward the back of All Tarted Up. His thoughts confused him.

Most of the patrons had slid out of the door and gone but Lil, Doll and Lee scurried back inside and stood close to the window where they had the best view of the chaos outside.

Guy, working like the professional big-city cop he was, moved economically to help Spike get Max and Tom on their feet and check for weapons. Tom Walen had a pistol hidden in a leg holster.

The women at the window sucked in loud breaths. "He coulda shot any of us," Lil said.

Here he sat, Cyrus thought, quiet and immobile, scarcely breathing and so quiet inside he felt hollow. Why hadn't he gone with the other men as he would have in the past, he wondered. Had he lost all the fire he used to have?

Max was the last to see Michele. As a concept, it sounded damning. But who was he to judge? He knew nothing.

While male voices rose outside, Cyrus looked at his hands, front and back. The voices seemed very distant. He didn't have soft hands, not priestly hands, but those of a gardener and handyman who happened to be a man of God.

The old shadow darkened him inside. Feelings, a man's feelings, battled with what he had chosen to become. He touched his forehead and felt sweat. This struggle was an old familiar. Eventually he would give in to it—the sooner, the better. The more easily he embraced his conviction that his personal choices were the right ones, the stronger he would become.

"He's another one."

Cyrus heard Lil but didn't concentrate.

"Oh, hush," Doll said. "You shouldn't say it."

"I will say it. Me, I'm glad Homer got his eyes opened. He needed takin' down a few steps. All puffed up like a broody hen just because he's engaged to that silly old Charlotte Patin who ought to know better at her age."

Cyrus heard that and took in the scene in time to see Lee O'Brien pushing a recording device back into the pocket of her skirt.

"If Charlotte had given you that job you wanted at Rosebank, butter wouldn't melt in your mouth, Lil Dupre," Doll said. "You'd be as sweet as pie to her face and behind her back, too."

Lil raised her chin and her tidily lined-up bleached curls bobbed a little. "She was afraid I'd be too good in that kitchen," she said. "That woman prides herself on runnin' everythin' and she plain isn't ready to give up control. There. That's all of it. She gets what she wants, and she didn't want me. But she bought that old goat, Homer, just like Vivian bought Spike. Those Devol men got no pride."

Cyrus found Jilly watching him, her expression horrified. He couldn't make himself say a word.

Sidney stood beside Jilly and he thought her eyes filled with tears.

THERE'S another one is wrong.

"And like I said," Lil added. "There's another one. That Guy livin' off Jilly. Me, I want to know what he does up there. Watch the television and sleep, I shouldn't wonder. He's even managed to lose his best friend."

Lee said, "What do you mean?" as if she weren't particularly interested in the response.

"Hush up," Doll whispered harshly.

"You know Nat Archer," Lil said, ignoring Doll's warning. "He and Wazoo got something goin'. Nat won't have nothin' to do with Guy anymore since he stayed here with his feet dry in Katrina. He knew he should have been back in uniform on the streets of New Orleans, him."

"Get out, you liar," Jilly said, her voice clear and steady. "Get out and never come back."

Cyrus jumped to his feet and hurried to meet Jilly as she came from behind the counter. "Hush," he said, holding her shoulders. "She doesn't know what she's sayin'."

The cruiser moved away and Guy ran back upstairs without looking into the shop. His face was set. The rest had dispersed.

"Yes," Jilly said. "Lil knows exactly what she's talkin' about. And if she says it anywhere ever again, and I find out, I'll sue."

"And Mr. Guy was down there in the water helpin' people till he couldn't move no more," Sidney said. "Days, he did it. And the sheriff and most the men in Toussaint. Mr. Guy, he just didn't do it with a NOPD badge is all."

"You go ahead Jilly. You pull the wool over your eyes and pretend." Lil pointed at Sidney. "And customers don't like bein' waited on by trash, remember that."

"We're leaving," Cyrus told Lil. "Now." He took her by the elbow and led her firmly from the shop.

"Oh," Sidney said. "She isn't gonna lose her job, is she?"

"I'm sorry, Jilly," Doll Hibbs said. "I shoulda put a stop to what she was sayin' but I…well, I just got carried away by it all, I suppose."

Jilly hugged Sidney and said. "Father will do the right thing. He always does." But if Lil lets her poisonous gossip get to Guy, Jilly would make sure she suffered.

Lee O'Brien stood quietly, looking at the floor.

"Lee," Jilly said. "I like you and I hope you'll do the right thing and leave all this out of the paper."

CHAPTER | 5

Business hummed at Pappy's.

Annie went over her numbers for the past month and felt good about the performance. Pappy still kept a close watch on what happened at the dance hall and eatery. He had just about lived in this office when he'd been completely at the reins. Most of his time was spent at home with his wife these days but he had a twin computer to the one that stood on Annie's desk and if she didn't get reports to him when they were expected, e-mail shot her way.

She flipped through a series of screens. The Swamp Doggies, a local band and great favorite at Pappy's, segued into "Toussaint Nights" and Annie smiled. Cheering broke out on cue and she heard the fiddle of Vince Fox racing away with the melody.

So why did she feel so bad? *Because she hadn't seen Max in days—and she had never felt quite so alone.* Each day she got to work early and stayed until the night manager, Jim Broussard, arrived in the early evening. When he was off, she stayed late into the night. Annie picked up a pencil by its worn-down eraser and doodled lightly over the top of a folder. Jim was due in tonight but she wished he weren't because she didn't want to go home.

Each day she made excuses to go in and out of her office at the time when Max used to come in. Only he didn't come in anymore and she'd known he wouldn't.

This place was her future. This was where she had the chance she'd hoped for, and she couldn't blow it.

A tap on the door and Wazoo stuck her head into the cramped room. With her hair up and tamed behind two shiny black combs, she looked different, and she looked sexy.

"Me, I can go away again if you don't want to see me."

"Wazoo sounding humble?" Annie said. "Well, what have you been mixing with your comfrey coolers?"

Sucking in one cheek, Wazoo slipped into the room and closed the door firmly. "You better watch how you talk to me, you. I had to make up my mind to do what I don't do natural. Me, I come here to help."

Annie plopped her bare feet on the desk. Her shoes had become too warm hours ago. By choice she would wiggle her naked toes in the air at all times. "Thank you," she said and glanced off at her screen. "I think you're helpful all the time, you just don't want to get the reputation for being soft."

"Anyone been in here to tell you about what happened?" Wazoo asked.

She got Annie's full attention. "What?" Her midsection did a nasty little flip. "Have they found Michele?" She already knew the answer but had to ask.

Wazoo sat on Annie's desk and wrapped her skirts around her legs. She shook her head, no. "Doll Hibbs is upset," Wazoo said. "Me, I'm tellin' you because I never saw her this upset before. Whole town went up this afternoon."

Annie stood up.

"Right there in Jilly's place. Big fight. *Big* fight. Bet you never heard of Tom Walen."

"I never did," Annie said, wanting to hurry Wazoo but too familiar with what could happen if she tried. This lady could make an art form of spinning out conversations.

"He's engaged to Michele Riley," Wazoo said. "He come lookin' for her."

"Oh." Annie went back to her chair and slumped. "That makes me feel awful just to think about it. Poor man."

"*Mad* man, if you listen to Doll. Come into Jilly's with steam comin' outa his ears and lookin' for Max." Wazoo's tilted black eyes turned mournful. "You gonna need my help, girl. You both gonna need it." Fumbling around she pulled a soft cloth bag from a deep pocket in her red-and-black striped skirt. "I gotta be around that Max more. Figure him out. At Rosebank, could be. Or could be not. Could be he dangerous to care about."

"Wazoo," Annie moaned. "Just give me the high points."

"Low points, you mean," Wazoo said, holding out the bag. "You put this away somewhere it'll never be found by anyone but you. Understand? If you need to do somethin' about it, we'll know. How about you put that in your purse?"

Made of brown cotton, a black cord tied the bag tightly shut at the top. The contents were lumpy.

Annie sighed. "I don't think I want this."

"You don't know if you do or not, cher. Do what Wazoo tells you. And don't you open it. That's a *bad* idea." She shoved it into Annie's hands. "Cyrus and Joe Gable was at All Tarted Up havin' coffee. Max Savage and his brothers was there, too. In comes Tom Walen—Doll said all this to me—and he thinks Max did somethin' to Michele so there was a fight. He said other stuff about Max, too. Ended up outside and Spike took the two of them off in his car."

"Max?" Annie blinked rapidly. She sniffed the bag absently. "Spike arrested Max?"

Wazoo shrugged and jumped from the desk. "I never said that word. Arrested. Spike, and Guy Gautreaux, Joe Gable and a bunch of other guys had to separate them two so Spike could take 'em off. Probably decided a chat would do for now. He can throw them in jail later."

Annie drummed her fingers on the desk. "Is Max still there with Spike?" She kept hearing his angry accusations before he walked out of her apartment the last time.

"I heard he took off with his brothers but this Tom Walen still wants to kill him."

"Oh," Annie said, miserable.

"I've decided you stay away from that man, Max, you," Wazoo said. "I'm not sayin' he's a bad man but we don't know and you already got trouble. He's got trouble, too, but he's hard to help. Too much anger in him—maybe enough he could kill. You hear from that Bobby man again?"

"No," Annie said, wishing Wazoo wouldn't make her think about things she'd rather forget.

"You will."

Annie rolled her eyes. "I think he saw me one day and got curious about what I was doing. So he decided to look me up. He won't be back." She wanted to believe it.

Wazoo twitched her skirts back and forth. "You have more bad dreams?"

"I don't want to talk about it."

"You did have more bad dreams."

"Not exactly," Annie told her. "Impressions. That's what I'd call them. But not nightmares." She would never tell Wazoo the last things she'd seen. The memory of Max's reaction to her confession still stung. He thought she'd made it all up.... She stared at Wazoo. How could he believe she'd be that cruel?

"Say what you thinkin'," Wazoo said softly, crooking a finger. "Let it come out. I see it in you."

"I don't think anything." But she did. Max's reaction, the way he'd lashed out, had been everything to do with his anger at her. She had shocked him. But she didn't know how she found out the names of the dead women. Max would think she'd dug around and found out the details. She'd looked at the computer and thought about it many times. If she dared, she might do it, but she couldn't face what she might discover.

"Listen to Wazoo. Be careful. Watch who is around you. I don't know where the evil will come from, but it will come. Don't be alone."

"I have to be alone and I want to be," Annie said. "But I love you for caring." Even if these warnings scared her silly.

Wazoo tossed her head. "Me, sometimes I just forget how much trouble helpin' people can be."

Annie smiled. "What was Bobby Colbert wearing when he left Hungry Eyes the other night?"

"Him, he wants you that one," Wazoo said. "Another angry man. And jealous of you. I don't know what he was wearing."

"A jacket with a hood?"

Wazoo squinched up her face and shook her head slowly. "Maybe. It was hot. It's always hot. Too hot for jackets. Me, I don't know. I gotta go. I got a date." She seemed about to say more, but gave a sharp shake of the head instead.

"Don't let me keep you from Nat," Annie said.

"You won't." She pointed to the brown cotton bag. "Keep that safe, you understand?"

"Uh-huh."

Wazoo hesitated. "You come, too. Come with me."

"On a date with you and Nat?" Annie laughed, dropped the bag into her voluminous purse and turned back to her computer screen. "That would be cozy." But Wazoo's out-of-character suggestion made her nervous.

She didn't look at Wazoo again but the woman hovered.

"Maybe you need someone to look out for you," Wazoo said. "Someone who knows what they doin'."

"'Bye, Wazoo. Thank you for everything. Give Nat a hug for me."

Wazoo snorted. "Every hug I give that man come right from me. It isn't easy for me to say, but Guy Gautreaux is one fine damn detective and he's for hire."

"Mmm," Annie said.

"You ignore Wazoo all you want. If one of them dreams you havin' comes true, you'll wish you listen to me."

"I can't afford to hire a detective," Annie told her, slowly typing "Google" in the search box. Just a little look at the Internet and she would back off, but she couldn't keep hiding from facts she might need to know.

"Maybe you can't afford not to," Wazoo said, and let herself out of the office. In seconds she looked around the door again and said, "Two things. I think I could have let Irene outside that night he went to the Gables'."

Annie's heart lifted. "That's great. I'll tell—"

"Please don't tell anyone. I went in to make sure I turned off the oven. The second thing is that Lil Dupre said bad things at Jilly's place. She got in trouble with Cyrus and poor Jilly."

Annie did look at Wazoo then. "What did Lil do?"

"This and that," Wazoo said. "She's in a bad way, but there was no call for her to spread gossip about good people. You hear any of it, you tell 'em they mouth gonna turn inside out and rot...then fall off. They don't die right away, but they want to." She left again and closed the door tightly.

Annie sighed and put the search engine to work. Max Savage, reconstructive plastic surgeon, wasn't hard to find.

Annie read entry after entry and printed each one out.

Son of financier Leo Savage and publisher Claire Worth Savage. Lists of Max's professional accomplishments with emphasis on face transplant research. Annie shuddered at that. She didn't follow links to his many published papers.

There was mention of twin brother, Roche, psychiatrist, also with links to published papers. Half brother, Kelly, was Leo Savage's son by a first marriage to Julia. Apparently Kelly worked for his father's firm. There were pictures of family members at black tie events and other shots of Max in scrubs, Max teaching, Max explaining surgical procedures. Julia, Leo Savage's first wife, looked stunning, an exotic woman. Annie could see Kelly in her but Julia's features were much more flamboyant. The woman stared at the camera with a sultry sneer. On the other hand, Max and Roche looked very much like their dark-haired mother. A big man, in early photos Leo had blond hair, and an autocratic face.

Studying Max's family and history made Annie feel like a spy.

Max was the star, and unfortunately scandal had tarnished a lot of the shine. She skimmed entries dealing with the two women he had supposedly been the last to see alive. Looking at their names, Isabel Martin and Carol Gruber, on the screen, chilled Annie. In both cases, no hard evidence had been found to link Max to the crimes. His cars had yielded no incriminating forensic specimens, or any sign of violence having taken place.

Annie read detailed descriptions of both deaths and exited from Google.

Her jaw ached and her teeth would not stay together. Her body felt stiff and too hot. Every gruesome specific of the murder scenes could have been plucked from Annie's nightmares, and her waking visions. The two women were assumed to have been snatched after Max dropped them off.

Questions rushed at her. Had Max's car been gone over for evidence this time, and his apartment? Did Spike think someone else had stolen Michele Riley away? If so, who? She doubted any of her ideas hadn't already been covered.

If Max was really being singled out for ruin by a murderous crazy, who was it? Toussaint wasn't big enough to hide anyone for long. Strangers couldn't get in and out without being noticed. Too many eyes belonged to too many people with time on their hands.

She jumped when Jim Broussard knocked and came in. Olive-skinned with straight black hair and dark brown eyes, his features were sharp. He worked hard and never let her doubt that he believed making her look good was a point for him, too.

With a hand at the back of his waist and the other held rigid against his belt buckle, he rocked his hips back and forth, and danced a mean and fancy two-step while he sang: "'A man with a plan with a pistol in his hand, hmm, hmm, doo-doo-doo. Victims of the darkness, what can they do? Victims of the darkness, they don't see the light.' Dance with me, Annie. Or maybe you can't two-step." His grin was supposed to soften her up and it worked.

The Doggies played the piece Jim sang and for a few minutes Annie matched him step for step, slapping her bare heels down first on the old wood floor.

Jim turned his mouth down at the corners when the piece finished. "You surely can two-step," he said, smiling again. He took her place behind the desk and she was grateful she had gotten rid of any evidence of what she'd been doing. "How did it go today?" he said.

"Very well," she told him, searching for an excuse to hang around but finding none. "It never slows down for long. Testimony to keepin' the kitchen quality up and the comped meals down. Getting those plates out of there fast is the key to makin' sure we aren't paying customers' bills for them."

"Yup," Jim said, already getting into the calendar of events for the week. "Wedding reception on Saturday afternoon. That's a good one."

"Sure is." Annie slipped her feet into her sandals, gathered her purse and said, "'Bye, call if you need me," before heading out.

Getting through the patrons took time but meeting and greeting went with her territory.

"Hold up, Annie." Bobby Colbert got up from a table close to reception, a great big smile on his face. "I was afraid you might be off duty."

"I am," Annie said and almost bit her tongue. "Got to get along and deal with the chores that don't do themselves."

"This is a great place," Bobby said. He wore a brown silk shirt the same color as his eyes and she could smell his cologne. "Not that I'd expect you to run a place that wasn't great."

"Thanks. Sit down. Your meal will get cold."

"Sit down with me." He looked around. "I'll get you a drink. Have you had dinner?"

Escape was all she wanted. "Not tonight, Bobby, but thanks for the offer."

The smile left his mouth. "Better things to do?"

Annie stared straight into his eyes. "No. *Other* things to do. Thanks, though."

He narrowed his eyes and she thought he would keep pushing her, but he sat down instead, pushed his plate aside and rested his chin on cupped hands.

"'Night," Annie said and walked away.

She didn't hear any answer.

At last she passed Blue the alligator and used a shoulder to open one of the swinging doors to the outside and the covered bridge over the shallow ravine that stretched a short distance in front of Pappy's.

Annie stood to one side of the door, chasing thoughts around in her head. There was something she had to do—sooner or later but not when it would soon be getting dark. She wouldn't dwell on it, or even let the idea stick.

A soft, warm breeze swept through and a clump of palms beyond the bridge rustled and clacked their fronds together. She walked out to the full parking lot and went to the row of spaces farthest from the building. Once inside the Volvo, she locked the car and sat there, frowning at nothing, struggling with indecision. The thought of going back to her apartment depressed her.

She hadn't needed to run into Bobby. He never failed to make her feel creepy. What she really wanted was to see Max.

From the way he'd treated her, she had to think he'd expect her to apologize when they did meet, yet she hadn't done anything wrong.

The loneliness freshened. She had nothing in common with Max. His life had been spent around successful people, rich people. And he had accomplished so much. She had taken note of his record as a humanitarian who traveled to operate on patients in other countries, patients who couldn't pay anything. And he had operated on war victims, mending their broken faces as well as they possibly could be.

She switched on the car. Why had he shown any interest in her at all?

They'd had sex. There wasn't another word for what happened between them, but she wouldn't change a thing about it—except for the embarrassment over the slight bleeding and maybe some of her wildness. She had seen Reb who verified that Annie needed lubrication. Reb had examined her and made oblique references to it being a good idea to take things more slowly next time.

Annie blushed.

The way she'd been with Max that night was no different from the way men were supposed to approach sex most of the time—she had needed it to happen. And now she had to pull herself together and move on.

Joe and Ellie would let her talk to them.

And what would she say?

There was Father Cyrus who made her feel welcome and as if he wanted to talk to her, but she didn't have anything to say to him, either.

Spike had enough to deal with. Her meandering ideas wouldn't help him—or her.

Annie drove between lines of cars to the exit from the parking lot and turned right. She couldn't go home, not yet. Since she got her first car, only about four years ago, she had used driving as a way to clear her mind.

The narrow roads and lanes were familiar in that they were the same as so many in the area. Although the light was failing, she had no fear of getting lost because her sense of direction rarely failed her.

Her breathing seemed shallow and she opened her mouth. When she rolled down the window, the breeze had turned to wind and she shuddered. A creepy feeling climbed her spine. The wind brought a needle-sharp, stinging sensation into the car. Like ice. Hot ice on the wind. Annie's heart beat faster and harder.

The truth was that she had no real human ties to Toussaint, or to any other place but Pointe Judah, and going back there would be admitting failure. Her cousins would never say as much, but they would know she hadn't been up to taking advantage of her chance to make a good, new life.

Headlights shone into her rearview mirror. Her eyes felt gritty and she pressed them shut for a moment. How long had there been another vehicle behind her? She couldn't make out what kind of car it was.

Now she was paranoid. No one ever promised her the roads were hers alone.

She drove on, repeatedly looking into the mirror, swallowing around stiffness in her throat, going a little faster, and faster still. The other vehicle kept right there with her.

This time he felt charmed. At first he hadn't wanted Max involved with Annie but he'd been wrong. He was going to make sure she helped him get what he wanted. "You go for it, Annie. I'll do what I can to help." He laughed. "I'll do everything I can to help you help me."

He kept her car in sight but didn't get too close.

CHAPTER | 6

Annie saw the sign for Loreauville and realized she had automatically taken the 86 loop road. She had driven north, not without thinking where she was going, but without considering what it really meant.

The headlights behind her had gone away.

Others had slipped in, two, sometimes three vehicles.

She wasn't being followed.

A side road, not much more than a track, cut west toward Bayou Teche, on the outskirts of St. Martinville. With no rain or fog, even in the near darkness she saw crooked tree limbs silvered by the moon. Heading north again, she drove as far as the bridge over the Teche before figuring out that she and Max hadn't needed to cross the bayou because they'd driven up from Toussaint on the opposite side.

"Idiot." She pursed her lips and rattled over the water—and pulled to the side of the road to see if she recognized any cars traveling behind her. A light colored pickup passed, then a nondescript sedan, also pale. Nothing else came immediately so Annie carried on.

The town was busier tonight. By the time Annie reached Main Street and bore left, she met with other vehicles—not many, but at steady intervals. The Pepper Festival could be coming up and when she'd lived in the area there used to be a lot of activity in town around that time.

She lowered her window and heard the rapid rhythm of a rubboard, the mad pace of a banjo, sounds of more than one good fiddler and an accordion. Foot-stomping music. Annie raised her shoulders and smiled a little. Farther along on the opposite side of the road she could see bright flags flying and colored lights. A small crowd had gathered there, dancing and clapping on the sidewalk.

A pretty town, St. Martinville, with a lot of good people. She just hadn't had a chance to enjoy living there.

She reached St. Martin de Tours Church and instinct took her to the little street where she turned left instead of right, as Max had on his route, and found the alley.

No headlights showed behind her.

Annie passed the closed bagel shop, continued on to the beaten-up street along the Teche, and made a right. A faint sheen wrapped the surface of the water like a film of ruckled black plastic and she saw it through moss hanging from cypress trees, their bark stripped to a smooth, pallid skin. She drove slowly, looked in one direction, then another. People who never came here, never saw how the land had ways of framing pictures in every direction even by night. The hurricanes had done their worst in so many places, but, like Toussaint, St. Martinville was mostly unscathed. But wicked storms would never manage to snuff out the breathy essence of the richness that was Louisiana.

Her hands slipped on the wheel and she wiped her palms, one at a time, on her gray pants. She pulled the Volvo to the overgrown verge at the spot where she thought she had followed Max over the fence and into the trees. And she sat there with the engine idling, peered through the passenger window, but couldn't see much more than a wall of trees. One thing she'd discovered was a pending contract on the site. Could Max have decided to buy it anyway?

A flashlight lay on the floor in the back of the car. Annie kept it there for emergencies. This counted as an emergency. No more pretending she wasn't exactly certain why she'd come. Tonight she would look for any sign that the ugly mental pictures she'd seen could have been real.

There had been no more imagined incidents for days. She was strong again and coming at a late hour could be the best decision since no one would expect her to be here. And, as deserted as it was, no one was likely to pass and see the parked car. Annie grimaced. A deserted stretch of abandoned road could well draw others looking for a quiet place.

Hammering on her window almost choked her. Thudding in her throat hurt and her heart went wild. She couldn't make herself look to see who it was.

"Annie." Muffled, her name came through the glass. A woman's voice.

She did turn then and looked into Wazoo's exasperated face.

Annie pushed her fingers into her eyes and shook her head. When she settled down a little she unlocked the door and got out of the car. "What are you doing here? How did you get here?" She looked around but there was no sign of Wazoo's van. "You scared me, Wazoo. I feel awful."

"You feel scared because you doin' somethin' dangerous. I parked on Main Street and walked. No, once I saw you goin' in the alley, I ran. Annie Duhon, you are a madwoman. They all say Wazoo's the crazy one, but they don't know 'bout you, girl."

"Go home," Annie said. "Now." She wanted to get on with what she intended to do and after the shock she'd just had, she'd be jumping at every pop or snap.

"Whatever you doin', I'm comin' with you," Wazoo said.

"No, you are not. You had a date—Wazoo, why aren't you with Nat?"

"Because a lady I like needs me to keep her alive."

Annie spread her hands. "What are you talkin' about? Why would you say a thing like that?"

"Maybe because there's a woman missing in Toussaint. I hear there could be more law called in anytime. But my friend is drivin' around in the night plannin' who knows what." She took a step backward. "Oh, excuse me, I'm probably intrudin' on a assignation. That must be it. You're out here to meet a lover and have wild sex in the trees, in the dark. All wet, slick skin and runnin' away naked when you want to be caught."

"Wazoo! I am not here for any such reason and you know it. You like to shock people with what you say."

"Why are you here, girl?" Wazoo stuck her face into Annie's. "And don't you tell me lies because they make me unpredictable. Just ask a few people about what happened when they lied to Wazoo. I'll give you some names. Ask Nat Archer. That boy scrubs every word he says to me before it slides outa his mouth. That's on account of him forgettin' he was tellin' a lie one time."

"Okay," Annie said. "Got it. I won't lie to you. I'm staying here on my own. You're goin' back to find Nat and quit worrying. That's the absolute truth."

"I'm not goin'."

"Yes, you are. I've got to do this my way. I'll be perfectly safe— I won't take any chances."

"Do what your way?" Wazoo said. She made a circle, looking in all directions. "This place is *empty,* Annie. You already takin' chances. There ain't one soul around here."

"So I've got nothing to worry about, do I?"

"What you goin' to do?" Wazoo stood so close, Annie had to stop herself from stepping backward.

"I'm going to sit in my car and think. I know this area well. I grew up in St. Martinville."

Wazoo's eyebrows rose. "You did?"

"Yes."

"You got family here?"

"Not anymore."

"You goin' to see someone else?"

Sometimes a little lie was the only answer. "Yes. Cousins. We've had our problems and I want to clear the air. That's why I came right here because I know it'll be real quiet and I can think about what I want to say."

Wazoo looked at the sky. "You got that little bag I gave you?"

"Yes." She hadn't wanted to leave it behind.

"Keep it with you." Wazoo turned sharply in a flurry of long skirts and started away.

"How did you get here?" Annie called after her.

"In my van. How'd you think I got here? I was behind you all the way—way behind. Good thought to pull off the road after the bridge and let folks pass. Only I see you goin' down there and had a need to stop for a little while myself. Just long enough for you to get started again."

"Sneak," Annie said, waving. "But thanks, Wazoo."

After the woman was out of sight, Annie waited another fifteen minutes just to be sure Wazoo didn't decide to come back.

With the flashlight in her hand, car keys in her pocket and her purse locked in the trunk of the car, Annie climbed carefully across the soggy, scrub-covered verge to reach the fence. Again she held the sagging top wire down so she could climb over. It wasn't easy to do, but she kept her flashlight off until she'd fumbled her way well into the trees.

Moonlight didn't make it past the dense overhead foliage. Annie turned on the flashlight and trained its beam on the fallen trunks, brush and overgrown vines snaking in every direction, like a treacherous jungle in some places.

She moved on, careful not to twist an ankle, until she reached the edge of the clearing where she'd seen Max. Annie swallowed, and swallowed again. Her throat felt filled with sand.

Breaking from what felt like her last connection to safety, she left the trees and walked slowly across uneven ground, sweeping the light from side to side. A line showed up in the dirt, and then another, and another. Max's lines made with a stick.

Annie followed part of the faded outline but made little sense of it. She supposed it must be his idea of how a clinic might have been built there.

She didn't know when Green Veil was supposed to open. People talked about continuing work, especially on the inside, but said the clinic could be ready to go in a month or so. They would need a lot of staff and most would have to come from places other than Toussaint. That would be good for the town, bring more business and fill up available housing.

Max's stick markings came to an end.

Annie continued to move her flashlight in one direction after another. She wouldn't find anything. A waking nightmare was what she'd gone through.

The small, white beam picked up a twig shaped like a sturdy wishbone, a black twig only inches from her right sandal. She bent closer, touched the stick with a forefinger and looked at it. Soot clung lightly to her skin.

Standing up straight, Annie checked around. All she saw was the

bumpy ground strewn with bits of debris and an occasional struggling bush.

The twig rested in the palm of her hand. Black bits had fallen off.
A piece of burned wood—in the middle of nowhere.

"Wise up," she told herself aloud and tossed the twig away.
"There are always pieces of burned wood lying around in places
like this."

But there were more scorched fragments scattered like a trail of
breadcrumbs. She followed them to the far side of the clearing and
faced another wall of vegetation. When she stood still and listened,
rather than silence, she heard a thousand critters skittering in there,
and the rustle of wind passing through leaves.

A single fat raindrop smacked her nose and Annie groaned. Still
sighting dark pieces of debris, she reached the first of the trees and
picked her way between trunks and over logs sprouting suckers.
Dead leaves lay thick enough to bury her feet with each step.

Another charred and rotten snag of wood and several small,
carbon-coated branches rested against some rocks. As if someone
had been carrying an armload and these few, and the ones behind
her, had been dropped in passing.

The sparse trail continued deeper into the trees. Annie kept
going. Several times she scouted the surrounding area but never
found pieces other than those in the meandering sprinkle.

A paper-chase? No accident but rather a deliberate attempt to
lead someone…where?

Water spattered her face, slid down her neck. By the muted
thumping overhead, the rain fell heavily. The thick canopy kept out
a good deal of the deluge, but she smelled the odor of moistened,
decaying leaves.

The singed trail petered out. And there was nothing to see,
nothing different. Just dripping leaves where some rain made it

through, deeply scoured tree trunks, and always the mounds of decaying material underfoot.

The front of her right sandal shot under a stick, jamming between her toes and the sole of the shoe. And Annie tumbled.

Immediately she scrambled to her feet again. Being on the ground made her feel vulnerable. The burned pieces didn't have to mean anything. Annie flicked the light back and forth, looking for any sign of…of what? Of a place where a person could have been buried?

Imagination was her blessing and her curse and in this place she felt the latter. Next she'd drift into the realm of scraping shovels and twisted bodies.

Annie turned around and started back. She looked for the same trail she'd followed in. Where were those sinister twigs now, darn it. Standing still, she breathed deep to steady her heart and decided she'd become disoriented and should be going the opposite way.

Her progress was too fast and she knew it, but getting out was all she cared about. The deep and deeper shades of darkness and the inky shapes flashed by, and she turned again, went another way with her arms held out in front of her, fighting off curtains of vines that scratched her skin, plucked her hair.

A sharp jab gouged her scalp.

Annie screamed and beat the air around her head—and dropped the flashlight.

She caught the next scream before it broke free, and held absolutely still. Still except for the sweat that drizzled between her shoulder blades and breasts and from her temples to her jaw.

Her breathing sounded loud, like water through a rocky blowhole where the ocean roared in and sucked out. When she bent over she saw the glint of the flashlight at once and grabbed for it. The thing had fallen on a teepee of roots and it slipped between them the instant she touched it.

The sound of the rain changed to what resembled a battalion of drum majors using tin sticks.

Hating to do it, Annie knelt and pushed her fingers between the roots. The light had gone out and that terrified her. What if the bulb had broken?

This way and that she reached, and encountered sodden mulch, then an opening that seemed to go under the roots. She closed her eyes and pushed farther.

A cold body. Sinuous, spineless, slithered across her wrist.

Annie gagged, but she didn't pull her arm back. On and on the thin snake slunk. She imagined it ready to strike.

The touch, the very tip of it, drew over her thumb and was gone.

She leaped up and stumbled straight ahead, holding out her hands, clutching anything she found in an attempt to remain upright.

Pounding in her head forced her stinging eyes shut. Her forehead connected with an overhead branch and she staggered back, flailing her arms.

"Stop it," she said and heard her words in a ghastly whisper. "Just stop and wait."

There was no way out.

She'd lost her bearings. But she never got lost. Her sense of direction never failed her.

A gush of water broke free of the leafy barrier and fell so close she saw it, felt its spray, but missed getting soaked.

Annie opened her mouth to breathe. She couldn't stay here all night until it grew light. Eventually, if she tried to walk in a straight line, she would get out.

Fighting the urge to run, she took measured steps. How could there be so much noise where there was no life to be seen?

Her cell phone was in her purse. Usually she hated the thing but she longed to feel it in her hand.

The going was hopeless. Every few steps she stumbled, some-times falling. Weakness trembled in her limbs but she didn't stop again. Each move brought her closer...to what?

Annie fell once more. Hard this time. And she scraped her face against a tree trunk—and thudded on things that were hard and jammed into her. She couldn't help crying out.

Great crashing sounds paralyzed her.

They came closer and closer and grew louder. A wild animal could have caught her scent.

This time not only the rain beat the air, but real thunder, distant and grumbling. Annie grabbed for the nearest handhold and found a broken snag. Slowly, she eased herself up...until a small bunch of something rough blew into her face.

The thrashing noise continued.

A gator could have come up from the bayou.

She brushed at the fibrous stuff clinging to her cheek and it landed in the crook of her neck. Annie swiped at it again. It itched. When she caught it, she felt filaments disintegrate between her fingers and she held them close to her eyes. Her heart seemed to stop. Whatever she held was invisible to her, but there was a scent. Damp. Equal parts of bruised magnolia and something burned.

Annie slapped it away. Sobbing, she flapped at her face and neck and wiped her palms down the bark of a tree. The crashing came closer and closer but she didn't care. An animal she could deal with, the remains of burned human hair were enough to explode her brain.

She didn't stop scrubbing at herself until every broken strand seemed gone. That was it, enough, she would get back to her car and go home for a long shower.

A light shone in her face, blinding her. Fear and anger made her strong and she lunged toward the beam, and the flashlight it came from, beating at the arm and hand she knew were there.

The new angle flooded diffused light over the newcomer and she looked into Max Savage's stark face.

CHAPTER | 7

Lee O'Brien approached Green Veil from the side that put the clinic between her and Rosebank Resort. Since there were few lights on in the renovated building and tall hedges almost hid Rosebank, she was probably safe from prying eyes, but she wasn't taking chances.

Oh, lordy, no, not when she could be about to get started on the biggest story of her life—if her instincts were as good as she thought they were and if she was really lucky. Whatever information she got could cost her considerably, but if what she suspected was true, she might enjoy herself every minute along the way. On the other hand, maybe she'd just get some leads and go on her way.

And that could be a real disappointment.

Next door there were plenty of upper windows with a view of Green Veil.

But it was late and dark.

"Hi, Lee. Glad you could make it," Roche Savage said, stepping from a doorway. "Come on in and I'll show you around. It's impressive, I think."

Lee didn't feel so sure of herself anymore. "I thought Kelly was goin' to be here." She'd made her arrangements to come with Kelly but Roche would do very nicely if he didn't clam up on her.

"He had to go out of town this afternoon. I was supposed to call and tell you he'd like a rain check." Roche shrugged and grinned. "You can't blame me for deciding to take his place. He'll be mad but you can always come back and see the place again with him—if you still want to."

Lee giggled, but felt a little uncomfortable. If she had her choice she'd rather be with Roche, but it was true that he hadn't really pursued her. After their last dinner he took her home and said good-night like an eagle scout working on a chastity badge.

"It's nice of you to step in for him," she said. Kelly had been careful not to show real interest in Lee when Roche was around, but she had felt his eyes on her and caught a few looks that were anything but cool. Lee figured she needed to get close to one of the two men if she hoped to get the *Toussaint Trumpet* noticed all over the country. "Are you sure it isn't too late for you to do this?" she asked. Kelly, and she assumed Roche, thought all she wanted to do was write a piece on the clinic.

"For me?" he said. "The later, the better. I'm at my best when the lights go out." His innocent chuckle didn't fool Lee. Maybe she'd do better with Roche, but she'd have to feel him out before she asked questions he wouldn't expect. Of course, she'd find clever ways to work them in.

He took her arm and led her into a wide side corridor painted a deep green with paler green marble tile on the floor.

"No real decorating has been done down here yet," Roche said. "The artwork and furnishings will change everything. I stay out of all that. Where do you want to start?"

Lee took a tiny recorder from her purse and smiled up at him. "Okay if I use this?"

"Why not?" His smile weakened her knees. She'd been away from the big city and any kind of male smorgasbord for too long.

"I'll let you lead the way," she told him, taken aback by a sinking sensation and a rush of shyness. Her cousin, Reb—and Reb's husband—would be amazed if they knew where she was, and they wouldn't be happy. But her life was her own and it was time she lived it—Reb and Marc were wonderful to her but they couldn't give her success or excitement.

They thought she was on deadline at the paper, and spending the night in her office. She would spend it there, regardless of what happened beforehand.

"You're quiet suddenly," Roche said, taking hold of her ponytail and tugging lightly—as he did whenever he saw her. He tilted his head to one side and she got the full effect of his lazy blue eyes.

"I appreciate you lettin' me come," Lee said. She smiled back. Just because she ran a small-town newspaper, she didn't have to come across as a hick. She hadn't always lived in Toussaint. "Do you like workin' with your brothers?"

"Can't think of many things I like better," he said, placing a hand at her waist and ushering her in front of him. "These are offices in this area. The administrative staff will be considerable.

"In addition to Max's reconstructive work, we'll provide extensive rehab, the best there is. Physical and occupational therapy. Sports medicine. General health and well-being. Self-image and psychological support is my job. I'm involved in every case from the beginning. There's a spa you won't believe. Our intention is to send our patients back to their lives in one piece. As close to the way they were before they were damaged if possible—better in some ways. I've heard talk of makeovers and fashion consulting but I get out of my depth real fast with that sort of stuff."

Lee held her recorder a little closer and said, "What's Kelly's specialty?"

"Money," Roche said.

"And he likes that, doesn't he?" Lee looked at him steadily, but his expression didn't change.

"You'd have to ask him about that."

A white T-shirt fit his physique very well. Black hair, slightly curly, reached collar length. The casual look suited him. He gave the same impression she had formed of him at their first meeting: a confident man who enjoyed power—a man who used a convincing veneer of quiet charm and good humor to soften intense sexuality. He was uncannily like Max to look at but their personalities were not even similar.

The corridor ended at an open area where the walls were the color of raspberries and an arch of tinted windows stretched to the level where a curved staircase reached the second floor. They had kept old wood and ironwork intact. "This is reception?" Lee said, glancing back in time to find Roche's attention in the region of her derriere.

His eyes rose to hers and he didn't smile. "Yes," he said. "It's going to be warm, welcoming—or so I'm told." He pointed to a bank of elevators with paneled doors the color of koa. "Patients' suites are on the upper floors. Terraces give them a place to walk outside in privacy until they're ready to move around with the others. That doesn't always happen at all."

"How long are these people here? I didn't think plastic surgery was that big a deal."

His expression changed. His mouth formed a straight line. "Max doesn't perform face-lifts. He reconstructs... Excuse me if I sound angry. I'm not. There isn't anyone like Max. He only takes cases other surgeons would rather not take—as long as he believes he can make a difference. Max always makes a difference."

"Sorry," she said, deliberately frowning. "I didn't mean to be offensive."

"I'm not offended." But a sharper light in his eyes made a liar of him.

Lee touched his solid forearm and said, "Thanks. My ignorance is showin'. I need to find out more about his history." Her wide eyes could fool anyone, they had put the toughest interview subjects at ease.

Roche looked at her fingers on his arm and patted them, the corners of his mouth turned up again. "I can tell you anything you want to know about him—as long as it's not too personal." He gave a short laugh. "We three share everything."

She just bet they did. And she wasn't surprised that Roche wanted to be in control of any questions she might ask about Max.

"You admire him a lot," Lee said, watching the steel in Roche's eyes.

"Everyone admires Max, they always have."

She avoided asking if they admired him when he was under suspicion of murder—twice—or if Michele Riley's disappearance had made them doubt wonderful Max. That would come later when she had more of Roche's trust, and it could take time. She tightened her belly against a thrill that felt dangerous.

"What angle do you intend to take on this story."

Lee gave him another wide-eyed look and breathed deeply. His glance moved down, to her breasts, and lingered.

At least she didn't blush easily.

She did tend to reflexive reactions. The pull came, the inner contractions, and she felt her nipples distend against her lace bra.

"Not sure of your angle?" he said, running the tip of his tongue along the edges of strong teeth. "Come on, I bet you could manage just about any angle if you really wanted to."

Lee swallowed. "It's amazing you and your brothers chose an out-of-the-way place like Toussaint for your wonderful clinic. I think the whole town is fascinated—a lot more than the town. People in little places can get taken up with what they're used to—simple, everyday life. I want them to read somethin' that'll make them proud of where they live. I want them to try to see it through your eyes. You must have thought it was beautiful and just the right atmosphere for all your poor...*injured* people."

She shut her mouth firmly. Babbling came easily enough in the course of whatever she was doing, but it wasn't usually the kind of drivel she'd just poured out. Polite should be Roche's middle name, he surely listened politely and smiled like he was interested. He would be thinking what a backwoods idiot she was.

"That's my angle," she said firmly, raising her jaw. She had experience with the art of bluffing.

"Mmm-hmm." Roche nodded and concentrated on her face. "Great. We'll want to use what you write. Patients will be touched by it, and we'll be grateful you put so much into something special."

She shrugged. "I'm a perfectionist. Whatever I do, I give it my all."

"That's what I'd expect from you," he said. "We'd better get to it, then. Remember, any photographs you want taken are yours. Shall we go up to the suites? Surgery and treatment rooms are there, too, and if you don't go wild over the spa you'll disappoint me."

They climbed two flights of stairs. Roche used a key card and put a code into a pad beside double doors that swung open when a green light showed.

When they were inside, the doors thudded softly shut. Lee had an urge to see if they could be opened by pulling on one of the handles.

"We have the security system to make sure no one who doesn't belong can walk in."

He'd seen her look at the door. "I thought so," she said. "It's warm in here." Really warm or she wouldn't notice.

"You haven't lived till you've gone through the kind of project we've got here. Contractors are a different breed. The air-conditioning quit earlier and the heat's building up. It'll be fixed when they can get to it. Would you rather go back down?"

"Of course not," she said, looking into a spacious room. "Is this a patient suite?"

"Yes. Go on in. Don't miss the bathroom."

Lee trailed self-consciously across blond wood floors to French doors and looked around the suite. "Unbelievable," she all but whispered. "So beautiful."

"Thank you. We think so."

One French door was open and a light breeze filled filmy white drapes. White silk-covered love seats faced across a glass-topped table. A pink ceiling drew Lee's attention. It sent a warm glow over the room, over a bed like none she'd seen in a hospital. This was king-size, with white eyelet lace trimming satin sheets and the subtlest shade of pink matelasse just showing at the edges of a snowy wisp of down blanket.

"Wow," was all Lee could think to say. "I love it. I don't think I've ever seen down blankets in Louisiana."

"I think when patients are recovering they often need extra comfort, extra warmth. And when the air-conditioning isn't defunct, the idea is a winner."

"I'm sure it is." Lee turned back to the windows and looked out.

All she saw were shadowy trees and, more distant, a few lights of Rosebank. "You're still stayin' at Rosebank?"

"Oh, yes. I doubt if I'll ever spend a night here. I'm looking for a house."

"That's nice."

Looking for a house. How must it be to have as much money as you needed to do whatever came to mind? She had started out with a nice financial cushion from her mother's will, but running a little newspaper, even with her friend Simon Menard shouldering some of the cost, strained her budget. Lee was careful how she spent, and didn't spend at all unless she had to.

"Where did you live before you came here?" she asked, already knowing the answer. Best to appear mostly ignorant of the Savages' background.

"New York. I thought everyone knew."

She shook her head. "I never heard it mentioned." The Internet and archives from some New York State newspapers had filled in a good deal, but she wanted to hunt down facts not so easily obtained. She wanted a *scoop.*

"Did you have a clinic there?"

"No. Walk into that bathroom. Go on, just walk in there."

He would only say what he wanted to say and that wouldn't include expanding on questions that didn't interest him.

The bathroom, at least half the size of the sitting and bedroom, astonished Lee. "It's huge," she said although Roche had remained in the bedroom. There was a Jacuzzi tub as big as a wading pool, a shower with no doors and a stone-tiled floor that sloped down so water wouldn't escape. Curved counters followed a curved wall and a plush swivel chair with arms was placed as if before a mirror, only there weren't any mirrors.

Lee backed out. The colors were stronger in there. A toned

down shade of the raspberry she'd seen downstairs seemed more intense when applied to the ceiling as well as the walls. Red veins showed in gold stone on the floors.

"No mirrors," Lee said and let out a gasp when she bumped into Roche who held her upper arms to steady her.

"Did the bathroom take your breath away, or is it me?" He laughed. "No mirrors until the patient is ready, or unless the patient insists on having them from the start. They lower into place electronically. Are you impressed?" He rested his chin on her shoulder and she felt his warmth on her face. He was testing her reactions to him.

"Very impressed," she said, not moving away from him. She didn't want to. Maybe he shouldn't, but he excited her. "It's going to be a great success."

"Yes. You're right. In surroundings like these, and with what we bring to them, we can't fail."

Unless it turns out the great surgeon is a killer.

"I want you to try that bed," Roche said, spinning her around and walking her toward the acres of white satin, eyelet, silk and glimpses of pink. "No girl can be complete until she's experienced that mattress."

In the company of Roche Savage? Lee's nerves stretched. His light, bantering tone didn't stop her from being on super-alert. If she planted her feet and said she was leaving, he wouldn't stop her. He couldn't afford the risk of nasty gossip—or worse.

Lee smiled sideways at Roche. If she did leave she might regret it later.

"Climb aboard," he said.

She put her purse on the floor, slipped off her shoes and lifted her denim sundress just enough to climb on top of the bed. Gingerly, she lay down, making sure her full skirt was modestly in place.

Instantly, every muscle stiffened, even her jaw and she clamped her teeth together. "So soft," she managed to say, and it was.

"Just relax," he said. "Close your eyes."

The last thing she wanted to do was close her eyes and leave herself vulnerable to a strong, sexy man who stood, staring down at her.

That old autonomic response reared its head at once.

"Do it," he said softly. "You won't believe how comfortable it is. If you go to sleep I'll make sure you get up in time for work in the morning."

And what would he be doing if she fell asleep? Where would he be? And where would *he* sleep? She looked up at him through her lashes and a quick inventory of his pants confirmed that Roche had more than the clinic on his mind.

This was more or less what she'd expected. No reason to be skittish now. Single women with healthy—maybe overly healthy— libidos enjoyed men with similar drives. She'd been cut off a long time and much as she knew Simon would like to be more than her friend and partner, she doubted he had enough passion or imagination to satisfy her.

Her eyes had closed. She managed to relax a little and waited for Roche's next move.

"Up you get," he said, taking hold of her hand and pulling her to a sitting position. "Don't forget your shoes. Are you ready for the spa? I'm not joking about that. Whatever you want to test or try, go to it. I'll be right behind you."

The questions she'd planned were piling up as the time passed. She must have been there half an hour already.

On the uppermost floor of Green Veil, Lee turned circles, trying to take everything in at once. "Why did you bother with the exercise equipment?" she said, giggling. "This is decadent. Look at all the divans. Who would want to work out here, or lift a finger at all?"

"If you come here, you work," Roche said. He put a hand on the

back of her neck and she was totally aware of his massaging fingertips. "I hope we haven't gone overboard. I don't think so. Max just
lets me do whatever I think is necessary."

The spa and exercise room filled the whole top floor of the
building. Colors had been chosen for impact.

"The previous tenants did have a plastic surgery mill. All the
spaces were broken down into cubicles. Their intention must have
been quantity. We had to gut the inside but we tried to save what
we could of the original house."

"Almost makes you want to get sweaty," Lee said, eyeing the
ocean of equipment, the treatment rooms that opened off the main
area, the aerobic floor. Roche followed her into a treatment room.
It had a big shower, a steam room, a massage bed and large pots and
bottles of products lined glass shelves. A facial steamer stood to one
side of the bed, and on a counter were a heater for stones, a micro-
wave and a wax bath. She smelled massage oils.

There were no windows, but a wall draped with shimmering
brown and beige curtains suggested there might be. Deep, leopard
print carpet swallowed the soles of her shoes.

"Let's work out, then see what other mischief we can get into,"
Roche said. "Would you like that?"

Lee sensed that giving her a choice was an afterthought but she
nodded and felt trapped.

"Terrific. Leave your things here." He stripped off his T-shirt,
stepped out of his pants but kept on his sneakers. The way he walked
showed he was perfectly at ease in front of her in his undershorts.
"Your bra and panties will be comfortable enough." He pointed to
a closet. "Hang your dress in there. We'll carry a wide selection of
workout clothes once we open."

He sat in a chair and took off his watch, checked the time and
began to adjust it.

This was the moment when she proved she wasn't an innocent little girl. The denim sundress came off over her head and she put it in the closet as she'd been told. Whatever she felt, she would move with confidence. As an afterthought she removed the small gold pendant she wore around her neck and her own watch. These she dropped into her purse.

She needed to think straight. "Ready," she said.

"Good," Roche said, glancing at her, apparently disinterested.

Lee didn't like that.

"You go on out. I'll grab us a couple of towels and some water bottles."

Self-conscious in her peachy thong and a lace bra with half cups, Lee kept her back straight, her abs tight, and picked out an elliptical machine. She'd used them before, used a lot of the machines in the room before, but not in her flimsy underwear, in a large deserted clinic, alone with a man she hardly knew.

No one had forced her to be here and the least she should get out of it was the article on the clinic from an intimate perspective. For the rest, the night wasn't over and she wouldn't lose all hope of digging up something sensational.

Conscious of her all but naked butt, she strode out anyway and the adrenaline started to pump. She knew she had a good body. Why not show it off?

Music, a woman's sultry voice, came through the sound system. Lee worked harder, until Roche spread a large hand on her buttocks and laughed when she jumped. Playfully, she slapped him away. "Get to work," she said, repeating his instruction. "I won't keep this up long."

He put towels and water bottles on a bench and hopped onto another machine like the one she used. His muscles flexed all over. From time to time he turned to her and smiled. He tossed her one of the towels and she managed to catch it. With the other towel he wiped his face and left it rolled around his neck.

"I don't suppose this was what you had in mind for your interview. We've always been a very physical family. We all work out every day."

"It shows," she said, and grinned when his face turned sharply toward her. "Well it does. You're in great shape."

"So are you."

Lee slowed down, jumped off and ran in place for several minutes, aware that the weight of her breasts made them bounce. She went into the stretching routine she should have done beforehand.

"Is that going to be it for you?" Roche shouted. His tanned skin shone.

"Nope." She wanted to stop but got on a bike and pedaled instead. The seat didn't feel good. It pushed the thong into uncomfortable places.

Roche approached and her heart quit beating when she saw his penis, erect and impressive inside his shorts. She looked away and kept pedaling.

He stood beside her and massaged her shoulders, knocking a bra strap down. With great care he replaced it. Then he ran a finger down her spine and rubbed back and forth at her waist. When his hand settled on her bottom again, she felt slick between her legs—and embarrassed.

"You've got a great ass," he said.

"Thank you, I think."

"Do you really want to make the *Trumpet* your life's work?"

"Absolutely."

He used his other hand to knead her flat abdomen, and to trail fingers up and down the inside of her closest thigh. Suddenly Lee's mind was clear enough to be cold. He intended to have sex with her—whether she wanted it or not.

CHAPTER | 8

"I should probably get home," Lee said. "Reb and Marc will wonder where I am." Her nerve had begun to crack. She'd look elsewhere for the breaks she needed.

"Kelly told me you were spending the night at the paper." His eyes didn't completely focus and he slowly pushed strand after strand of her hair back. "You aren't afraid of me, are you?"

"Of course not." She smiled widely and let her head hang back while she smoothed sweat from the tops of her breasts. He scared her crazy and he hadn't even done anything, except insist she exercise in her underclothes. And put his hands pretty much all over her.

"Great. You're jumpy though. Let's get you cooled off and feeling good enough to go home and be ready for another day." He brought his face so close she thought he would kiss her. His breath smelled of mint, and brandy?

Offering his hand again, he assisted her from the bike and walked, swinging their arms back and forth, to the room where they'd left their things.

"I can't let you go immediately, you understand," he said. "A hot shower first."

"I'll take a shower when I get back."

His answer was to turn on the water.

Lee wondered if she'd have locks to contend with if she tried to get out.

"In you go," he said. "I'll use the head at the other end if that's okay."

"Go right ahead," she told him and stepped in—still in her underwear.

From the edge of her vision she saw Roche strip off his shorts and get into the other end of the shower. She washed vigorously, even rubbing soap over what little she wore.

Roche's sudden laughter made her look over her shoulder. He faced her, water beating down onto his head and face, and indicated that she hadn't undressed completely. "Come on. Are you shy? Don't you want to take those off? I won't promise not to look."

"They need a wash," she said, feeling stupid. "I sweated on them."

His eyes remained crinkled at the corners.

Lee couldn't stop herself from lowering her gaze again. The guy was ready to go but he scared her to death. So much for her sophistication. She wanted him, but she couldn't stand the thought that he'd find out she wasn't so experienced. Not that she hadn't had plenty of sex.

Roche turned off his showerhead and reached around her to turn off the second one. He got out and used a fresh towel. When she didn't move, he gave her another charming smile, put a hand around her waist and drew her toward him.

Her heart beat hard.

"So quiet," he whispered, massaging her belly and ribs. "I think you *are* afraid of me."

"Of course, I'm not."

"Lie on the table," he told her and he wasn't giving her a choice.

She grabbed a big towel and wrapped it around her.

Roche pulled it off. "Over here first." He took her to one of the counters, removed the lid from the wax bath and plunged in her hands, ignoring her indrawn breath at the heat. He dipped her fingers in twice more. "Hold them out," he said. The wax turned opaque almost instantly. "Sit on the table. Now."

She did as she was told. "Now what are you up to?" She didn't want him to know she was scared, but he'd started to really frighten her.

"How old are you?" Roche asked. He slid gloves over her hot hands, followed by electric warming mitts which he plugged in. "Soak up the heat, baby."

Fleetingly, Lee imagined what kind of reaction she'd get if she told this part of the story in the paper.

"I asked how old you are," Roche said.

"Old enough."

His mouth turned down but he didn't press her.

"Seaweed," he said, lifting down a transparent container filled with a green material. "The woman who demonstrated this for me said it draws impurities out of your skin—or something like that. It feels damn good and that's what matters."

Frozen, she watched him open the big jar and scoop out a handful of what resembled green slime.

Her skin had turned cold and covered with goose bumps. She shivered.

He smoothed the slippery goop over her legs, sweeping up from foot to groin, making her jump, then reaching beneath to take far too long on her rear. Lee felt stiff enough to snap. Why not just say all she wanted was a good story on Green Veil and she'd like to go home now?

Because she feared he'd refuse. He might also turn nasty. What did she know about him?

The green stuff, when he smeared it on her middle, felt warm and slightly grainy. Roche spread it as if his hand were a huge butter knife. Back and forth, back and forth, lingering over every inch.

"How is the sex with your boyfriend, Simon?" he asked, catching her offguard. "Does he satisfy you?" He covered her skin, but avoided her bra and thong.

Roche held her arm and shook gently. "Come on, you can share secrets with me. You tell me yours and I'll tell you mine."

"Simon is a good man, a nice man. I don't talk about my friends."

"That's the way it should be. I hope I'm a friend." He leaned close enough to settle his smooth, hard crotch against her leg.

Lee didn't move a muscle. "You're a friend," she said in what she hoped sounded like a calm voice. "Why would three sexy guys like you and your brothers settle in a backwater like this?"

He didn't miss a beat. He showed his white teeth in a throaty laugh. "We sexy guys have all seen things we like around here." Undulating lightly, he applied more and more of the seaweed mud. For a few seconds he straightened and looked down at her. Then he set the next dollop on her décolletage, swept over the rise of her breasts. "On your side," he said and once she was there, made sure she was a study in green from all directions.

The electric gloves made movement awkward. They also meant she couldn't interfere with anything he decided to do.

Without warning, he spread his hands beneath her breasts and pushed them up. "Very nice," he said. "Very, very nice. Oh, yeah, baby—we've got places to go and things to do."

"Not like this," she said, wiggling at the sensations he'd started.

"You bet like this." The hot gloves hit the floor. "Leave the wax. We'll make the best of it. Come on."

To Lee's dismay, he led her from the treatment room, across the floor of the gym and opened another door into a dark room. "We're messing up the floors," she said

Roche shot his arms around her, lifted her into the room, and shut the door again. "Forget the floors," he said.

"Turn on the lights," Lee said.

"In time. Show me how you make a man happy."

She felt her skin grow hot under the mud, then blanch. Her breath came in short spurts.

"C'mon," he wheedled. "Just a little encouragement. I'll make it worth your while."

"Why are you doing this?" She kept her voice steady.

"Oh, don't try the innocent on me. You came here to get fucked and who am I to disappoint a lady."

"Maybe I've changed my mind," she said, shivering.

"Really." His hands spanned her waist and he slipped them slowly upward until they supported her breasts then, in a move that shocked her, he caught at the front of the bra and snapped it in halves with a single yank.

"Don't," she said, even though it was too late.

A sheen caught her eye. She jerked her face to look toward a wall. Shapes, moving shapes, her own and Roche's. Even in near darkness she discerned they were surrounded by mirrors.

So rapid she had to clutch at his biceps, he shifted her until her back met glass. And the lights went on.

She closed her eyes.

"Don't do that," he told her. "There's nothing sexier than watching yourself making love." He raised her chin, leaned his weight against her and sent his tongue deep into her mouth. With fingers and thumbs he tugged on her nipples, shook them.

She reacted to him, had been reacting to him, couldn't help herself. Her hips came away from the mirror and pressed into his.

"That's the way," he murmured. "I thought I was right about you. You like it, don't you. The more the better. The harder, the better. And I just bet you like to experiment."

Her heart beat painfully but excitement wiped out any reluctance. Jutting his pelvis, he sent his smooth, notable penis between her thighs and pumped back and forth slowly in a parody of what he intended to do next.

"I only came to get a story," she said in a croak when he raised his head and she felt as silly as she was sure she sounded. Marshaling her pride, she said, "What a lot more I'm getting."

He laughed with her and slid her over the mirrored wall.

"The glass!" she said. "It'll be filthy."

"Not my worry," he said. His face seemed feverish. He ate her up with his eyes. "Touch me."

It took her a moment to gain courage. Then she held up her hands where ragged wax trailed. "I can't."

"It'll feel good," he said.

Carefully, she slid her hands between them and took hold of the biggest, hardest man she'd ever encountered. Fire flashed through her body. He made keening noises while she stroked him, moved her hips against him. She tried not to look at herself. Or at herself pressed and straining against him.

"Let's make pictures," he said, suddenly, loudly. His laughter came, also loud, and too high. "Yes, Lee, pictures. This first." She slammed against the mirror this time and he held her there by the neck.

Her hammering heart made a louder noise. He was dangerous, maybe unbalanced.

With his free forefinger, he circled a breast, the circles getting smaller and smaller, and stopped suddenly. His lips and teeth replaced the finger and he sucked her nipple into his mouth, bit just hard enough to cause pain, sucked until she cried out—loving what he made her feel.

She rolled her back, thrusting her other breast toward him, but he ignored it in favor of rubbing between the slick folds of her labia. "I can't take it," she breathed. "Please, don't tease me anymore."

"Would I tease you?" he said and increased his pace until she went over the top and her knees sagged while ripples of pure pleasure took her. "We're just beginning." He bit her ear—and he drove three fingers inside her, used them the way only a man who knew how to please a woman could do.

Lee felt her mouth fall open. She ached. Her breasts felt heavy and sensitive. He brought her to another climax and she screamed silently.

"Pictures, pictures," he said. "Before you dry out."

Roche rotated her and all but threw her onto the mirror. He pulled her arms wide and moved them as if making snow angels. Then he yanked her away, spun her again and rushed her to another wall of cold glass. Her shoulder blades hit first but he didn't give her time to complain. He turned his back, leaned his buttocks into her pelvis and applied pressure. Once more he sprang away, pulling her, pointing and saying, "Best ass prints in town."

She couldn't laugh anymore. Fear turned her cold and where he'd banged her on the hard surfaces, she felt bruised. "The best," she said and tried to collect herself. "That was fun but I am in a time crunch." The waves of sensation hadn't completely faded.

"A time crunch? Is that right? We'll, I'd better help you hurry then. You want to even the score, don't you? Yes, I know you do."

This time he pressed her, face first, to the glass again and lifted her from her feet. He smeared her up and down, laughing all the time. "You're a great sport, Lee. I won't be able to wait until you come again."

If she had her way, she'd never lay eyes on him again.

Clamping her on the cold surface with her feet at least a foot off the ground, he held her there with one arm. With the other he pulled her hips back and he slid her gently down, guided her over his distended penis, and stepped back again, carrying her.

"Payback time," he almost sang out. He pushed her until her head hung down and her legs were behind her, clasped on either side of his hips to save herself from falling.

"Ride that pony," he yelled, pulling and pushing, beating into her and capering.

She shouldn't be so stimulated, so excited by him that she didn't want it to stop, but that's how it was now. Lee did her best to help him and he grunted his pleasure before he stood still, grinding rapidly, then staggering, slipping to the floor with her squeezed hard against him.

Lee closed her eyes and smiled. An adventure, the kind she'd only read about. And he wouldn't want a word about his kinky predilections to get out, not in little old Toussaint. Secrets could make for a really close intimacy—even a compulsion to share everything. Telling her about his family's troubles could be a relief to Roche...

"Mmm," she said, snuggling against him and pretending to be tired. Rarely had she felt more awake. "That was so good."

"It was a start," he murmured. "You and I have a great future."

She didn't dwell on what he meant. After all, she'd just had the best sex of her life. Why not look forward to more of the same?

"Are all three Savage brothers amazing lovers?"

He gripped her too tight. "That's not what I've heard."

She grimaced. A sore spot had been touched. "I'm getting cold."

"I'm not."

"Do you like your brothers?"

"Dumb question. Of course I do."

"I had a brother, still do somewhere, and I don't like him."

"My brothers are extraordinary at what they do. Especially Max. We all knew he was amazing from when we were kids. He could make the folks swell up with pride without trying. They gave him all their attention and that way he kept them out of our hair. He knew the deal but he didn't mind taking the fall."

"Doesn't sound like a fall, sounds like he was the fair-haired boy."

Roche sat, then sprang to his feet. She saw what a mess they both were.

"There was never any favoritism in our house."

He hadn't made it sound that way. "Kelly's mother is gorgeous."

He grew still, like a stone. "Yes, she is."

From his expression, she could assume she'd scratched a raw area for Roche. "How old was Kelly when his parents divorced?"

"How do you know they divorced?" he asked through his teeth. He hauled Lee to her feet and bent threateningly over her. "Maybe his mother died. What business is it of yours?"

"I'm a journalist," she told him, holding her ground. "I research most things. Did your father meet your mother before, or after he and Kelly's mother—"

"Keep your nose out of our business." He was making sure she knew where he was vulnerable.

She rolled her eyes. "No offense meant. I was interested, is all. You and Kelly must have suffered with all that scrutiny Max got after those women died. It's not fair when we suffer for other people's problems."

"You have been doing your research," Roche said. "Is that why you came here and behaved like a bitch in heat? Because you're digging for a big scoop? Were you ready to lay Kelly—but you decided it didn't matter which one of us you got *close* to?"

Sickness caught at Lee. "Of course not." She twisted her face into an unhappy mask. "How could you say things like that?"

"Don't try to dig dirt on Max. There isn't any."

"Okay," she said. "Is Kelly as protective of him as you are? I've heard the way he talks and I think he sounds jealous of Max."

"It's time you went," Roche said.

"Okay," she said and walked, her destroyed thong hanging by threads, to the treatment room. She threw away what was left of her underwear, took a rapid shower, and pulled her denim dress over her head.

Roche didn't show.

So she'd leave. The evening had been more entertaining than any she recalled enjoying before. And without Roche saying much, she'd got the idea that at the very least, there might be some dirt to dig about the Savage family, about Leo Savage and his two sexy wives—and how much their boys suffered in the wrangles of divorce and remarriage.

Max could be so damaged he hated women. She rubbed her hair, tossed it back and fluffed it with her fingers. He wouldn't be the first man, twisted by his suffocating mother, who turned to killing and mutilating women.

"That's some smile," Roche said from behind her.

Lee faced him and smiled even more broadly. "You gave me something to smile about." He had, she noted, come by a pair of jeans and some boat shoes. He looked cool and relaxed.

"Glad to have been of service," he said. "Let me see you out."

He disquieted her but she picked up her purse and looked around for anything else she might have put down. And she frowned, searching through the purse.

"Something missing?" Roche asked, leaning against the doorjamb, his arms crossed.

"I don't see my recorder. I expect I left it downstairs." Just as well, she thought.

"Is this it?" Roche asked. He dangled the little chrome instrument before him. "It does a great job."

Lee held out her hand. "Thanks for findin' it."

"You didn't lose it," he said, his eyes hard. "I carried it along all the way."

"Yes," she said, still holding out her hand. She didn't like being here anymore.

Roche switched on the tape and she heard herself sobbing and climaxing, and goading him into more.

He switched off. "Insurance," he said. "You've got quite a way with words, to say nothing of with your body. You're a natural whore."

She winced and anger built. "Give me that. And I never want to set eyes on you again."

"Keep your mouth shut," he told her. "Whatever you think you know, forget it. There's nothing to know and if there were, you wouldn't find out about it."

Lee lowered her eyelids. Staying calm counted. Figuring a way out really counted.

"I didn't mean to make you angry," she said. "We had fun. Thank you." She'd like to claw his eyes out.

"Yes, we did."

Lee smiled and walked past, wiggling her fingers goodbye, as she went.

He didn't even guess she'd snatch the recorder from his hand and run with it. When she did, he failed to react quickly enough.

The elevator was open and the door slid shut the instant she hit the button to close it. Roche all but lost his face trying to force his way in.

At the bottom, she shot out and made for the front doors. The one she'd used to come in would take too long to reach.

"Ah, ah, ah," Roche said, gripping her around the waist and hauling her away. The doors had been locked anyway.

She kicked at him with her heels, caught him hard and he dropped her.

Before she made it out of the lobby he was on her and they went down together, writhing, Roche going for the recorder she continued to hold in her hand.

Her skirt rode up and air around her hips reminded her she'd abandoned her thong.

His weight pinned her. "Just give it to me nicely," he said, deliberately fitting himself between her legs.

"Okay," she said, smiling at him. And with her free hand she grabbed him where she knew it would hurt most and squeezed.

The noise he made was unintelligible. He curled off her, doubled over, and she took off.

"Never underestimate a small-town woman," she yelled, running down the side corridor. Her throat hurt. She went as fast as she could, slammed into the door and shot outside, stuffing the recorder into her bag.

Roche caught up with her beside her car and held one of her arms in a grip she wasn't going to break.

"Let me go!"

He held her against the car, looked from her one empty hand to her purse and took it away so easily she wanted to cry.

"Let's see what we have here," Roche said. He tipped the bag upside down and the contents scattered on gravel. Still holding her, he scooped up the recorder. "Thank you."

"Get off me." She kicked at him but missed.

He let her go and stepped backward at the same time. "My pleasure. But I do think we'll have to meet again."

She frowned at him.

"We both enjoyed ourselves, remember? Why waste a good thing?"

CHAPTER | 9

"Annie. Annie!"

Max's shout tore into her.

"Don't say my name," she told him, grabbing for the flashlight. "I'm nothin' to you." She couldn't feel her feet or hands.

"Stop it." His left wrist caught her neck hard and her breath rushed out. "Back off. Get hold of yourself."

With one brush, he bruised her windpipe and she held her throat. "Okay," she whispered, her stomach roiling. She would not throw up in front of him. "I can't stop what you're going to do, so do it. But I'll fight you. You should have stopped the killing. You've gone on too long. This time you're makin' a mistake and they'll get you for it."

She took several short steps away from him but he followed, shone the blinding light directly into her face.

"You figured out I'd come back here eventually, didn't you? You were right. Here I am and you intend to make sure I don't bother you anymore. You've been watching me, haven't you? Waiting for me?"

"No," Max said.

"How did you know to come after me tonight?"

"Don't worry about it," he said.

"You think I deliberately found out the names of the two women you killed. Why would I do that? Your ego is so huge, you can't imagine I might have issues of my own. You aren't the center of everything for me."

The moment she moved again, he reached for her. He missed.

Great breaths barely reached the tops of her lungs. She saw red, flaming red. "Stay away," she said. The crimson hung deeper in the trees.

"Come here. I mean it, Annie. You're going to calm down and listen to me."

He wanted to overpower her with as little noise as possible—not that anyone would hear if she screamed. "I'm not doing anything you say. Who did you have watching me? Guy Gautreaux? Did he tell you I'd headed this way? Poor Guy. He believed you cared about me."

Kicking up clots of rotting leaves, she rushed at Max again. She clawed for his face, aimed for his eyes, but he fended her off.

"Damn you, Max Savage." Annie hit out again. She ducked her head and cannoned into him. She wanted his blood under her fingernails to lead the police to him.

And she did it. The neck of his shirt was open and her fingers landed there. When she pulled her hand away, she dragged out hairs from his chest.

"Goddammit," he yelled, shoving her. "Stop it. I've never hurt you, you little fool. You're mad."

Annie's heel came down on something hard and slick. She fell, caught herself on her hands—and quickly curled her fingers around a rock that dug into her palm.

Following his flashlight beam he loomed over her, gradually got closer.

She tried to twist away.

Max caught her by the shoulders, lifted and landed her on her feet. The light shone straight up and she couldn't see his face anymore.

With both arms she tried to break his hold. She didn't have a chance, but she wouldn't give up. Her head felt light and she saw firebugs glint.

Not in the rain. "Not in the rain," she said aloud. "Firebugs don't come out in the rain." There were embers in the air, floating from a fire. He'd lighted a fire. "No! Don't do it. I can't stand it again. Don't burn me." Her own thin scream jolted her brain, deep pains ripped at her temples.

"It's okay," he said. "I won't hurt you. Never. I came to make sure you were safe. Annie, someone called and said they saw you heading toward St. Martinville. I don't know who it was. He sounded… forget that. Remember what happened here before? You had some sort of hallucination and went crazy."

"No!"

"You're doing it again, now. You saw fire then, didn't you? You're seeing fire now."

It crackled behind the trees. Sparks spat and spun toward the leafy canopy. "You don't know what I'm seeing." Annie shook her head. Again sweat soaked her body and quickly turned icy. "It's getting worse. It never used to happen when I was awake."

"What is it?" he said. "Tell me. Explain it to me."

She couldn't stop her legs from trembling. "I can't. What are you going to do?"

"Get you back to Toussaint and ask Reb to see you." He sounded angry. "Better yet, Roche will look at you."

"I don't need a shrink." Had she gone mad? "I don't need anyone."

"Dammit, Annie. You do need someone and you're coming with me now."

In an arcing motion, she swung the rock.

The blow made a sound, like a bullet hitting a range target. *Thud.* She made out the way his head whipped sideways from the impact.

Annie whirled about and staggered forward. Getting lost, out of Max's sight, might be her only chance.

"Annie, don't run. Please, Annie. This is my fault."

She stumbled, grabbed at vines and climbed over logs, pushed through bushes. In front of her, a shadow arose, thin and wavering. A faint moan came from whoever, or whatever it was.

Closer, it came.

"Who is it?" Annie said. In the darkness, and with her eyes stinging, she scarcely saw anything. "Stay still, please."

Her head felt light and she blinked. Her body shook. The shadow moaned again and she smelled it, scorched flesh, burned hair.

Somewhere a shovel scraped on stone. Annie's knees buckled and the world turned suffocating, and black.

Max threw himself across the final space separating him from Annie. She wasn't like this. If he believed in possession he'd think her mind had been taken over.

Damn, now he was thinking like Wazoo and other folks like her around here. Stress could do this. Cases of duress leading to complete mental and physical collapse were common. He hadn't come across any of them, but they were hardly in his area of exper-tise.

She huddled on the ground, her arms and legs folded beneath her.

His forehead hurt but it could have been a lot worse. Her blow had glanced off but he did feel blood above his eyebrow.

Careful where he trod, Max worked his way to her head and crouched beside her. "Annie?" Gently, he touched her back and rubbed her shoulders. "Come on, let me help you."

She stayed where she was.

He had stopped bleeding from her scratches at the open neck of his shirt. His skin stung. That wasn't something the Annie he knew would do. That and the way she'd swung a rock at him.

For a moment he recalled the evening he'd spent in her apartment. Annie had been wild...

But he couldn't get rid of the notion that her behavior had been out of character. What was happening with these bizarre episodes—there had been no sign of them when they first met?

Walking away from her wasn't an option anymore. He cared too much.

"Okay," he said. "Let's get out of here."

When he gathered her up into his arms she fell against him, limp and boneless. He put his cheek near her mouth and nose to wait for escaping air, couldn't help it, instinct always kicked in. Annie breathed, shallowly, but breathed and that was all he cared about. He shifted her weight to check the pulse in her neck. Thready, but she'd been through shock after shock.

Darth Vader had called again, sending him to St. Martinville.

How the hell did the man know what Annie was doing and what he was doing? Annie stirred in his arms, but only to turn more toward him. She muttered, but he didn't make out what she said. Heaviness settled deep in his chest. Annie had entered a darkness where he couldn't reach her. It coincided with her knowing him. Not at first but soon enough. How could he doubt he was responsible. If she'd started projecting, why couldn't it be because she had found out about the women he'd been accused of killing, then moved on to a fear that he would do the same to her.

And now there was Michele. Spike told him how Toussaint, and areas for miles around had been searched and searched again. He'd also hinted that the lack of a body—and a single linking clue—was all that kept Max a free man after so many days had passed.

Her fist, thumping his chest, jarred him. "It's okay," he told her, although her eyes remained shut...for a few more moments.

Annie looked at him, her eyes luminous by flashlight. Recognition came into her stare. She buried her face against his chest, but planted her hands as well, and pushed. "Put me down," she said clearly.

"It'll be easier if I carry you."

"No." Her voice rose as if she held back tears. "It's over now. I have to leave. I have to go to work."

"You finished at Pappy's for the day. You should be at home. When you go, it'll be to bed."

"You don't decide what I should do." She became more shrill. "You don't understand me. I don't want you to. Are you going to kill me?"

He caught his breath and felt almost ill. "How could you ask that? I care about you—we're not strangers or just lunch companions."

"Yes, we are."

"We are not, Annie. You can't hide from the truth. We had sex. We made love and it was good."

She struggled, kicked her legs. "Don't talk about it again. I know what happened and what I did." She choked on her next breath, and coughed. "I'm not sorry. At least I... It was important but I want you to forget it."

"I never will."

"Put me down."

"Not until you admit you're wrong to be afraid of me."

She remained silent.

"Annie? It's damned wet out here. I want to take you home." Cautiously, he set her feet on the ground.

"She's still missing," Annie said. "Michele. I just have to believe a whole lot more is being done about it than we think. That poor man she's engaged to is staying at the Majestic all this time."

"Search parties have been out every day." Each morning he awoke, tense and listening for footsteps in the hall at Rosebank. He expected the arrival of Spike at his door, with deputies, come to arrest him.

"They need more than search parties. Toussaint should be crawling with official types."

"It is," he said, biting down on his back teeth at the thought. "Spike has called in help. The latest he told me was that they're watching for Michele all over the country. Some think she ran away."

"What do you think?"

"I think she's dead." He'd stopped pretending. "Annie, you've been seeing things, haven't you?"

If the episodes she had got around, she'd be branded as crazy. Who knew how Pappy would react if the news got to him?

"Don't hold back," Max said. She heard him struggle with his temper.

"I've already said too much," she told him. "Don't push me."

She felt as if she could reach out and touch his exasperation.

"Okay," he said, taking her by the arm, none too gently. "Let's go." He hurried her along.

"Did you think I'd be vulnerable here? Alone? Did you think I could somehow spill my guts and help you? What do you think I know?"

"You can't blame a man for hoping. What happens in these visions you have, or whatever they are?"

She resented his tone. "Forget about them. They're probably a hysterical reaction. Isn't that what they always call emotional or uptight women, hysterical?"

"You are so angry. Why be angry with me? I'm on your side."

Leaving Toussaint might be the best answer. Her stomach clenched. Leave Toussaint, leave Pappy's—and leave this man she couldn't bear to be without, even if he did frighten her, puzzle her.

What was the matter with her? They said some women wanted to be victims. No, she wasn't one of those people.

The evidence against him was too strong to ignore.

Annie opened her mouth to breathe. If he killed her here, and buried her, chances were she'd never be found. She thought of Wazoo and got some comfort thinking that the other woman knew where she was.

"You don't trust me." Max stopped. He continued to hold her arm. "Do you? You believe I've killed people for the hell of it."

I'm not sure what I believe. "Of course I don't." This wasn't the time or place to invite more trouble.

"You look at me as if you think you're about to die. You asked if I was going to kill you. How the hell do you think that makes me feel?"

"How do you think it makes *me* feel? I can't be sure. I have feelings for you, a lot of good feelings, but look at the evidence." She had shouted and she lowered her voice. "I'm so afraid, but I can't make myself believe you're a killer."

Another flashlight was switched on without warning and she saw Guy Gautreaux. "Let go of the lady's arm," he said. Guy, rangy, built like a tall, whiplash-proof cowboy, braced his booted feet apart and held a gun in a way that spelled business. *"Do it!"*

Max looked sideways at Annie. "Do you even have a cell phone with you?"

"No, I forgot it," she said. "And if I did have it with me, when would I have had a chance to call Guy?"

"Just do as I ask," Guy said. "Then we can all keep calm and get through this without getting hurt."

"There's nothing to get through." Max spoke through his teeth. His lips were pulled back. "You aren't needed here."

Guy's stare didn't waver. "Her arm," he said.

Max released it.

"Why are you here? I already know about Annie, but not you. Did you ask him to come?" Guy asked her.

She couldn't look at Max. "I'm only here to look around. Me, I was here the other day and thought it a beautiful place, so I thought I'd come back and see if it was just as pretty at night."

"In a storm?" Guy said. "On your own. And Max here just happened to think it was a good night for trompin' in the woods, too. You got a flashlight, Annie?"

She tried to breathe in without much success. "I dropped it somewhere." Airily, she waved a hand. "I couldn't find it."

"What have you done to your face?" Guy said.

Automatically, she put both hands to her cheeks and recalled walking into a tree. "Bumped myself," she said.

He moved his beam over Max. "And you. Looks like you messed up your face and neck." Guy moved in closer. "Rough out here, huh? Scratches. You been scratchin' this man, Annie. Hitting his head, maybe?"

"No...yes, it was my fault. I slipped and he tried to catch me. I'm afraid Max got the worse of it."

"You always fight people who try to help you? I'll bear that in mind."

Her heart beat a little faster, a little harder. At last the rain had beaten down the leaves and fell hard enough to soak all of them. "Guy, I was alone here and Max came to find me. I got scared when I heard someone else. I went a bit nuts."

"You fought him. Good. Me, I make it a rule to fight people who creep up on me in the dark, too."

"Yes," she said, aware of how quiet Max was. "So you understand?"

"Did you fight him before you slipped and he tried to save you from fallin'...or after?"

He was letting her know her half-truths, lies, conflicting comments, weren't going unnoticed. "I'm unsettled," she told him and it sounded weak. "But it's okay here, really it is."

Max kept his mouth shut and listened. He couldn't blame Guy for being suspicious and he wondered who had sent him here. Most notable of all was Annie's defense. She'd be a nut not to at least doubt his innocence, but he did believe she cared for him. She humbled him—even if he didn't understand her.

"I want a few words with you, Annie," Guy said.

From what little Max knew of the man, he liked him. But he didn't want him removing Annie to see if she'd tell a different tale.

"Annie?" Guy said.

"Surely," she said, and walked away from Max, a little unsteady on her feet, her eyes fixed on the obstacles underfoot.

Either she would keep up her story that Max was okay or she wouldn't. This wasn't the first time Max had been dependent on the kindness, and the support of others.

"It's okay," Guy said when Annie reached him. He pulled her to one side so he could keep his weapon trained on Savage. Guy lowered his voice. "You don't have to talk with me. A good friend of yours asked me to check you out. I'm doing that."

"I appreciate it," Annie said and realized how much she meant it. "Wazoo called you?"

"My clients expect me to be circumspect. What's goin' on here? Say the word and I'll get you out."

She wanted out, but Max hadn't tried to do something bad to

her. He'd hurt her, but only because he'd had to stop her from taking lumps out of him—more lumps. "He came because he's worried about me." Annie made up her mind what she needed to do for now. "May I come and talk to you in your office if I need to?"

He regarded her intently. "Yes. Yes, you surely can." He dropped his voice even lower. "If you need help now, just fold your arms."

She left her arms at her side. "If I do need help, you're going to be the one I call. I don't believe Max did any of the things they reckon he did. I'll come in and tell you what's been happening to me. Will late tomorrow be okay?"

"You've got it. Goldilocks is a love so don't let her scare you."

She frowned at him.

"One of our dogs. She likes to sit inside the door to my offices. Baby—he's the younger one—he's upstairs. Sometimes they scare people but they're a pair of softies."

"Dogs don't scare me," Annie said, thinking, and not for the first time, that Guy was an interesting type and she could understand why free-spirit Jilly looked at him as if she couldn't wait to get him alone.

"Hey, Max," Guy said. "I'd like to get back. You want to walk out together? This place is a maze."

"Sure," Max said, joining them as fast as he could. "What did you decide? That I'm a lady-killer—literally?"

"Go easy," Guy said. "Put yourself in my shoes. You do realize this entire town knows pretty much all about what happened with those women?"

"Sure I do."

Annie faced him. "Guy knows I don't think you had anything to do with the murders. We're going to walk out together. Three pairs of eyes could help."

"Got it," Max said.

As they went, they didn't say much. The two men automatically placed her between them and helped her clamber through the underbrush.

"Max once thought he would build his clinic here," Annie said, uncomfortable with the silence. "Then he and his brothers found Green Veil."

"Not exactly here," Max said. "The next lot over."

Annie pulled up. "Did I wander that far away? I left the land you liked?"

"Easy to do," Max said. "It all looks the same. I've bought the parcel next door, the one I showed you."

She looked into his face. Even in the darkness she could tell he wasn't smiling. "It's beautiful," she said. It wasn't her place to press him about his reasons for wanting that particular piece of real estate.

"I think so. When some of the trees are cleared on the bayou side there'll be a great view."

"You intend to build another clinic?" Guy asked, and Annie was grateful the responsibility for finding out had been taken from her.

"No. A house. I intend to live there. It's not so far from the clinic and I love the spot."

Annie felt warm. He intended to have a home here—that meant he intended to really settle in.

They reached the clearing on Max's lot and walked across the mushy ground in a relentless downpour.

"I'd like to drive you home," Max said. "You're in no condition to drive. We'll come back for your car when you've slept and seen a doctor."

"I'm fine to drive. I'll take it easy." She didn't want to be in debt to him for anything. But she did want to find a way to prove his innocence. Annie also figured she'd better go to Spike in the morning and bring him up to date.

The long trudge took them back through the trees to the road along the bayou.

"I'm going to follow you," Max said.

Guy cleared his throat. "And I'll be right behind."

Annie thought all this was a fine idea. "Thank you."

"I appreciate you looking out for Annie," Max said to Guy.

She liked hearing him say it, Annie thought. She liked any tiny piece of attention he showed her. A dangerous thing when they couldn't seem to get along anymore.

"What time did you leave Toussaint?" Guy asked, talking to Max.

"I'm not really sure. I got a call suggesting Annie might be coming up here on her own and left."

"Who called you?"

Max sighed. "I don't know. A man. He cut out before I could ask him anything."

"You have trouble with getting anythin' you say backed up, don't you?" Guy said, mildly enough.

Max was noncommittal. "Seems that way."

"You haven't spoken to Spike since then."

"No." It was hard to keep on walking. Max's gut tightened up and not for the first time tonight. "Why would I?"

"Cyrus called in to report Madge's dog missing. Apparently she can't even talk about it."

"No!" Annie said. She speeded up. "Madge never lets Millie out of her sight. Everyone says so."

"Lil was going into Loreauville and the dog needed to see the vet for a shot. Lil volunteered to take her and apparently Madge couldn't figure out how to refuse."

"It's late," Annie said. "Lil would be back long before now."

"Spike called Ozaire. You know Ozaire? Lil's husband. He helps out at Homer's place and at the church. He said Lil was probably with her sister in Loreauville. The sister says she went back to Toussaint hours ago."

"I'm going straight to the rectory," Annie said. "They might need help."

"So, what did Lil do with the dog?" Max asked.

"If they could find Lil, they'd ask her."

CHAPTER 20

"A sheriff knows things are out of control when the whole damn town moves a meetin' about a crime to the *rectory*," Spike said, clattering into Cyrus's kitchen, the heels of his boots ringing. "What happened to this kind of get-together bein' held at the station?" He nodded at Guy who gave a sloppy salute.

Cyrus's kitchen was pretty crowded and he forgave Spike for sounding off. The man was up to his eyes in missing women and the breaks weren't coming his way. "It's because Lil's expected back here—we hope," Cyrus told him. "We want to be around when she shows up. We're not meetin' about a crime as far as we know."

Spike ignored Cyrus and pointed at Annie. "Dr. Reb told me she's on her way over to take a look at you." His attention shifted from Annie to Max. Spike's eyes narrowed. "You'd better get in line for medical attention. What the hell's goin' on around here?" He glanced at Cyrus. "Sorry, Father."

"Never could keep his mouth clean," Homer said. He slouched

off in a corner by himself, his elbow propped on a white-tiled counter.

Spike stared at Max again. "Your old buddy Tom Walen's blown any cover you thought you had in this town. He's made sure folks are thinkin' you could save us a lot of grief and money by lettin' on what you did with Michele Riley."

Max knew any response he made would sound defensive.

"That's like accusin' him," Annie said. She turned a lighter shade of pale so the scratches on her face glared. "They couldn't even try him on those two other women. He's bein' trapped by gossip."

"If he's trapped, he'll do it himself," Spike said. "Or maybe I should say he's already done it himself. You'll need to account for your movements today and this evening, Max. Unless Lil shows up first—alive and healthy."

"Now you're tryin' to say he's done somethin' to Lil?" Annie jutted her chin. "That's just wrong, Spike."

Nothing was good about the situation, but Annie's attempt to protect him eased Max's pent-up anger.

The smell of coffee, good as it probably was, turned Annie's stomach. Max might get arrested because some people could turn rumors into facts.

No one broke the silence. Most wouldn't look at one another.

Annie could scarcely bear to see Madge. As worried as she must be about Lil, Annie had figured out that for Madge, little Millie was the recipient of all the love the woman couldn't give to… Annie glanced at Cyrus and her eyes filled with tears. He watched Madge like a desperate man. He had made the Church his bride, but he cared deeply for Madge, and not just as a friend the way they both pretended. Did they fool themselves? Annie wondered.

"I want to hear it again," Spike said and cleared his throat. "From the top. Everything any of you can remember about Lil's movements today. Sometimes you hear somethin' you didn't notice before."

"From the top," Homer muttered. "You'd think we were havin' one of those musical rehearsals."

Spike shook his head. He went to the coffeepot and poured a mug, starting a trend. "Before we get to that," he stepped aside to let Guy get at the pot, "I want to know where everyone is. Folks shouldn't be taking out their own search parties without keeping us informed."

Madge, seated at the kitchen table, stirred and looked up. "Marc Girard, Joe and Ellie Gable. And I heard Tom Walen is out there, too—Michele *is* his fiancée. All kinds of people from around town and the outlying areas are out there. Jilly went with the Gables."

"Great," Guy said, cradling his mug. "I should have told her to stay home." Since he followed Annie and Max back to Toussaint, he'd been a watchful shadow. He had a big, black, mostly Lab at his heel. Each time Guy stood in one place long enough, the dog flopped down and rested her head on his feet. Goldilocks traveled in the car with him most places.

"Work, would it?" Cyrus said to Guy, who frowned. "Tellin' Jilly to stay home?"

Guy pulled in one corner of his mouth.

They all heard an engine draw into the parking lot out front. Footsteps crunched on the gravel path around the house and the kitchen door opened with a bang. Wazoo marched in first with Charlotte Patin, Spike's mother-in-law, right behind.

"This is what I thought, me," Wazoo said, glaring in all directions. "Our dear friend, Lil, is missin' out there and where are all of you? Drinkin' coffee in God man's kitchen and *talkin'* about it. Where's Ozaire?" She peered from face to face. "He'd better be searchin' for his wife."

"He's out along the bayou," Madge said in a small voice. "Gator Hibbs is with him, and his boy, Wally."

"So what are you waitin' for—Lil's giblets delivered in a pie?"

"Wazoo!" Madge stood up and left the room.

"Sometimes you're a bit harsh," Charlotte Patin said. Her short gray hair stood up in spikes. An attractive woman, small and vibrant, she spoke to Wazoo but settled her eyes on Homer who appeared to whistle soundlessly. He avoided her eyes. Charlotte, who wore Homer's diamond ring, didn't look a happy woman.

"I'm harsh?" Wazoo said. "We got women droppin' like flies around here, and I'm harsh?" She sidled closer to Max. "Me, I got nothin' serious against you, but if I don't say it, someone else will. How come you're here chattin' like a member of the community? You couldn't find one soul who doesn't know all about you."

Although he'd wondered the same thing, Max kept quiet.

Annie made fists. "What's gotten into you?" she said to Wazoo. "Surely we all know the bad luck Max's had, but you better remember there's been nothing proved against him."

"Let's calm down," Spike said. He gave Wazoo a hard look. "Might be a good idea if you learned to keep your mouth shut now and then. Think first. There's nothing' bein' said here that isn't general knowledge—or won't be shortly."

In other words, Max thought, even if he was a serial killer, it didn't matter what he heard. "What does that mean?" he blurted out to Spike, surprising himself. "You'd just as soon have me where you can see me?"

"No," Spike said. "You're puttin' words in my mouth. I meant what I said. We're not discussin' secrets here."

Wazoo gave a bark of laughter. "What he means is we don't have no secrets here because we can't keep any." She winked at Max. "Anyways, we know what you know so it's all the same. And when we hear all about where Lil's been, either you'll be findin' out news, or listenin' to old news."

He considered that and decided giving her a wink in return was best.

"Okay, Sheriff," Wazoo said, looking pleased with herself. "What's next?"

"You women stay here and hope Lil shows. The rest of us better get to the command center at the station."

"Where you'll make more plans to make more plans?" Wazoo said. "Tell it like it is. You don't know where to start lookin' and neither does anyone else."

Madge came back in and got herself some coffee. She didn't appear any less subdued.

Max went near the window and stood next to Annie. "How are you doing?" he said.

"Doesn't get much worse than this."

"Uh-uh. Thanks for sticking up for me. Don't shut me out again, Annie."

She looked around but no one was taking notice of them. "I'm tryin' to believe in you. I want to."

"I'll take whatever you can give me," he said.

Annie turned her scratched and bloodied hands from side to side, checking them out. "I don't know what's going to happen," she said. "All I want is to find Michele and Lil—and poor little Millie."

"I want that more than I can say." He looked at his feet. "That's an awful small dog."

Annie crossed her arms. "That doesn't mean she can't survive."

"Who's tellin' the story?" Spike asked loudly. He stared at his father. "From the top."

"As long as you don't expect Homer to do it, there's hope," Charlotte said in very unCharlotte-like tones. "He's gotta sulk. Hard to talk when you're sulkin'."

"Anybody *not* know the whole story?" Spike asked, his mouth drawn tight.

"I don't," Wazoo said. She turned to Annie. "You got that bag I told you to keep?"

Annie had forgotten all about it. "Yes."

Wazoo gave a short nod. "Get on with it," she said to Spike.

"Correct any mistakes I make, please, Madge," Spike said. "You probably know the story better than I do."

Madge nodded, yes.

"This afternoon Lil said she wanted to visit her sister in Loreauville and drop off some food," Spike said. "The sister hasn't been well."

"Excuses," Wazoo muttered. "Anythin' to get out of work."

Spike pointed a warning finger at her. "Save it. Madge, you were plannin' to take Millie to the vet in Loreauville, but Lil said she'd take her. Right so far?"

Madge nodded again.

"When Lil wasn't back by eight, you called Ozaire who said she sometimes spends the night with her sister."

"And I called the vet," Madge said, getting paler as she spoke. "Lil had taken Millie in for her shot. I called Lil's sister and she said Lil left hours ago. She hasn't been seen since and neither has Millie. Lil doesn't believe in cell phones. Your people have covered all the roads between here and there, Spike. No accidents. It's hard to search in the dark but that's already underway regardless." She pushed her mug aside. "And that's where I'm goin' now."

Cyrus held her arm. "I'll come with you."

"No," Spike said. "I've got folks runnin' in all directions and not a plan between 'em. It'll be light in a few hours and I want to wait till then."

"No," Madge said. "It's wet out there. She's little and she doesn't have much body fat...and there's critters..."

"With any luck Lil lost her way and she'll show up," Guy said rapidly. "Going every which way in the dark isn't likely to help."

"It might if we heard something," Madge said. She didn't have to add that she was thinking about Millie's bark.

Homer still hadn't acknowledged Charlotte. "I wouldn't let Vivian come," she said to Spike. "She wanted to."

"She'd have gone right back home," Spike said at once. "Worry's the last thing she needs about now."

"What's your problem, Homer Devol," Charlotte said suddenly. "You look like you swallowed somethin' nasty. And while we're at it, where have you been all these days?"

With interest, Cyrus watched red climb Homer's thin cheeks.

"He's got a bug up his ass," Wazoo said. She pushed out her lips and shook her head slowly from side to side. "But it's his bug and I sure wouldn't want to touch it."

"What time is it?" Madge asked, ignoring Wazoo.

"Almost two in the morning," Max said.

"Your brothers left the same time I did," Charlotte said. "Think they were going to the station."

"Which is where I'm headed,'" Spike said. "Any of you who feel like gettin' organized and ready to go—come on. Rest of you can stick around the rectory, wait to hear somethin', and talk about how no one does anything right around here."

"Watch your mouth," Homer snapped. "Just because your wife lets you get away with it, doesn't mean the rest of us are easy to push."

"Stop it," Madge said. She wound her fingers tightly together. "I'm going to the station, too. It's because she hasn't been missin' twenty-four hours, isn't it?" she said to Spike.

"What is?" He looked puzzled.

"That's why you aren't out there now. You don't count someone as missing for twenty-four hours."

Spike said, "That's not it. There's an alert out. The switchboard's fully manned at the station. And there's groups out there. I'm worried some of you will get into more trouble if you start out now, and we'll be lookin' for you, too."

Spike got a call and looked relieved at the interruption. He spoke low and while he did, Charlotte stood close to Homer and he dropped his head close to hers.

"This is making me crazy," Max said. "Everything's so disorganized."

"If something's happened to Lil, they won't be able to suggest you did it," Annie said. She smacked both hands over her face. "I didn't mean that the way it sounded."

"Sure you did. Depending on the times involved you could be right. Didn't anything bad ever happen in this town before I came along?"

"Of course it did," she said, moving nearer to him. "What's goin' to happen?"

"Lil will be found. Dead or alive."

She drove her fingers into his arm.

"Well, am I wrong?" He stared into her eyes. "Then they'll…then Michele. We'll know what happened to her—more or less."

"What do you mean?" she whispered. "More or less."

"That's all they got on Isabel and Carol. More or less. If they'd had anything definite, maybe they could have found the killer." He had to believe he could convince Annie he wasn't that killer. The way Spike curled around his phone, his voice inaudible, only increased the tension.

Another vehicle approached. This time Marc Girard's wife, Reb O'Brien Girard, let herself in through the kitchen door. She carried a medical bag and put it on the table. "Did Marc leave?" she said.

"He's at the station with another group," Guy said.

Spike continued to talk on the phone and Charlotte didn't even turn around.

"Hey," Reb said. "I see my patients." She went directly to Annie and Max. "Let's take a look at you two."

She looked closely, first at Annie's face, then at Max's. She opened the neck of his shirt wider, then checked their hands. Annie expected Max to protest at being ministered to, but he didn't.

Minutes later Reb had swabbed scratches, applied a butterfly bandage to the cut on Max's brow, pronounced the marks on Annie's face superficial and stood back where she could look at them. "Bruises. Cuts. And you look like hell. I suggest the two of you go to bed and get some rest."

Silence followed.

"Could be if you weren't so tired, you wouldn't bang into hard objects, or fall down, or whatever you've been doin' to yourselves."

"Thanks," Annie said, casting Max a warning glance. She could almost see him trying to figure out how to ask the doctor to check her over more thoroughly.

Max cleared his throat and offered Reb a hand. "Thanks, Doc," he said.

"I never thought I'd be the one patchin' *you* up," Reb said, and gave him a quick grin while she tossed stuff back in her bag. "It's always good to see you, Max. We'll have to get you and Roche out to the house again. And Kelly, of course." Long red hair slid from a twist at the back of her head and her green eyes didn't miss a thing. She glanced quickly from Annie to Max and he could see her making correct assumptions.

Max smiled at her. "We'll look forward to it." He wanted her to give Annie a physical but this wasn't the time to say anything. And if he did get to it, he couldn't be sure Annie wouldn't dig in her heels and refuse. Yes he could—she wouldn't go for it.

Madge had taken to pacing. Now and again she opened the back door a few inches and peered outside. Then she'd wander from the kitchen and along to the front door where she repeated the process.

Annie wanted to hug her and try to make her feel better but she knew how she'd feel if Irene went missing.

"If that isn't the dumbest thing I ever did hear, Homer Devol," Charlotte Patin said, her voice rising. With her hands on her hips, she planted her feet apart. "You have the nerve, at a time like this when people are in real trouble, to complain because I've got more money than you?"

"Oh, my God," Max said, but not quietly enough. "I don't believe this."

Madge ran out of the kitchen again.

"Listen up," Spike said, he gestured with his phone and bounced on the balls of his feet.

"You listen up," Charlotte said. "Your father says he's not having people think he's a kept man the way you are." She turned to Guy. "You, too, Guy. Your wife's got a business and you're a hanger-on. Did you know that?"

Guy's response was a huge smile. "Better talk to Jilly about that. I'm not havin' any problems."

"I told you not to say anything like that to Charlotte," Spike told Homer. "You old fool. Listenin' to gossip."

Homer stood up real straight. "Old fool, huh? I guess it's time for me to be movin' on."

He strode toward the door but didn't make it before Charlotte cut him off and slammed her engagement ring into his hand. She rushed out of the kitchen, probably following Madge.

Homer stared at the ring, his face set. He put the diamond in his pocket and banged out of the back door.

"I've got news, dammit," Spike said. Muscles worked in his jaws.

"A woman was just taken to the emergency room at the hospital in Breaux Bridge. Sounds like Lil."

He had the attention of everyone in the room.

Cyrus hurried into the passageway and called, "Madge, get in here. Wait please, Spike, I want her to hear this." Then he went out back and returned with Homer who must have been hanging around.

Madge and Charlotte came running, Madge with red eyes.

"We think Lil just arrived at the emergency room in Breaux Bridge," Spike repeated. "From the description it's got to be her."

Marge shook visibly. "Either it is or it isn't. Is...did she have..."

"I don't know," Spike said. "I'm sorry. I'm going there now."

Guy raised his brows at Max. "It is Lil, or it isn't," he said. "Or is this woman too seriously injured for them to be sure."

"She's injured," Spike said. "I don't know how badly. But she's not talking."

CHAPTER 2

"Why did you make sure everyone knew you were driving with me?" Max said, swinging his car out of the upper lot at the rectory.

"You didn't want me to?"

He looked sideways at Annie. She stared out of the window at darkness, unbroken but for the headlights of other cars leaving for Breaux Bridge or the sheriff's offices. "You know I want you with me. You also know it may not be the best idea."

"It's obvious we're friends," she said. "Why pretend anymore? Do you think Spike would have said as much as he did in front of you if he thought you were potential enemy number one. If you were the bad guy you wouldn't be hanging out the way you are. Why not decide things are coming to a head and they're goin' to change? I still think if folks see I trust you it can only help your case."

"I want to kiss you," he said, staring straight ahead.

Annie chuckled. "That would be nice, but I'd rather you keep this sparkly little car of yours on the road."

"Where's your sense of adventure?" He gripped her above the knee and stroked her thigh.

She caught his fingers and wound them into hers. "I guess we shouldn't waste opportunities."

In other words, she did think his world would fall down around his ears but she wanted him to know she cared for him anyway. "We won't do that," he told her.

"Your name is goin' to be cleared."

His lungs expanded fully for the first time in ages. "I want to believe that. Annie, I also want you to have a physical." He knew he might be pushing his luck.

"Where did that come from?"

"I've been thinking about it for days. If...look, there's some reason for these episodes you've been having. Put it down to professional habit but I'd feel better if I knew you were well and the aberrations will pass."

Aberrations wasn't a word Annie liked much. "A physical won't—" She frowned at him. "Sometimes people have problems. Who knows why? There isn't always a way to find out, is there?"

She had him there. "I guess not. We're going to Spike's offices?"

"Are we? Is that where you want to go?"

"You know it's not. I want to find out how Lil's doing firsthand. And I can't stand waiting to find out about Madge's dog." He might as well be completely honest.

"The hospital in Breaux Bridge then. Don't be surprised if we get kicked out."

Max smiled at her. "We won't get kicked out—not unless Spike flips and accuses me of something he has no proof of."

"I see." She slid lower in the seat. "The doors will open wide for Dr. Savage."

"Something like that." He couldn't get rid of the feeling that

Annie had a hidden side, that her reactions weren't always spontaneous. "The way I figure it, if I'd done something to Lil, I wouldn't confront her in the hospital in front of the law."

"You're right," she said and laughed. "I should have thought of that."

"When we're done at the hospital, can we go somewhere together?"

She turned sideways in her seat and inclined her head, watched him until he had to look at her. "What?" he said.

"You don't beat about the bush, do you?"

He smiled. "You could be jumping to conclusions. Could be I just want to talk."

"True. Is that what you want?"

He kept his eyes on the road but with the backs of his fingers, he rubbed her cheek. "Come back to Rosebank with me."

She put her heels on the seat and wrapped her arms around her legs. "I'd be embarrassed if someone saw me."

"They don't have to."

"I don't like sneakin' around," Annie said.

"Then don't. We're grown-ups."

She didn't give him an answer.

"Have you seen Bobby Colbert lately?" Max said.

She had done her best to forget about Bobby. "He was at Pappy's one evening but that was nothing to worry about. I'm goin' to hope he gives up on me."

"But you worry about him? He's been on my mind ever since he shot his mouth off at Hungry Eyes." He knew his mistake at once.

"What did he say?" Annie said.

He gave himself a few moments to look for an escape route. "He tried to convince me you'd been a wild child." Better to approximate the truth than outright lie. "The idea makes me laugh. I can't see you as a drugged-out rebel."

"I wasn't," she said. "Did Bobby say I used drugs?"

"No." *Sheeit,* he should have said yes, now he'd have to look for a different exit from the conversation.

"So what did he say?"

"Nothing sensible. The main thing is that he sounded unhinged and if he does pop up again, I want to know. I'll get him warned off officially."

She thought about that. "I'm glad you're on my side."

"I hope I can always be there for you, Annie."

Did he mean what he'd said?

Did he mean what she thought he did?

"If I ask you a question," Max said, "will you try not to get mad?"

Which meant he was about to ask her something that would make her mad. "I'll do my best." She found a comb in her purse and ran it through her tangled hair. "A shower would be nice."

"You can do that at my place."

He wasn't the kind to give up. "How close are we to the hospital?"

"I'm following Spike's directions. Can't be that much farther. I've wanted to say I'm sorry I went roaring out of your place that night. You didn't deserve that."

"I'm more or less over it now." She was and she wasn't. He'd said things that still raised issues for her.

"Okay, that question I want to ask. The things you've seen revolved around fire."

Annie took a breath and held it.

"You've got to face it sometime. I talked to Roche about what little I do know. I told him the physical symptoms you showed. He wonders if you did know something about my background before the episodes started, but you've blocked it out."

"I can't talk about it."

Max slowed down so much, other cars passed them. "You can't talk about it. When it happens, it's terrible, right?"

"Yes," she whispered.

"You described it to me—pretty much. Annie, why would you meet me, then dream up something that had changed my life? Just like that? I don't believe it could happen that way."

She curled into an even tighter ball. "You'll have to because it's true."

"Okay. Will you talk to Roche?"

"I don't want to."

He felt her misery. "But will you? He's a nice guy, the nicest guy I ever met."

"He's your twin. You're biased."

"True. Will you see him?"

A wise woman knew when to throw a man a scrap. "I'll think about it."

"Good. I think that's Breaux Bridge up ahead."

"It is," Annie said.

"Sometimes I forget you're from around here," Max said. "Do you think you ever heard about, you know, a case where the victims died the way you've seen in your mind?"

"*No.*" An explosive sensation swelled in her head. "No. Don't talk about it again. Until last night it was days since it happened. I want it to go away. Please."

"Okay. Okay, cher. Isn't that what they say around here?"

She nodded. "Only you say it 'shar.' Look, I only want to say this once because I can't deal with it. Some people do have a sort of second sight. I could be one of them. I don't expect it to stick around, or I hope it doesn't. Once before I had visions, or whatever you want to call them. They stopped. That was after a trauma. I could be supersensitive and now I'm picking up on something else."

"Okay."

"You don't believe me," Annie said.

"I want to," Max said. "I'm prepared to go with your theory until a better one comes along——cher."

He made her smile at the darkest times. "There's that word again," she said.

"I like it."

"So do I. Max, it's stupid but I wish…well, I wish things could be different but then I think that you and I are an unlikely couple. You'd never have come to Toussaint if bad things hadn't happened to you and then we wouldn't have met at all. But I'm not really your type. You need a smart, educated woman."

"Don't say that again."

His sharpness made her tingle. "It's true." But she felt embarrassed by his anger, then foolish because she had no proof he thought of her as other than a convenient distraction.

"You are a smart woman. And there isn't a particular type of woman for me."

"I shouldn't have brought it up."

He glanced at her once more. "Yes, I think you should. Rather that than have you dreaming up some other myth. Let go, will you? Let go and let things happen if they're meant to."

Another myth?

A policeman stood outside a cubicle in the hospital's emergency department. The walls of the cubicle were half-glass and Annie saw Lil on a gurney inside with medical types moving around her. Spike and Deputy Lori stood by her, and her husband, Ozaire, hovered at her other side.

Max felt Annie tense up. "Cool it," he told her. "She doesn't look in bad shape to me." Not that he could tell so much from here except that the woman had apparently found the ability to talk. He saw her mouth moving rapidly.

"Have you been in?" Cyrus asked from behind Max.

He turned to see the priest with Madge. Of course she'd want to come. Not that she'd find any little black and white dogs around here. He felt sorry for her.

"Spike's in there," Max said. "We'll have to wait and see if we're allowed in."

Annie rubbed Madge's shoulder, then, awkwardly, gave her a hug and held still when the other woman started to cry softly.

The door to the cubicle opened and Spike came out. He approached Max and said, "I think it would be a good idea if you talked to her. Remind her you're a surgeon and give some sort of medical reason for being in there. Interested party or somethin'. I don't know. I'd like to see her reaction to you."

No kidding. Max smothered a smile. This truly was small-town law in action. Spike came right out and told a could-be suspect how he might manage to incriminate himself.

But it could be that complete honesty ought to give a man comfort.

"Okay?" Spike said, and when Max nodded, continued, "Let me get back in there, then give me a couple of minutes. Be patient, the rest of you. She'll be wantin' to tell her tale to each of you."

"What's she been saying?" Madge asked.

Spike puffed up his cheeks. "That's another thing. I'm not sure what to make of what she is sayin'." He sniffed. "Maybe one of you'll figure out what I mean."

"Millie?" Madge said, and bowed her head. "Sorry. I know I shouldn't be fussin' about a dog now but she's all I've got."

"Lil hasn't said," Spike told them with a mildly horrified expression. He hurried back into the cubicle.

"They'll want to give Lil time to talk things through at her own pace," Max said, with a curious glance from Madge to Cyrus. His face had the kind of stony expression Max hadn't seen on the man before.

"Of course," Madge said. "I feel so stupid and weak."

"If there's one thing you're not, it's weak," Cyrus said, and he sounded ferocious. "You've got more guts than most people could ever hope to have. Stay here."

He tapped on the glass door to the cubicle and let himself in. A nurse smiled at him and shut the door again.

"Power of the collar," Max said but got no response from the two women.

Cyrus went to Lil who immediately clutched the hand he held out. He began to talk and Lil nodded, her face relaxing a little. Cyrus pointed to where Madge and Annie stood with Max and talked some more.

Lil's expression changed, went blank, then crumpled. Max and Annie embraced Madge between them as Lil started to cry.

"She's gone," Madge said softly. "Millie's gone. I was afraid to love her so much."

Max met Annie's eyes over Madge's bowed head. "You can't love too much," he said. "My mother is a very wise woman, and she told me that."

Annie swallowed and held on tight to Madge's shaking body. Platitudes rushed forward but Annie swallowed them. Suggesting Millie might still be all right wouldn't help.

"I'd better go in," Max said. "Spike's giving me the eye."

"We'll be okay," Annie said, and felt him take a second too long studying her before he turned away.

"I'm glad Lil's okay," Madge said when they'd watched the patient interacting with her audience some more. "She doesn't look scared of Max to me."

Annie felt briefly irritated. "Why should she? Whatever

happened to her, it's obviously nothing like the thing with Michele Riley in Toussaint. And Max wasn't involved with that."

"No, of course not."

"Oh, Madge," Annie said. "I'm sorry I snapped. What is going on around here? One thing after another. I'm so confused."

"That's because you're in love with Max Savage," Madge said. Her body had stiffened and she stood straight.

Annie opened her mouth, but closed it again.

"You can't argue, can you?" Madge said. "Be careful, Annie—you know what I mean. But don't you give up on that man. I'm supposed to be a good judge of character and I don't feel anythin' bad about him."

Annie could have kissed her. "Neither do I. But I'm not a fool. I was hurt before…you know how it is. We all have our brushes with thinking we've found Mr. Wonderful."

"I know how it is. Here comes Cyrus."

Once he was alone with them, Cyrus drew them to a row of chairs along one wall. "Sit," he said. He remained standing. "She says she thinks she had some sort of "turn" and went off the road," he said. "Ended up in a ditch and doesn't remember getting out of her car. Thinks she got disoriented and wandered off."

Annie waited.

"She says Millie was with her," Cyrus said. When Madge looked up at him, he failed miserably at an attempted smile. "That was before she went off the road. She didn't think about her afterward."

"Where's the car?" Madge said, shifting to the edge of her seat.

"They're looking for it now. Lil's pretty unclear." He touched Madge's hair and dropped his hand immediately. "There is something else, though. Lil says she was frightened off the road."

"You said she had an attack."

"Uh-huh. After she got frightened."

Annie's muscles had tensed until they ached. "Is that it? Just vague talk?"

"Not quite. She says someone ran across the street like they were going in front of her car. Instead he rushed at her window. That's why she thinks she swerved."

"I would, too," Annie said. "How awful. Did she recognize the person."

"No. You know how dark it must have been. And she says it was raining then. All she saw was a good-sized man. She's sure it was a man. In a jacket or coat with a hood pulled forward."

CHAPTER 22

Max:

Tonight should have taken Annie out of the picture. She should have realized you're a dangerous man. I am getting very angry with interference in my affairs. I will not wait forever.

What do you think you're doing with the country girl? You know you're poison to any woman. She's a complication I don't need or want but if anything happens to her, we'll know who to blame.

I like that! You didn't think I had a sense of humor, did you?

Don't worry, I won't lose my focus. I know exactly what must be done. All there is left for me is to wait and watch, then act. Soon I will write again and tell you how the end will come.

CHAPTER 23

"You're sure you've got something?" Spike said, dropping inside Guy Gautreaux's gray sedan in the hospital parking lot.

"Sure," Guy said. "You didn't mention me in there? About it being me who called you?"

Spike yanked the creaky door shut. "Nope. When I go in again I don't want a bunch of questions about you comin' here. What's up?"

Guy took his time working a notebook out of a back pocket in his jeans. "How's Lil doin'? Still not talkin'?"

"She's talking now. Once she saw me she wouldn't shut up. I'm not sure she's okay. She's quieted down in the last half hour. There's a pretty good bump on her head. They're doin' more blood work. And they're fussing over bruises on her neck."

Guy looked sideways at him. "Why?"

"Beats me." Spike shrugged.

Guy pushed his rangy body deeper into his seat. Even in semi-darkness the prominent bones in his face showed. "We could go round some more on this one but I'll wait," he said. "Who's with her?"

"Cyrus and Max."

"Max, huh?"

"He wasn't invited to come. I figured if he was so eager to find out if Lil was talkin' I'd see if she announced he was the thug who scared her when she was driving."

"You didn't mention that," Guy said.

"I haven't had a chance," Spike said and told Guy a brief version of what Lil had said.

Guy drummed his fingers on the steering wheel. "That's interesting," he said. "There wasn't an opportunity to tell you about Max and Annie."

"Other than how they look like they've got something going?" Spike said. "Do they?"

"Could be. She's protective of him. Wazoo persuaded me to keep an eye out for Annie last night. She'd gone to an undeveloped lot near St. Martinville. She went on her own."

Spike considered the thought of Annie going to some deserted place at night, alone. "Why was she there?"

"She's going to have to explain that herself. I found her with Max."

"At this lot?" Spike asked.

"Yeah. Things were tense, I'm tellin' you. I didn't hear much before they saw me but he was tryin' to persuade her over something and he wasn't gettin' far. She'd made the marks on him—the ones we saw at the rectory. I think she'd fought him."

"What about the marks on her?" Spike said. He looked toward the hospital. "They're together. They were standing together at the rectory."

"Annie reckoned she fell. She had a lot of thin excuses. She's coming to see me late tomorrow—today now."

"I think I need to step in right away," Spike said.

"On what grounds? What reason do you have apart from what I say I saw? She's with him of her own will. You saw her run after him at your place and asking to ride with him. Would she do that if she was afraid of him? When I started to intervene she told me to back off."

"So let them be?"

"He'd be a fool to lay a finger on her when everyone knows they're together. Max Savage is no fool," Guy said.

"I'll want directions to where you found them. Sounds like we gonna have to take a good look at it."

"I can see that," Guy said.

"I don't like the two of them bein' together, alone," Spike said. "I want them followed. You said you've got something on Lil's accident."

"If it was an accident."

Spike leaned a shoulder against the window and waited.

"Where did she say she was goin'?" Guy said.

"Home to Toussaint." Spike took a stick of gum Guy offered and folded it between his teeth. "She'd been to Loreauville to visit a sister and take Madge's dog to the vet. She was going home."

"That's what I thought you'd say." Guy did some chewing of his own. "Only she wasn't."

"She what?" Spike sat up straight. "Where the hell do you think she *was* goin'. Lil isn't the secret-life type."

"People can surprise you. If she'd been headed to Toussaint from Loreauville, she'd be going northwest. If I'm right, and I know I am, Lil went off the road on Landry Way."

"I'll be..." Spike slipped his Stetson to the back of his head and rubbed at his beard stubble. "Landry Way. Landry Way? Gimme a minute."

"It's—"

"I know where it is now, dammit." He laughed. "Just didn't recognize the name. Drive it every day. I never think about what it's called. It's the cut between the road Rosebank's on and the main drag into Toussaint. If you're right, Lil did lie, or she didn't bother to tell the real details."

"Question is, why?" Guy said. "After Loreauville she must have driven away from Toussaint."

"Not far, though," Spike said. He tapped a wobbly hula girl cemented to the dash. She bobbed on her spring. "You think Lil drove around a half mile south, more or less, and turned onto Landry Way. Do you know how far she got on Landry before the accident?"

Guy pressed his head into the rest. "She was maybe a hundred yards from the road to Toussaint, only she was driving toward it, not away."

"How do you know?" Spike said slowly.

"Skid marks—and a flare. You didn't ask why I was on Landry."

"Gimme," Spike said, beckoning.

"I decided to go looking for some sign of where Lil went off the road. Couldn't figure out why your guys didn't find anything. I couldn't either at first. But I'd passed Loreauville before I knew it, so right away I took the first side street. That was Landry. Then I made a U-turn and started back. There were the skid marks. And residue from a flare."

There had better be more than skid marks to place Lil at that site. Spike said, "And?"

"She drives a blue Hyundai. Two door. I think she saw the guy she told you about and speeded up instead of slowing down. She lost control. I found the vehicle buried pretty deep in the trees there. It must have been really movin' to go that far. The plates checked out."

"But you're sayin' she got out of the car, got back to Landry and lit a flare? And then wandered away and wasn't found for hours?"

"No, I'm not saying that. Did she tell you she lit it?"

Spike gave a single shake of the head. "No."

"That's because she didn't do it."

"Who did?"

"The man in the hood. Looks like a setup to me. He threw down the flare and waited for her."

Spike couldn't fault the logic, nor could he buy it whole. "She'd have told me. I don't suppose there was any sign of Madge's dog?"

"No, I wish there had been. Lil wouldn't tell you if she's got something she wants to hide."

Spike let out a long breath. "If the Hyundai isn't where you say it is, I'll know small-town life is getting to you."

"That man who scared her," Guy poked a finger into Spike's arm. "He wanted to make sure she kept whatever secrets she's got."

"Maybe," Spike said. "Maybe."

CHAPTER 24

"I still don't see why Spike said we should leave the hospital," Annie said. She stood in the middle of Max's sitting room, exactly where she'd been for the five minutes since they arrived. "Not the way he did. He dismissed us."

"He's got a lot on his mind," Max said. He hadn't liked being "dismissed" as Annie put it, not when the action had picked up. First he was sent out of Lil's room, then he'd seen a new doctor go in and have a nurse put screens around the bed. Next came a lab technician followed by another doctor and Max wished he could find out what was going on. He hadn't liked the changes he had noticed in Lil's condition.

"I should have stayed at my apartment," Annie said. She had insisted on going there first to shower and to check on Irene. The cat hadn't been pleased when they left.

"I'm glad you didn't stay there," Max said, keeping his distance from her. He didn't want to do anything to scare her off completely. "Would you like a drink?"

She shook her head, no.

"You haven't had anything for hours. I can make coffee, if you like."

"Coffee keeps me awake."

Their eyes met. "I wouldn't want to do that at this time of the morning." He tried a smile. "You need your rest."

"Don't we all?"

Did they? "Yes." He could hardly grasp that she had agreed to come back to Rosebank with him—even if she was expressing doubts now. She'd brought a small bag of things she'd taken from her apartment and insisted they come into the house just as he would on his own. Not that it made any difference when the place was silent and they hadn't encountered anyone on their way through the front hall, up the stairs to the second floor, and along another hall to Max's rooms.

"You feel awkward, too," Annie said.

"Not really." Just like a man hanging from a frayed rope over a tub filled with eggs. "Please sit down."

"It's a nice room." She meant it. A man's room, classy, clubbish, with dark wood paneling and leather furniture. Books hogged horizontal spaces, some in bookcases, a lot in piles—some open and turned facedown, others stacked on the floor. He favored landscape paintings and the ones he had looked original and old.

"You don't look comfortable, Annie."

Green velvet draperies stood open over linen roman shades. "Neither do you. We'll get through it." She liked the way that had sounded. Sophisticated. Nonchalant.

Spike's announcement that Lil had mentioned a man in a hood had shaken Annie badly. An immediate check of Max's expression revealed no reaction, but it was fact that after he stormed out of her apartment on the night they'd been together, she'd seen a figure in a hooded garment pass the gate to the alley outside. And she was almost sure she saw the same or a similar person at St. Cécil's, only she'd been waking from a dream and didn't trust much of what she'd thought at the time. But the coincidences were piling up.

"If I haven't already told you," Max said, "I'm happy to have you with me in what I call home these days."

"Thank you."

Annie waffled, unable to decide whether to mention her own sightings to Max. He would think she had piggybacked onto Lil's comment and dreamed up hooded menaces of her own. Spike would probably decide the same thing.

"Bobby Colbert came into Pappy's yesterday evening."

"Yes, so you said earlier," Max said. She couldn't tell if he was worried or furious.

"I didn't intend to mention it at all. I don't know why I did."

"Yes, you do," Max said. "The guy scares you. I've seen it in your eyes when he's mentioned."

Of course he was right. She had brought up Bobby's name deliberately. "He was nice to me." Yet there had been that one sideways stare that menaced her.

"He's not nice," Max said. "He…"

"What. He what?" This wasn't the first time she believed Max stopped himself from saying more about Bobby.

"He bugs me. I wish he'd stay wherever he's supposed to be. Doesn't he have a job?"

"I think so. He always worked in his father's insurance office." Her voice trailed away. Bobby Colbert's parents were people she had tried to wipe from her mind. "Let's not talk about Bobby anymore."

"Did he try to get cozy with you?" Max asked.

Men were always suspicious of any potential competition. She shouldn't expect Max to be any different. "No," she said. He didn't need to get hot under the collar because Bobby pressed for a date.

Max narrowed his eyes as if he were deciding whether to believe her.

"I'm good at looking out for myself," she told him.

His hand shot out so fast, he had a tight hold on her arm before she could react. "I want you to stay away from him."

She looked at his hand but it stayed there. "I didn't ask him to come by."

"Promise you'll call me if he comes near you again."

Men didn't get to push Annie Duhon around anymore, no matter what excuse they thought they had. She wrenched her arm away. "Thanks for your concern."

He looked her in the eyes and nodded. "Sorry. I got carried away. Put it down to…" His chin rose. "I care what happens to you. Friends are allowed to do that."

"As long as they don't get overbearing," Annie said. She scarcely recognized herself as she was now, determined, at least outwardly, even when she was shrinking inside. She patted his arm. "Thanks for caring." Again she felt proud of sticking up for herself. She'd come a long way.

Max smiled, a gentle smile. "It's good to know what you like."

"I feel so awful for Madge," Annie said to change the subject. "Millie isn't likely to survive, is she?"

"Probably not, but it isn't cold, so that's not a problem. We can always hope. If there weren't so many animals around out there, and if I thought she had any skills to take care of herself… Poor little devil."

Annie looked away. Her eyes stung and she didn't want him to see her reaction. Would Madge stay at the rectory tonight, or come back here? When Annie and Max left the hospital, Madge and Cyrus were still there, sitting on chairs outside Lil's cubicle. Annie wouldn't like Madge to see her at Rosebank and know she'd been with Max all night. If she decided to leave, Max would have to drive her.

"I like your desk," she said. The silences were long and awkward. "It's big. Looks like it's meant for a man."

"Thanks," he said. "I'm glad you like it."

"The whole room looks as if it was done with you in mind."

He smiled and bowed. "Thank you. That means I know what I like. And you understand me. The furniture's mine."

His delight amused Annie.

The smiles faded and with them, the slight thaw.

She had come to sleep with him. They both knew it. Annie smiled again. And Max smiled back. He came close enough to put a finger under her chin and tilt his head sideways to study her.

"In a day or so you'll hardly see any marks on your face," he said, vaguely removed, professional even. Then he looked into her eyes and there was nothing professional about that look. Intensely, deeply blue in the warmly shadowed room, his gaze probed for answers. He expected to make love to her and he was searching for clues to how she felt, what she wanted, how to break through any doubts she had.

Annie didn't turn away, or even try. "I shouldn't have hit you with the rock."

He finally moved his attention to her mouth. "No, you shouldn't have. But I don't blame you. You were shocked and you were scared. And the other thing was going on—the fire stuff."

She swallowed, tried to swallow again but her mouth was too dry.

Max frowned. "Are you afraid of me?"

"No."

"Too fast, cher. Think about it. You know my history, and you know I'm under suspicion now. The only reason I'm not in custody is because they don't have any evidence—or a body. Are you sure you're not scared to be alone with me?"

Annie stiffened her spine and kept her head up. "I'm sure." And she was—almost. A telephone call from a stranger had sent him after her in St. Martinville. "But I do wonder how you found me."

Of course she did, Max thought. "I got—"

"A call," she finished for him. "And you don't know who it was."

"No, I don't. Annie, I automatically went back where we'd been before. You had that episode there. I thought you might be there trying to figure it out."

"You're starting to know me, too," Annie said.

"I followed your flashlight. Then it went out. I was trying to get to you without scaring you to death."

Her wraith of a smile, the flash of humor in her eyes reminded him again why he liked her so much.

"I believe you," Annie said. "But Guy's goin' to tell Spike all about it and who knows what he'll believe?"

"I know," Max said. "All I can do is wait. I don't expect anything from you. It's just good to have you here."

"But you want something from me."

No smile from her this time.

"Don't you?" she said.

"Yes, I do."

"Then we're even. Too bad the stuff before, the dancing around each other, scares me nuts." If she was a fool to tell him the truth, she'd be a fool.

"You call the shots," Max said.

"I think I did that last time. Mostly."

"And it still wasn't easy on you, was it?" He moved in and held her head, rubbed little circles at the sides of her face with his thumbs. "So what's the answer?"

For once she wished someone else would make decisions for her. She could tell him that, straight out, only her breath blocked her throat.

Above his eyebrow, where the rock had landed first, a circle of skin had gone leaving raw redness and specks of blood behind. A thin welt spread into his hair. Her blow hadn't been too solid.

Annie spread his collar apart and saw where she had scratched him. She'd been thinking about DNA because she expected him to kill her. Now she was alone with him in his rooms.

And glad. If he'd wanted to get rid of her he'd already had his chances.

"Wish I could read your mind," Max said, even though he wasn't so certain he'd like what he saw.

"I've never attacked anyone before." *Only been attacked.* Impetuously she blew softly on his marred skin. "My mom used to do that if I hurt myself."

"Oh, yeah, you can blow on me anytime."

She closed her eyes and her lashes flickered.

Max hesitated. She seemed so vulnerable. *Get on with it or stop.* He kissed her. Kissed her again. And Annie stood there, her face turned up to his, her arms at her sides, responding with her lips alone.

If she wanted to unnerve him, she'd succeeded, but the taste of her, the feel of her mouth, spurred him on. He was hard. Looking at Annie was enough to arouse him. Kissing her, sensing her warmth, imagining her naked in his hands—against his body— drove in the fiery stake.

"You feel good," he said between kisses.

Annie opened her eyes, soft blue eyes. She took a moment to refocus on him. Soft to touch, soft to look at—warm and responsive to hold. When he stroked it, her pale hair flew, fine, reminding him of watching a child blow on a dandelion puff in the sunshine.

Pull yourself together, Savage. He didn't usually have to remind himself he was a scientist, not a dreamer.

"Max," Annie said. "I owe you something. You need to know some things about me."

"You've got a criminal record? Oh, good. That makes me feel better."

Annie frowned at him. Some men couldn't resist turning serious moments into jokes. "This isn't easy for me."

He rested his forehead on hers. "I'm not usually flip."

"I'm..." No, she wouldn't ask him to decide where she should start. How did he know?

Max kissed her again, for a long, hot time, and shifted his hands from her waist to her breasts. He spread his fingers and rubbed, and Annie's belly tightened. Her breasts felt swollen and sensitive. She put her arms around his neck, her hands in his hair, and he covered her bottom, ground her pelvis into his.

No pretending this time. "Max, I want to show you something."

He groaned and pulled her face into the crook of his neck.

"I know," she told him. "I don't want to stop, either. Let me go, please."

His sigh, his convulsive grip on her, didn't help. Max dropped his arms and stepped backward but Annie wished she had done this a better way, sooner, before she'd excited him.

"I'm going to take my clothes off," she said. "Is this the best place?"

Confusion clouded Max's eyes. He scrubbed at them with the heels of his hands. "Are you going to put me on a roller coaster whenever we're together this way?"

For a moment she couldn't make herself say another word.

"I don't think this is a good idea," he said when she'd been quiet too long.

Annie cleared her throat and looked over her shoulder to the only door in the room. "Could we go in the bedroom?"

His expression cleared. "I don't understand you, but be my guest."

She went toward the bedroom, picking up her bag as she went. Her hips didn't sway, the walk wasn't studied, but she had the most desirable ass he'd ever seen. Looking at her started something he used to think only happened to men without minds, men led around by their penises.

He followed her, closed the door behind them while she dropped the bag on the floor and stood by his bed with her back to him.

Remembering, he turned off the lights.

"Don't do that," she said, her voice sharp in the darkness.

"I thought you preferred it."

"I don't."

He obliged her by flipping the wall switch. Low light spread from the bedside lamps again.

"I like this room, too," Annie said quietly.

"Thanks."

She held the hem of her white tank top and pulled it off in one motion. Underneath she wore a pink satin bra. Her skin was as pale as he'd expected.

He crossed his arms and gripped his biceps while she folded the tank.

Blue linen pants slipped easily to her feet and she stepped out. Once again she folded the garment. Max couldn't look away from pink satin hipsters. They fitted smoothly and they weren't demure. Laces crisscrossed an open vee that plunged to the cleft in her bottom.

She reached back and undid the bra, slipped out of it and put it on her neat pile. And Max shook his head. He was also just about out of control. "Annie—"

"Don't touch me!" She faced him. "You'll be kind. That's who you are. But you'll never know how I feel inside or how it is to be crazy about a man, or to have sex with him and feel like you're cheating him while he's makin' love to you."

"You didn't cheat me."

"Come closer."

He started to go to her but she held up a hand before he reached her. "See," she said, pointing to a thigh. "That's the least of it."

Burn scars. "I see. I wondered about your hands but you never said anything, so neither did I."

Wriggling her hips this time, Annie skimmed off her panties. She held them in both hands and turned her head away.

Max looked at her pelvis. His first thought was that he should have noticed from the feeling alone. He took breaths to stuff down the urge to question her.

"You got quite a burn," he said when he could. "I'm sorry you went through so much pain."

But why did she think he, of all people, would be horrified, or disgusted?

"It wasn't fair to hide it away from you the way I did. You deserved to make up your own mind about this."

"You've got scars," he said. "They're well healed." But they had been third degree in most places. He hated how they curled back between her legs. No wonder she'd bled. If she hadn't had sex since it happened, he'd probably broken dry skin.

She shook. Standing on one foot, trying to put her panties back on, Annie wobbled.

"That's it," Max said, closing in and lifting her by the waist. He sat her on the bed and took away the panties. Gently, he rubbed the smooth marks on her thigh. "You know I want you to tell me how it happened, but let's get something straight first." With the pads of his fingers, he stroked the other scars, soothed them. "I don't care about this—why would I? You're lovely, and sexy. Annie, you are so sexy. Accidents happen—forget it." His laugh didn't lighten anything up.

"It wasn't an accident," Annie said.

Very little made Max recoil, but he looked at the location of the old injuries and went cold. And he made up his mind. He stripped, fast, determined to be naked before she could argue too much.

"Max—"

"I'm in charge," he told her. "Enjoy it." He heard her indrawn breath.

He had anticipated they could be here like this eventually. This time he'd make sure nothing took away from her satisfaction. A bedside drawer held what they needed.

Seconds later Annie pulled up her knees. "That's cold."

"It'll be warm very soon," he told her, easing her legs down and working the jelly into places that started her writhing and reaching for him.

He coated her belly, her thighs, smiled a little and slicked her midriff, and her breasts. "I'm taking advantage now," he said. "I'd be a fool not to." She closed her eyes tightly and he made sure they would slip together like melted butter, even though handling himself almost brought him to his knees.

Annie slitted her eyes to see him. He had shown her he didn't care if she had ugly scars—he also didn't know the full extent of them, but perhaps he'd guessed.

"I see you, sweetheart," he told her. "You ready for me?"

She nodded, burning up inside.

Max bent over and kissed her long, deep and slow, and he held her breasts, incited her nipples with his thumbs. Her hips rose from the bed.

Looking at her, he kissed her again, and slid his forearms beneath her shoulders so he could rest on his elbows. If she'd wanted to touch him she couldn't—she couldn't reach.

He nudged himself into the folds between her legs and her eyes shot all the way open.

"It's okay," he whispered. "If you hurt, tell me and we'll figure out what to do next."

She didn't hurt. Max prodded against her, came close to entering but drew back to press at her sweet spot some more. He held her hips while he continued. Then, when her legs jerked and she couldn't keep her hips on the bed, he held his penis and stroked at her faster and faster until Annie threw her arms over her head, and rode an unbearably strong climax.

His breathing seemed to fill the room. Standing, pulling her up and astride his hips, he bounced inside her and she used her feet and strong legs to urge him on.

It all shattered, explosively, and she arched away from him, out of control.

Max cushioned her as best he could but they fell in a heavy heap on the mattress. She kept her arms around him and held on tight.

Heavy, sleepy, he lay like that, holding her. Finally he felt sweat cool on his skin and the warm sleepiness lifted. Max didn't know how much time had passed and Annie hadn't spoken at all. He shifted, slid her head onto a pillow, then stretched out beside her.

She wasn't close enough. He slid an arm beneath her shoulders and pulled her against him. Annie settled her head into the hollow of his shoulder and pressed her body to his. He heard her sniff, and felt her tears fall on his chest.

Max swallowed. She had burdens and they were heavy, too heavy to bear alone. He wanted her to share them with him. "You're special, Annie," he told her, stroking back her hair. "I'm a lucky man to have found you."

"I don't want to talk yet," she told him. "Just hold me. Pretend the wolves aren't circling."

CHAPTER 25

I didn't expect another car to arrive at Rosebank, not so late.

Or to come up right behind it. Shit, all I could do was duck under the dashboard.

A few more minutes and I would have been away clean. But I knew I had to keep calm and make sure I didn't blow my cover.

This night has thwarted me one time too many. I wanted to write to Max again but with that fool Lil still alive, it wouldn't make much sense.

It was hard to wait around at Rosebank, listening, and worrying someone would see my car and decide to check it out.

I should have known I'd be okay. I always am. I parked well back between the trees so I wouldn't be noticed.

Lil's a problem, but that story isn't over yet. I can't stop thinking about it. I don't like loose ends.

Max and Annie puzzled me at first, walking into the resort in the open like that. It's all clear now. Max has conned Annie into helping make abso-

lutely certain he looks like a pussycat to anyone who finds out about them, and everyone will find out. He wants her to help him seem innocent.

I only stuck around after they went in the house to make sure Annie didn't sneak back out before the place woke up.

Damn, I had a lot on my mind waiting there like that. Max doesn't deserve what he's got and I'm going to make sure he doesn't keep it.

I didn't know who could be driving the two cars that came after, but I kept my head down just in case.

The second car—I recognized it by the rough engine—it started up again and drove back out. I waited to see if the other car would follow but it didn't.

What I heard was the front door of the house closing.

When I took another look I saw Madge Pollard's Camry parked, so she must have gone inside. The car I heard leave had to be Father Cyrus's old Impala.

I wasn't interested one way or the other.

Max has made one big miscalculation. Sleeping with Annie and letting everyone know about it won't save him—or her.

CHAPTER 26

Madge turned back at the foot of the stairs. Leaded panes beside the front door reflected the final winks of the Impala's vanishing taillights.

Rosebank felt huge—it was huge—and in the silence of early morning its bulk settled heavily around Madge.

Lil wasn't doing well. After Max left with Annie, the doctors had allowed Cyrus in again for a little while, but said that Spike and any other members of the law must stay out because the patient needed to be quiet. Please let Lil be okay. She could be maddening but she was one of Toussaint's own, a fixture who could surprise you with a kind deed now and then. And she took good care of Cyrus.

Madge sat on the bottom step.

She didn't want to go up to her rooms.

How long would it be before someone suggested she should get another dog to "replace" Millie? She'd have to smile and understand people said those things because they wanted to be kind and couldn't think of a way to be comforting.

To her left, its door open, stood the sitting room. Charlotte and Vivian had kept the room and its exotic furnishings much as they had been when Vivian's uncle had owned the house. From inside, the faintest of glows tickled the gloom. They left a single floor lamp burning all night. "Just in case," Charlotte had explained to Madge without elaborating.

Walking softly, Madge went through the door. Striped hangings draped from the center of the high ceiling to the tops of the walls and then to the floor. Whenever she entered the room she thought of a desert tent. Sometimes Madge read in here, in a comfortable chaise. She had it in mind to sleep in that chair tonight, rather than go up and face the bed without Millie's little weight against her back.

Her phone rang in her purse and she fumbled wildly to get it out before it awakened someone.

"Yes?" she whispered into the mouthpiece, and held the phone away to see who was calling. "Cyrus?"

"Ozaire called and I'm goin' back to the hospital," he said. "I don't want you to wonder where I am in the morning—just in case I'm not at St. Cécil's."

She pressed the phone hard against her ear and sat on the edge of the nearest chair. "It's Lil, then?"

"They've found a clot—a hematoma in her head. She must have hit the steering wheel harder than anyone thought. Subdural hematoma, they called it. They've got to make a hole in the skull to release the pressure from the swelling."

"Will she be all right?"

"Probably. They said it's not a big clot. She'll have to be quiet for a few days—stay in the hospital. Max Savage said something to me about her not looking too good. Guess he knows his stuff."

"I like him," Madge said.

"Me, too. Ozaire says he's told Spike whatever he heard Lil say. Not that she's makin' much sense."

Madge curled over her knees. "What did she say that doesn't make sense?"

"Stuff about being chased when she got out of the car, and pushed down, then left when someone came close on an off-road bike. She keeps talkin' about a man—must be the one who ran at her car. He caught her, then dumped her. A lot of pain. That keeps coming up. He hurt her but she's not clear about it."

"What did they decide about the bruises on her neck?"

"Nothing as far as I know. Madge, you know how…"

"I know," she said quickly. "I know you feel badly for me. What's so awful is thinking about Millie suffering. She never did anything but be sweet and loving. I'll be all right though. Don't worry about me."

"Please don't shut yourself away with the sadness," Cyrus said. "I know you. If I don't stop you, you'll hold it in."

He really did take care of her and that must be enough to make her happy. She smiled and pushed back in the chair—and started violently. "Oh, Vivian," she said. "I didn't see you there."

"Sorry," Vivian mouthed. "I didn't know how to let you know without scaring you."

"Madge?" Cyrus said in her ear. "What's going on?"

"Nothing. I just realized Vivian's here. I jumped." She laughed. "Should I come to the hospital now." An excuse to stay busy appealed to Madge.

"No. You get to bed. There wouldn't be anything you could do and I'd appreciate you being at the parish to field questions in the morning."

"Poor Lil. Poor Ozaire! He'll be beside himself." She smiled at Vivian who sat in Madge's favorite chaise, her pregnant tummy covered by an orange quilt.

"You wouldn't believe what a mess he is," Cyrus said. Madge could hear the *knocka-knocka* of the Impala's engine as he drove. "Says he's got to make somethin' right with Homer and if I didn't know better I'd have said he was close to tears while he was talking."

"Drive carefully," Madge said. "Ozaire's upset about Lil is all. He puts on a tough face but he relies on her for everything."

"Yup," Cyrus agreed. "Hold things together at the church—if I'm late back."

"You've got it," Madge said. "Later."

She hung up. "Vivian, I didn't see you there. What are you doing?"

"Waiting for Spike," Vivian said, her short black hair slipping forward at her jaw. "I heard your conversation. Lil's not doin' well?"

Madge didn't want to worry Vivian more than she already was. "She's shocked from the accident and needs more rest. What happened really frightened her and I don't blame her."

"Neither do I," Vivian said. She cleared her throat. "I don't have the right words to say about Millie. I'm still hopin' she comes home."

Madge wanted to hope but the odds were poor and she was a realist. "Thanks." Vivian had a Chihuahua called Boa who spent her nights with Wendy, Spike's young daughter. The two dogs had done well together.

Vivian shifted, pushed another cushion behind her head. "They haven't quit searching for the nurse, y'know. Michele Riley. That's where Spike is now."

"Physical therapist. Why would they be out there at night?"

"There was a tip so they're following up. They may bring the bloodhound in again—even though the scent only gets weaker. I made the last bit up—I don't know what those bloodhound noses can do."

Madge raised her brows. "I didn't know they'd ever had a bloodhound. Makes a lot of sense, though."

"That's how they figured out Michele probably went straight out the back door of the Majestic. Right after Max dropped her off."

Madge hadn't heard anything about that either and figured Vivian was tired and uncomfortable enough to be repeating things Spike had mentioned without expecting them to be passed on. Vivian could even have heard Spike on the phone and not realized the information wasn't common knowledge. She didn't get out much at the moment.

The information that Michele had left the Majestic right after Max dropped her there could be good news for him—and for Annie. Madge worried her bottom lip. She should probably keep quiet, but it didn't seem fair for Max not to know.

"I don't sleep well if Spike's not here, especially when I'm like this." Vivian smiled. "Never would have thought I'd be the clingy type. I only seem to need Spike more and more."

Madge smiled. She got up and went to sit closer to Vivian. "The baby's healthy and it won't be too much longer now. Wazoo says this one's going to keep you running around till you wonder why you wanted him so badly."

"Him? We don't know the sex of the baby. We told them we don't want to know. Could just as well be a girl." Apart from the belly, Vivian remained a slim woman with eyes that missed nothing and a thoughtful smile.

Madge stared at Vivian's abdomen. "He's busy in there." She felt odd, watching the movement and wondering what it would be like to feel her own baby moving inside her.

"Put your hand here," Vivian said, patting a spot.

Tentatively, Madge got up and did as Vivian suggested. At first she didn't feel anything, but then Vivian's tummy tensed, swelled on one side and Madge felt a little pointy something pass her fingers. "Oh!" She breathed through her mouth, screwed up her eyes and concentrated. "He is playin' football in there. Vivian, that's just wonderful."

"Isn't it? It will be when it happens to you, too."

Madge straightened. She met Vivian's eyes but looked away. "Yes. Wazoo says you're having a boy and Wazoo says she knows these things, so I'm buying you some blue booties."

Vivian laughed, and sobered as quickly. "I don't want you staying down here because of me. I'm just fine on my own."

Always sensible, Vivian. Madge rested a hand on her shoulder and raised her own face. Easier to control any tears that way. "I don't like leaving you here," she said.

"But you're tired and you need to get to bed," Vivian said and chuckled softly. "You go on up. I'm more comfortable here than in my bed these days. I'll be fine."

"Let me get you another blanket."

"Uh-uh, but thank you. I'm warm enough. Night, Madge."

"Night," she said and walked with leaden feet to the stairs. Slowly, she climbed, and slowed even more when she got close to the top. There was nowhere else to go. She had no family left that she knew of. A room could always be hers at the rectory but she couldn't take advantage of that. Tongues would wag.

She smiled through filmed eyes. Too bad there wasn't anything worth those tongues wagging about.

In the morning she would be off again, back to the job she mostly loved, tied up in other people's lives…avoiding her own.

Her rooms were all the way at the end of the first corridor on the left. Max Savage lived closer to the stairs with Kelly next to him. Roche was one floor up, as was Wazoo.

Madge stood in the corridor and let her head hang down. In the future she'd be able to lock her door like everyone else. She'd gotten into the habit of leaving it open a little so Millie could get in and out.

She went through the door. Sparely furnished, her sitting room appeared cold. Madge had collected few personal possessions and kept what she had simple. The place looked as if it belonged to someone with no roots.

Didn't it?

Not a single chair in the place invited her to sit down. Madge went directly to the bedroom. What was left of this night wouldn't be easy. The sooner it was over, the better.

She liked the bedroom with its chintz drapes and comforter and two small, overstuffed chairs.

A scratching noise sounded and a really small black and white dog pushed herself from beneath the bed, her leash trailing behind her.

"Millie!" Madge clamped both hands over her mouth. Her heart jumped in her throat. It hurt. She shook uncontrollably and whispered, "Millie."

No dog could look more pathetic, more sorry for herself than Millie Pollard. Before Madge could gather her wits, Miz Millie, her tail tucked between her legs as far as that much tail could be tucked on that much dog, half jumped, half dragged herself onto a chair and from there made it to the bed. There she sat, oversized ears flattened to her round head.

Madge found her feet, and her ability to move. She dashed to sweep up the dog and hug her until Millie squealed. Madge rained kisses on top of the dog's head. These were tolerated, but the ears stayed down.

"Where have you been?" Madge said, holding Millie away and looking at her. She put her on the bed and ran her fingers through her fur searching for injuries. No wails of pain came. "Your feet? Let me see them. Oh, Millie, you've walked so far, poor cher."

Carrying the dog again, Madge hurried into the bathroom. Looking at the pads of Millie's feet could be a problem since the animal would decide, usually correctly, that her claws were about to be clipped—and do somersaults to get away. This time Madge held

Millie up and peered in the mirror to see if her feet were bloody stumps.

"There's nothin' wrong with 'em," Madge said. She still trembled. "Where have you been, you little horror? How dare you run off and scare me that way? Just you see, tomorrow you get no food and no water and I'm shutting you in here all the day, and don't you go showing me up by making a fuss."

She held the dog up and stared at her, nose-to-nose. "You aren't big enough to go exploring. You saw the main chance and took a run for it, didn't you? I don't know how you got home without hurting yourself, but the dog angels were watchin' over you. Not that you deserved it. Shows how much I can trust you. Ooh, I could..."

Millie licked Madge's nose.

"You don't need to be down here with me, Mama," Vivian said. "It's time you disabled that kid-monitor of yours. I'm too old for you to worry about now."

"Hah," Charlotte said. She had arrived minutes earlier and curled herself into a chair near Vivian's. "You wait, girl. When that babe of yours is born, your life will change forever. Won't matter if you're a hundred, you'll still be worrying about your kid—or kids. Won't be long before Wendy's driving you and Spike to drink because the boys come around."

"She's still a little girl," Vivian said promptly. She knew her mother was trying to help her pass the time, and hoping maybe she would fall asleep somewhere along the way.

Charlotte reached across and held Vivian's hand. "You love that man of yours. I knew I was right to encourage him."

"Mama! How many years ago was that?" Vivian shook her head. "But you're right, just like you were right then." She did love him, so much it scared her sometimes. When he was out so late she didn't settle until she'd set eyes on him again. "Wazoo says we're goin' to have a boy."

"Then we'd better get blue booties," Charlotte said, squeezing Vivian's hand. "That woman isn't wrong when it comes to babies—or a lot of other things."

Vivian wouldn't argue about that. "That's exactly what Madge said—including the blue booties bit. Sometimes I wish Wazoo wouldn't say some of the things she does," she said. "She can scare me a bit."

"She means well," Charlotte told her.

"I know she does and I love her to pieces. Wouldn't it be somethin' if she married one day?"

Charlotte hummed and seemed to get lost for moments. Then she said, "It would. We'll see. Most of what I'm thinking tonight is about Lil. When you spoke to Spike last I suppose he was a closed-mouthed toad, like always."

"Mama! Don't you call Spike a toad. He isn't even very closed-mouthed anyway—he could say a lot less than he lets out sometimes but he's too trusting. He just doesn't waste time talkin' when he's got work to do."

"He doesn't fool me," Charlotte said. "He likes folks to think he's happy-go-lucky and informal, but he keeps more to himself than he ever lets on."

Vivian avoided responding. "Lil's not doing as well as they'd like but she is coming along. Madge was at the hospital earlier and she told me when she came in." She and her mother looked at each other and sighed. "She's doing her best about Millie."

"Hard," Charlotte said. "You do know Spike's like his dad, don't you? They both keep too much to themselves when it comes to feelings."

Vivian decided not to touch that.

"Ornery old fool, that Homer," Charlotte said, so quietly Vivian felt sad. "I know what it's all about, y'know, that man's stupidity. But don't you ask me to tell you 'cause it'll only make you madder than would be good for my grandson."

Vivian giggled and rubbed at her tired eyes. "So this is definitely a son I have here. If you don't mind, Mama, I'd as soon you didn't talk like that in front of Spike. He wants to be surprised."

"Oh, no, no, no," Charlotte said holding her hands, palm up. "Not a word of it'll come from me. Did Spike say anything else about Lil? More than you heard from Madge?"

"I haven't talked to him for hours. I can't figure out how Lil would drive right off a road she's been using all her life."

"Neither can I," Charlotte said. "I feel bad about...well, she came to ask about a job and I didn't hire her."

"Lil did?" Vivian couldn't believe it. "You didn't mention it before. She's been with Cyrus forever. She'd never leave the rectory."

Charlotte fidgeted with piping on the arm of her chair. "I think money's a problem. We both know Ozaire sees himself as an entrepreneur. If his schemes panned out it would be great, but mostly they don't. Even adding his part-time from the church to what he gets from Homer, he can't bring in much."

"I bet Cyrus doesn't know Lil came to you," Vivian said. "Why doesn't she talk to him about a salary raise. He'd find a way."

"Cyrus always does find a way," Charlotte said. "For everyone but himself."

Vivian laughed. "He has what he needs—and what he wants. Cyrus is a happy man. Mostly." She met her mother's eyes briefly. There were few subjects they didn't discuss but Cyrus and Madge was one of them.

"Madge could probably help figure out what to do," Charlotte said. "When she's settled down a bit, I'll talk to her."

Footsteps pounded down the stairs.

Charlotte held up a hand to Vivian and whispered, "Who can that be?"

"Bet it's Madge," Vivian said in a hoarse voice. "I don't know what she's goin' to do without that dog of hers. She sure isn't going to like being on her own up there."

The dog beat Madge into the room and leaped into Charlotte's arms.

"Lordy," Charlotte said. "Look who I've got and she doesn't ever come to me."

"Or me," Vivian said.

Madge came in, her face flushed and her eyes bright, even though she'd obviously been crying. "I don't understand it. She was upstairs under my bed. And there's not one mark on her. I think she's been here all day."

"She couldn't have been," Vivian said. "We'd have seen her. If she's here and you're not she doesn't just stay in your rooms."

"Anyway," Charlotte said. "Wazoo said Lil took Millie to the vet in Loreauville."

"She did," Madge said, out of breath, her face flushed. "Her sister backed that up and the vet said he gave Millie a shot."

Charlotte cuddled Millie. "Is she hurt? Do we need to get her back to the vet now?"

"She's absolutely fine." Madge's dark eyes glowed. "I've checked her out. Not a mark on her and even her feet aren't injured. They look as soft as ever."

"This is great," Charlotte said.

"Great," Vivian agreed.

Madge said, "She hasn't run miles, has she? She didn't have to find her way home."

"No," Charlotte and Vivian said in unison and Vivian added, "She must have been brought back here."

"Who would do that and not let me know—or one of us?" Madge said.

"*Why* would they?" Vivian added.

CHAPTER 27

Sometimes there was no right way to deal with idiots.

Roche wished he could shut out Kelly's pacing. Unfortunately his brother made sure he walked back and forth only feet from Roche's nose.

"It's always been like this," Kelly said, at least keeping his voice down. They were in the residents' dining room at Rosebank and even with the door closed Roche didn't feel safe from passing ears. "Don't you do that freezing out thing with me," Kelly said. "It gets you by with Max but it doesn't work with me."

"Leave Max out of this," Roche said. "And remember Max and I don't want you running to Dad just because you want to make points." He knew his mistake at once.

"You shit," Kelly said through his teeth. "You fucking superior upstart. No, don't try to interrupt. This time Max gets pulled in and we sort out the thing you've got about me and *our* father. I've had it—"

"Shut up," Roche said succinctly. "It's time to get over being jealous of Max and me. And we don't have time for sibling rivalry—not now."

"Jealous of you and Max?" Kelly laughed but his eyes stayed hard. "It's time *you* got over thinking you've got to cut me out whenever you can. I'm the oldest son, remember. I'm not in competition with you. Not with you or Max. Max is the one in competition with me."

"You are jealous," Roche said. This had been a long time coming and was overdue. "Dad and Julia couldn't get along. They divorced. Dad and our mother met and married. Mom always treated you like her own son. Jeez, Kelly, whenever you're around her butter wouldn't melt in your mouth. And Mom had nothing to do with the divorce, except in your mind—"

"Shut the fuck up," Kelly said and Roche heard his teeth grind. "I didn't accuse Claire of anything. She's a good woman. It isn't her fault my father made a mistake when he broke up with my mother."

Let it go. Roche hoped he could.

"You pull off your little act nicely," Kelly said. He took his coffee mug from the table they'd been using and went to the laden sideboard for a refill. The residents' morning spread was invariably impressive. While they hadn't been in this morning, usually the Devols and Charlotte also grabbed breakfast there, and the kitchens would want to keep them happy.

Kelly went to the window that overlooked gardens at the side of the house. From there, the chimneys at Green Veil were visible.

"I'm waiting," Roche said when he couldn't contain himself anymore. "What act am I pulling off?"

Kelly pulled back a sheer drape that hung to the floor and stood closer to the window. "We're going to miss the lousy wet weather," he said. "Looks like it's going to burn us up and wring us out today. Damn, I hate humidity."

"Don't avoid the question," Roche said.

"Okay." Kelly swung to face him. "You put up a good front— you've got most people believing you're Dr. Nice—but the quiet, reserved act doesn't fool me. You resent Max. I pity you that, because I'm sure enough of myself not to care if everyone bows down to him. I just make sure I don't get swept away in his dust. But you hate it because as well as you've done, you can't touch Max. I've seen how you look when Dad and Claire are fawning on him." He sighed. "I don't blame you. Where is he anyway? He knew we were getting together this morning."

Roche simmered. "Max is my brother, my twin. I'm glad for any success he has and I hate it that he's going through so much he doesn't deserve."

"How reasonable," Kelly said. "I hope he's got himself covered for every minute of last night."

"Why?" Roche opened and closed his hands. "Don't fool around, just spit it out."

"Lil," Kelly said. "Last I heard she was going down for the third time."

"She's critical?" Roche frowned. "I should have checked on her condition last night."

"You were busy."

"Okay, you've made your point. Why would they think Max had anything to do with hurting Lil?"

"They're going to think he's got something to do with anything that happens around here. Did you hear anything else about it?"

"No," Roche said. He felt a light sweat break out.

"Call the hospital. You can always get the information you want."

"They won't tell me anything," Roche said. "Damn, just what we need, more complications. I'm sorry about the woman, of course. But no one's going to suspect Max in this one."

Kelly gave a one-sided smile. "Do you wish they would?"

"You…" Roche went around the table, but Kelly made sure he didn't get too close. "What kind of thing is that to say? God, you're eaten up with envy. You can't even stand it that Max and I are twins. You don't like how close we are. And you hate it that you couldn't make it in medicine. Go on, admit it."

Kelly's eyes went flat and lost any shine. He drew the corners of his mouth down. "If I'd wanted medicine, I would've had it—and I'd have been better than either of you. Damn, you medical types think you're gifts from God. And I still say you wish you were the star, not Max. Maybe you're right. You think about that, don't you?"

"Why do I bother with you?" Roche said. He took a long breath that didn't calm him down and dropped his hands, limp, at his sides. "I'm proud of my brother. He makes a difference and that's okay by me."

"Sheesh, I wish I was as perfect as you. You don't fool me. How does it feel when they say only screwed up people become psychiatrists? Nutcases and people who couldn't cut it in most fields of medicine."

"No one ever said that to me," Roche said mildly. "They may have thought it, but so what, I'm doing exactly what I want to do. You might want to make an appointment."

Kelly frowned.

"Short-term cognitive therapy might work for you," Roche said, enjoying himself. "The way things are, I can fit you in every day until the clinic's ready to go."

For an instant Roche expected coffee in his face, then Kelly sighed. He shook his head and grinned. "We don't stop, do we? You and I have been needling each other since you started talking. But even if you don't get it, I want the best for you. I think you deserve it."

What Kelly had already said wouldn't be so easy to forget, but Roche grinned back. Some of what his older brother said was true, Roche didn't always feel as unconcerned as he made sure he seemed. The reasons were complex and who knew when they'd all get worked out.

"I saw you with Lee," Kelly said. He sat down at the table again.

Seconds passed while Roche digested what Kelly had said.

"I got back early. You were supposed to call her and ask for a rain check—for me. But you decided to take advantage of an opportunity. It wasn't pretty."

Roche's pulse felt faint. He kept his gaze steady on Kelly's. This had better not be what he feared it was. "What's that supposed to mean?"

"Don't worry, I'll keep it in the family. But rough sex—"

Max came in and closed the door behind him. "Did I hear someone say 'rough sex'?" He went straight for the coffee. The heat must already be turned up outside. A blue chambray shirt stuck to his back.

"You've got to get your mind on the right track," Roche said. He hoped Kelly wouldn't continue whatever he'd been about to say.

"Yeah," Kelly said. "That's what I said, rough sex. Roche here has been having too much fun and if he doesn't watch it he could bring the town down on our heads."

Max didn't immediately face them. His life was changing, again, and he wanted to concentrate on it—not on his brothers' arguments.

"You hearing me?" Kelly said.

"Yes." Max turned around and drank some of his coffee.

"You're late," Roche said and Max felt his twin's discomfort. "One of the building inspectors is coming today and we're agreed we should be there, not just the contractor."

Kelly rapped a knuckle on the table. He hadn't stopped moving since he arrived. "More important than that is the human resources woman. I'm not wasting my time hiring office staff. Where were you last night by the way?"

"Minding my own business."

"I didn't think you got to do that anymore," Kelly said.

Max didn't rise to the bait in Kelly's last comment. "You're in a great mood," he said. "You're right, we had a breakfast date but we didn't set a time. I was late getting in last night. This morning I had to drive Annie to work first, but I'm here now." The two of them had decided they wanted openness, even if it did carry a price.

"Huh?" Kelly said.

"You heard," Max said.

Roche smiled and offered Max a chair. "Annie spent the night with you? Go, bro'. You always were a stallion."

"Yeah, a real stud." Max felt more angry than sarcastic but he had to keep his temper under wraps. "Annie is special to me. Really special. She's off-limits to guy comments—from either of you."

Kelly put his elbows on the table. "Have you lost your mind?" he said to Max.

"Not the last time I checked."

"Max, it's too dangerous. For her. She can't be with you all the time." He jumped up and clasped his hips. "What if she's alone and... You know what I'm thinking."

He did. "Thanks for the concern," he said. "I'm laying down some ground rules. When she's not with me, there'll be someone else keeping an eye on her. This thing with Michele has to be cleared up. If anything's happening, I don't know about it. Spike pretends he's a good ol' boy who shoots off his mouth. The problem is he never really says anything."

"Who will you find to watch Annie for you?" Kelly said. "Where do you think you are, Manhattan?"

Max intended to approach Guy Gautreaux. He liked him, and trusted him. The big question was whether or not he'd take on the job. "Leave it to me," he told Kelly. "What's with you, Roche? You don't look so good."

"I'm fine, thanks, Doc."

"He's fine all right," Kelly said, stacking his hands behind his head. "You should have seen him in action last night."

"Damn you! You didn't see anything. You couldn't have." Roche made a threatening move toward Kelly. "Leave it, will you?"

"Lee was a mess and you were no better," Kelly said, smirking. "Drowned rats. Did you use one of the baths or something? Nothing like sex in a great, big bath. Roche had Lee O'Brien over at the clinic. When I saw them he was saying goodbye—on the floor in reception."

Max shot out an arm to stop Roche from rushing Kelly.

"Matter of fact, she looked dead," Kelly said. "Did you fuck her to death? Hope you made a good job of getting rid of the body if you did."

"Let me at him," Roche said but Max made sure he'd have to come through him to get to Kelly. "Out of my way, Max."

"Quit," Max said. "What's the deal? You didn't get rough with Lee, did you?"

"Forget it," Roche shouted. "You aren't in charge around here. My sex life is my business. Drop it, both of you, or you'll wish you had."

"You and Lee at the clinic," Max said. "As you say, it's your business but it isn't a place I'd choose."

"No," Roche said, "you prefer to take women to your rooms, in front of anyone around."

"Not women," Max said. "Annie. And the choice was hers. I agreed."

"Lucky you," Kelly said under his breath. "Dad's on a cruise."

Max frowned. "Where did that come from?"

"I want to let him know what's been going on here."

"Roche having sex in reception, you mean? And Annie and me getting together?"

"Michele Riley," Kelly said. "Have you forgotten? Her boyfriend or whatever is still over at the Majestic spreading hate about you. The whole thing has to be ready to blow. Now there's Lil Dupre. I don't want Dad reading it in the paper before we say anything."

"We've been through this already," Max said. "Dad's a strong man. And Mom takes most things in stride. I don't want to say anything yet. We could get lucky and have this go away."

Kelly skewered Roche with a glare. "You're careless. What made you turn on all the lights at Green Veil? I wouldn't have gone over if I hadn't wondered about it. You've got a clean reputation—why dirty it up?"

"Drop it," Roche said. "Lee and I understand each other."

Max didn't like either of his brothers' attitudes. "We're all wearing thin," he said. "Let's ease up, huh?"

Heavy footsteps in the hall preceded Spike's appearance. He threw open the door and walked in looking as if he'd missed a few nights' sleep.

"Coffee?" Max asked, looking him over.

"Yeah. There's a few things you ought to know." He threw down a copy of the *Toussaint Trumpet* and pointed at it. "We'll get to that later. Can't get into it now. But if I'm readin' the code right, someone around here could have some explainin' to do."

Both Kelly and Roche stared at the paper. They weren't the only ones who wanted to get their hands on it.

"What else is on your mind?" Max said to Spike. He poured a mug of coffee from a carafe. "Did you eat? There's still food here."

"I ate. Around ten donuts, I reckon. I couldn't tell you this before, Max, but Michele Riley went into the Majestic when you left her there."

"I know. We've known that from the outset."

Spike dropped his chin to his chest and took a breath. "Let me get through this my own way, okay? She went in, and straight out the back—or that's what we think."

"How would you know that now?" Max asked.

"We knew it within hours of learning about her disappearance. Bloodhound followed her scent. Only problem is the scent ran out a few feet from the door to the parking lot. The back door handle had been smeared with lanolin so there were no prints. Without the dog we wouldn't have had anything."

The skin on Max's face tightened. "Does that mean something to you, other than it sounds like Michele got into another vehicle?"

"Bingo," Spike said. "But we don't have anything else from then on. Forensics went over every inch. Nothing interesting. So many vehicles come and go there you can't tell one track from another and there weren't any useful footprints. By the way, Tom Walen got here the same day Michele did."

Max's spine jerked straight and he couldn't feel his hands. "He flew in the same day?"

"Drove. Says he didn't trust you with Michele so he came down, too."

Roche tapped a foot and Max wished he wouldn't. "From what he said at All Tarted Up, he'd flown in later, once Michele was reported missing," Roche said. "He showed up at the shop and wanted to rip Max apart."

"There's no law against stayin' in a motel out of town because you want to make sure your fiancée's safe," Spike said. "He had plenty of reason to worry, didn't he? He knows all about you."

"But why lie about being here?" Max asked, wondering why Spike was giving them the information. Rather than bring any hope, his revelation made Max feel he was waiting for the handcuffs to come out. "If he drove, he would have had to leave New York before Michele did. He'd have to have an excuse for that."

"He does," Spike said, but didn't attempt to explain.

"Have you checked out his car?" Max said.

"Sure. He volunteered. All we got were a few hairs that matched with Michele's mother's DNA, but Michele was in Tom's car all the time. She'd be bound to leave hair and fibers. No blood."

"You didn't ask for my car," Max said.

Spike shook his head. "We might have turned up a hair or two but you're too smart to leave evidence around."

"Blood would still show. I want it looked at. Take it apart if you like."

"I don't need you to explain basic forensics to me," Spike said.

Kelly cracked his knuckles. "Yeah, look at Max's car. Hell, take all of our cars if you want 'em."

"That won't be necessary," Spike said. "Now, listen up, Max. I want you to think real hard about that night when you dropped Michele off. Did you see a vehicle in the vicinity of the Majestic? I mean coming or going from the back?"

Max shook his head, "No."

"Just thought I'd ask," Spike said. He set his Stetson more firmly on his head. "At least it looks as if you got lucky with Lil."

"*Lil?* You saw with your own eyes that she didn't react when she saw me last night."

"I know," Spike said. "But from the direction things are going, if she'd died you'd have been tried and convicted by some. I've got to call and see how she did with the surgery."

Max inclined his head in question.

"Surgery?" Kelly said. "We thought she wasn't expected to live, so this is better news."

"No one said she wasn't expected to live," Max said. "But they weren't talking surgery when I was there."

"She had something called a subdural hematoma. Clot in her head somewhere, don't ask me." Spike showed signs of growing very restless. "They were going to make a hole to let the pressure out."

"I wasn't sure about her condition," Max said thoughtfully.

Spike started toward the door. "Can I see you in the corridor?"

Without a word, Max followed Spike from the room and into the front hall.

"Listen to me," Spike said quietly. "We don't have much to go on and what we do have I don't feel good about. Guilty or not, you're the patsy, though."

"I think we all figured that out," Max said.

"Some are sure you killed Michele. They want you fried."

Max looked at him. "Which camp are you in? I did or I didn't?"

"Jury's still out," Spike said. "Lee O'Brien's written an article in the *Trumpet*. You'd better read it. She's a better reporter than she ought to be in a town this size and she wants to make what she does count for something. This may just be one of her attention-getting schemes, but there aren't too many people who could sort of fit what she's suggesting. You know the drill, she doesn't use names. But she writes a bunch of innuendos, some sort of accusations— and there could be a threat or so there. Whatever, you'd better tread lightly, all three of you."

"I'll go back in and get the paper," Max said.

"There's another one over there," Spike told him, indicating a demilune table against one green silk-covered wall. "I understand you and Annie spent the night here."

Max stared at him.

"Word gets around," Spike said. "And in my book, Annie Duhon's future just got a whole lot more uncertain. Maybe it'll be good for your reputation if everyone knows you two are real close. Be real careful, though. If somethin' nasty happens to Annie it won't look good."

Max flinched. He was leaving now and knew exactly where he was going. "You're right there," he said, smiling. "Nice to talk to you, Sheriff."

He'd just been warned that he was still the prime suspect in Michele's disappearance, and that nothing had better happen to Annie.

CHAPTER 28

"Hey, Annie."

A hand closed on her wrist and she stopped. She still knew Bobby Colbert's voice. "Yes," she said, facing his table rather than cause a scene. "I didn't see you there."

"You're still too busy being the boss around here." He released her and smiled as if they were the best of friends. "It's a nice place."

"Thanks. You said you liked it the last time you were in."

"So I did, but you were in such a hurry to get away I wasn't sure you heard me. Sit with me." He pulled out a chair on his right. "You're the boss around here. You can decide when you want to take a break."

"I'm the manager, not the boss," she told him. "Anything goes wrong and it's my fault. I'm on duty."

"You don't have to be so superior. Just because you've come up in the world."

Annie weighed her options. She hated drawing attention to herself. "Okay. Just for a few minutes." She walked behind him and slid into the chair. There was always a chance she could persuade him to leave her alone. "What is it, Bobby? Why are you working so hard to talk to me?"

He reached as if he would stroke her cheek but Annie jerked away.

"Sorry," he said. He put his hands on the table and studied them. "We both had a hard time back then—when we were kids. We weren't old enough to make the decisions we needed to make. I want you, Annie. Don't just react to the past and shut me out. Give me another chance."

A nice-looking man, in good shape, shouldn't need to chase around after a woman he'd dropped years earlier, in a part of her life Annie wanted to forget.

"Annie?"

"Move on," she told him. "I have."

"With the famous surgeon?" His expression wasn't pretty. "Why would he want you? Have you wondered about that?"

Annie moved to get up but Bobby took hold of her arm and held her there. "Don't be a fool. He's usin' you. That scares me because I know all about him and I couldn't stand it if something happened to you. We were always meant to be together. I knew it the moment I set eyes on you in St. Martinville. Before that I was drifting but one look at you and I figured it all out. We made a mistake when we let each other go, but it isn't too late."

From when he was young, Bobby had been the all-American boy. Facing her this morning he'd still be the one to put on a poster advertising something wholesome. But inside him something had gone horribly wrong.

"My folks said I was too young for you." His eyes slid away. "I should have been strong enough to stand up to them but I wasn't. They wanted someone—something different for me. If I didn't do what they told me, I was going to be sent away to one of those military schools."

"You're older than me," she reminded him. "It doesn't matter anymore. We aren't even the same people we were then. I'm sorry it was hard for you." He'd never be able to imagine how hard it had been for her.

Bobby studied her. "You're successful. You've got to be or you wouldn't be running a place like this. It's a gold mine."

Annie wanted to escape, and she didn't want him to bother her again. "It's not my gold mine."

"What do they pay you?"

She stood up, wrenched her arm away from his renewed attempt to detain her. "I don't want to do this," she said, making sure she wasn't overheard. "But if you keep following me around and bothering me, I'll go to the sheriff and complain."

"Don't be like that," he said. "I came on too strong. You know I'm not good at saying the right things." He laughed. "My mother says I was born with both feet in my mouth. Will you think about having dinner with me? I'm a good cook."

Annie didn't just turn cold, she felt flash frozen. "No," she said, aware that she might have to report this encounter. "Like I told you, I've moved on. I like my life. But I hope you'll find the right person for you real soon."

She sensed a change inside Pappy's and frowned.

"I saved your *life,*" Bobby said.

"Thank you. I'll always be grateful." He was partly right but he would never have been there after she was attacked if her mother hadn't met him by chance and brought him home that evening.

Guy Gautreaux, Jilly's husband, strolled among the tables, turning heads as he went. He found a place by the windows, sat down and put a newspaper down in front of him. Annie didn't realize she was staring at him until he looked back at her, and smiled. She had a ridiculous urge to rush and ask him to get rid of Bobby. The impulse passed as Guy started looking the menu over.

"You okay?" Bobby said. "I didn't mean to upset you."

She saw a different window, this one in a dark room where flames sent shadows leaping over the walls. A man wrestled to open the window.

"You don't have to go weird on me. I'm leaving. I'll come back when I can figure out the right things to say."

Pain shot into her legs. She heard her own scream. The man couldn't budge the window. He shrieked and rushed to the bed, tore her hands free of the bonds he'd tied.

"'Bye, Annie."

Bobby knocked her aside as he passed. "Sorry," he said and she saw his face again. Panic. Bobby Colbert panicked because of something she'd done, or said.

"Are you okay, Annie?" Guy stood at her shoulder with a hand on her back. "You don't look good. Was that man bothering you?"

Disoriented, she gave herself a moment to calm down before saying, "He's someone I used to know a long time ago. Bobby Colbert. We both grew up in St. Martinville. For some reason he's trying to strike up a friendship again—that's all." At least the vision had faded. "He's pushy. I should tell him to get lost. I thought I already had but I guess I wasn't nasty enough."

Guy held her shoulder. "I guess you weren't, but that doesn't surprise me. You probably wouldn't know how. Don't worry about him—he's makin' himself too public to be dangerous. He'll get the message you don't want him around. I will mention him to Spike if it'll make you feel better."

"You don't have to, but thanks." Somehow she figured Bobby's name would come up to Spike no matter what she said. "Did you get waited on?"

"Not yet. I'll get to it. Pappy's can't compete with All Tarted Up but it's a close second."

"Thank you, that's quite a compliment. Enjoy your meal." Guy's calm manner relaxed her. He was right about Bobby being too obvious to take seriously.

Annie wondered why Guy would come here, rather than All Tarted Up, but he could have business in the area.

Pappy's was busy, which was great when there was still an hour or so before the very start of the lunch rush. Toddlers and pre-schoolers played on the dance floor while their mothers visited over coffee. That had been one of Annie's ideas. She had supplied large foam blocks and at any moment a house or fort, a barn or two were going up, while others were pounded down amid shouts of laughter. One morning a week was advertised as a "Mothers With Tots" session and the idea had caught on.

Between pillars surrounding the dance floor Annie had a view of the lobby, or of the back of Blue the Alligator and some of the lobby. She looked in that direction because a lot of motion caught her attention.

And a raised voice.

Rather than run and create a stir, she walked briskly.

"It'll be okay," Guy said, falling in beside her and keeping up easily with his long strides. "Looks like Carmen is already there."

"Carmen isn't supposed to be here at this hour," Annie said, speeding up. "I'm glad he came in. What a ruckus. What's goin' on?"

She hurried past Blue and her questions were answered. Max held Bobby against a wall and took the man's wild punches to the body. Carmen, minus his Elvis duds, including the wig, stood just out of punching range with his meaty fists on his hips. Completely bald, pink and smiling happily, he was more appealing in his own identity.

Carmen saw Annie coming with Guy and shook his head.

"Does that mean we shouldn't do anything?" Annie said.

Guy caught her elbow. "Yes. *Hoo mama,* that old friend of yours is pushin' his luck. If Max decides to hit him, really hit him, he's not going to feel the same for a long time."

"Max wouldn't hurt anyone badly," Annie said, outraged. "What do they think they're doing? This is a family place."

"Families fall out sometimes," Guy said mildly and Annie gave him a disbelieving glance.

She shook off his hand and started off as if she intended to go to the hostess's desk. The instant she was out of Guy's range, she ran at the two men, grabbed one of Bobby's arms and hung on. "Stop it, you two. Right now or I'll have Carmen throw you both out."

Max, much taller, used one hand at the base of Bobby's neck to hold him off. "Stand back," he said to Annie.

She clung to Bobby's arm which he stopped trying to use on Max. With his other fist, Bobby continued to punish his opponent's ribs.

"You look so silly," Annie said. She caught Guy's eye and he grinned. "What are you laughing at? Help me stop these goons."

"You're doin' just fine," Guy said. "They're not hitting you. They'd knock the shit—excuse me. They'd hurt me."

Annie smiled, she had to. And she yanked on Bobby's arm. "Stop it, you two," she said. "Stand still or I'll call the law."

Max shook his head. "Tell him," he said, nodding at Bobby.

"He had it coming," Bobby said, breathless. "He walked past like he didn't see me and I know damn well he did. He's high and mighty—just like you. Maybe you deserve each other after all. What do I care if he decides to add you to his list?"

He quit hitting Max who waited a few seconds before releasing him. "What list would that be?" he asked quietly.

"Any list you want it to be," Bobby said, rubbing his neck. "You're good at violence, but it's not so easy to push men around, is it?"

Max shot out a hand but Guy deflected it. "Let me buy you a cup of coffee," he said to Bobby. "You're having a bad day."

Bobby's response was to flounce away, muttering to himself, and walk through the front doors.

"Ass," Max said. He swept a newspaper from the floor and stuffed it under his arm. "Thanks for stepping in, Guy. Carmen offered to smash him but I got him to hold off."

Carmen pulled his upper lip toward his flat nose in his version of a smile, showing off a wide gap between his front teeth. "Miz Annie don't like her lobby messed up," he said and wheeled away to plod toward the jukebox he revered.

"I need to get back into town," Guy said. "When I get outside I'll check on the other guy to make sure he isn't still hanging around."

"Thanks," Max said. "For everything."

When they were alone Annie felt abruptly and forcefully awkward. She glanced up at Max who looked steadily back at her.

"Did he talk to you?" Max asked her.

"Yes. He's tried to before but this time I didn't see him in time to get out of his way. From what he said to me, he's been working on turning me into the future love of his life but I think I popped his bubble today. I don't think he'll bother me again."

Max gave her a speculative look. "Good." He didn't sound convinced. "He lost it when he saw me. Let's hope he doesn't do a whole lot of that in future."

"He was just lettin' off steam. He hoped for something different from me and I disappointed him."

"If you say so," Max said. "Did you see the *Trumpet* this morning?"

"No time," she said.

"I want you to look at it now. Your office okay?"

Things were under control. "Okay." She led the way, acutely aware of him with every step she took.

Max opened the office door for her and followed her inside. "Can we make sure we're not interrupted?" he said, and stepped back to allow Wazoo to whirl past him.

"Shut the door," she told him over her shoulder. "*Annie.*" Wazoo's eyebrows shot up to her hairline and she flashed what Annie assumed were meaningful messages at her.

"Hi, Wazoo. I don't think I've ever seen you here at this time of day," Annie said.

Once more the dark brows rose and fell, and drew tight together in the middle. "I'm outa here soon enough. You gotta give Irene more loving by the way. That poor critter is terminally confused. One day you gonna come home and she'll be lyin' on her back with her feet in the air and her eyes poppin' outa her head. She'll have lost her mind, that poor Irene. That's how lonely she's gettin'."

Annie admired herself for not laughing. "It has been a bit hard on her lately. I'll be stayin' home this evening and I'll make a big fuss of her. But don't you pretend you aren't spoiling her rotten. She lives in the shop when I'm out. And she's getting fatter. Are you feeding her goodies in the café?"

"Don't you change the subject," Wazoo said. She went to Annie's desk and wrote on a piece of paper. "These are things you need to remember," she said, handing over her note.

"Thanks," Annie said, casting Max an apologetic glance. She read the note. "*Show me the bag I give you. If it's in your purse, nod. Your sexy man won't know.*"

Annie felt pink. "Thank you. Yes, I understand what you mean." She nodded.

Promptly, while Max lowered himself into a folding canvas chair, Wazoo whipped back the note. "I'll just make sure you don't forget to take this home." She reached under the kneehole in Annie's desk and pulled out her purse as if she knew exactly where it would be.

Plop, the bag landed on the seat of Annie's chair and Wazoo, with her back to Max, pushed the paper into the purse and felt around inside at the same time.

"How are you doing?" Max said to Annie. "You look wonderful."

"Thank you. You don't look so bad yourself." She smiled at him.

Wazoo made sure Annie saw her roll her eyes. She worked out the brown cotton bag that had sunk to the bottom of the purse and held it in both hands. Her eyes closed.

Annie smiled at Max again, grateful he'd decided to riffle through the pages of his newspaper.

The intensity of Wazoo's stare grabbed Annie's attention. Her pale face had become red and her eyes glittered. Slowly, she approached Annie until she stood in front of her, so close Annie had to hold herself where she was.

The brown bag, slowly raised in Wazoo's hands, looked no different, until she squeezed it, carefully, pausing from time to time and holding it out to show Annie. A faint smell, a mixture of dirt and old things, like incense residue and burned wax, tickled her nose. Wazoo grasped one of Annie's hands and placed it around the cheap cotton.

The contents felt lumpy and softer in some places than others.

Annie winced and Wazoo took the bag from her at once. "See," she said. Sharp ends of wire stuck through in many places. "I hoped it wouldn't be so, but this is the proof. The effort is costing him plenty, but that man, he is getting closer and coming in the open because he can't get to you no other way."

"What are you talking about?" Max said sharply.

"Quiet," Wazoo said. She refocused on Annie and continued to feel the bag. "This isn't all bad. It's good as long as we don't mess up with the timin'."

She pushed the smelly bag to the bottom of Annie's purse again.

"I don't understand," Annie said, but her stomach clenched hard.

"Things have gone wrong for him. He's gettin' scared and scared people do crazy things. Watch yourself. We can't know when he'll strike again."

"Who is *he?*" Annie asked.

Wazoo raised her shoulders. "I don't know yet. If we're real unlucky, we never will—until it's too late. But he's a killer and he's startin' to crack up."

CHAPTER 29

"Are you going to tell me what that was all about?" Max asked.

Wazoo had dropped her amazing comments and left, announcing her intention to find "that mind-changin' man, Nat Archer," and "spend some good lovin' time with him."

"I don't know," Annie said, honestly enough. She didn't want to bring up the...whatever she had in her purse that didn't belong there, not with Max. "I say we don't give it another thought."

"'He's a killer and he's starting to crack up,' that's what she said." Max had tossed his paper on the floor. "Of course I'm going to give it another thought. Do you really think she knows things other people don't know?"

Annie stood over him, looked down into his eyes. "Dr. Savage, what would your colleagues say if they heard you ask a question like that?"

"They won't. You're the one I'm asking. Wazoo likes to act out, but I've heard too much about her to dismiss her completely. Guy believes she's got some sort of powers, and even Cyrus hinted at them."

"Maybe she does," Annie said. "She has told me about things she shouldn't know. I always look for regular ways she could have found out but I don't find any."

Someone tapped on the door and this time Max's eyebrows rose, and he rolled his eyes. "Whatever it is, if you can get rid of it quickly we really do need to go over something."

"Okay." She raised her voice. "Come in."

Madge was first, then Cyrus.

"Cyrus brought me over to show you something," Madge said. Her movements were jerky and she wore the same dress she'd had on the previous night. She glanced down at herself and looked sheepish. "I haven't been to bed. I just couldn't. Cyrus is doin' his best to calm me down and persuade me to go sleep at the rectory but I can't till I've seen everyone I need to see."

Cyrus rolled onto his toes, and when she looked at him, turned a sunny smile on her. "We'd better make it quick. I've got a parish to run and these people have their own responsibilities." No one could miss the warmth in his expression when he looked at Madge.

"We know there are some really strange things goin' on. There's a lot that makes no sense, but Millie's okay. Can you believe it, she's fine. She was in my room waiting for me when I got home from the hospital last night. Charlotte and Vivian and I sat up the rest of the night just being happy about it. And tryin' to figure out what happened."

That's when Annie noticed something moving inside Cyrus's plaid shirt, one of the fraying few he used when he worked in the rectory garden. She stared until a wet, black nose appeared between two buttons.

Cyrus looked apologetic. "I know you can't bring dogs in here, but Madge says she isn't goin' anywhere without Millie."

"Never again," Madge said, her eyes bright with tears. "Give her to me."

Cyrus unbuttoned his shirt and Madge held her hands out to Millie. The dog squirmed up Cyrus's chest, causing him to wince when her claws dug into his bare skin, and arranged herself over his shoulder. A sigh lifted her entire body and she set about licking Cyrus's neck, his ear, the side of his face.

"Look at that," Madge said. "She's mad at me and makin' me pay for all she's been through. Of course, she's got good taste. She knows when a man is too good to let go."

Annie's silences didn't help Max. He wanted her to read the piece in the *Trumpet* and see what her reaction was without hearing his opinion first. Afterward, ideally, they would discuss what Lee O'Brien might or might not mean by what she'd written. He knew what he hoped Annie would not think, but there were no guarantees.

After a visit with Madge and Cyrus that had lasted longer than Max had expected, both he and Annie had more on their minds than ever. But Max also found some hope in the uncertainty over where the dog had gotten out of Lil's car and how she had arrived at Rosebank without a scratch, or even a sore pad. Somewhere there was a lead.

"I think Lil was left for dead," Annie said. "She'd hit her head hard and when the off-road bikers roared through and whoever attacked her ran off, he could well have believed she'd already been killed."

"She thinks he was trying to make sure she was dead," Max said. "Lil talked about him holding her down and hurting her more— and a lot of pain. She blacked out when the pain got really bad. I'm not sure if she's only talking about pain in her head but it's likely."

Annie had asked for coffee to be brought. One of the waitresses knocked on the door and bustled in to set a tray on top of littered papers as if she hadn't noticed they were there. "Coffee, cream, sugar, honey," she said, pointing to each item. "Ice water. Iced tea. Baby crab cakes, fried shrimp and a plate of pralines left over from the kids today."

"Thanks, Josie," Annie said. "Whose idea was it to give the kids pralines? Pure sugar isn't going to help their mothers keep them calm."

"It was all of us," Josie said and Annie recalled how loyal the woman was and that she was a great team player. "We watch the kids so the moms don't have to worry so much and the kids get to do what they wouldn't at home. Including eatin' sugar and gettin' high. We figure they sleep real well later."

Max ate a praline and licked his fingers. "Every kid should have as many of these as they want," he said, grinning and taking another one. "Thanks for bringing them."

Once they were alone, with Max demolishing the pile of shrimp as if he were afraid Annie might get one, she wished their lives were simple and she could think about him without the specter of disaster hanging over them.

She poured iced tea and when Max nodded, gave him the glass and got another for herself.

He wiped his hands and mouth on a paper napkin. "I forgot how long it's been since I ate."

"You've got something more than food on your mind."

Max inclined his head and looked her over slowly. "I do. You. You're on my mind all the time, but that's not what either of us mean." He picked up the paper, opened it to a page he'd obviously read before and folded it back for her. "I'm not sure what to think about this, but Lee O'Brien is angry. I think this is a threat."

Annie took the paper and read:

DON'T MESS WITH THE NATIVES
A SMALL-TOWN, LOUISIANA PRIMER FOR FOREIGNERS
BY
LEE O'BRIEN, EDITOR

"What does she mean by *foreigners?*" Annie asked. The piece had been given a prime spot on the editorial page.

"People who aren't from around here," Max told her.

Annie shook out the paper.

FOLKS WHO ARE BORN AND BRED HERE IN LOUISIANA, ESPECIALLY IN LITTLE TOWNS LIKE TOUSSAINT, DON'T UNDERESTIMATE THE LOCALS. EVEN A FEW SMART OUTSIDERS SOON FIGURE OUT THAT SOME OF THE WISEST PEOPLE LEARN ABOUT HUMAN NATURE FROM OBSERVING LIFE, NOT JUST READING ABOUT IT.

SOMETIMES IT'S THE NEWSPAPER'S JOB TO LOOK OUT FOR ITS READERSHIP AND I'M GOING TO DO THAT NOW. I CAN'T NAME NAMES OR SOME SMART CITY TYPE WILL SUE THE SOCKS OFF THE *TRUMPET* AND WE CAN'T AFFORD THAT.

THERE ARE THOSE WHO SETTLE IN OUR MIDST BECAUSE THEY THINK WE'RE STUPID. TOO HARSH? NO, JUST TRUE. THEY THINK WE'RE GULLIBLE AND UNWORLDLY, AND THAT THEY CAN TAKE ADVANTAGE OF US. I WANT YOU TO WATCH OUT FOR ANYONE LIKE THIS, THEN WATCH OUT FOR YOURSELF IF YOU COME ACROSS ONE.

WOMEN ARE MOST AT RISK. WOMEN WANT TO THINK THE BEST OF OTHERS AND THEY CAN GET SUCKED IN AND USED—SOMETIMES HORRIBLY USED AND LEFT SO EMBARRASSED THEY'RE NEVER THE SAME. BUT THEY DON'T SPEAK UP BECAUSE THEY'RE WARNED THEY WILL LOOK THE FOOL IF THE TRUTH COMES OUT.

AS I'VE ALREADY WRITTEN, I CAN'T NAME NAMES, BUT I CAN STILL WARN THE WOMEN OF TOUSSAINT. IF A MAN COMES INTO YOUR LIFE FROM A DIFFERENT WORLD, WITH A BACKGROUND THAT SEEMS EXCITING, AND LETS YOU KNOW HOW SOPHISTICATED HE IS—BACK OFF UNLESS YOU'VE CHECKED HIM OUT. SO FAR I DON'T THINK ANYONE'S BEEN IRREVOCABLY HURT BY ONE OF THESE PREDATORS, BUT IT COULD HAPPEN. THE DANGER IS THERE.

WHAT I DO KNOW IS THAT ONE WOMAN GAVE HERSELF TO A STRANGER WHO THOUGHT NO MORE OF HER THAN HE WOULD IF HE'D PICKED HER UP ON THE STREET. HE DID THINGS NO MAN SHOULD DO TO A WOMAN. AND HE MADE SURE HE HAD A RECORD OF WHAT HAD HAPPENED THAT WOULD MAKE HER LOOK BAD. HE WILL MAKE HIS DISGUSTING EVIDENCE PUBLIC IF HIS VICTIM EVER TRIES TO USE WHAT HE DID AGAINST HIM.

HE'S MADE A MISTAKE.

THIS REPORTER KNOWS THE WOMAN HE ALL BUT RAPED AND SHE'S MAD. MAD AND GUTSY AND IF SHE DOESN'T GET SATISFACTION FROM THE MAN, SHE'LL GO AFTER HIM. EVERYONE WILL KNOW WHAT A PERVERT HE IS.

AND TAKE NOTE, IF SOMEONE WANTS DAMNING EVIDENCE TO HOLD OVER YOU, THEY'RE GUILTY OF SOMETHING THEMSELVES.

THAT'S ALL I CAN WRITE FOR NOW, BUT WATCH THIS SPACE AND AS I CAN, I'LL SHARE MORE. MEANWHILE, DON'T SLEEP WITH STRANGERS.

"Oh, my, goodness," Annie said.

Max watched her face as he'd watched it all the time she was reading.

"I think Lee's done something dangerous here," Annie said.

"Dangerous why?"

Annie looked up. "She's accusin' someone of a sexual attack—right here in Toussaint. It doesn't sound as if she has any evidence except hearsay stuff. She could make someone furious enough to do her harm."

"Do you always think about someone turning violent if they're cornered?" Max regretted saying that.

"No!" Annie folded the paper convulsively. "Not usually. Just when weird stuff's been happening around here."

"I'm a foreigner in the way she means," Max said, waiting for any change in Annie's expression. "So are my brothers."

"So are a bunch of people. We've got construction workers—you know that. Most of them were brought in from other places. I've got a couple of new, out-of-town hires here. Then there's even Tom Walen hanging around. And *Bobby*. Dr. Reb's got an assistant helping out at her clinic and he came from Mississippi."

"That would make him really foreign," Max said with a smile.

Annie sighed. "Right."

"Spike showed the piece in the paper to me."

"He's worried about Lee's safety?" Annie asked.

Max thought about how he should put Spike's suggestion. "He wondered if Lee could be writing about you and me. He intends to speak to you to make sure I haven't been taking advantage of you."

Annie's mouth dropped open and stayed that way.

"He says Lee's a crusader and it would be like her to take your side and try to fight me."

"Good grief," she murmured. "She'd have no reason to make suggestions like these." She flapped the paper, then looked sharply at him. "No, Lee isn't talking about us, she's talking about someone else and I'm worried about her."

Relief crashed over Max. He hadn't believed Annie would think Lee was talking about them, but he couldn't be sure unless she reassured him. "She'd have had to make most of it up anyway since she wasn't there," he said with a wink. "And find out about the dominatrix stuff and put that in. Oh, yeah, are you a turn-on in black leather. I love those nipple holes."

"Max!" Annie glanced at the door. "Keep your voice down, you clown."

"I am. It just sounds loud because you're shocked. I kinda enjoy shocking you. Or should that be, I enjoy underestimating you?"

Annie got up, put the paper on the seat of her chair and came to lean over him, her hands on the arms of his chair. Her face was close and got closer. "I do believe you may underestimate me," she said. She left him and checked to be sure the door was locked. "We don't have a lot of time, so cooperate."

"Sure thing."

He hadn't finished speaking when she sat astride his lap and kissed him hard. She opened his mouth and probed deep inside with her tongue, then her lips gentled and she nipped at him and pressed his mouth repeatedly.

Max's hand circled her neck and he kissed her back, drawing her in, loving the taste of her. And Annie unbuttoned her shirt, undid the front closure of her bra and carried his hands to her breasts. "No nipple holes," she said, coming up for air, "but you can have every-thing instead."

She tried and failed to unzip his pants. He did it for her and with her skirt pulled high on her hips, she pushed him past her panties and inside her.

"Annie," he said, hearing his own strangled voice. "We can't do this here."

Without warning, she braced her feet on the floor and bounced up and down on him. Her breasts jiggled before his eyes and he lowered his head to capture a nipple.

He found the spot he wanted between her legs and rubbed. Finesse wasn't easy when he was losing control.

Annie let her head hang back and the word, "Yes, yes, yes," jarred from her lips.

She climaxed beneath his hand, and immediately climaxed again as he drove into her. He held her breasts and lifted his hips from the chair, meeting her each time she came down on him. The fireworks went off and he entered the world of red and black, and the best damn, sweet pain there was.

They moved, slower and slower, for moments. Max pulled Annie against him and she opened her mouth against his neck.

"And you said we couldn't do this here," she murmured.

"Foolish of me. But of course, I took advantage of you, didn't I?"

Annie smiled and raised her head, and as quickly frowned. She gripped Max's shoulders.

"What?" he said. "What's wrong?"

"Do you think the woman Lee wrote about was herself?"

CHAPTER 30

She was there, right where the guy behind the counter at the paper had said she'd be.

Working on a laptop computer, Lee O'Brien sat at a window table on the left side of All Tarted Up. Roche didn't relish what he had to do next, but there wasn't a choice, he and Kelly had discussed options and there weren't any, only this, to confront Lee.

The bright pink door of the shop sported a new coat of paint but the Pepto Bismol hue hadn't changed. Roche paused another moment and went inside the shop.

A few tables were in use but the place wasn't nearly full. The mid-afternoon rush would have passed by now. He watched Lee. She was fast on the keys and leaned way over her machine as if shielding the screen from prying eyes.

Roche approached her table but she didn't look up until he stood beside her. "I'm going to sit down," he said and pulled a chair around so he could sit beside her, effectively cutting her off from any attempt to leave.

She turned off her screen and sat with her hands in her lap.

"What you did wasn't very smart," he said.

"What would you like, Dr. Savage?" the girl, Sidney, who worked for Jilly said.

He didn't want anything. "I'll have a shot of espresso, please. That's all for now."

"Lee?" Sidney said. "Anythin' else?"

"I'll take a refill," Lee said, pushing her coffee mug across the table. Sidney filled it and left.

"Anythin' you want to argue about?" Lee said. "Make sure you talk plenty loud. There's lots of people in this town who want to know who attacked that woman I wrote about."

"No one attacked her," he told her through his teeth. "She was a willing participant. A very enthusiastic participant. From what I've heard, the lady really got into it. She wouldn't even quit when it was time to go."

"I was trying to get my tape back. I want it now."

"I just bet you do."

"Give it to me and I won't write anythin' else in the paper."

Roche smiled at Sidney while she set his coffee down.

"Is it with you?" Lee asked, with hope in her eyes.

"Lady, it's never going to be used unless you try to drag my name or the names of any members of my family through the mud. If you do, I'll have to set things straight and tell the truth. You'll look like a hooker."

"And you'd look like a bastard."

"I'm not going to let you take me down over this when it was your idea in the first place," he said.

She crossed her arms. "My idea? How would I know about mirrored rooms and mud? You couldn't make that excuse hold up."

Roche drank some of his strong coffee and enjoyed the way it felt going into his veins. "A nice girl doesn't invite herself to an empty building, at night, to meet a man."

She pinched her mouth shut and narrowed her eyes. Then she said, "I asked if I could come to talk about the new clinic. Kelly was supposed to be there. I didn't expect to see you, or have you set on me."

Roche tilted onto the back legs of his chair. "Funny, we don't seem to remember everything exactly the same way." He let the chair bang back onto all legs. "Sure you expected Kelly, but you decided you were going to get some sort of scoop. You were ready to do anything to get it and it didn't matter which of us gave it to you. You started asking questions about Max's business as soon as you were through the door. You weren't subtle. Max had no part in whatever has happened to Michele Riley. And he did nothing to those women years ago. Someone wants to frame him."

"I was only asking questions anyone would ask," Lee said. "Why would someone try to frame him when he was a high school senior? Doesn't make any sense. Everyone knows Max has been accused of murder. He will be again when they figure out what he did with Michele Riley."

"Shut...up," Roche said, looming closer to her. "My brother was not accused of murder, not officially. He was questioned. They couldn't arrest him because they didn't get any evidence. I've told you he's innocent."

"But they never found anyone else, did they? No other killer?"

"Other killer?" Roche said. "You're doing it again, accusing Max. He never did anything to anyone."

"You're his twin," she said. "I wouldn't expect you to say anything else. But I don't care about him right now. No one does what you did to me without payin' for it."

"What did I do that offended you?" Roche asked. "It sure wasn't the sex. You loved it. You're an alley cat."

She lifted her hand to strike him, but put it on the table. "You made a fool of me."

"Ah, and now we get to the truth. It was going to be fine for you to make an ass of me by suckering me in, but it doesn't work the other way around."

"Get me that tape."

"Which one," he said. He checked his fingernails.

Lee was quiet until he looked at her. "What do you mean?" she said.

"Nothing. Do you like pictures with your sound? I do."

"Pictures? Damn you." Tears looked out of place in her eyes. "I don't believe it. You're just trying to scare me."

"I have scared you and I'm not pretending about anything. I had fun in bed last night watching my big plasma screen. There's nothing like a sexy film to spice things up. I think this one might be saleable."

"Oh, sure, and you'd love your face viewed by all those sleaze-bags."

"You can't see my face. What do you think I am? And you can't tell where the action takes place either, everything's too close. Real close. You can about see the pores in your skin."

"Okay." Trembling, she pushed her computer away and wrapped her hands around her mug. "You want something. What is it?"

"Very little," Roche said. "Respect would be a good start. And no more vitriolic pieces in your pathetic rag. Then you're to keep your mouth shut about the whole thing and help squelch any negative gossip about Max. The gossip's not true. That should make you feel good about doing the right thing."

"I hate you," she said under her breath. "I was just doing my job."

"And I was just doing mine. A very nice job it was, too. I forgot to tell you the other condition."

She glared at him.

"Listen," he said softly. "I enjoyed you and I'm prepared to forget you were stupid enough to think you could get back at me. We're going to meet again."

"No, we're not."

Roche smiled and heard her swallow. He turned her on and he intended to use her appetite. "Have you ever had sex on a stair stepper?"

"No," she whispered. "And it wouldn't work. Stop this."

"I know how to make it work just fine—if it doesn't kill you. There's always a danger of bruising your diaphragm."

She took a moment to decide what he meant then turned the corners of her mouth down. "That big, huh. Funny, I don't remember that."

"You will next time. I'll show you all the ways you can use that exercise equipment—all the ways the gym staff won't tell you about."

"You're sick," she said.

"No, just horny sometimes," he told her. "But we'll get to talk all about that. Just be ready for my call."

"I won't."

"Aw, Lee." He caught her chin and pulled her toward him. "You're something, you know that?" He stuck his tongue quickly into her mouth and withdrew.

"So easy," he said, risking a brush of the back of his hand over her breasts. Despite the disgust he felt for Lee, he was getting excited.

Roche stood up. "Be where I can find you. And keep your mouth shut about the other."

She stared at him, her cheeks pink and a sheen of sweat on her upper lip and brow.

"See you later," he told her. "Take a nice bath. Make sure you're all soft for me—everywhere."

Lee curled in a ball beneath the sheets on an airbed in a small room off the print shop. Early in the morning she'd call in her part-time staff of two. This would be another important run of the paper—a special edition. There was rarely more than one issue a week.

If Roche Savage thought he could scare her into submission she'd have to teach him a lesson. One thing she'd learned as a reporter was never to give in to intimidation.

She turned on her side. The room had no windows and even with the door left open, the air was stifling and laced with odors from the old press they still used.

Roche was hot. Who would have guessed from the quiet act he put on? Too bad he was also a snake. A breeze would feel wonderful, and the scent of magnolias, a glimpse of purple bougainvillea brilliance while she sipped a julep under some trees.

Now she was hallucinating. She smiled and closed her eyes.

"Don't turn around." A voice, muffled but definitely male came from immediately behind her.

Lee began to roll toward him.

"Don't." A slap to her rump was no love pat. Her skin stung.

"What's wrong?" she said, forcing her voice to be steady. "What's happened?"

A hand came down on her arm and she heard a ripping sound. So fast she had no time to react, the intruder rolled her toward him, unwinding a roll of what had to be duct tape around her at the same time. He left the sheet between her body and the tape and worked rapidly, not stopping until there were at least three bands holding her fast like a swaddled mummy.

Her heart beat harder and harder. "Why are you doing this?"

He backed away, reached for the wall just inside the printshop and threw a switch that flooded light on behind him.

Mostly in silhouette, but not entirely, she saw his shape. She saw he was large, well built, but a surgical hood and mask disguised his face.

Lee bucked, she rocked from side to side and tossed her head. "Let me go," she cried. Her lungs expanded, puffing out her chest, pressing down onto her stomach until she felt acid rise.

Her scream rang in her ears.

He didn't say anything.

Wearing a surgical gown, his raised hands swathed in surgical gloves, he looked down on her from what felt like a distorted height. She couldn't see his eyes. Goggles hid them.

Deliberately, he snapped the wrist of each glove. Sounds like small caliber gunshots, one, two.

Sweat sprang out on her body, and her face. Her eyes hurt.

He turned his back and she saw him fumble with the gown, pull it to one side. When he faced her again, he held a hypodermic needle.

Lee blinked, pressed her eyelids together and focused again. His thumb was on the plunger.

"Don't! What is that?"

"Something to make you feel quieter. You'll like it."

"I don't do drugs. Please. Please let me go. Whatever you want, I'll do it."

He laughed.

Lee rolled her head to the side and bile oozed into her throat. She heaved and spat, tried to clear her mouth.

"Calm down," he said, holding the needle at the level of his face.

"Max?" she said, weeping, choking on the tears that ran down the back of her nose. "I'm sorry, I didn't mean anything against you. I was just looking for a story. That's what I do. It's my job. Please don't kill me."

He sank to his knees and leaned over her. Through the goggles she could see the glint of his eyes.

Once again she screamed, then kept on screaming.

She stopped.

Still he knelt there, needle in hand, swathed in his anonymous healer's uniform.

"Look," she said. "I can help you. I can start a campaign that'll stop people from saying bad things about you."

"Look over there," he said, indicating the wall farthest from the door.

"No."

"You're being very silly. Once this is over with, you'll wonder why you made such a fuss. Look over there."

She started to scream but he shouted, "Be quiet, or I'll hurt you. Now do as you're told."

"I can't."

"If you move, this could kill you," he said. "Be very still."

His head came closer. She reared up, attempted to butt him.

For a moment he paused, then he slid the goggles on top of his head and she gasped.

The needle slid into her neck with a sensation like a giant mosquito bite, and she didn't move because she didn't dare.

"It'll be quick," he said, getting up.

Lee tried to speak. Her vision clouded.

"Be brave," he told her. "Make me proud."

When the pain exploded, she arched from the bed.

She couldn't see.

The mosquito was eating her eyes.

CHAPTER 3

Carmen picked up the two men by their collars, Tom Walen in one hand and Bobby Colbert in the other. He hauled them to the front of Pappy's, kicked open the door and went outside with them.

Annie left her office in time to see the threesome disappear.

"I saw that coming. Not many men could move Tom Walen that way. Did you see him kick?"

"No and I'm glad." She glanced over her shoulder at Guy. "I didn't know you were here."

"Just stopped by," Guy said, but he gave his lopsided grin and slouched on one leg and they both knew Annie had figured out why he was spending so much time at Pappy's.

Annie put her hands on her hips and grimaced. No point in making a fuss. Max wanted an eye kept on her when he wasn't around to do the job himself. She should be flattered. She was. And embarrassed.

"Do you know what happened?" she asked. "It's not good for business to have people fightin' in here."

Guy nodded. "We're gonna have to make sure they behave—if they come back."

Annie had thought Bobby would get lost after their earlier skirmish.

"Walen's spoiling for a row with anyone he can rile," Guy said. "Bobby was it, tonight. Tom asked him what he knew about Max Savage's woman and Bobby hit him in the mouth."

"Wonderful." Denying her attachment to Max would be too little, too late.

"Bobby sees himself as your champion and he surely didn't like hearin' Walen call you Max's woman."

Annie pushed her fingers into her hair. "Why can't this be all over?"

"Because we haven't found Michele Riley. By the way, latest theory seems to be she took off because she didn't want to marry Moose Walen."

"I hope that's true," Annie said. "Maybe she'll show up like some of the women do in those cases."

Guy snorted. "If she does, she's gonna have to mow a lot of lawns to make up for what she's cost us. I talked to Nat Archer—you know him? He was my partner when I worked for NOPD."

"I heard that." One thing she couldn't imagine was Guy Gautreaux being afraid to go anywhere or do anything and she understood those were must qualities for NOPD. "Wazoo says a lot of nice things about Nat."

Guy grunted. "I see him when he comes down to take Wazoo out. He reckons the greased up door handle at the Majestic puts the lie to Michele decidin' to take off. I agree, although it's a nice thought. He thinks she wouldn't either know how, or bother with keepin' her prints off that door the way it was done. Also she'd at least take her car and abandon it when she was far enough away to make a start."

"Maybe abandon it so it would look like she'd been abducted in her car?" Annie suggested.

"Could be. But she didn't do any of those things. Spike's on board with the same conclusions. I'd better go see what's going on outside."

He didn't have to. Max came through the door with Carmen. Max's expression wasn't pretty but Carmen looked like a man who'd just finished the best plate of ribs he ever ate.

"Hey," Max said when he saw Annie. His glance never failed to nail her. It was as if he wanted to see inside her head. "You okay? Hi, Guy."

"Carmen had things under control," Guy said lightly. "Time for me to get home, I think."

"What happened here?" Max said. "You can't get two sensible words out of Carmen. He has informed the sheriff's office though. I'm going to ask—no, on second thoughts, would you mind asking to have those two followed up. See if they've got records and find out what their situations are now."

Guy gave a two-fingered salute. "Got it. I was on my way to set that in motion, anyway."

The moment Guy left, Annie said, "Is Guy working for you?"

Max looked her in the eye and said, "He's a great guy. Smart. Lots of contacts. And he wants to help me. Guy believes in me, imagine that."

"I can't imagine anyone not believing in you."

For an instant she thought he would pull her into his arms, instead he placed a forefinger on her lips and said, "Thanks."

"I can't get that newspaper piece of Lee's out of my head," Annie said. "Not one soul has given me a sideways look, but I keep thinking people are starin' at me."

Max looked wicked. "Fess up," he said softly. "You really want to know what that was all about. It definitely doesn't say the woman was raped. For all you know she's feeling guilty for having a good time."

"Max!" Annie scanned the lobby quickly. "That's evil."

"Uh-huh."

Annie punched his arm. "I can leave now. Just let me get my purse."

She ran into her office. Making sure Max hadn't followed her, she opened the purse and reached to the bottom for the brown cotton sack Wazoo had given her. It had been on her mind. Her fingernails dug into gritty dust and she grimaced.

With her stomach flipping over, she withdrew the thing. It seemed to be deteriorating with every day yet she hadn't done anything to damage it.

Annie looked at it closely. Surely enough, bits of wire poked through the cloth—more now than when Wazoo had pressed her to hold it. Annie couldn't bring herself to open the top. Cautiously, her nerves jumping, she gently felt the contents. Then she felt them again and her face seemed to grow tight.

She knew what was in the bag. A sensible person would dump a doll of this kind. Annie held it over the wastepaper basket.

The scent of incense and old wax instantly grew intense. She tried to drop the sack but couldn't make her fingers open. This was silly, a hysterical reaction to what bits and pieces she'd been told about voodoo.

"Annie?" Max said from the doorway and she shoved the doll back into her purse. In the morning she'd talk to Wazoo about this.

"I want to go out to Cloud's End," she said, facing Max. "That's where Dr. Reb and Marc live. It's not far. Lee lives there, too. She's Reb's cousin."

"So?" Max said. The worry lines in his face suggested he had a good idea why Annie wanted to see Lee.

"The more I think about it, the more convinced I am that she made a terrible mistake writing that piece in the *Trumpet*. If she did run into the type of man who took advantage of her, hurt her, even, she shouldn't have antagonized him."

"So you want to go out there and tell Lee you know she's the woman she wrote about?"

"No!"

"How else will you bring it up?" He blew out a breath. "Rather you than me."

Annie felt silly. "I guess I buried that angle under all the enthusiasm to fix things. But I'm still going to do it. Don't you worry, though. I'll call Reb and ask if I can go out there. I've got my own car."

"You're not going anywhere on your own."

She stared at him, took him by the sleeve and led him outside the dance hall. "Did you just say what I thought you did?"

"Probably. Did I say something wrong?"

Annie looked at the sky. The moon showed faint skeins of silver cloud trawling over its surface. A hot wind didn't cool the humidity one bit. "You said I couldn't go anywhere on my own. You don't get to tell me that."

He didn't answer, just settled a big hand on the back of her neck. "Things are changing with us, Annie. If you don't understand it, I'll try to explain. But I think you do understand."

Annie stood on the covered bridge and looked at the ground. She could read a lot into what he said and most of it would make her happy—if he knew and had accepted the whole truth about her. "Not one thing is stable for us. I know that." And she had held back too much about herself. She knew that, too.

"Nothing stays the same." He walked her forward. "All of this will pass. And you can avoid reality for now if you want to, but I'm a patient man. I'm not going anywhere."

She hoped he wouldn't change his mind about that.

"What will you say if we go out to see Lee?" he said.

"I don't know. I kind of thought I'd trust that I'd know once I got there."

"Never go to a meeting without being prepared," Max told Annie.

"This isn't a medical symposium," she said. "I won't be talking to a room filled with experts on something, just Lee."

"Okay, then." He swayed her toward him, kissed the top of her head. "Whatever you say, I'll be along to back you up."

He didn't like any of this. Max parked in the small lot behind the shabby *Toussaint Trumpet* building. "Too bad Lee wasn't at Cloud's End," he said.

"Yeah," Annie said. "I surely don't like this place in the dark. I can't believe Lee feels good about spending nights here."

"Relax," he said. "You aren't on your own."

"Do you like it here?"

He laughed. "You're something. I'm the big, tough male around here. Afraid of nothing. Of course I like it. Annie, will you promise me something?"

"Maybe?"

"You are one independent woman." He liked her that way but it wouldn't be a bad thing if she'd go along with him on this one.

"I wasn't always independent," she said. "I had to learn."

He could imagine Annie being shy, reticent. Even now she was generally careful of what she said. But under the circumstances it was unfortunate she'd chosen to fight Lee's battles.

"What you do and say is up to you, but do you think it might go better with Lee if you approached her as a concerned friend, rather than coming out and telling her you saw through what she wrote?" Of course Lee had been writing about Roche, damn his hide. Max knew his brother well enough to be certain he'd had plenty of encouragement but that didn't justify whatever had turned ugly enough to make Lee so mad.

"We'd better get this done," Annie said. "Don't worry, I'll be diplomatic. When she wrote about not trusting a person who wants something to hold over you, do you think that meant the man really had something? I mean, actual physical evidence?"

Max had kicked the same concern around all day. "It's more likely he compromised her and told her he'd talk about it if she gave him away." Max hadn't finished with Roche and he anticipated an ugly scene to come, but threatening women wasn't Roche's style. Lee could well have been adding more drama to her editorial.

Annie hopped out of the car but didn't shut the door until he also stood on the uneven lot. He offered her a hand and she held it quickly. Her breathing was too loud, and shallow.

"Backing out of this wouldn't make you a coward," he said.

Predictably, she pulled him to the back door which, according to Reb, was the one Lee used when the front office was closed.

An uncovered lightbulb shone from a fixture on the wall. Max rang the bell and stepped back. A glass, wire-reinforced panel gave a dusty view along a passageway inside.

"I've never been here before," Annie said.

He shook his head, watching for Lee to appear. "We should have called first." *Or not come at all.*

"I know. I didn't want to risk Lee saying she didn't want me to come."

He pressed the bell again. "If she told you that you'd know you should stay out of this."

Annie pulled on his arm. "Men and women are different. Women usually want to help other people if they can."

"And men don't?"

"Not in the same way, and I don't want you gettin' all touchy on me."

"Maybe she's gone out to eat," he said. There was a car parked in the slot closest to the door but she could have walked somewhere.

"Yes," Annie said. "You really want to give this up, don't you?"

He really wanted to do whatever was best. "I'm half expecting a disaster if you do talk to her."

"Her car's here," Annie said.

"I noticed."

"I've got this feeling I'm supposed to do something for Lee." Annie turned the handle and the door opened. She let it swing wider but stood where she was and frowned up at him. "Would she leave the door unlocked?"

"If she's just gone out for—"

"She shouldn't. Anyone could walk in."

He grinned at her. "But most people wouldn't, and small towns are famous for being more trusting, aren't they?"

"This town has one woman missing and one woman in the hospital who says she was forced off the road." Taking her hand away from his, she walked into the building.

With a sigh, Max followed. He knew better than to try to change her mind.

At the other end of the hall a door stood open. Reflections from front windows wavered through darkness in what was probably the main office.

Annie walked on tiptoe. Max didn't point out that making some noise would probably be a good idea. Instead he called, "Lee? Lee, it's Annie Duhon and Max Savage. You here?"

Annie shot around and stared at him, then let her shoulders relax. She listened with him.

"We should go," he said. "If she walks in and sees us, all we're

going to do is shock her to death before she realizes who we are."
If Lee was furious with Roche, Max would be one of the last people
she'd be glad to find waiting for her.

A wedge of dull light shone from a partially open door just
beyond Annie. She glanced at it and gently poked the door wider.

"You don't give up," Max said.

If she heard him, she didn't react. In she went and said, "This is
where they print the paper, I think."

"Come on," Max said, grinning. He wouldn't change her but
she might give him less to worry about if she showed more
caution.

"Max! Come here."

He went after her, all but running by the time he arrived in the
middle of a room filled with old but immaculately kept printing
equipment. Annie stood just inside another door that opened
inward. "What is it?" The foreboding he sensed was too familiar.

"I don't know." She put on the light. "I'm not sure."

He joined her and looked down on Lee O'Brien. Wearing a
T-shirt and panties, she lay facedown on the floor with one foot on
an air mattress covered with a fitted sheet.

Rapidly, Max stepped over her and crouched down. Her eyes
were open and horrified.

Her lips were drawn back from her teeth.

"Is she dead?" Annie whispered. "Is she?"

"Wait in the other room," Max said. "And call 911."

On his knees beside Lee he felt for her pulse, knowing he
wouldn't find it.

He didn't.

What he did discover was a body that felt about as warm as his.
Whatever felled her had happened very recently. He whipped her
to her back and started CPR. If she'd had a seizure of some kind he

could get lucky. There was nothing to lose. "911," he told Annie again, between breaths.

No blood evident. No obvious injury that he could see with each brief look he got at her. "Come on, Lee. Come on."

She wouldn't respond. "Nothing, dammit." He pulled back his right arm and landed a single, hard blow to the center of her chest. "Come on!"

He felt for her vitals again, and heard sirens at the same time.

"She's gone," Annie said and he looked at her. Tears slid down her face.

"Yes," he said.

CHAPTER 32

Reb O'Brien Girard, arms tightly crossed, sat down with Max and Annie in a dilapidated lunchroom across the hall from where Lee lay dead.

Even from their removed spot, Annie blinked at white light that seeped from spotlights at the death scene. Photographers were at work. She tried not to think about strangers taking pictures of Lee lying helpless like that.

"Why are they photographing someone who died of..."

"That's why," Max said. "It looks like natural causes but they do it just in case."

"But what natural causes?" Annie persisted. "A heart attack, I suppose. As young and fit as Lee was and she just went off with a heart attack."

"We don't know what went wrong yet," Reb said, her voice strained.

Max said, "There isn't anything I can say that'll make a difference, Reb. But I'm sick you're going through this."

"I can't believe it. Lee was the most alive person I knew." She shifted and blinked, raised her face to stop tears from falling.

Reb had insisted on being there, not just to identify her cousin's body, but in the capacity of medical examiner.

"You don't have to do this," Max said. "They can bring in someone else."

From her expression, she knew what he meant and shook her head. "I want to be here for Lee. I want to be the one to touch her and care about what I'm doing. That's all I can do for her now, the last thing I can do for her. I'll go back in when the photographers leave."

Annie made a sound in her throat as if she'd come close to choking.

"You okay?" Max asked. She had a cool head. Even though what she'd seen had wounded her, she didn't panic or show any sign of falling apart.

"I'm as okay as I can be," she said. "Do you have any guesses about what killed her yet, Reb?"

"No, it's a mystery so far," Reb told her. "There'll be an autopsy and I don't think we'll know much more before that. She wasn't the type who showed up for physicals, but I took care of any medical issues she did have and she was a healthy woman. If it was a heart attack or a stroke I didn't see any warning signs."

Max hoped Reb wouldn't start blaming herself for something she probably couldn't have known. "I thought I heard Marc's voice," Max said of Reb's husband.

"He came with me. He's talking to Spike. Everyone's going to feel so awful about Lee. She rubbed people the wrong way often enough but they liked her."

"Does she have other family?" Annie asked.

"I'm the closest. In a way I should be glad she was here with us.

I'm not lookin' forward to telling Simon. I think it was understood they'd get together when they were both ready to settle down."

Max glanced at Annie. She looked as blank as he felt.

"Simon Menard," Reb said. "You probably never met him. He's been overseas—Egypt, I think—on special assignment for a magazine. Simon owns half of the *Trumpet,* but I know he got involved so he and Lee would have a reason to keep getting together. I'll have to track him down."

"Rotten luck for the guy," Max said.

"Reb?" Spike walked in. "As soon as you're ready Lee can be...moved."

Max stood up. "Is it okay if I come with you?" he asked Reb, who nodded, yes. "Will you be all right here, Annie?"

"Of course."

He smiled at her and she tried to smile back but the result was more of a grimace.

Spike, Marc Girard and Guy stood in the printing room. Max was surprised to see Guy there and said so.

"Heard it on the radio," Guy said. "Some habits don't go away." He took Reb into a quick embrace. "Sorry, kid," he said.

"I'm expectin' a crowd anytime," Spike said, with his wry grin. "Listening in to official bulletins is a local pastime."

Two medics arrived with a gurney and body bag and Max looked swiftly at Reb who stared straight ahead. Marc Girard held his wife's hand and took it to his mouth. When they were together his dark eyes rarely strayed from her. Tonight he worried about her and it showed.

Wazoo flapped into the room, her hair wild. "What's happened?" she said. "Me, I got to know. Who you got in there?" She pointed to the sleeping cubicle.

"I told you," Spike muttered to the room at large. "Listening in. It's a local pastime."

"You told me nothing, you," Wazoo said, her expression dark. "I got the feelin' is all. I thought on it. I tried to see who was calling to me, but there was only the cold. Then I heard the bulletin on my radio so I come right away."

Wazoo got "feelings," Annie got "feelings," hell, he'd even gotten some odd feelings himself. Max looked at the small, dark-haired woman in her swirling black lace and wondered what had happened to his well-formed opinions on the order of things.

"Annie's across the hall," he said. "In the lunchroom. She could use some company."

"Just the one I want to see," Wazoo said. She angled her head toward the cubicle. "Who is it, Reb?"

"Lee. She's dead."

Wazoo's very black eyes narrowed. "Me, I didn't expect that," she said, shaking her head. She sped away, muttering as she went.

"Strange woman," Max said.

"She's got a good heart," Reb said and went back to her cousin's side.

Max joined her. "It was probably quick," he said although they both knew every platitude in the book.

"Not so quick—she was terrified when it happened."

"That's how it looks," Max said. "But sudden pain could cause that."

"We're done," one of the photographers said while he disassembled equipment.

The medics hovered outside. Reb knelt again and touched Lee's face, "I'd have tried CPR, too," she said. "This is how helplessness feels, isn't it?"

"Yes," he told her quietly. "But we know from the beginning that we won't be able to save them all."

"I looked her over and I swear there's no sign of anything

external. I think she died lying down, or at least she didn't fall that I can see." Reb rubbed her face. She ran her hands over Lee's body again, bent to kiss her cheek and blushed.

Max looked away. "Do you have any reservations about this being a natural death?" he said quietly. "I'm not trying to upset you, just being objective."

"I don't have a good reason for reservations," she said. "But I've got them just the same. I feel as if I've missed something but I don't expect to find it."

More of those feelings.

"May I?" Max said and when Reb nodded, he examined both sides of Lee's arms closely.

"If she'd been a drug user I'd have known it," Reb said.

He went over the body. Her back and buttocks were already darkening slightly as blood began to pool.

Reb had closed Lee's eyes. Her fair hair made a cushion under her head. Not a blemish showed on pale skin. He automatically ran his fingers behind her ears and down her neck. "What a waste," he said, sitting back on his heels. He bowed his head closer to see a tiny mark on the side of her neck. It was almost invisible in a crease of skin.

"Did you see this?" he asked Reb.

She knelt beside him and peered up close. "No. Could be a tiny red mole or an insect bite, even. Wait, I've got a magnifying glass."

"Here." She took it from her bag and gave it to Max.

He brought the area into tight focus and Reb shone her flashlight on the spot. Wordlessly, he took the flashlight from her and handed over the magnifier.

"She could have…" Reb began.

"You think she could have done this herself? And lying on the floor in a dark room?"

"No." Reb's fair, freckled skin all but shone against her red hair.

"No," Max said. "She was given an injection here."

Annie listened for the gurney to leave. She couldn't help staring at Wazoo who had come into the room and immediately gone into some sort of trance. Standing, her feet apart, her hands at her sides, with eyes closed she turned her face toward the ceiling.

And she'd been there for several minutes.

Voices grew gradually louder as if someone was coming slowly toward the lunchroom.

"*Ooh, ya, ya,*" Wazoo said, spitting it out venomously. "The conscious world has no sense of timin' because it senses nothin' it can't see or touch."

"Wazoo," Annie said. "This is a really stressful time."

Wazoo pointed from Annie to herself. "Just for you? I think for me, too. Where you got that bag I give you?"

An involuntary shudder rocked Annie. "It's in my purse and I don't want it anymore. I know the kind of thing it is and I don't believe in any of that."

"Hush!" Wazoo shot the heels of her hands toward Annie. "Don't you offend. Open your purse."

Annie did as she was asked but wouldn't put a hand inside. Wazoo had no such reservations and whipped the brown bag into the harsh artificial light. Making a crooning noise, she cradled it in her palms. "Here," she whispered to Annie. "Come close and see." She smiled a purely delighted smile.

Looking at the nasty bag wasn't high on Annie's list of preferences but she went and looked at the thing Wazoo held out. "It's a mess," she said.

"Mmm." Wazoo nodded and grinned even wider. "It's workin'. They don't know what's happenin' yet, but they will. There's many things hidden from all of us and a few we see clearly. I see someone gettin' too scared to be clever much longer."

"What do you mean?" Annie asked softly.

"You take care of yourself," Wazoo said, putting her magic or whatever it was back into Annie's bag. "I'm doin' my best and you got that big man who cares about you, but you be careful. He could only help if he was there when it happened. All I can do is warn you."

Annie prickled all over. "Warn me about what?"

"You aren't safe. But your enemy's gettin' weaker and more careless."

"I don't have any enemies," Annie said, mortified by her squeaky voice.

"Not in the way you mean, maybe, but there are other ways."

"What ways."

Wazoo threw up her hands. "Me, I don't know everythin'."

CHAPTER 33

Dear Max:

You fool. You might have gotten away with Michele Riley, but you've blown your chances.

It's all over the radio that a body was found at the newspaper offices and you were there when the cops arrived. I thought you were smarter than that.

And what was the deal with not getting rid of the body? You're losing it. You should have taken the body and done what you always do after one of your killings.

You panicked.

Or are you trying to change your M.O. Serial killers never do that—not the best ones.

Did you pretend you'd walked in and found this one dead? If you did, how long do you think it will take them to figure you out? Dr.

Savage, the man involved with the killings of three women already.

What do you think you are, bulletproof?

They're going to take you in this time.

CHAPTER **34**

They watched the sun come up. The early boat traffic eased back and forth on the Teche. A trail of pirogues, each with someone wielding the oar at one end, took children to school. With the ease of long practice, the kids held their places, single file, in the middle of the narrow wooden craft. High voices carried on air barely warm before the hot day to come.

Annie sat close to Max on a slab of rock. He leaned forward, his forearms braced on his knees, and she looked at his black hair, ruffled by a breeze, and the breadth of his shoulders. Max had become familiar to her but not someone she could take for granted.

"Sooner or later we're going to have to get more sleep," he said. "We can't make it on a couple of hours."

"You're right."

"Making love to you is unbelievable."

She flushed. "Do I say, 'thank you,' or, 'ditto'?"

He laughed and looked at her over his shoulder, squinting one eye against the heightening sun. "Both," he said. "Then I'll say both and we can go around and around."

"As long as we use every hour in bed the way we did last night, we won't get more sleep," Annie pointed out. "But it's okay with me." It was so okay. And she was so troubled and afraid that what they'd found together could be stolen away.

"You were the one who wanted to be out here before sunup," he pointed out.

She said, "Yes, and I'm glad. I've got a lot to say to you, Max, and I wanted to be outside where I feel free, not in my apartment. And I think we should go to the rectory to support Reb and Marc when they talk to Cyrus about Lee this morning."

He deliberately avoided mentioning that he would leave her later in the day to be present at Lee's autopsy. So far he hadn't told Annie about the mark he and Reb had found while examining the body. If it meant nothing, why make what was already awful even worse?

"Would you mind if we do that?" she said. "Go to the rectory, I mean?"

"No. I'll be glad to go." The only peace he'd found in weeks had been in Annie's arms. He turned back to the bayou and blew into a fist, attempting to take his mind off southerly parts that wanted Annie in his arms again—for a start.

"I told you what I saw," Annie said. "Or thought I saw in my nightmares."

That snapped his moment of bliss. "Yes."

"I didn't lie. It was true."

"I know you aren't a liar. I'm sorry I blew the way I did when you first told me about it."

Annie set a hand on his back. "You asked a good question. You wanted to know how I could imagine things that had been real parts of your life. The burnings. The names. I can't explain the names at all. I've thought about it and I think it's partly coincidence. I had a bad experience with fire. I had horrible dreams afterwards, and I'd wake up still seein' the same scenes, but they went away in time. Then they started again a month or so ago, but I don't know why."

"Put it behind you if you can." Max wanted to. If he could, he'd never think about any of it ever again.

"One night in St. Cécil's I thought I saw a man in a hood."

Max swung to look at her. "What night? What man?"

"Just a night some time back when I couldn't sleep. I took a walk and ended up at the church. I felt safe there. But I had a nightmare. And I saw a man in a hood. I think I did."

"Lil saw a man in a hood rushing her car. Are you sure you haven't muddled that in with your own story?"

She narrowed her eyes. "I expected that. No, I didn't get anything muddled. I saw the same thing again. The night we argued and you left. I went through to the back of the apartment and looked out the window. I was looking for you. I saw your car drive out of the alley, then, just for a moment, I saw a man wearing a hooded jacket of some kind. He was hunched over and he hurried past the gate. You left the gate open."

"Because I was too angry to think straight," Max said, searching his memory for anything he might have seen when he was getting into his car that night. "So this person was in the alley while I was with you. That makes a whole lot of sense."

"It doesn't make any, but I've wanted to tell you, that's all."

"You should. And we should tell Spike," Max said. "Today, I should think. I like him, y'know. A lot. I'm still not sure where I stand with him. He behaves as if he trusts me but puts me on warning from time to time."

"Spike's a good man and I'm sure he knows you are, too. Look what he's got on his hands? And this is a little place with a small law enforcement department."

"Yeah," Max said. "I think he'd be just as happy if all he had to think about was speeding tickets."

Annie laughed. "He used to be a cop in New Iberia until he fell out with his boss for bein' too eager and showing everyone else up. That kind of puts a hole in your theory."

She was right but he only gave her the pleasure of seeing him shrug.

Along the far bank of the bayou, sun rays reached what was left of the night's fog and turned into faint, gold strokes. Water hyacinth bobbed on the surface and one patch moved faster than the rest where it probably rested on the back of an alligator in transit.

"I've had a more checkered life than you know," Annie said.

Max heard the complete strangeness of her voice and sucked in his belly. "You don't have to tell me anything that makes you uncomfortable. We were all kids, and we all got into little scrapes."

"I want to tell you about things that changed me. In a way they were helping me get where I am today. Right here, I mean, with you. And in Toussaint. You need to know."

"Whatever you say." But he wished she didn't sound resigned, as if he would disapprove.

"I think I'd forgotten how to dream," she began. "Or forgotten how to get started on a dream, maybe. In a way everything started ten years ago, beside this bayou only up near St. Martinville. If I hadn't kept a date with Martin Samuel, nothing would be the same as it is today—for me—except for the much earlier stuff with Bobby."

Annie heard children on the water again, and felt herself slip away a little. She could tell Max now, without picking her words, just flat out say it the way it was ten years ago.

* * *

He was late. That probably meant he wasn't coming.

There she went again, being negative. Of course Martin would come for their date.

A fluttering in her belly felt familiar—and it didn't feel bad. How long was it since she'd last known she didn't feel bad? If the fluttering wasn't a dream (now and again she did have a sort of fantasy sensation where she saw colors in her head) it could be something to do with hope. Whatever it was, she'd take it.

The bayou was low and she sat on the bleached knee of a worn-down cypress tree. Scummy pea-green water had retreated enough to leave the stump all but dry at the base and from there she studied the way the water gently heaved. Annie had lived in Louisiana all her life, in St. Martinville, St Martin's Parish precisely, and her mama said they hadn't had such a long dry patch since Annie was a skinny little girl.

Didn't feel natural.

Most things didn't feel natural.

Sure was hot enough. Her cotton dress stuck to the skin on her back and sweat drizzled down the sides of her face. She jumped at the sound of a splash and watched a fat, white nutria pulling its thick-tailed body out of the water. A time was when she would have tried her hand at catching the tasty rat for dinner. Her mother made the best nutria pie in the parish.

Today she wanted to look decent more than she wanted to see her mother smile, and if that was mean, then so be it. She really wanted to look pretty. Time came when a girl had to look out for her own needs.

Maybe he wouldn't come after all.

Until three weeks ago, Annie hadn't had a plain old date since the third year in high school when she got pregnant and had to find a job. She didn't like to think about all that. Her little girl had been born too early and her lungs hadn't been properly developed. They couldn't keep her alive.

That was then, almost five years earlier, and this was now. She wanted to start over. All because of a pair of kind eyes looking at her over beer froth on the top of a glass, and the way a man put the glass down so slowly, never glancing away, Annie thought she might be coming alive again. He was to meet her here today. At first she wouldn't believe he had actually known her before she'd seen him at Petunia's Gumbo in town. But he had. Martin Samuel reminded her how they'd exchanged glances at a library in Lafayette six months earlier.

Hoo mama, *how a little thing could change your life. Annie took classes at the junior college, traveled there three evenings a week because she was going to make something of herself. She had her GED, but now she needed real qualifications to work her way up from boxing cakes at a local factory. She wanted to be a cook. People looked up to a good cook and Annie just knew she'd always have a desirable job if she could run a kitchen. Could be one day she'd have her own place—something like Pappy's Dance Hall down by Toussaint.*

Maybe she'd call it Annie's Dance Hall. Best eats and best music around.

In that library she'd sat across from Martin. Just once. When he mentioned the occasion, she recalled seeing him and thinking he was one of the nicest-looking men she'd ever seen. But they hadn't met again until three weeks ago. Martin said he'd been looking for her. How he had found her, she couldn't guess. They'd had four dates and today would be the fifth. Why not ask him how he had been clever enough to search her out?

Clouds slid over the sun and the trees threw darker shadows on the water. Faint nets of shading cast by mossy beards hovered between reflected branches.

"You givin' up on me, Annie Duhon?"

She smiled and looked at him over her shoulder. "What makes you think you've been on my mind at all?" Warmth gave her a little giddy feeling, warmth from being happy.

"Oh, don't you be coy with me, young lady. What you doin' here, sittin' on that stump, if you aren't waiting for me?" He walked toward her and showed no sign of concern at the damp ground pushing up around his shoes. "Answer me that, girl. And remember, tell the truth and shame the devil."

Annie laughed. He was one of those tall, rangy Cajun men. Black hair, black eyes, olive skin and too appealing to be healthy—for a woman concentrating on getting to be a real good cook and changing her life.

He drew close, bent over and put his big hands on his knees. "I do believe this is the best view I've ever had of you," he said, not smiling anymore. "You're a lovely woman, Annie, with the nicest smile I ever did see. Everything else about you is nice, too."

Annie felt her cheeks get red. She turned her head away from him and remembered her mother's warning. "Don't you ever forget how a sweet-talkin' boy got you pregnant and cost you more than any girl should have to pay. This time it's a man and the only difference between a boy and a man is a man is bigger, stronger and slicker. Men and boys want the same thing, it's all in how they go about gettin' it."

The heat in her face throbbed. That had been before her last date with Martin. This time Mama didn't know where Annie was or what she was doing.

"What is it?" Martin touched her arm. "Have I offended you? Come on too strong? If I have, I apologize and I'll be more careful in future."

"You were nice," she told him and jumped from the cypress knee to stand on the soggy dirt. Finding him so close surprised her but she stayed right where she was. "I've had some busy years trying to make a life for myself and I'm out of practice with pretty talk."

He offered her a hand and she held it. Well, they'd met five times now and he'd shown no sign of trying the kind of things Mama feared he would. Why shouldn't she hold his hand?

"I brought us a picnic," Martin told her. "After a bit I'll run back to my car and get it."

"Lunchtime's gone," she told him quietly, smiling up into his face.

"But dinner isn't," he said. "I thought we'd wander over to a little spot I know and talk awhile. When the sun goes down a bit more and we're hungry, why, then we'll eat."

They strolled along the edge of the bayou before Martin led Annie up a little rise where a faint path showed, to a rotted-out wooden bench in front of a willow tree. He sat on the bench and indicated for Annie to join him.

Gingerly, she perched on the silvered slats. "It'd be a shame to spoil this bench by falling through it," *she said, and giggled. Gradually she wiggled her way to lean against the back.* "Well, I'll be. Would you look at that? You can still see the water from here. I thought it would be hidden."

"Not hidden," *he said.* "An inlet curves around there and comes this way. Did you tell your mama you were meeting me today?"

"No, not this time. Why?" *She hadn't wanted another lecture.*

He put an arm along the back of the seat behind her. She didn't mind. "The other day I thought you didn't seem yourself. You were edgy."

"I was fine." *She most certainly had been edgy.*

"Annie——" *He turned so he could see her face and pulled up a knee.* "I would like to meet your mama."

"Why?" *That was an inappropriate response but he had shocked her.*

"Because you and I aren't children. We know somethin' special's happening with us and it's happening fast. Don't you think your family should be included?"

"We've only met five times," *she said quietly.* "Six if you count the library."

"Exactly, and I think about you all the time." *He shook his head.* "Forgive me. I'm goin' too fast for you but this never happened to me before. I haven't known many women because I always figured I was looking for one special one. Now I've found her I want us to share our happiness with those who care about us. Next weekend I hope you'll let me take you to meet my folks in New Orleans."

Annie's heart thudded so hard it hurt. "I see."

Martin was quiet awhile.

"I like sitting here with you," *she told him.*

"But you didn't understand what I said to you—about feelin' something special between us?"

Annie messed with a thread hanging from a button on his shirt. "I do understand." She leaned closer and wound the loose piece around and around beneath the button so it wouldn't fall off.

"Do you feel the way I do, cher? Would you hate it if I asked you to marry me?"

Her head buzzed and she thought she must have misheard him. Things like this didn't happen to Annie Duhon-the-loser. Now, she shouldn't put herself down like that. The nice people who helped her get well after... She'd made mistakes in the years after her little girl died, but those people at the rehabilitation place taught her how to respect herself again. She'd never touch drugs again.

She looked at Martin and he smiled at her. With his free hand he gathered up both of hers and held them against his chest.

"I like you a lot," she said.

"Enough to marry me?"

He wasn't making fun of her after all. "Well," she said, tentative. "Yes, I like you enough for that."

"Poo-yi—" He let his head hang back and he laughed. Then he hugged her to him. "I was scared to ask but I'd made up my mind I would. Once I make up my mind I don't change it. You have made me a happy man."

Annie's pulse fluttered and she couldn't get quite enough air.

"Do you like this?" Martin kept on holding her but reached into a pocket. With Annie in the crook of his arm, he showed her a ring. "Would you do me the honor of letting me put it on your finger?"

"It's beautiful," Annie said of a dark ruby in an antique gold setting. She held out her hand and he slipped it on her finger. "I don't think I should take it," she told him. "You don't really know me."

"I know you as well as I need to. That was my grandmother's ring. She gave it to me for the woman who becomes my wife. That's you, Annie."

What would her mother say? She would like Martin, how could she help it?

The ring looked elegant on her long-fingered hand. She started to giggle, couldn't help it. She and Martin were engaged to be married. They'd never as much as kissed. He treated her with so much respect, just like you'd expect a gentleman to do.

They both faced the bayou but Martin pulled her close. "I don't want to wait," he said. "We don't need to go through all the ritual. Talk to your mother and see how dates work out for her—we'll do it together. Three weeks should be all we need to get ready."

Annie's heart got tighter. Her life was going to change. She'd known it would, but not so soon.

He stroked the side of her face. "Would you like to give up your job and go to school full-time? You know I travel. I want you to do whatever makes you happiest so you'll be busy while I'm gone."

School full-time? Annie covered her face and let her hair fall forward.

"Hey, hey, cher." Martin rubbed her shoulders and neck and kept his fingers there beneath her hair. "You wouldn't be cryin', would you?"

She shook her head. Tears ran down her cheeks but she laughed and hiccuped.

"I have rushed you," Martin said.

"No, no, no. I'm so happy."

Annie looked into his face.

He wiped the tears from her cheeks.

She wanted him to kiss her and brought her mouth closer to his.

Martin put a finger on her lips and touched his own to her brow. "I sure do want you, Annie."

He wanted her. A man like him who could have any woman he wanted. He must expect her to say something but she couldn't think what. Please don't let him get mad about her not saying anything.

"Listen to this place," he said, his voice gentle. "Some would think it silent, but everything's talkin'."

Annie's stomach quit hurting. "I like it here," she said. Waving willow branches swished and cast shadows over Martin's face. Small animals skit-

tered in the brush, crickets clacked and she even heard faint creaking in the cypress trees and the sound of dry Spanish moss catching against peeling bark on the trunks.

"It's noisy," she said, smiling at him.

A pirogue swayed through the water, a man standing at the oar and two small children sitting one behind the other in the middle of the narrow wooden boat. The children screeched with laughter.

"It's hard to find a little peace that lasts," Martin said, sounding annoyed. "Let's go, it's time for our picnic. I don't like an orange sun. Looks like it's bleeding to death."

The orange sun he spoke of lowered in the sky, sending fiery shafts through the trees and lightening the color of the water. Annie thought it beautiful. "We should eat," she said. "I'll help you bring the food from the car."

"It's getting cold," he said, although Annie hadn't cooled off one bit. "We might eat in the car but that isn't what I had in mind. Maybe we could go to your house and eat. We could wait for your mama. We need to talk."

"Mama won't be back till late. She's with her sister."

At first his silence worried her. He was working out how they would do things. Men didn't like it if you messed with their plans.

"You're right," she said. "It's comfortable at my house and we could wait for Mama to come home."

She could see he liked the house. It was a single story, surrounded by trees, and Annie and her mama kept bright potted flowers along the gallery.

"It's nice out here," Martin said. He parked his car facing the narrow lane leading from a rough road to the Duhon place. "Secluded. You and your mama made a good choice."

"My folks bought it. Dad died two years ago and left the place paid for so we get along fine."

Martin got out and came around to help her from the car. He ruffled her hair and said, "We're going to need a house of our own—in New Orleans.

Your mama won't like that, but she'll feel better when we tell her she can be with us whenever she pleases."

They climbed to the gallery and Annie let them into the house. "The kitchen's at the back and the window's so close to the trees we can pretend we're picnicking after all," she said. It felt funny to be in the house with Martin—alone. Not that she didn't know she could trust him.

"I want to tell you something," he said suddenly. "I should have made sure you knew everything about me before I asked you to marry me."

He walked past her, straight to the kitchen and leaned against the sink with his arms crossed.

"Don't look so unhappy," she said. "We all have things in our past we wish we could forget."

"You couldn't have anythin' bad in your background. You're untouched. Annie, I was married before but my ex-wife wasn't a good woman. I had to divorce her."

Of course he'd had a life before they met. So had she. "I'm sorry," she said. "You wouldn't have done it if you hadn't had a good reason. I had a baby, Martin. When I was in high school. She died and I still feel sad about it."

"Thank you," Martin said. "Thank you for believin' in me enough to tell me that. We're going to be so close, cher. Come here and let me hold you."

He met her in the middle of the kitchen and they clung together.

"We've made a commitment," he said.

Annie whispered, "Yes. I never expected to have this much joy."

"This is just the beginnin'. Purging the soul takes time. Annie, I'm exhausted. I didn't get much sleep last night and it's been the kind of day that wrings you out. Maybe I should go. Your mother won't appreciate a man who's fallin' asleep while he talks."

A panicky feeling shook Annie. "I don't want you to leave me. Not now."

"And I don't want to leave you—ever—but I need to be sensible."

"Take a nap till Mama gets home. She'll be another couple of hours. Sleep here."

He shook his head. "That wouldn't look good."

"Oh." Her face felt hot. "Why, it'll look just fine. You can sleep in my room and I'll bake something for after dinner."

"You're tempting me."

She smiled. "Good. Oh my, how long is it since you ate?"

"I'm not hungry now but I will be later, in time for your baking."

"Come on, sleepy boy," she said, leading the way to her room at the front of the house, across from the tiny sitting room. She opened the door and walked in ahead of him. "Don't laugh at the frilly stuff. Mama likes it and I think she pretends I'm still her little girl."

Martin came behind her and put an arm around her neck. "It's okay for her to think of you that way. Innocence is easy to love." He kissed her ear, ran his tongue around the inside. "It's so easy to love you. I shouldn't ask, but would you lie with me? I need to feel your warmth."

She struggled to find her voice. "I shouldn't."

"No, of course not. Forgive me. I'll go now."

"You stretch out on that bed. I'll hold you till you sleep."

Without warning, Martin picked her up and dropped her on the bed. He sat beside her, held her wrists above her head and kissed her. Annie could scarcely catch her breath. She'd never been kissed like that before. His tongue reached into her throat and flicked back and forth. When he raised his head his face had flushed, and his black eyes shone bright. "You're so beautiful," he said. "I bet you're beautiful all over."

He excited her. Inside, she trembled.

"Can I do the things I want to do? We are goin' to be married."

Annie stared up at him and drew in a sharp breath when he sat astride her hips. He released her hands, slid the straps of her dress from her shoulders and pulled the bodice down to her waist. She didn't wear a bra. Panic bubbled into her throat. She watched the top of his head, the glimmer on his dark hair when he licked her breasts, bit her nipples. "This isn't right," she told him, not wanting him to stop.

His response was to pull her arms free of the straps. Once more he took her hands over her head but this time he produced lengths of twine and tied first one, then the other wrist to the rails of the wrought iron bed. Her finger stung when he wrenched off the ruby ring.

Annie screamed.

She tried to fight him, she struggled, but his body pressed down on her and she was no match for his strength.

"I want to stop," she said clearly. "Please let me go, now." Be firm, she'd been told. Don't do anything you don't feel comfortable about.

"That's not what you said to the boy who fucked you in high school. Or to the men who paid your rent and kept you in drugs in New Orleans for years."

She couldn't speak, couldn't think. Why would he behave like this? Why would he put a ring on her finger and talk of marriage, then do this? How did he know about her shameful past after the baby died? Annie started to cry.

"Shut up." He pushed her skirt up to her waist and tore off her panties.

"Don't," Annie said. "I'm not a bad person, not anymore. If you think I am, why did you want me?"

He laughed. "When you went down in the woods today, you shouldn't have gone alone," he sang. "Those people in the pirogue spoiled everything. No one comes up that inlet. I should know, I've studied it. Everything would have been perfect. You were going to drown and no one would ever figure out how. This is so much messier." He pinched her belly hard and laughed when she cried out. Pitching his voice higher, he said, "Mama won't be back till late."

Annie shook so badly her teeth clattered together. "I'm not sure when she's coming home. I knew there was time for you to nap and feel better is all."

"You're terrified," he said. "I like to see a woman terrified. I like her to struggle and wish she'd never met me. Women like you wouldn't get punished without men like me. A woman like you made me HIV positive."

The panic roared out of control. Annie screamed again, and Martin slammed a hand over her mouth before he ripped her bodice apart and crammed fabric into her mouth. She gagged. He caught hold of her hair and turned her head to one side. "Oh, no," he said. "No choking to death till I'm ready, tramp. Once a tramp, always a tramp."

Blood pummeled her eardrums. The orange sun had died and shadows filled the room, turned it black and white in her eyes.

She felt him tie one of her feet to the bed and kicked at him. He finished and grabbed her flailing ankle. With her legs splayed wide apart, he secured the second foot and immediately stuffed her cotton panties between her thighs.

"There," he said, still at last. "You lie there and think about the things you hookers do to decent men."

From his pants pocket he took an old lighter. He eased it apart and dripped stinging fluid between her legs. With the lighter back together, he flicked a flame to life.

Annie's eyes filmed over. When she wailed her pain, the cloth in her mouth moved deeper into her throat. She smelled burning hair, felt scorching skin.

From somewhere close she heard her mama call, "Annie, whose car is that outside? Who is with you? I've brought someone you used to know. He's been lookin' for you. You're gonna be surprised."

Martin turned toward the door, his features stretched wide, tight. He started in that direction, then returned to wrench the twine from her wrists. "Lyin' bitch," he muttered. "Filthy, lyin' whore."

Annie struggled to sit up, beating at the already dying lighter fluid flames.

And a man shouted, "Something's burning. In that room. Call the fire truck."

Mama had come home early. She and a stranger would come in here.

The fire was out but Annie hurt so badly she gulped to breathe. The air tasted oily.

Staring about, his eyes wide and glassy, Martin spun around and rushed the other way, banged into the foot of the bed as he went.

He ripped back the lacy curtains.
Martin couldn't get the windows open.

Silence lasted so long Annie felt tears sting her eyes. He hated what she'd told him, especially the parts he'd known nothing about, the worst parts.

"And it was Bobby your mother met somewhere and brought home?"

"Yes. It turned out he was back from college and wanted to take up where we left off."

Max stood up and stared across the bayou. Why had she thought he might accept what she told him and tell her it didn't matter?

"Did you start seeing Bobby again?" he asked.

"No. I couldn't have forgotten how he left me alone when I was pregnant. Not that I had any right to be choosy."

He faced her. "You have a right to be choosy, you always did." Sitting beside her again he hugged her until her ribs hurt. "Bastards, both of them. Martin——"

"He's in jail. It turned out I wasn't the first woman he'd attacked. I was just the first he'd…mutilated."

"You are not mutilated, dammit. You haven't seen mutilated. You belong to me, got that?" Giving another crushing embrace he pressed his cheek to hers. "If I set eyes on Bobby Colbert again, I'll kill him."

"He didn't do what——"

"What he did was just as bad. Worse. He destroyed your confidence so the other freak could take advantage of you."

CHAPTER 35

The ice cubes melted as the tea hit them. And the tea came out of
the refrigerator.

"Damn, it's frustratin'," Spike said, whipping off his Stetson and
wiping his brow with a forearm. "Every turn I take goes nowhere."
He slapped the hat back on and took a glass of tea from the old picnic
table out back of the rectory.

The meeting planned for that morning had been postponed until
later in the day, until after the autopsy on Lee. They were waiting
for Reb and Marc to arrive. Max felt out of place in the gathering
on Cyrus's dried-up lawn. Cyrus, Madge, Guy and even Annie
looked at home but he was an interloper. He couldn't even fathom
why he was so welcome given the amount of hostility he'd met from
some people in Toussaint.

And he couldn't find Roche. That was what ate him up—his twin
had gone missing and Max didn't dare ask if anyone had seen him.

Kelly knew he wasn't around and worried the same as Max did, but Kelly wouldn't be back in town until tomorrow.

Annie wore a blue-and-white striped polo shirt, a blue cotton skirt that hit her just above the knee and white sneakers. She looked pretty and fresh—and sad.

She took two glasses of tea and brought him one. "Is everything coming to a dead end?" she asked.

"You sure that's the term you want?" he said and grimaced. "Sorry. We're all getting punchy. Some cases do fade away without solutions but I can't believe this will. If there's a link between the things that have happened here, I wish someone would figure it out."

"That's the million dollar question," Guy said. "The mystical *link*."

As usual, big, black Daisy rested beside Guy, her head on his foot. Madge's Millie made running attacks, landed on Daisy's head repeatedly and got no more response than the flick of an ear or a loud snort. Annie was reminded of a horse swatting at flies with its tail.

"It's too hot," Madge said and got a laugh out of the group. "Yeah, I know, that's obvious and it's almost always too hot around here. But when you're hot *and* worried, it's worse."

"Sure is," Cyrus said. He did the unusual and removed his shirt, hung it on a pigtail belonging to a kid member of the bronze statue on the lawn. They called it the Fuglies.

Annie sized Cyrus up frankly, surprising herself. He was no soft man, not one teeny bit soft at all. And he had spent enough time working outside in the yard he loved—without the shirt evidently—to be both tanned and muscular.

She tried not to, but glanced at Madge anyway.

Madge rolled a glass of iced tea back and forth on her forehead—and cast Cyrus sidelong looks.

"We're marking time," Max announced. "All this standing around is getting under my skin."

Spike strolled in his direction and Max steeled himself to be told he wasn't needed here.

"Any ideas about a link?" Spike said. "You were with Reb at the autopsy. Anything at all?"

"I don't know."

Spike jutted his head forward. "You don't *know?*"

"Science isn't always perfect," Max told him. He dropped his voice. "I don't feel right talking about it when Reb is in charge. I haven't done an autopsy in longer than I want to remember. I was along for the ride today." And because Reb had wanted his opinion on the neck wound they had found.

"But you *might* have seen something interesting, or suspicious."

Max filled up his cheeks with air and kept his eyes firmly on Spike's.

"Okay," Spike said. "I get it and I even understand. Damn, I wish Reb would come."

"Hard day for her. And Marc. They feel responsible for Lee."

"Responsible," Spike said. "She was too old—"

"Yeah." Max cut him off. "Since we're talking about things people shouldn't feel responsible for, you've got to know I've heard the stuff about Homer and Charlotte. Charlotte isn't happy, but you know that."

Spike kicked up a small cloud of dust. "You mean I shouldn't feel responsible for it, but you figure I do?"

"I can tell when a group of people are suffering."

"Okay." Spike put an arm around Max's shoulders and led him on a slow downhill walk. "You asked. Nobody else has said a word because they don't want to get caught up in a family feud. But you asked and I'm glad 'cause now I'm gonna let it all out."

"Sure," Max said, wishing he'd kept his mouth shut.

"My father is a horse's ass."

Max wiped away all expression and made sure he neither nodded nor shook his head.

"My father listened to some gossip from someone in this town and fell right in the hole they dug for him. He's making all our lives a misery, includin' Vivian and this is not a good time for that to happen. In fact, if my father doesn't make a move to put things right real soon, I'm going to run his…I'm gonna get real mad. I'll flatten him if he doesn't fix things. Charlotte's miserable. Vivian's miserable because Charlotte's miserable and Wendy's miserable because Charlotte and Vivian are miserable *and* because her grandpa, who is just about her favorite person, is a miserable son-of-a-gun."

"You've got trouble," Max said.

"You don't say much, do you?" Spike said.

Max pulled in the corners of his mouth, then gulped at his tea. "Want me to talk to Homer?" *No, he hadn't just said that.*

"You?"

Max was so grateful to hear amazement in Spike's voice. "I didn't mean to be presumptuous. Forget—"

"Damn good idea," Spike said. "Homer has a lot of respect for the medical profession. I'd truly appreciate any help you could give us." He slapped Max on the back. "Thank you."

Max breathed deeply through his nose and before he could get himself into more trouble, Reb and Marc emerged from the side of the house.

"Fan my brow," Spike murmured. "This is hard on everyone, but look at these two." He glanced at Max. They both nodded and went to greet the newcomers.

Reb and Marc looked haggard. They had Reb's old apricot poodle, Gaston, with them. The poodle looked suddenly puppyish when he saw the other two dogs and took off into the fray.

"You didn't bring the children," Madge said, but stopped talking with her lips still parted.

"They're better with Amy," Reb said. Amy was Marc's sister who also lived at beautiful, rambling Cloud's End.

"Of course they are," Madge said, turning pink. "That was a dumb thing to say."

Reb smiled at her. "No, they love coming here because you spoil them. They know you dote on them."

"This wouldn't be a good time, though," Madge said. She offered tea to Marc and Reb. "Sit down and rest."

"Thanks," Reb said, accepting her glass. "I think I'd rather cover the things you're wondering about first." She leaned on Marc and he slipped a hand around her waist.

She shaded her eyes as Max and Spike joined them. "How much did you tell everyone?" she asked Max.

"I was waiting for you," he told her.

"Okay," Reb said. "There's not much to say anyway. Lee was, as I suspected, a very healthy woman. We think she may have died of an embolism in her brain. There will have to be further tests that can't be done here so unfortunately this will drag on longer."

Max wasn't surprised she didn't mention the evidence they'd found of foul play. Reb made the briefest eye contact with him but it was enough to let him know she'd decided against any too-detailed public announcements.

"You mean a blood clot," Annie said. "She hadn't hit her head or anything, had she?"

"No," Reb said shortly.

Spike crossed his arms and looked ready to interrogate her.

Guy took Annie and Max by the elbows and moved them to a bench beside a stubby palm with a bulbous trunk. "Looks like a good time to break things up a bit," he said. "Take a seat. I've got a couple of pieces of news. One isn't big, or it doesn't look that way. The other is interesting—especially if we're still looking at Michele Riley having taken off under her own steam. You'll probably want to share some of this with Spike."

Max hoped for good news but feared the worst.

"Bobby Colbert was kicked out of some military school back east and came home to work for his father," Guy said. "Apparently his folks sent him to the school because he was hard to handle."

Annie looked at Guy's belt buckle. Just how much had he found out about Bobby?

"Haven't we decided he's mostly a nuisance with a crush on Annie?" Max asked.

Annie held her breath.

"Mostly," Guy said. "But he's hangin' around and it looks like he tries to hook up with women who have money."

Annie laughed. "Why would he want me, then?"

"Because he sees you're successful. Apparently he's talked about you driving a fancy new Porsche, living in a big apartment and making a lot of money at Pappy's."

Max remembered the bagel shop in St. Martinville. "You drove the Boxster in St. Martinville," he said. "That's when you ran into Bobby again. And you have a nice apartment. And I doubt Pappy's stupid enough to underpay you."

"It's not my Porsche. Joe and Ellie don't charge me enough for the apartment and it hardly has any furniture in it—not that Bobby's seen it—and Pappy's doing me a favor by givin' me a chance. He pays me decently, but it's not a fortune." This made her angry and she flipped a hand. "Who cares about Bobby, anyway. Not me."

"Good," Max said, planning to keep an eye open for an opportunity to have another chat with Bobby Colbert.

"He got let off on a charge of theft by his father," Guy said. "A friend of mine got this from a friend of his. The father contacted the cops in a rage and said Bobby was stealin' from the safe. Had him taken in for questioning. Then Dad showed up, apologizing all over, and saying he found the money he thought had been stolen. End of case. Baby boy went home but he hates it there. Dad insists he work and Bobby isn't interested. He's lookin' for a way out. I don't think he's a problem."

Annie didn't want to think about the man at all. Spike came toward them again and she waved at him, grateful for any diversion.

"Movin' right along," Guy said and paused until Spike arrived. "I found out Michele Riley was breaking off her engagement to Tom Walen. She told him a few days before she came down here. Apparently he was devastated."

Max felt tension ratchet up between them. "She didn't mention it."

"He must have set off to meet up with her when she got here," Spike said. "What do you bet he thought they'd have a better chance of workin' things out in neutral territory?"

"Maybe," Max said. He felt agitated, excited. Even though Tom hadn't endeared himself, there was still no reason to wish the man harm. But given what Max and Reb were theorizing about in relation to Lee's death, Tom could become very important. Not that Max could think of any connection between Lee and Tom. He thought about it, but his mind kept wandering to Roche. He didn't know where to start looking.

"Come back to us, Max," Annie said, tapping his arm. "Are you okay?"

He shrugged his shoulders up and down. "Lot on my mind," he said. "We can't toss unproven theories around, but Reb and I think whoever killed Lee had some medical knowledge."

"*Killed* her?" Spike said.

Max bowed his head. "I shouldn't have said that. We'd better get Reb over here."

CHAPTER 36

"Will you be glad to come home day after tomorrow, Lil?" Ozaire Dupre asked. "You've been in this hospital long enough, I reckon."

Lil fussed with the edge of her sheet. "I want to be home," she said. "You need lookin' after. Then there's the rectory. Goodness knows how Father Cyrus is getting by."

A nurse paused outside the room, she smiled but she also tapped her watch. It was long past time for Ozaire to leave and let Lil sleep.

Lil didn't want Ozaire to go. He hadn't arrived until late and she could tell he didn't want to leave. Thinking about the dear man and how worried he'd been about her warmed a body. When you'd been married a long time, well, the bloom could seem to be a bit off. She'd been wrong about that. Her husband still loved her and more than a little bit.

"I'll hold on a few more minutes," he said. "They don't mind. Bein' in a proper room's a whole lot nicer than the emergency."

"That cubicle felt like a cage in the zoo," Lil said. "Look at this.

My own room, a TV and a phone, and folks comin' to see me all day. And there isn't a nurse who comes in and doesn't say I've got more flowers than anyone she's ever seen."

"That's because you've got so many friends," Ozaire said. "And we could have lost you if things had gone worse than they did. I can't figure why they don't have the car yet, though."

Lil could. She had to talk to a few people and set some things straight. She wasn't sure how much she wanted to do that and every hour she delayed made it worse. She'd tried to tell Ozaire but couldn't make herself do it.

"It's too bad you have to all but die to find out how many people care about you," she said.

"You should have known, Lil. You just never thought about it. Folks look up to you."

Lil couldn't remember crying, not for years, but tears prickled in her eyes. "I've got to tell you somethin'," she said. "I should have talked about it before now."

"Lil," Ozaire said, looking at his work-roughened hands. She didn't think he'd heard what she said. "I've been tryin' to give you some news ever since I arrived. It's why I was late. They needed an extra hand to drive the ambulance and I'm the first on the list."

"Who was it for?" All jumpy inside, Lil looked into Ozaire's face. "Who? It's someone close to us, isn't it?"

"It was Lee O'Brien," Ozaire said. "They found her dead at the paper offices."

Lil's jaw felt slack. "Lee?" She felt sick, frightened and confused. "How could she be dead?"

"I haven't heard how it happened yet, but I knew you'd want to know."

He was wrong there. Lil wished she'd already gone to sleep. She wished she could turn the clock back and change everything. "Poor girl. She was sassy, but that's because she had a job to do and reporters have to be a bit pushy. Oh, I hate hearing this."

"Mr. Dupre?" the nurse said from the hall. "I don't like to sound like a school matron but Mrs. Dupre needs her beauty sleep." She stepped into the room and straightened Lil's pillows and sheets.

"That's okay," Ozaire said. "I'll be back sometime tomorrow so you can throw me out again." He grinned at the nurse. Lil looked at both of them and hoped she wasn't going to be sick.

Not Lee. How could Lee be dead and why?

Ozaire pecked her forehead and left, popping back one time to give an extra wave.

"He's a nice man," the nurse said. "Now you get to sleep. It'll only be a few hours before you'll be gotten up for breakfast."

With the lights out Lil did her best to settle. The bed was comfortable. What people meant when they complained about hospital beds, she'd never know. But it didn't matter tonight because she knew she wouldn't be able to sleep. She'd made terrible mistakes. One of those mistakes could have had something to do with Lee's death. Oh, she couldn't be sure, but it was possible. Lil closed her eyes. She would have to tell all of it now—not hold anything back.

The building had that night silence about it. Kind of heavy and a bit lonely. A nurse or doctor going along the corridor outside her room would be the only movement until the place started waking up.

Lil had a lot on her mind. It all kept coming back, much as she tried to shut it out. For a moment she'd convinced herself it was better Ozaire interrupted her before she could tell the truth about her accident. Sometimes you kept your own counsel and it turned out better. Not this time. And sooner or later they would find the car and the questions would start.

If she'd told the truth in the first place they would already have picked it up. But she'd been embarrassed to admit what she'd been doing when she crashed. She had explained some of it, about the man running at the car, but the rest would make her look a fool. Why had she set off for Rosebank to apologize to Charlotte for being rude about not getting the job in the kitchens there? It could have waited and the way things turned out, she hadn't seen Charlotte anyway.

At least Madge's dog was okay, although Lil still wasn't sure how she'd gotten home.

For all she knew they already had found her car but they were waiting until she was stronger to get really mad.

She would try to shut everything out and think about it tomorrow. Could be she should tell Father Cyrus and ask his advice. He always knew what was best.

It could wait for tomorrow.

Lil closed her eyes, but they opened again immediately. There was a murderer out there. First Michele Riley, now Lee O'Brien. She, Lil, had a small connection to Lee. Could it be enough to make the killer come after her? Had he already come after her, before he got Lee? She knew he had. She was supposed to have died in the ditch on the night of her "accident," and there was no reason to think the threat wasn't still there.

CHAPTER 37

"You're staring at me," Max said.

Annie deliberately looked away. "I didn't mean to. I think I'm waiting for someone to tell me what to do." She opened the refrigerator in her kitchen and studied the contents. Irene joined her, purring and apparently surveying possible treats.

"You're hungry?" Max said.

"We had coffee early this morning and I haven't eaten since. How about you?"

"Same."

"Then you're hungry, too. We'll have red beans and rice—and jambalaya, sausage jambalaya."

Max leaned into the kitchen. Longer than usual, his black hair curled forward just above his collar and his intensely blue eyes showed he was tired. "I thought those things took all day to cook."

"Not when you do the sort of things I do. I'll have to make the rice, but the rest is cooked and frozen already. I love to cook but it's hard to get it done just for myself so when I do get in here I make enough for several meals."

He wasn't listening. Annie saw his focus wander and he turned away. Moments later she heard him leave a message on someone's phone, a cryptic message: "Max. Call me." He didn't return and he got through to someone else on his phone. "Anything?" Max had walked farther from the kitchen. "No, for God's sake, of course I don't think he did. I do think he could be beating himself up over whatever went on at the clinic." Annie could hardly hear him now. "Sorry. I know. We both are." He talked longer, or so she presumed, but he had gone into the rooms at the back of the apartment.

An image, fast, there and then gone, turned her stomach. Lee, half on and half off that air mattress, her eyes open.

Annie found Irene a piece of chicken and closed the refrigerator door.

The sound of Max's footfalls, purposeful, hurrying, unnerved her. She walked out of the kitchen—and met Max. He pulled her against him and held on so tight the pressure hurt.

She stayed quiet.

"Annie, do you know how much you mean to me?" he said

"Max—"

"Just answer me." His voice rose and he shook her once. "I love you. If anything…I want you with me. Not just now and again but all the time." He spread a hand over the back of her head and pressed her face to his shoulder.

She didn't want to cry, darn it. But it was too late not to and her throat clogged. Even if she knew what to say, she couldn't get a word out.

Annie caught at the sides of his shirt and hung on.

Max loosened his grip enough for her to look at him.

He wiped the tears from her face.

"If I thought I wouldn't see you again I couldn't bear it," she told him in a rush. The tension she felt in him scared her. A kind of desperation showed in the way he looked at her.

"I would never hurt you," he said.

Annie put her hands on his shoulders. "Do you think I don't know that? I feel safer with you than I've ever felt."

"You've been through too much. I wouldn't blame you if you were afraid of men."

"I'm not afraid of you." She smiled, sniffed—and laughed. "I don't know how I got lucky enough to have you want me, though."

He put his face close to hers. "I'm going to teach you to stop saying, or even thinking things like that. I've hit gold and you're it."

But he wasn't either a happy or a satisfied man. From childhood she'd been taught not to press for personal information. The thought felt strange but she would have to ask him questions until he told her everything that was on his mind.

He loves me. He said he does.

"If I made the arrangements, would you consider going away for a while?" he said.

Annie stared at him.

"Just until everything settles down here?" he said.

"No," she said. "I can't believe you'd ask me."

"I'm asking because I want you somewhere safe. There's too much—"

"*No.*" She interrupted him. "We belong together. You said so. You think I would run and hide while you're here on your own? I'm not a kid. I know there's big trouble ahead. I shouldn't ask but I'm going to. What did you and Reb find out about Lee's death—the stuff that made you say someone with medical knowledge killed her?"

"My mouth got out of line. I shouldn't have said anything."

"But you did. And then you and Reb went off with Spike and Guy.

You were telling them what you'd discovered." She couldn't stop a fine tremor in her limbs. "And now you want me to go away. Tell me why?"

"It's like a war," he told her. "But I don't know anything about the enemy except he knows me and he's close. It can't be any other way."

And he didn't want to tell her all the details, Max thought. He didn't want to frighten her more than she already was.

"That means you really need me now, and I need you," Annie said. "I've got to know you're okay."

"I'm not afraid for myself," he said. "It's others. Already—" Hell, he hadn't intended to say that.

"I intend to stay safe," Annie said. "I won't go anywhere without you."

She still wore blue, but she'd kicked off her sneakers and her feet were bare. Everything about her pleased him—and turned him on. And this wasn't the time for that.

"You have the clearest blue eyes," he told her. "And your mouth is soft."

She smiled a little and said, "Thank you. You take the blue eyes prize."

They both laughed but he couldn't feel anything but her breasts pressing his chest, her hips fitted to his. If she didn't feel his reaction to her... She felt it, he saw her smile fade and watched her suck her lower lip into her mouth.

"I'm usually pretty controlled," he said and felt like an ass.

She lowered her gaze, but not fast enough. He'd seen the heat in her eyes.

Annie spun away. She returned to the kitchen, her bare feet smacking the floor rapidly. She opened two upper cupboard doors and stood back to see inside. Standing on tiptoe, she reached in to slide a casserole dish out. Her arms shook with strain.

"Put it down," Max said, standing behind her.

"I've got it."

He pushed his hands under her soft cotton shirt and swept up to hold her breasts.

"Max." She moaned. "That's not fair."

"You don't like it?" He threaded his thumbs inside her bra and flicked them back and forth over her nipples.

The dish hit the shelf with a clatter. With her fingertips she gave it small shoves to make sure it was safe. Then she hung onto the shelf.

"You're a very sexy woman, Annie."

"You make me feel sexy. You make me want sex. I've never been this way with anyone else."

Max found her ear with his mouth and licked it. He nibbled the lobe. Every instant he held back cost him, but he knew better than to rush her.

Annie released her grip on the shelf. She pulled up her shirt, reached back and undid her bra. Her breasts filled his hands and as he pulled on her nipples, she rubbed her bottom against him.

"I'm not thinking straight, sweetheart, but I like it this way. Yes, push on me. Come on, bounce. Annie, Annie."

"You're burnin' me up," she said, panting. "I ache. I can hardly stand up."

"Grab the shelf again, then," he whispered in her ear. "Let me do the work."

Shuddering, she did as she was told and Max gritted his teeth, counting the cost of holding back a few more seconds. He couldn't. The short skirt rose above her waist as if anti-gravity took it. She wore a thong, a testimony to how her trust in him had grown, and he sank to his knees to kiss her. He liked the little crease where her bottom met her thighs, liked it even more when his tongue there caused her to writhe.

Annie tried to face him but he clamped her where she was by her hips, leaned over her so she couldn't move while he undid his pants. He stripped the panties to her ankles before he urged her even farther forward and nudged at the wet entrance waiting for him.

"Max," she said, her voice high. "Is this okay?"

"Very okay," he told her, his head beating in time to the heavy pulse in his loins. "Go with it. You'll feel more than you ever have."

Sweat broke on his brow, his back. He drove into her and their rhythm matched instantly. Cradling her breasts, he let any restraint go and pounded into her.

Annie made a sobbing noise and Max pushed one hand in front of her, slid his fingers between her legs and into the slick hair he found.

He couldn't wait any longer.

With his fingers he chafed harder and faster.

He poured into her, his legs jerking, doing what they needed to do without any help, and Annie cried out. The spasms of her climax clutched at his penis and still they came together, again and again.

CHAPTER 38

Lil Dupre hadn't slept.

For what felt like hours, she had tried to figure out how to tell Spike—and it had to be Spike—that she had lied to everyone.

She was convinced that if she'd spoken out at once, right after the accident, Lee would still be alive. The burden crushed her.

The covers on her bed were too heavy. Lil threw them off.

Her mama and papa, older when they had her, did their best even if they didn't understand children. "Just you tell the truth," Papa had said from when she was real little. And Mama would nod and smile and it was as if the three of them had an agreement.

She rubbed at her eyes. What must they think of her now? What had they been thinking all these years when she'd forgotten sometimes and made up a story to be real mean to someone—like Homer and Charlotte who never did her any harm.

Charlotte Patin, when she'd said she couldn't see her way to hiring Lil, told her, "I couldn't do that to Cyrus," and she'd offered to talk to him about the way things cost so much more these days. Lil had turned down the offer—and set about covering up her disappointment with a nasty trick. She knew how a man like Homer had his pride and she'd tried to take it away from him with her rumors.

Now she was too cold and she huddled under the white sheet and cotton blanket again.

First thing in the morning, she'd call Spike. She'd call Cyrus, too, because he deserved to know. She smiled a little. And she wanted him to come because he'd forgive her. Cyrus forgave everyone, even that wicked little Millie when she chewed his one good pair of shoes.

Lil thought about the way the black and white piece of warm fur would come to be picked up, and how she'd licked Lil's face and put her head on her shoulder. Oh, that was just about the best dog around. She needed to grow up a bit more was all.

They'd even dimmed the light in the corridor. If someone passed and they weren't alone, they whispered so low, Lil couldn't hear a thing.

Ozaire had always wanted to open a gym. He'd been given a bunch of equipment and had it stored out at Homer's who reckoned he was going to drop it all in the bayou, only he never would. Homer grouched a lot but he was a decent man.

When she could work on it, Lil would help Ozaire find a place to open his gym. He deserved that. As long as she'd known him he'd been trying to make something more of himself. He liked raising dogs, too, German shepherds. If he wanted, she'd encourage him. Look at that Daisy that Ellie Gable had—that dog had probably saved Ellie's life once and that was because Ozaire trained Daisy so well.

Tomorrow wouldn't be easy, but there was a lot of love in this town—and Lil had her own love for the place. Cyrus was going to help her straighten out.

She felt warm and relaxed.

Her muscles softened. For the first time in days tension didn't hold an ache in her temples.

"Mrs. Dupre?"

Lil opened her eyes slowly. "Mmm. That would be me."

"Just making my rounds and I thought I'd drop in. How are you doing?"

She smiled at a doctor who approached her bed. He put his coat over a chair and picked up her chart. Must have better eyes than she did to see it in this light.

"Doing well, are we?" he said, standing beside her.

He was tall. "Yes, thank you. Going home day after tomorrow."

"I just want to check your vital signs and give you a shot," he said. "You relax and close your eyes."

"Better put the lamp on," Lil told him. "You'll never read my blood pressure otherwise."

"Just close your eyes—I can see well enough in the light from the corridor. I didn't want to disturb you but the nurse insisted."

"Why?" Lil asked, suddenly anxious. She sat up.

"Nothing to worry about."

He had on the things they wore in the operating room. And big, dark goggles. His voice was nice enough but not clear coming through the mask.

"Why do you have to wear a mask in here?" Lil asked. "The rest don't."

"It's a good idea."

Her stomach clenched. "I've got somethin', haven't I? I expect one of those tests they ran showed it. Is it serious?"

He laughed. "Not at all. We believe in taking precautions, is all. Now, I want you to lie back down. None of this will take long and then you can be off to dreamland."

Lil maneuvered her hand, very carefully, to the switch for the bedside lamp. A bright glow shot over the room.

Why would he wear dark goggles, just about black goggles?

He looked over his shoulder, toward the door, and Lil planned her next move.

Encased in rubber gloves, his fingers were icy when he took her pulse. He made a notation on her chart. "Very nice," he said. "Lie down so I can listen to your heart."

She didn't need to lie down for that. And she wouldn't. The dark coat on the chair started to slide. The fabric was thin, could be black cotton but there was a lot of it. A string snaked across the floor— from an eyelet at the neck of a hood.

Trembling turned her cold. It was him, the man who caused her to go off the road. He had followed her into the ditch and hurt her when she got out of the car. He wanted to hurt her again.

He wanted to kill her.

Shot? He wasn't giving her any shots if she could help it.

"Lie down," he said. "You're wasting my time."

She didn't have to see his mouth to imagine his teeth were clenched.

Lil sat where she was. She prayed one of the staff would come, and inched toward the call button pinned to her bottom sheet.

"I said, *down*." One shove across her neck flattened her on the pillows, he held her face away from him and she heard a small, popping sound.

The cap coming off a needle...

Lil reached the call button. She depressed the center and held it there. Instantly the bell outside her door chimed intermittently.

"Goddamn *bitch!*" The pressure of his hand left her. "You're gone, anyway, sweetheart."

But Lil didn't wait for what he planned next. She rolled to the floor on the other side of the bed and made a run for the door.

He cut her off. With the hooded coat already in his hand, he caught her by the arm and threw her in a corner where she connected with the walls and slid down.

"Oh, Nurse," she heard him say. "You're here, good. Help me with this. Mrs. Dupre is having a seizure."

CHAPTER 39

*M*usic blared. A horn-player in black-and-white striped satin blew his horn and high-stepped, twirled a circle and pranced on, his knees reaching as high as his elbows.

On his head rested the top of a miniature black satin umbrella. A skullcap fixed the fringed thing in place. And the fringe swung, back and forth, back and forth.

Along an alley where people clustered to watch, he went.

"Didn't he ra-amble?" the gathering sang, their voices full. They kept the rhythm with waving arms and looked past the strutter, back toward the place he'd come from.

Annie stood among them and she leaned to see what they were looking at.

"Didn't he ra-a-amble?" the crowd sang.

Another man came, not high-stepping or twirling, but staggering from one side of the alley to the other, weighted down by the woman he carried over his shoulder. A woman in white, her face thumping his back with each step, her hands swinging. The man held her with an arm across the backs of her knees and Annie didn't know why he struggled and sweated; the woman was small.

Annie walked behind them, left the crowd behind.

Leaves covered her feet and she walked faster to keep up with the strutter, the man and the woman in white.

He turned, the man, and smiled at her. With one finger he beckoned, then away he went and Annie broke into a run to keep up.

Her own white dress reached her ankles and twisted around them. It dragged on her legs. She kicked to free herself and stayed behind the little group, up a hill, into a lot of trees.

The horn-player had left. She heard the man with the woman breathe. She heard wood snap. Bushes snagged her dress, sticks punctured the fabric and tore her legs.

The man with the woman in white had forgotten Annie. They went such a long way. Annie's feet dragged. She tripped and fell, and got up, and fell again.

Deeper into the trees, they went. Underbrush got higher. Annie scrambled, used her hands as well as her feet to keep moving.

The woman slid from the man's shoulder. Slowly, she slipped sideways and floated down among brambles.

The ground opened, peeled back by the man. He took the woman in his arms, held her over the hole he'd made, and dropped her.

Not a sound.

Annie stood alone, looking down at the twisted figure in white.

A scream issued, long, choked, ending in a gurgle.

One pale hand reached out on the dirt floor below Annie. The fingers closed on a flashlight and turned it on, shone it on the woman's own face. She reached to bare a shoulder where a triangle of skin was gone, showing the raw flesh underneath. A neat triangle with straight edges.

The flashlight belonged to Annie.

The face was Lee's.

* * *

"Annie, hush." Max lifted her from the bedroom floor and put her back on the bed. She flailed her arms and jackknifed her legs to her chest. She was as wet as if she'd showered. Her hair stuck to her head and dripped on her shoulders. "Annie," he said into her ear. "Can you hear me?" He wiped his brow and squeezed burning eyes shut.

He knew fear, the kind of fear he'd never had to feel because he'd never really loved a woman before. Max loved Annie so much he ached to see her like this.

She stiffened and he turned her head to the side. If she were epileptic she would have told him, wouldn't she?

Max chafed her arms and then her legs. Her heartbeat was strong if irregular. "Come on. Come back to me. Open your eyes."

She did open her eyes and rather than light blue, they were all but black and staring at him from a distance.

Max let out a breath. "Just relax. I'm here and I'm not going anywhere."

Slowly her eyes cleared and she took several deep, shuddering breaths.

"Stay where you are," Max said. "I'll get a cool cloth. Don't move. That's an order."

"Yes," she said.

In the bathroom he soaked a washcloth and returned to wipe Annie's face and neck. He swept her hair back with one hand and took her pulse with the other. The pulse was slow and regular.

"Do you have any medical condition you haven't mentioned?" he asked.

She rocked her head from side to side.

"Do you remember if you had a bad dream?"

Annie kept looking at him. He sponged her arms. "You

screamed. I thought someone had broken in. I ran out of the room and heard you fall."

"I'm okay now," she said. "I'm sorry, Max, I had a dream. A nightmare." She scrunched up her face. "I need a shower."

"I don't want you doing that."

"You can come with me," she told him, with no hint of suggestiveness.

Within minutes he stood with her under warm water, soaping her body, washing her hair. She seemed insubstantial and weak, but determined. He couldn't quite turn off his reactions to her.

She stood like an obedient child while he rubbed her dry, and sat on the toilet lid swathed in a dry towel while he dried himself. One big fence had been climbed, Annie didn't try to hide her scars from him anymore.

"I have to go out," she said.

Max finished wrapping a towel around his waist. "The only place you're going is back to bed."

"You go back to bed. I've got to go get something."

"Tomorrow."

She shook her head. "Now. I'll be fine."

"You're wobbly and you sound as if you're still asleep. Come on. Back to bed."

Annie stood and he sighed with relief. He didn't want to haggle with her.

"I'll take my cell phone," she told him as she left the bathroom.

Max looked at the ceiling. *Give me patience.* He followed her.

She already wore panties and had started putting on a bra.

"*Annie.*"

"Don't worry." She pulled on jeans and a cotton sweatshirt, slid on her sneakers and walked from the room.

He grabbed his own clothes and hopped into them all the way to a closet in the room overlooking the backyard. Annie took out a bulky canvas bag stamped with daisies. "Look after Irene for me— if you decide to wait here till I get back."

Calm and matter-of-fact, she intended to do whatever she'd gotten into her head. "Okay," he told her. "I'm coming with you, dammit."

"You are?" Her sudden smile transformed her. "Thank you. I didn't want to do it on my own."

"Do what?"

"Find my flashlight."

CHAPTER 40

"We've been told to make sure you don't get excited," Spike said to Lil, pulling a chair close to the bed.

Cyrus sat on the other side and patted Lil's hand.

Maybe if he'd been a priest, Spike thought, he'd be good at things like patting hands and making folks feel cared about.

"Thank you for comin'," Lil said in a croaky little voice.

Immediately Cyrus got up and bent over her. "You're all banged up again, Lil. Now don't you go worrying about a thing. Are you sure you don't want Ozaire in with us?"

She shook her head, no, and winced. "No. I'll ask you to explain everythin' to him afterwards. He'll take it better from you." Turning up her hands, she added, "Men, y'know, they can get all het up around women."

Spike looked steadfastly at the wall.

"Whatever you say," Cyrus said. He glanced at Spike and whispered, loud enough to be heard, "Did you want to make reconciliation."

Lil had several reddish bruises on her face but she blushed and they seemed paler. "No," she whispered. "He's gotta hear this." She twitched her head sideways at Spike.

Cyrus resumed his seat.

"I've done wrong," Lil said hoarsely. "I will surely go to hell for the evil I've caused."

"Lil—"

She shushed Cyrus. "Not a word till I get it all out. Understand?" Each of them got a sharp-eyed stare.

They nodded.

"Charlotte was looking for a cook at Rosebank. I asked for the job, but she said she couldn't take me from you." Cyrus got a glance. "She was right but I got mad and made up a story about how Homer is a kept man on account of Charlotte havin' a lot of money and him not havin' much."

While Lil took a breath, Spike pulled one booted ankle onto the opposite knee.

"They got unengaged because of me and I'm sorry. We gotta put it right."

"Right," Cyrus said.

"Not a word," she snapped. "Not till I'm done."

The three of them were silent for several seconds.

"I lied about what happened the night I came in this place," Lil said. "I had Madge's Millie in my car and I was headed home from Loreauville. The dog was supposed to go to the rectory. But I got this fool—no, it was a good idea—I got this idea to go to Charlotte and apologize. Me, I wasn't brought up to be mean.

"When I drove past that new clinic the place was all lighted up so I thought I'd go take a look through the windows. We all been wondering what it'll be like. I parked right by a hedge at Rosebank and ran up the drive next door. Imagine my surprise when I got to them big windows in front and saw what I saw." Folding her hands carefully on her stomach, she flapped her fingers.

Very carefully, Spike sat straighter.

Cyrus ran a finger under his clerical collar.

"What did you see?" Spike said. He couldn't stand the wait any longer.

"It was awful."

"Mmm," Spike murmured.

"You gotta let me get it out my own way," Lil said. "It's embarrassin'. On the floor they was…" She put a hand over her mouth. "I got scared and took off. I drove my car as fast as she would go, right down that little road toward where you turn toward Toussaint. There was a flare in the road. It was rainin' but I saw the flare, all wiggly pink light through them wipers.

"Well, I slowed down, didn't I? And then he come at me, runnin' across like he'd bang right into the car. Wearin' a big coat with a hood. It was on that very floor tonight." She pointed across the room.

Spike kept his mouth shut. He'd already been told the story of what had happened an hour or so earlier in the evening. He figured he'd have to hear it again from Lil but there was no point rushing into it.

"So it was like I said about goin' off the road, just a different road. It was Landry Way." Her throat clicked when she swallowed and her smile was a sad affair. "He banged me all up again tonight. See." She held out her bruised arms. "He said he had to give me a shot only I knew somethin' was wrong."

"It's terrible," Cyrus said. "Spike's already got deputies out searching for him and asking questions. The folks here in Breaux Bridge are helpin', too. Everyone's looking—it's on TV."

"What I told you about him hurtin' me some more when I got

out of my car was true," Lil said, big tears welling in her eyes. Spike noticed she addressed Cyrus now. "He likes pushin' at your neck. He did it then and I fell and it felt like I got stung. That could have been a shot only I didn't get sick—except for my head, but that was the crash. He pushed me again tonight only it didn't sting the same way. That night it was like I said, I think the sound of them noisy bikes scared him off. He ran, I'm tellin' you. Did I say he had on that mask and hood thing, and the big, bug-eyed glasses? Wore them tonight, he did. Big, black glasses in here like I was too stupid to notice."

"People underestimate other people," Cyrus said with sympathy. "You did everything right tonight. You saved yourself."

Lil gave a pleased little moue. "And I've got a clue," she said, and pulled a clear plastic cap from beneath a hip. "I heard it go down and I got the nurse to find it for me afterwards. She should have gone after him sooner, but... This is from that needle he wanted to put in me. There, so you know I'm tellin' the truth this time."

Spike rose from his chair, searching around for something to drop the contaminated evidence into. It should be useless, but he could hope for a miracle.

"Use your head, young Spike," Lil said. "He had on rubber gloves and even if he hadn't, the nurse and I would have ruined any prints by now, wouldn't we?"

Cyrus grinned and Lil looked even more pleased.

"What did you see at the clinic?" Spike said, beside himself. "We'll listen real quiet, Lil."

Once more her face flamed. "I don't know what happened to that darlin' little Millie but I thank the Lord she got home safe."

"Seems simple enough to me," Spike said. "Either she got out of the car when you got out—at Rosebank—or she got out when you got back in. End of story. She went home."

Both Cyrus and Lil gave him reproachful glances.

"Sorry to interrupt," Spike said, feeling no remorse. "You were going to tell us the awful thing you saw at the clinic."

"Yes." With a firm nod, Lil raised her chin. "And awful, it was. A disgrace, but I wish I never saw it because now it's my fault. They were on the floor, their hair all wet, rolling around. I was mortified, I can tell you. She had somethin' she held away from him and he reached for it. Then she grabbed his…him…you know where and she was up and off while he was holdin' himself. She was leavin', I suppose. Well, I was leavin', too. I never ran that fast since I was a girl. All the way to my car.

"But I reckon I was seen and somehow he got down there faster. I had to go all the way along the drive and out by the hedge at Rosebank, see. He must have been quicker. Then he got away after he did that to me with the flare and everything, and look what's happened. He's killed her, hasn't he?"

"Who?" Cyrus asked gently.

"Lee, of course. That's who he was with at Green Veil, poor Lee." She pinched her lips and frowned. "Me, I know what they'd been doing. It was all over them."

"What was?" Cyrus said.

"That *look*. All mussed and pink in the face." She closed her eyes. "And she didn't have no panties on."

Spike couldn't even turn his eyes in Cyrus's direction.

"It's always the quiet ones," Lil said. "But who would have thought it of that Roche Savage? At least, I think it was him and not the other one."

CHAPTER 4

Grit eddies flew up from the cleared area on Max's lot. A stinging speck landed in Annie's eye and she tugged one lid over the other. Blinking, she tromped on, following the wide beam from a camp lantern Max carried. She had insisted on hauling her own bag of gardening tools.

Tonight Annie was glad she hadn't thrown the lamp out. Night? There couldn't be many hours left until dawn.

"Now what?" Max said, standing with his weight on one leg.

"Your heart isn't in this."

"Darn right." He shifted his weight to the other leg.

"I've got this feeling, though," Annie said. "It's strong. I saw something when I was asleep and it made me think."

"You see a lot of things while you're asleep," he said.

Annie tried to take the lamp but he lifted it high. "Go home," she told him. "Go anywhere. You're in a rotten mood. And you're mean."

"Can't imagine why," he said, a dangerous glint in his eyes. "Where are we going to find this thing?"

"I told you. I couldn't understand why it disappeared the way it did."

"But we had to come now—we couldn't wait until we'd put a few hours' sleep together? And if I go home, what are you going to do? Walk?" He put the lamp on the ground and spread his arms. "Okay, let's stop and take a breath."

Annie breathed deeply but she fumed, probably because she couldn't blame him for not being enthusiastic about one more of her "visions."

Being wrong stunk.

If she was wrong. And they'd never know if they didn't check out her hunch.

Hunch was a new word that fitted her purposes: she liked it.

"About a hundred volunteers turned over every leaf on this lot," Max said.

"I know," Annie said. "But they didn't find my flashlight."

"Argh! Where do you want to start looking?" Max said.

"There's only one place, I thought you knew that. It's over there." She pointed toward the densely treed lot next door. "Where I dropped it the night you just about scared me into cardiac arrest."

"Of course," he said. "On the next lot. I forgot you'd wandered over there. So why are we here?"

"Because," she pointed to her desired destination, "I don't think you can get there from anywhere but here without a machete. Why did there have to be more tests on Lee?"

"What?"

In the light from the lamp Annie saw the thrust of Max's chin. "Lee. After the autopsy Reb said there were tests that couldn't be done here."

"Don't dwell on that."

"I'm dwelling, and if you can't tell me I'll just have to dream up my own answers."

"Not a good idea." He crouched, rested his elbows on his knees and sighed—loudly. "At the paper Reb and I noticed a mark on Lee's neck. We think it was from a needle, an injection, only we couldn't prove it. But we were pretty sure she'd been wrapped in something, probably the upper sheet from the air mattress, before she died. Fibers on her front side matched fibers from the bottom sheet."

"She was on her stomach," Annie pointed out.

"And off the mattress, like she'd been rolled, maybe? Wait before you say anything. We are almost sure she was taped inside the sheet at some point."

"How could you know that?"

"Whoever did it wasn't quite careful enough. That could be because we interrupted him with the doorbell. He didn't want to leave her in the sheet because he hoped the death would look natural. It almost did. There were two spots where the tape took the skin off. One on her left calf and one on her left shoulder."

"Her shoulder," Annie repeated almost under her breath. If she had second sight, she didn't want it.

"It's ironic," Max said. "He could have been trying for an air embolism by injecting air, or gas into the jugular. It can work—kill someone I mean—but it's just as likely to fail. This time we think the embolism occurred and he'd have been away free if he hadn't gotten careless with the tape. I think he restrained her in the sheet and planned to take her away in it. They know an intruder got out through a window—or someone did—and it fits. The body's at an FBI lab. We'll see what they turn up. So far there are no toxins."

"Lil had bruises on her neck," Annie said. She had a bad feeling almost all the time but it was getting worse. "Do you think—"

"Yes, I do, but nothing conclusive was turned up. The guy who attacked her probably—in my opinion—got the shot in but it either missed or didn't work."

Cold sweat popped out all over Annie. She did some more deep breathing. "Can we get started now, please?" What did she think she'd find? A subterranean chamber hidden by a carpet of grass with Michele lying on the bottom? A body couldn't be in two places at one time—as far as she knew. "You'd probably be glad if I lost my nerve and went home. But I'll never have any peace until I get these questions out of my head."

Max picked up the lamp and took hold of Annie's hand. "Let's do it. The sooner we get back, the better. Don't get all worked up at me, I'm just tired and a bit short-tempered. And I'm worried." If she asked him why, he was ready to tell her.

"You're worried about all this?" she said. "There isn't something I don't know about?"

Of course she asked. "I can't find Roche. I haven't heard from him in twenty-four hours and Kelly and I haven't been able to get him on the phone. This never happened before."

Annie changed her grip, threaded their fingers together and squeezed. "I'm sorry. We'll go back to Toussaint now. I didn't know."

"I didn't tell you." He kept on going and speeded up until they ran. "Kelly should be about back by now. He'll call if Roche shows. Which he will." Max knew he was trying to convince himself. He took out his cell and switched it to vibrate rather than ring. "All we'd need would be a sudden noise. They'd be picking us out of the treetops."

Annie chuckled, and jumped. Her own phone rang at her waist and she snatched it up. "Yes?" She sighed and clicked off. "Wrong number. Sheesh, who makes calls at this time of night—or morning?"

"Took years off my life," Max said.

His phone vibrated. "Here we go again. Grand Central Station," he said and slid open the cell. "Yeah?" The readout said, "private number."

"It's Roche," his brother said.

Max released Annie's hand. "Where are you?"

"First, where are you?"

"I asked—"

"Not now, Max. Is Annie with you?"

"Yes. We're at the lot. She lost a flashlight here and we're looking for it."

A slight pause. "At this time of the morning? Forget I asked. Do something for me."

"Anything," Max said. *Just like I always have.*

"Stay put and I'll find you. I don't want you running around. I'm all messed up. I need you with me—and her if she's important to you."

"She is," Max said quietly, his heart beating loud enough to roar in his ears. "Tell me what's happening?"

"I've found something you're never going to believe. You've been set up for sure. It's sick—horrendous. Be patient and just don't leave. And don't talk to Spike or Guy or anyone else yet."

"What would I talk—" The connection died and Max cursed softly. He closed the phone. "That was Roche. He wants us to wait for him here."

"What a relief," Annie said. "I'm grateful you've heard from him."

"Yes." He wasn't grateful for the near desperation he'd heard in Roche's tone, or the suggestions he'd made. "I don't know how long he'll be. We'll carry on with what we were doing." Anything to keep his mind off whatever Roche might be going to tell him.

Annie turned and sniffed. She caught a glint and looked upward.

Over the trees where they were going, an ember whirled in the night sky.

"Campers?" Max suggested, following the direction of her gaze. "That'll put a crimp in things. The timber's pretty dry, too."

"It's too dangerous to light campfires in places like this," Annie said. "You might get away with it on this spot where it's cleared, but that's all underbrush and trees over there. Shall we call for the fire department?"

"Not for one spark," Max said. "Not until we see what it is. Hurry, and be quiet about it." He turned off the lamp and they moved as swiftly as the conditions allowed. Max didn't want any accidents.

Snapped branches were inevitable and they sounded like gunshots.

"I get disoriented in here," Annie whispered. "I'm not sure where I was that night. I could have been quite far from your place."

"Let's hope one of us recognizes it. First we check for pyromaniacs."

"I smell burning."

Max pulled her to a stop and sniffed the air. "Yeah. Do you hear anything?"

She didn't.

"We have to be quiet. I wish someone was playing loud music and breaking beer bottles, then I'd know what to do."

Annie squeezed his upper arm and he paused. "Up there," she said. Several more embers whirled but went out quickly. "It's not raining but the bits aren't staying alight," Annie said.

"The fire can't be going too well, which is a good thing," Max said.

Annie didn't just stop, she took several steps backward and put her hands on her knees, breathed in great gasps.

"Sweetheart." He went and bent over her. "What is it?"

"Don't ask."

"I am asking."

"What if it's him? The fires I saw, Max. The bodies. Remember what I told you."

"How could I forget. But that wasn't real."

She stared at the sky again. "Maybe."

He helped her stand up straight and massaged her back. Gently, he kissed her mouth. And he said, "Whoa, back off, boy," supposedly for his own benefit.

"You can always make me smile," Annie said although she wasn't smiling in her mind.

They didn't speak again for some time. Side-by-side, they crept forward, not knowing where they were going.

The wind grew stronger and the suggestion of burning turned into a stench. "It smells damp?" Annie said.

"I think it does. Try to relax. I think we're going to find a fire someone thought they'd put out but it's still smouldering."

"You do?" Annie blew out air. "Wow, I hope you're right." She tried not to breathe so loudly.

"Mmm," Max murmured moments later. "It's not so dense up ahead." The going had gotten even rougher and more difficult to get through.

The trees thinned and Max led Annie into an open patch of land. From the feel of it underfoot, grass grew there so there must be more light by day, that or most trees were less mature than Max's.

Scorched earth. The smell was sickening, overpowering.

Annie pointed. Occasional sparks seemed to escape from a small area of ground and behind the sparks, pacing back and forth, she made out the figure of a man. She spun away but Max stopped her from running. He put his mouth to her ear. "Keep quiet."

"Could be, you know, magic...voodoo conjure?" she said close to his face. "It's still a big thing here. I'm not staying."

"Get hold of yourself. I've got a gun. You'll be okay."

"A gun?" Her mouth opened with each word but no sound came out until a squeaky, "Oh."

The man stopped pacing and approached the place where the little sparks spewed and fizzled. He bent, braced his legs, grasped something and heaved. A hole opened up and black smoke laced with a few burning floaters curled out.

Max said, "No heroics," and pushed Annie behind him.

Heroics were out because she felt like melted rubber, but she moved along in his footsteps. Why did they have to do this? So someone was pacing around a smoking hole in the ground in the middle of nowhere. Was it her business?

"Hello," Max called out suddenly. "Looks like you've got a problem, can I help?" At the same time he put the lamp down and turned it on full. It blasted out yellow light.

"God, no," Max said. "Kelly?"

"Well, shit," Kelly said. "Did I invite you to my party?"

Max ran to take his brother into a bear hug. "I'm here, Kelly. It's okay."

"It's not okay. We've lost Roche. He's gone because you've made it too hard for him to stay. I'll never forgive you for that."

"Roche is fine," Max said. He wanted to get Kelly away from here. He'd never seen his older brother completely out of control before.

Kelly blinked at him and he had red rims around his eyes. "Nothing's fine. Nothing's ever going to be fine for you again. But Roche knows I've stuck by you. Dad's going to find out I stuck by you, too. And you don't have to worry. I'll make sure the cops never get their hands on you."

Max took Kelly by the shoulders, trying to figure out if he was serious or in an altered state. "Have you been drinking?" He didn't smell alcohol, although with the stink from the hole, who would?

Kelly broke away and looked down again. He picked up a long pole and poked it around in the hole. "I've bought this lot," he said. "Right next to Roche's. I'll have to keep him safe from your backlash."

"That lot belongs to me," Max said.

Kelly laughed and shook his head. "They tried sinking salt basins here. Not much more than holes in the ground. They were on the plat maps. That's what this is, an open salt basin. There are two more over there." He pointed to his right. "They were just left and stuff grew over them. I found this one when I fell in." He coughed on smoke and choked before he could carry on. "It wasn't finished so I didn't have much more than a few feet to fall. I put the side of a wood shipping crate on it. See? A grand piano crate. I covered it up, and now I've got me a perfect hiding place. Pretty ingenious, huh?"

"What are you burning?" Max asked. The ghastly odor flooded the air.

Kelly tilted his head to one side. "Things I don't want anymore," he said. "That's one thing these basins are good for. Getting rid of useless stuff. How did you know I was here?"

"I didn't." Fear for Kelly grew stronger. "I came looking for a flashlight. Annie dropped it here another time."

"I know she's over there." Kelly laughed. "I can see her but I don't want to embarrass her. Bit old for sex in the mud, aren't you, bro?"

This would be a poor time to punch Kelly out. "That's enough."

"Come here," Kelly said and Max stood beside him. "Look down there."

Max looked, he knelt and tried to see past the thinning smoke. And he felt Kelly move. Before Max could stop him, Kelly jumped to his feet and ran toward Annie. "Hey, Annie," he called. "Come on and join us. This is going to be my lot. Right next to my brother's. We're going to need each other."

"She's fine where she is," Max shouted, getting up, but Kelly had already taken hold of her. He swung her up into his arms and ran back. "Put her down," Max said.

"Just helping out," Kelly said.

Annie couldn't speak. She felt she might pass out.

"You're okay, Annie," Kelly said. He smelled of sweat. "I'll take good care of you. Max and I have got to make a decision."

She craned her neck to see Max. He walked slowly toward them.

"Ah, ah," Kelly said. "Not a good idea to come close. I've got a grenade."

Max halted. "Where the hell would you get a grenade?"

Kelly made a rapid detour and ended up beside the hole. "Just joking," he said. "You know me. I've always been a joker. But I'm not joking now. Listen up, golden boy, or Sweet Annie takes a tumble."

He would drop her in that smoky, foul-smelling pit?

"You're right," Max said. "You always were a joker."

"Lil Dupre saw Roche with Lee that night," Kelly said. "Getting it on at the clinic."

"You're sure?" Max said.

"I saw her. Luckily I was fast enough to head her off. I didn't want her smearing Roche's name. Unluckily, I was interrupted and she didn't die like she should have. Death is the only final silence, remember that, bro."

Annie held still but Max could see her wide eyes.

"Let her go," he said.

"Unless we shut Lil up, that woman will tell everyone what she saw and conclusions will be drawn. They'll think Roche is the guilty one.

When they start putting things together, they'll think he tried to frame you for the killings. He dated the first one—Isabel—before you did."

"No, he didn't, you did." Max shut his mouth. Aggravating Kelly was too dangerous. Max thought about the gun. He couldn't use it without the risk of hitting Annie. He couldn't shoot Kelly anyway. As far as Max could tell the man needed psychiatric help.

"I dated her to keep Roche away from her. She was no good for him. Roche always wanted the women you went for. He'd deny it, but he still wants to be the one women get all heated up for. Remember how he talked about Michele Riley wanting to come here because of him?"

"Sure," Max said, buying time. "You're right."

"They've taken Tom Walen in for questioning," Kelly said. "That wasn't what we wanted, was it?"

"I don't know," Max said. He saw no way to get to Annie if Kelly decided to throw her down. "If he hurt Michele it's what we want."

"But he didn't." Kelly laughed. "Come closer. I don't like shouting."

There was no choice but to do as he was asked. Max approached slowly.

"It's not burning," Kelly said. "The fire's gone out. Fix that for me."

Max stared at him, then at the rapidly thinning spiral of smoke.

"*Do it,*" Kelly shouted and Max flinched. Annie looked at him, aghast.

"Do it how?" Max asked in an even voice.

"Go down there and get it burning again. I shouldn't have closed it up so soon. I made it go out. It's your fault. I saw you coming, you know."

"Kelly—"

"Do it!"

"I can't. I can't even see what's in there."

"You're not in charge," Kelly said. "I am. I'm the oldest. You shouldn't have tried to take my place. I will have my way. I'll have what's mine."

Max knew the deepest fear he'd ever felt. "You're a good older brother, the best. Roche and I have always said so."

"You've always taken my place," Kelly said. "Ever since you were born, Dad preferred you because you were *brilliant*. Well, I'm brilliant, too, and so is Roche. You've made our lives hell."

Max took another step toward Kelly.

"Stay put," Kelly said. "She can do it for you." With that, he spread his arms and Annie fell, without a sound, into the opening in the ground. Straight down, she went and Max heard a thump. She did scream then.

"That was your fault for not doing what you were told," Kelly said to Max. "Learn your lesson. Don't come any closer. Here's a lighter, Annie." He tossed something and it glinted before it disappeared. "Baby, light my fire. *Now.*"

"Annie, I'll get you out. Stamp on any sparks. Keep calm," Max said. "She won't be setting fire to anything. She's coming out of there. I've got a gun, Kelly."

"And I've got a grenade," Kelly said.

"Sure you do, joker. Lie down on your face."

"Max?" Annie called and he heard her panic. "Please. Please get me out. Please. It's hard to breathe."

"I'm coming."

"Nope," Kelly said extending a hand.

Max looked and whispered. "Where did you get a grenade?"

"You can get anything you want. I'll throw it in after her if you try to interfere."

Even if Roche did find them, he wouldn't be able to help. Nobody would—without getting blown up.

Kelly did throw something and Max instinctively fell, facedown, and covered his head.

Only Kelly's laughter followed. "Just a penlight, bro. So your little piece of ass can see to do as she's told."

Max shot to his feet, his heart thundering. He started toward Kelly who held up the grenade, a finger and thumb on the pin.

Annie screamed and kept on screaming.

"Let me get her," Max said. He was begging and didn't care.

"All your life I had to walk behind you," Kelly said. "Now it's my turn out front. They should have put you away the first time your girlfriend bought it. But, no. You were bulletproof, only you're not anymore. You're going to do whatever I say, when I say it.

"First you'll have to help me finish that Lil Dupre bitch. It's Roche's fault she isn't dead. He'd never make a sleuth. I don't know how he figured out where I was but he followed me around today. I was afraid he'd come into the hospital after me. I was in too much of a hurry and I botched it with Lil." He gave a secretive smile. "Roche only wants to look after me, I know that, but he made it harder for me."

Early dawn had begun. In the lightening shades of gray behind Kelly, a man crouched a way off. He hunkered down every few steps before running toward them again. Max had felt Roche before he saw him. They could all die here.

Max couldn't do anything to stop what happened next. Roche rushed Kelly from behind, tackled him around the waist and threw him down. "Get Annie out," he said to Max, lying on top of Kelly.

"He's got a grenade," Max said, staring at Kelly's outstretched hand and the grenade he still held.

"He can't throw it from where he is," Roche said, struggling to get control of Kelly's arms.

"You don't have to pretend you care about him anymore," Kelly said to Roche. "Help me. He won't get a chance to tell Dad what happened."

"Just hold him down, Roche," Max told him. "I'll get the grenade."

"Don't even try," Kelly said. "Lil saw a doctor in scrubs in her room last night. And she'd already seen him beside the road after she played Peeping Tom at Green Veil. She *thought* he was a doctor. It was me. I acted fast and I was prepared. I got away from the clinic in time to head her off. I wanted to see *you* finished, Max, not Roche. She had to wonder if it was him who went after her on Landry Way. Her head injury bought some time but she's recovering fast. After last night she'll identify Roche for sure." He chuckled. "Imagine how sorry Dad will be for me when he finds out how I've been used by my murdering half brother all these years. And he'll be so grateful to me for saving Roche from you."

CHAPTER 42

The indescribable odor of the thing she could not look at almost obliterated the smell of burned garbage underfoot. Pressed to a rough, curved wall, Annie shone the tiny penlight on one piece of debris after another.

Burned away in places, only scorched in others, a sheet lay on top of the heap. Since she couldn't bring herself to touch it, looking for duct tape was out of the question, but she thought she saw patches of dull silver.

The men's voices carried to her. She heard every word and felt physical pain for Max and Roche. Particularly Max who had grown up with someone who hated him enough to kill innocent victims, then try to get him blamed and ruined for the crimes.

Annie hadn't fallen badly. Her tailbone might be bruised and she was bumped and scraped, but for the rest she thought she was all right. Except for her mind. She pressed her knuckles into her eyes. The putrid stench raised her gorge and acid ran repeatedly into her throat. Each time she swallowed, she retched, and she tried not to look across the pile of debris at what lay beyond.

Kelly had a grenade.

She slid the phone from her waistband and opened it. Looking upward, afraid Kelly's face would appear at any moment, she dialed 911. She faced the wall and cupped her mouth. The dispatcher dealt with Annie's whispered request as if all callers rasped out their problems.

After saying she couldn't stay on the phone, Annie switched off and covered her nose and mouth with her hands while she tried to figure out how long it would take for help to come. There wasn't even an address she could have given.

"Why did you start following me?" Kelly said. "Tell me the truth. I've got to know what made you do it."

Neither of his brothers responded.

"Roche," Kelly said, "I was supposed to be out of town. You knew that. I needed everyone to know that. The first time I thought I saw you I couldn't be sure. Last night outside the hospital, I knew it was you. You ruined everything."

"*You* ruined everything," Roche said quietly. "You started when we were all not much more than kids and you killed for the first time. But I've played my part now. I told myself I had an excuse to take what Lee offered, but I didn't. And I pushed too far. I wanted to make sure she kept her nose out of our business and quit looking for dirt on Max, but that wasn't an excuse for what I did."

"Hush," Kelly said in an unfamiliar, soft tone. "She wanted what she got. She lured you."

"No," Roche said. "If I'd just let her go that night you and Lil wouldn't have had anything to see when you were sneaking around. But I didn't let her go. What she wrote in the paper would have gone away if you'd left it alone, but you had to kill her."

Annie closed her eyes. Roche wasn't to blame, but she understood why he felt guilty.

"She had to die," Kelly said. "It was for you. She wasn't good enough for you. Work with me and we'll get everything we've ever wanted. Whatever happens here will be in self-defense."

"I've got your journal," Roche said, his voice rising. "You *wrote down* everything you did, damn you. You wrote letters to Max— letters you never sent. You wrote them like he'd done the things *you* did. It's all there."

Annie braced herself, expecting Kelly to blow them all up.

"That's private," Kelly shouted. "For me. You went in my rooms? They were locked."

"I needed a copy of the clinic plans. You said you'd leave them for me but you didn't. You've always tried to keep things to yourself. I borrowed a key. Why wouldn't Charlotte lend me one when I'm your brother? You hid the plans, didn't you? You *hid* the plans just because I said I wanted to look at them. In your bedroom. On top of that thing padded to match the curtains. Over the windows. Did you think you could just get away with *anything?*"

"You couldn't have found them," Kelly said. "You had to have known they were there. You must have watched me."

"Sure," Roche said. "That must have been it. Only it wasn't. I used a chair to check on top of the wardrobe and when I turned around I saw the plans. And the journal."

"You read my journal?" Kelly sounded petulant.

"To me it was something else you hid and probably didn't want me to see. I'm only human, thank God."

The sky had lightened beyond the opening above Annie's head. If she moved some of the garbage she might be able to get high enough to pull herself out.

"Kelly," she heard Max say. "We'll work it out. Give that thing to me and take some deep breaths. We've always stuck together."

Kelly sounded as if he cried. "Roche is going to realize what a dud you are. He'll turn to me. It's taken me too long to finish you, but it's worth it."

"We're a team," Roche said. "That won't change."

"You and me," Kelly said, sounding querulous. "Max has been treating us like children. Putting things over on us, laughing at us. He's been taking what's mine. I don't need a second hand to pull the pin. Give me the gun, Max, or I'll push the grenade in the hole."

Annie shook. The early dawn light didn't brighten the salt basin and she made herself train the minuscule penlight on a dark shape across the salt basin. Blackened, just as she'd seen in her twilight horrors, what had once been a body lay mutilated beyond recognition and left to decompose.

"The gun," Kelly raged. "Now, or the grenade goes down."

"And you go up," Max said calmly.

"We'll all go together, when we go," Kelly sang, his voice cracked. "Or we can stay here until one of us falls asleep. It won't be me. You know I don't need much sleep and I don't need any at all now."

Annie would not believe that they were going to die. Not like this. She looked toward the disintegrating body and retched again, and felt pity so deep she could not cry. Ambition and hatred had done this to an innocent. And jealousy.

The final minutes of night slipped away. A lemon sheen stained the smoky pallor in the east. Roche remained sprawled over Kelly who held the grenade just out of reach. Max sat with his legs crossed, his gun in his hand.

Kelly had scarcely blinked and Roche kept his eyes trained on the grenade. Max had an idea but no way of transmitting it to Roche secretly.

Roche had told Kelly he had to lie on top of him to make sure he didn't get hurt and Kelly had accepted the lie with another mysterious smile.

From time to time Annie coughed. Max had heard her sniff occasionally, and he'd heard her get sick. The familiar foul odor of old death that rose from the salt basin intensified his hatred for Kelly. To think of Annie trapped down there in close proximity with a corpse was unbearable.

No less horrifying was the certainty that they had found Michele Riley.

He felt Roche looking at him. With his eyebrows raised, he turned his eyes to the grenade, then back to Max. Max couldn't think what his twin had on his mind but something was about to happen. His belly tensed. Within minutes they'd be free, or scattered over the area in little pieces.

In one, heaving motion, Roche levered his body higher on Kelly's, pinned his shoulders with his knees and took one of his wrists in each of his hands.

"Now what?" Kelly said, laughing. "That took you a long time to figure out. What's next? Don't worry, it's up to me."

Max was already springing from his position. He got to his brothers just as Kelly strained to hook a finger through the grenade pin. With one foot, Max delivered a smashing kick to Kelly's right wrist and said, "Yes!" when he cried out.

The grenade shot away, rolled a few yards down an incline that had looked like nothing from Max's position on the ground. On his feet, he leaped past Kelly and Roche. Kelly grabbed Max's ankle as he passed and landed him hard on the stony ground.

Max leveled his gun at Kelly's head.

His sight lined up not on Kelly, but on Roche. Kelly had vaulted behind his younger brother and had him in a hammerlock. "Relax," Kelly told him. "I'll protect you."

Roche managed to buck Kelly hard enough to knock him sideways. Still Kelly gripped his brother in the crook of a steely arm and clung to Max's ankle.

A shot rang out.

"Shit, no," Max said under his breath. Reinforcements, oblivious reinforcements, had arrived. The shot had been a warning. He and Roche needed help but that grenade was still too close for comfort.

Through the burning sweat in his eyes, he saw a group spreading out along the perimeter of the trees. A dog barked and Max figured they could thank the canine for finding them at all.

Behind Kelly and Roche, the top of Annie's head was above the rim of the basin. She got her elbows onto the ground and hauled herself out of the hole. Max just wished she had stayed where she was safe, regardless of the conditions she'd been trapped in.

"Get down and stay still," Kelly told Max. "Your buddies aren't going to help you. They're going to find out what you've been up to for years."

"You're insane," Roche said.

"Don't you tell me that," Kelly cried. "You don't have to pander to Max anymore. I'm the one you'll care about."

"Give it up," Max said. "You know the evidence Roche has on you."

"He'd never show that to anyone," Kelly told him. He looked toward the phalanx of people moving slowly forward across the field. "Help," he shouted. "I don't know how much longer I can hold him."

Kelly saw Annie. "Come here," he snapped. "Come here or I'll hurt your lover boy."

Annie didn't hesitate—she walked to Kelly.

All Max needed was one clear shot. At the moment, even if Roche was out of the way, Annie could just as well be in line to take a bullet.

"Whatever you're thinking of doing, forget it," Kelly said to Max. "One wrong move and I'll break Roche's neck. Neither of us want that."

The dog barked and sounded more excited. From the number of people circling them, several agencies had to be involved.

Kelly's left foot was visible to Max. Visible and an easy shot.

Max pulled the trigger without moving any part of his body but the necessary finger.

Kelly screamed. He screamed and when Roche threw him off, grabbed Annie convulsively instead. "Come any closer, you fucker, and she dies. My foot. You've ruined my foot."

Max stood, held his weapon in both hands and trained it on Kelly and Annie. He would wait for his opportunity and he felt nothing about killing his half brother. He felt nothing for him but hate.

With gigantic effort, Kelly got up, hissing through his teeth at the pain he must feel. He held Annie in front of him and shuffled backward—toward the grenade. "You don't think it's real." His eyes half-closed but instantly opened all the way again. "You think I'm bluffing."

He struggled on until he reached his goal and, watching Max and Roche, fell to his knees with Annie still in front of him. He folded the grenade into his palm.

Holding it so close to Annie's face it almost touched, he took hold of the pin.

Annie looked directly into Max's face. He looked back and he felt as if they touched. His mind wound in one direction after another, looking for a way to save her.

He realized the reinforcements had stopped moving forward. They would have glasses trained on the unfolding drama, including the weapon Kelly used as the ultimate threat.

Kelly pulled the pin from the grenade.

Max ran at him.

Roche ran, too.

Annie clutched Kelly's hand, the one gripping his precious weapon, with both of hers and pulled it against her.

Roche made an inhuman noise and stopped running, but Max couldn't stay away. Whatever happened, he would be with her, he would give survival his all, just as she was doing.

"Get down," Roche shouted. "We can't do anything."

A gurgling shriek sounded and Max turned his head from side to side, forcing his sweat-soaked vision into focus.

And he was almost upon them. Annie had driven a heel into Kelly's mangled foot. With his mouth wide open, he choked out his agony and slid down, left the grenade in Annie's hands.

"Throw it," Max shouted to her. They had a few seconds. Maybe six, maybe two.

She cocked her arm and lobbed the grenade into the salt basin. "Get down," she yelled.

The explosion ripped at his eardrums. The earth shuddered and his feet left the ground. A plume of fire and smoke swelled out of the hole, and Max landed, spread-eagled, on his back.

CHAPTER 43

Rosebank. Six weeks later.

Annie studied the exotic salon at Rosebank, and all the people in it—there for her and Max—and for a moment felt like the insecure girl she used to be. She drew herself up, reminded herself she was a competent, successful woman, and plastered on a smile. Then she caught the eye of her cousin Finn Duhon who had come from Pointe Judah to give her away, and she giggled.

Finn, tall, black-haired and every inch a still-impressive former Army Ranger, waggled his eyebrows at Annie and hugged his wife, Emma. The looks on their faces didn't need translation; they were thrilled for Annie and Max.

"I put in another good word for you with Cyrus," Roche said softly and rested an arm around her waist. "I told him our mother is Catholic and Max and I were brought up Catholic."

Annie held a glass of champagne, which she placed firmly into Roche's spare hand. "Take a drink," she said. "It'll settle you down."

He frowned and tipped the glass. The men in the wedding party wore gray tuxes and on the Savage men they were spectacular. Roche looked almost as good as his twin, but, Annie thought, that was the most he could hope for.

Standing with his parents near the massive white stone fireplace, Max's head was bowed as he listened to Leo and Claire Savage.

"You were brought up Catholic," Roche said. "That's different, of course."

"Cyrus already knows Max's history, and mine."

"No harm in making sure, though," Roche said.

"Mmm."

"I didn't think it would hurt to put his mind at rest."

Annie had no idea what he meant.

Roche smiled and said, "I assured him that I'd be a godparent and make sure the children go to mass."

Annie took back her glass. "Would you like some coffee?"

"No thanks. I'm feeling really good."

"I noticed," she said.

"But you're not noticing that your husband keeps waving his arms at you. Looks like he's trying to fly."

Annie fiddled with the skirts of the white chiffon wedding gown Max had tricked her into buying. Actually, he'd said he'd lie on the floor of the shop and refuse to leave if she wouldn't have it rather than something simple and short.

Bending, Roche looked closely at crystals and beads in points from the waist down the skirt of the dress. "Prettiest dress I've ever seen." He stood up and smiled at her. "And you're the prettiest woman I've ever seen. Your husband's still trying to fly."

Annie waved at Max, threaded an arm beneath one of Roche's

and walked gracefully to join the little group by the fireplace. With Kelly in prison awaiting trial, Annie wondered how much the Savages could celebrate anything.

"You think I'm drunk, don't you?" Roche said.

She looked up at him and he smiled wide enough to show most of his perfect, white teeth.

"I'm not. I'm just so bloody happy I can't stand it." He stood still and put a hand over his heart. "If I could change what happened, I would. I hate it that Kelly's ruined his life, but I hate what he did more. Even all of that can't take anything away from thinking of you and my brother having each other."

Impulsively, she turned toward him and rested her forehead on his lapel. He held the back of her head but after a moment said, "Look at Max now."

She did and laughed aloud at the sight of him with his fists on his hips, glowering in their direction.

Roche held her back a few more moments. "We'll get other chances to talk but I want you to know I'll be here for you if you need to talk. Or if you don't think you can be comfortable with me, I'll make sure we find just the right person."

"Thank you," she said, sobering. They would both have their demons to conquer and she wouldn't make any speedy decisions about how to deal with hers. Unless Max had talked about them, she had issues Roche didn't know about. But Annie believed in the power of love and hers was strong. With Max, she felt she could overcome anything.

"Let's join Max before he starts rolling up his sleeves and looking for seconds," Roche said.

She walked lightly beside him. There had been a few bad dreams for some weeks now and those that came were different than before, and understandable. They passed when she awoke, or when she felt Max close to her.

Max couldn't get enough of looking at Annie. He had wanted her to have the kind of wedding a girl dreams of, the kind she probably imagined before reality changed everything.

"Hi," he said when she reached him, and kissed her cheek sedately. "My brother's been hitting on you, hasn't he? And at our wedding. Excuse me while I take him outside."

Annie laughed.

"I'd insist on making you do what you just threatened," Roche said, "but Annie would be mad at me if you were unconscious on your wedding night."

Max met Roche's eyes. They smiled widely at one another. This happy day was the best medicine for the Savage family.

Annie had taken off her veil and wore small white orchids in her hair. "You smell wonderful," he said, to her only. "How long do we have to stay?"

Annie smiled at her parents-in-law while she slipped a hand beneath Max's coat and pinched his back. She looked at him sharply when he said, "Ouch."

"It's convenient to be able to stay here at Rosebank," Claire Savage said. "The house is huge. I would have loved to see it exactly as it was."

"From what I've been told," Annie said, "apart from some additions, the renovations were made without changin' the look of what was already there."

Claire looked interested. "I wonder how they feel about showing people around? Not tonight, of course."

"They're pleased to be asked," Max told her. "The place belonged to Vivian Devol's uncle and apparently he was quite flamboyant. Did you ever see so many brass animal feet on furniture, or monkeys carved in odd places?"

"None of this is accidental," Claire said. "The collecting must have taken years but it's beautifully done. Very 1930s colonial—India primarily, I should think. With the Asian influence, of course."

"When I give her some spare time," Leo Savage said, "Max's mother is an interior designer."

Claire smiled. It was from her that the twins got their dark hair and blue eyes.

"Wazoo is absolutely the best with the history of the house," Annie said. "She has all sorts of theories—some of them *way* out there."

The Savages looked puzzled.

"Wazoo lives here, too. We'll make sure you meet her."

"Good," Claire said, looking at her impressive, silver-haired husband. Shadows showed in her eyes. "Are we ready to go up, Leo? Since the bride and groom don't leave until tomorrow, they won't mind if the old fogies give up for tonight."

Leo smiled, but Annie felt his relief. This must be harder for him than the rest.

Claire hugged her and said, "Max is a lucky man, but he deserves you." She laughed. "How's that for a compliment?"

"I guess I'm glad to have it," Annie said. She and Max walked his parents to the stairs before returning to the reception.

"Look what a good time they're having," Max said. "They won't miss us if we go upstairs, too."

"Don't you tempt me, sir," Annie said. "We're supposed to circulate again."

"I'm starting to wish you hadn't read that wedding etiquette book."

Spike and Vivian, Vivian in red with bugle beads swinging and her black hair shining, walked toward them.

"You look like a beautiful flapper," Max said to Vivian when she got close.

"A very pregnant flapper," Vivian commented. "This has been a fabulous day. Thank you for havin' us."

"*Hoo Mama,*" Spike said. "I've got to make this woman get off her feet. D'you know she even danced tonight?"

Vivian gave an angelic smile. "Anything a girl can do to help matters along, y'know," she said. "Keep on bein' happy, you two."

"You do that," Charlotte Patin said, joining them with her left hand around Homer's upper arm. The diamond ring sparkled there again. "I want this man to head for home while he's still sober."

Homer reddened on cue and mumbled something. He patted Charlotte's hand and she beamed before the four of them moved on.

Groups of people from out of town, Max and Roche's friends, hung together deep in conversation. And just about every familiar Toussaint face could be found somewhere in the room. Even Lil and Ozaire were there, Lil seated in a comfortable chair and from what Max could tell, probably telling her story to yet another polite listener. Spike had told him she'd placed him or Roche at the clinic with Lee—until she heard Max had an alibi. He just hoped she wasn't saying anything at all about that aspect of the incident.

Cyrus came to stand between them, a hand on each of their shoulders. "I just wanted to let you know everything's going to be okay," he said.

Max frowned at him. "What does that mean?"

"Cyrus." Madge, stunning in yellow, planted herself in front of them. "Me, I know this man too well. I see it when he's plannin' one of his jokes. And they are rarely, I repeat, rarely funny."

"Joke? *Moi?*" Cyrus spread his fingers on his chest and managed the most innocent and wounded expression. "It's no joke that I have Dr. Roche Savage's assurances that this marriage will be lived in a strictly Catholic manner. Or that he, Roche, will make sure the children—he expects a number of them, he says—are brought up with strict religious guidance. His own."

"Roche must be drunk," Max said, and his ears turned red.

Annie knew enough to keep quiet until the pair wandered off to huddle with Guy and Jilly, and Guy's NOPD friend, Nat Archer, who turned a great many female heads.

"That reminds me," Max said. "Didn't we invite Wazoo? She should be with Nat."

Annie slapped her forehead and looked at her watch. "Whoa, I thought it was later than it is. Wazoo's been in and out, but she's busy organizing the kitchen staff. I promised I'd spend a few quiet minutes with her in—" she checked the time again "—about five minutes, or four, I guess."

"I can't spare you," Max said. He put his lips to her ear. "Seriously, I just want to be alone with you. I've had it with the fuss."

"Soon," Annie said. "That's what I want, too. We'll start our goodbyes as soon as Wazoo's said her piece. I was glad Reb and Marc came to the church."

Max rubbed the back of her neck. "They won't get over losing Lee easily. We're going to have to keep an eye on Roche in that area, too. He pretends he's fine, but he blames himself. He's talking about how he shouldn't have invited Michele to Toussaint as well. I was more responsible for that than he was but he's not hearing me."

"Give him time," Annie said, although she knew too well how long it could take to get over some things.

"Here comes Wazoo," Max said. "And right on time. I can stay with you, can't I?"

Annie looked at him. "She said she wanted to talk to me alone. Can you handle that?"

"No," he said as Wazoo arrived in front of them. "I'll have to make you pay for it later. And not much later, if you don't mind." He left them and was immediately commandeered by slender little Wendy Devol, Spike's daughter by his first marriage. With her hands on her hips, apparently very earnest, she looked up at him through her glasses as she spoke.

"She's askin' him if he does breast implants," Wazoo said.

"She is *not,*" Annie said. "Shame on you. She's too young to have breasts yet anyway."

"Wendy thinks ahead," Wazoo said. "I told you I gotta show you somethin'. We could just step outside a moment and hope we're not followed."

Annie didn't want to leave, but she followed Wazoo into the vestibule and out through the front door, which Wazoo closed firmly. She took Annie by the hand and hurried her down the steps and off to a potting shed near the rose garden.

"I can't go in there," Annie said, indicating her dress.

"We don't have to then," Wazoo told her. "This can be done right here."

She flourished a plastic grocery sack. "Know what's in here?"

Unfortunately, Annie was certain she did know. "Don't tell me you're still carrying that nasty doll around. You said you'd take care of the thing."

"And I have. I'm gonna prove it worked. It's already proved it worked." She peered into the sack, carefully removed the infamous brown bag and untied its top. The contents she dumped on the ground in a pool of light spilling from a lamp on the potting shed. "Look at that. Nothin' left but dust, bits of rag and bits of wire. It did its job. It unraveled, and he unraveled. The wicked one got taken down."

Annie shook her head and stared at the mess. "A few bumps inside my purse and it fell apart," she said. "Cheap doll."